A PANE
OF GLASS

R. BYRON STOCKDALE

R. BYRON STOCKDALE

ISBN-13: 978-1983506048

R. BYRON STOCKDALE

For the victims of child predators.

R. BYRON STOCKDALE

CONTENTS

"It is my hope that by 1993 girls may go to church or to school, or even take a harmless walk in the fields or woods, without danger of being waylaid and murdered by their 'natural protectors'..."

Elizabeth Akers Allen, poet

1893

R. BYRON STOCKDALE

−1−

THE BEGINNING

All the young girl could do was be afraid. Her screams were not loud enough to be heard, and she couldn't cry; there were no more tears. Beyond the plaster walls of the small empty church, the same awful sound from the night before was getting closer. Through the hole in the roof she saw the headlights sweep across the tops of the trees and knew that the bad man was coming again.

She pulled against the cable that was locked around her neck and bolted to the floor. It was just long enough to reach the dirty mattress in front of the window and the bucket she used for a toilet across the room. Her body felt weak and broken; she could barely walk, but she had to get back to the mattress because that's where he had ordered her to stand whenever he came. If she did what she was told, he would leave the bottle of water and the piece of bread when he left. If she didn't, he would hold her hand over the candle and burn another finger.

The boards nailed outside the windows kept the building mostly dark, but the moon's glow had found its way through the roof and where a board had fallen from the window above the place where he had told her to wait. And standing there now, she looked up into the stained glass and found the face of the bearded man dressed in the golden robe. The baby was there too, cradled in his arms, glowing within a halo of orange light. The man's gaze was upon the child; its little eyes closed and face calm as if taken by a wonderful dream.

For a short while during the afternoons, the sun would shine through the roof in a way that would let her see the rest of the beautiful picture. Some of the glass was gone and some was cracked or clouded; but she could still make out most of the image that remained: his hand gently resting under the infant's head; the other raised high into an exploding star of yellow cutting across a blue-glass sky; little children gathered all around, each radiant in their own circle of light; all seemingly waiting for a chance to sit with the bearded man in the golden robe.

Tonight the moon bathed the girl in the colors of the glass and, for a fleeting moment, they let her forget who would soon be coming through the door.

Then she heard the rattle of the steel bars… the click of the lock.

Sadly, she surrendered her cheek to the sill and pressed her blistered fingers to the glass. Through it she felt the cold and thought of the window in her room next to her bed. She yearned to be there again, to crawl under the warm covers and listen to her father's voice reading her stories of magical, far-away places.

…and the door creaked open.

She released the glass but could no longer stand like she had been ordered; her legs would not hold her. She slumped to the floor between the wall and mattress and sealed her eyes closed as tightly as she could, as if behind them she was hidden from the approaching evil. Everything was beyond her understanding. She waited for the needle he would bring without knowing where it would stab her naked flesh; she no longer cared that it hurt because something inside told her that what happened next, after she fell asleep, was so much worse.

His smell was near…

Terrified and frozen in the pool of colored light, she whispered to the God she tried to love but hardly knew; quietly she pleaded for Him to somehow bring her daddy to this place, so he would save her from the horrible man.

...and the needle pierced her skin.

She wanted to die but wasn't yet old enough to know about death, and she was too young to recognize that her fear was a voice from deep within her, telling her she was never going home.

*****

–2–

A WORLD APART

Communications Sergeant Tim Smith climbed onto the narrow rock ledge where the lead weapons expert from his unit was keeping watch over a lonely stretch of the AH77 road. Barely a dirt trail, the 'seventy-seven' cut across northwest Afghanistan and followed the fertile valley lying at the foot of the Paropamisus Mountains. Smith squatted to his knees and leaned against a boulder to catch his breath in the high altitude air. It was too dark to see much of anything under the starless night sky.

"So, how's it going B.R.?" Smith asked.

Bryan Rhodes was sitting with his back propped against the mountain, scanning across the black expanse through infrared goggles. He swept the foothills below him and each flank for hostile visitors before setting them down. "Just another ho-hum day in paradise, Sarge."

"Copy that. You'll be glad to know I finally fixed the SAT-COM; had to use parts from both busted phones to make one good one. I just talked to the Battalion Commander. The target convoy turned south on the Kandahar Highway; that's why they never showed up. It looks like we got to sit this one out. We're booked at the PZ for an extraction at 0600—day after tomorrow. We'll have a drone and one Warthog circling overhead for top cover." For no reason, Smith picked up a fist full of sand and released it over the side into a light breeze. "The good news is our little Reserve Unit gets to go state-side after we close this op. I guess our life goes back to being boring again."

"You mean like sitting on top of a cold rock for two weeks doing nothing?"

Smith chuckled. "Yeah, something like that." He took off his helmet and scratched his scalp. "Sure be good to get a hot shower and a warm bed." He handed Rhodes the satellite phone. "The S-1 said your wife's been trying to get a hold of you for several days; it sounds urgent." He grabbed the goggles and stood up. "Call home, B.R. The signal's weak; so you better do it before you lose it. Take my advice; call now—family is everything."

The sergeant swept the horizon before settling his focus on the glowing ridgeline fifty miles to the west. The low sky was painted orange, but sundown had occurred over six hours ago. "It looks like the enemy is looting Herat again. You know, I feel sorry for the poor bastards in that town; the only thing they have left to take is their lives." He lowered the goggles and turned to Rhodes. "So, B.R., how long do you think this *conflict that never happened* will go on happening?"

"Until it doesn't."

*****

Bryan finished punching in the fifteen-digit number and pressed send. There was a long pause before he heard a voice on the other end of the call. It wasn't his wife.

"Who the hell is this? Where's Mary?" The response was garbled; he could hardly hear it through the static. "*What?!*"

The signal was gone; Bryan was shaking. He spoke slowly into the dead phone, his voice hollow and broken.

"My little girl is missing?"

*****

–3–

TURNER'S WOOD
(8 years later)

Winter ripped across the naked landscape and frozen river, swirling snow into drifts against the rocky embankment, dead thistle and sycamore roots that marked the edge of Turner's Wood. Although narrow, the river split the land decisively in a crooked, deep line and held the forest from spilling into the adjacent meadow at spring's thaw. Overhead a silver tapestry of branch and twig were gripped in an icy glaze and hung like frozen willow, crying against the brutal wind—a million glass ornaments rattling in eerie concert with the howling air. Even for early March, the storm had been fierce and sudden, burying northeast Iowa under a mantel of freezing rain and almost a foot of snow.

The hunter knelt at the river and filled his canteen from the hole in the ice he had made easily with the heel of his boot. Despite the bitter cold, the water moved too swiftly to freeze more than an inch thick, and out in the middle of the channel, where it flowed even faster, the ice was thinner still. To get home, he needed to reach the county road on the other side where his truck was parked along the old railroad spur, but he wouldn't dare to attempt to cross here; here the ice would never hold his weight. He had traveled too far south from where he had crossed that morning, and he now realized his carelessness had cost him valuable daylight that would soon be gone.

He cursed himself for coming up with the brilliant idea of hunting turkey out-of-season. Since dawn he had found scarce evidence of only one roost, and it looked to have been abandoned for some time; even the birds had had more sense to find better shelter from the storm. As he pulled a long drink from his canteen, he decided that the day had been just a series of bad decisions and tried to ignore the fact that he had been right about the one thing he now wished he had gotten wrong: it was a month before the spring turkey season and he would have the woods all to himself.

The shortest path back meant crossing here, but he realized that would be impossible. Not far down stream, perhaps a mile or a little more, the channel grew wide and shallow and turned abruptly east, falling with the contours of the rolling land, coaxing the water to flow faster toward the Upper Iowa River and farther on to the Mississippi. Surely the ice would be even thinner there if it existed at all. To the north he remembered a spot he had fished a few summers ago where the channel ran deep and slow, meandering through an area of steep, crowded hills. There the ice would be thick enough, but he guessed it was several miles away and at least a four-hour walk. He knew that somewhere between there and here he had crossed that morning, but there was no way he was going to find it now. His gear was soaking wet, and the cold had crawled deep into the joints of his bones. The weather had not improved just as the forecast had promised. It was getting late and daylight was dying in the woods behind him. He prayed that his flashlight had stayed dry.

The hunter turned his attention to surviving the night ahead and to do so meant finding shelter from the weather and soon. He had packed light for the day: his canteen, shotgun and ammo, some deer jerky, lighter, his favorite hunting knife and the flashlight, and all of it would help him get through the night. Thankfully his clothes, although heavily soaked, were well insulated and would save his life if he could get them dry. With any luck, he might be able to find enough wood to sustain a fire and thaw his legs and maybe keep from freezing to death before daylight. He would get an early start with the sun; surely everything would be better in the morning.

*****

Turning his back to the river he headed up into the woods, pushing perhaps a hundred yards through the dense undergrowth to where the forest floor opened up below a dominant stand of old-growth pine and some occasional cedar and oak. He swept the frozen ground ahead with his flashlight, its throw narrow and dim from the weakening batteries. The tall, straight trees punctured the snow almost in a regular pattern like timber columns rising and branching out high overhead, forming the vaults of an imaginary forest cathedral that reached into the black above. Their stoic presence humbled him and compressed his thoughts so that his mind couldn't wander much beyond the sliver of light and the bitter cold.

He picked a spot to make camp on the lee side of the storm below a deep ledge of exposed limestone that would hold some heat from a fire and give him decent protection from the wind. Luckily, the overhang had prevented the snow from accumulating below it, and the ground was relatively dry; it would make a good shelter until morning. An old hobbled oak tree clung to the side of the outcropping, and its shape would help him more easily find it again when he came back from searching for wood.

After unloading what little gear he had, he worked his way out in widening arcs, dragging his feet through the snow like a rake, collecting any deadfall he could carry that would burn. Then he gathered the few dry leaves he could find from under the ledge and started a small fire, adding the low branches he snapped off a dead cedar just a short distance from his camp. It didn't take much to coax them to burn. When the fire grew strong and steady, he ringed it with layers of wet limbs so they would be dry when he needed them later. Next he grabbed his knife to cut saplings that he would cross layer for a bed to insulate him from the frozen ground.

As he walked away from his camp he looked back just once to check the fire and saw the crooked oak eerily animated by the pulsing flames as if it was dancing in the rising heat. By now, complete exhaustion had taken control over his numbed mind, and he would have to focus hard to push back the strange thoughts that were beginning to invade his imagination.

He searched for a long while, yet found himself far from the fire with his hands still empty. What young growth there was had been laden by the freezing rain and pulled to the ground, buried under the heavy snow. Except for the trunks of the trees that seized the dark nave above him, all he could see and everywhere he looked was nothing but a silent blanket of whiteness. And beyond the reaches of his fading electric lamp, the world abruptly and completely disappeared.

Something peculiar caught the edge of his vision. He would have missed it, but he had brought his light around one last time before turning back to the fire and saw it just ten feet away; a black hole in the snow like a void in the forest floor that didn't belong. He stood motionless and a bit confused, instinct overriding his brain's ability to sort through an explanation for what he saw *or what he believed he saw.* He sensed that he should ignore it and leave, yet he was unable to turn away. Guardedly, he moved to the side but not toward it, careful to keep a safe distance, caution and curiosity balanced. The pale light shook in his hand and made the void appear foreboding; the urge to escape pulled him backwards. His breathing was short and nervous; the noise of his boots punching through the snow confused him even more. Were the sounds his own, or did they belong to something else?

Damn it! It's just a fricking hole in the ground. But he unsheathed his knife anyway. He filled his lungs with cold air and held it as he backed away, staring defensively into the hole as he did, and in the changing light he began to see the scene differently. It wasn't an opening in the earth at all but a dull object in the woods that the snow had refused to cling to— *just like a bag of trash.* Still, he could relax only a little; there was something wrong in this place. He thought to dismiss the feeling and get back to his fire, but he couldn't. In these dark, empty woods, so far from everywhere, he knew of two things that didn't belong: him and this black blister in the snow. The odds were inconceivable, and he needed to know what it was. In a hundred-square-mile haystack of winter emptiness, the hunter had found another needle.

He moved beside the swollen shape and poked it with the toe of his boot. Like a stone embedded in the ground, it did not give way. Nearly two feet long and a foot-and-a-half wide, its taut surface, dull and worn, absorbed the remnants of the hunter's light. A tear split the length and width in the form of a cross and ice had collected in the crevices hiding what lay below. *The ripped seams of a coat?* He pulled air through his nose, but there was no smell or taste to it. As best he could, he looked around in the near darkness for something to help him understand, as if finding more strange things would explain the occurrence of the one, but there was nothing.

Cautiously, the hunter began to clear the snow from around the shape with the side of his boot until he hit something hard and stiff. *A root?* Reaching down he found the end of a thick steel rod; the top flared broadly from being driven into the ground. With his other hand, he uncovered a heavy chain that ran from a ring welded at the base of the stake and disappeared somewhere under the dark object, and as he cleared more snow away he began to see, first one, then another and another. From the sides and end of the leathery shape, the gnawed bones of human arms and legs emerged like the broken branches of a petrified log. He stumbled backwards and fell, kicking franticly against the snow to push away from the horrible corpse; putting distance between him and it was all that mattered. The flashlight rested in the snow where it had fallen. It flickered for a long, frightening moment, strobe-like, to capture the bleached jawbone and faceless skull of a man picked clean by the scavengers of the woods.

Then, suddenly and finally, the light was gone.

*****

−4−

EMMA

L ooking down he's rewarded with his daughter's bright smile. Her eyes, squinting slightly in the early sun, now find his.

"Daddy?"

"Yes, Emma."

"Will you hold my hand?"

"Always I will."

She pulls his hand to her face and snuggles her soft cheek against it. He can feel the warmth of her skin on his.

"Daddy?"

"Yes, Sweetheart."

"I love you."

"I love you also."

"Can you hear the siren, Daddy?"

"What siren, Emma?" He points down the street, "Look young lady, here comes your school bus. Don't forget your things."

He holds the backpack as she works her little arms into the straps; he squats to adjust the clasps and gently kisses her forehead.

"Thank you, Daddy; will you come with me?"

"Someday soon I will, Emma."

"Pinky-swear?"

The long shadow of the approaching bus glides over them and softens the glare of the low morning light; it rolls silently to a stop. There is no other sound, just his voice and her voice. Then he hears it also: the faint howl of a siren, but it seems very far away.

"Yes, I promise, Emma.   Now sit near the window, so I can wave goodbye to—" His words trail off abruptly.

"What is it, Daddy?"

A tall, dark form glides across the lawn and merges with the shadow of the bus. "Get going, Emma—find yourself a seat." He thinks to himself: 'Who the hell is pulling up so close, doesn't he know there are children?'

"What's wrong, Daddy?"

"Nothing; just climb up and sit by the driver; tell him to close the door behind you." He releases her hand and points to the steps. "Emma, do as I say! Get inside!"

He's standing alone now—thinking—looking. A large brown delivery van has rolled to a stop and is idling at the curb, its bumper just inches behind the back of the bus. Black smoke leaches from below, drifting up the side and through the rungs of a ladder tied along the edge of the roof; the lettering and logo are obscured under blood-red paint. The loud clatter of the diesel engine masks the sound of the siren and he can't hear it anymore. He takes a few steps farther up the lawn so that he might see in the cab more clearly. As he does, the school bus begins to pull away and passes through the limits of his vision trailing its shadow with it, but he stays focused on the van. He cups his hands above his eyes to adjust to the sudden brightness. The glare is painfully irritating; he needs to see the man sitting behind the glass.

"Hey idiot!" he yells to the shadow figure hiding from the

daylight, "What the hell is wrong with you? There are little kids around here!"

Streaks of smeared dirt arc across the windshield and obscure the formless shape beyond; it ignores his shouting and remains motionless, looking forward. It is tracking the bus as it pulls away. He moves toward it but the diesel roars to life and the van begins a slow retreat backwards up the road. As he walks faster, the van retreats faster too, and the distance between them grows rapidly. He starts to run but soon everything's a hallucination, morphing into a kaleidoscope of skewed green, brown and gray. The van, street and homes are bending upward and receding as if he's racing through a tunnel, and the other end is being pulled into a vacuum—strangely warping, stretching, up and away from him. His legs and heart are burning, but he runs harder, his head dizzy from the contortions of the scene that he is trying to chase. At the center of it all the van suddenly shrinks to a tiny speck inside a tightening circle of twisting light—then completely disappears.

"Emma?" His anger is instantly overwhelmed with panic; he can barely breathe. 'Oh my God, I didn't see her get on the bus!' "Emma!"

At the opposite end of the street the school bus is turning the corner and beginning to vanish out of view. He races toward it, running across the driveways and lawns, struggling to see through the windows; reflections from the houses, trees and clouds dance across the glass and play with his mind. "Emma, let me see you! Please God; please let her be there!"

Sirens are wailing all around him now, drowning out the sound of his breathing and the desperate cry of his screams. "EMMA!!!"

In that horrible instant he can see clearly. There is no one on the bus.

*****

Bryan awoke with the suddenness of breaking glass. On the nightstand beside the bed, the clock mocked him with its pathetic whine. *Please, not again.* He wiped the sweat from his face and neck with the twisted bed sheet, pulled loose from the mattress sometime in the night. With the palms of his hands, he tried vainly to relieve the ache that lived behind his swollen eyes; they throbbed against his brain and kept annoying cadence with the pulse of the damn alarm. It silenced under his heavy fist.

He stared at the red numbers as they blinked from 4:30 to 4:31, trying to gain some focus to his vision. Exhausted with the awful images still crowding his mind, he rolled over on his back, letting his open hand fall tenderly on the vacant side of the bed and waited. It wasn't long before his thoughts grew still and his breathing slowed; the memory of his dead wife always helped him to not think about the dream. As his mind cleared, the tide of reality that flowed in and out of their room began to pour over him again; he sat up to escape the rushing feeling. His large shape glowed crimson in the dresser mirror opposite the end of the bed; the features of his face painted red in an eerie and unnatural glow. Under his eyes, two dark, haunting circles revealed his fatigue. It had been a long and restless night just like all the others.

"What is it?" He growled at the reflection staring back at him. His mouth and lips whispered the answer out loud, but he thought he heard the words come from the man in the mirror. "It's nothing, Bryan—*just nothing.*" He switched on the lamp clipped to the headboard beside him, above where his wife used to sleep, and waited for his eyes to adjust to the light. As they did, the soft emptiness of her pillow pulled on him until he surrendered back down to the bed, resting on his elbow beside it. *I had the horrible dream again, Mary. I know it's just a dream but she was so real; I can still hear her voice. The pain was so real too. I lost her all over again, and I don't know how many more times I can live through that. I wish you were there in the dream with us; maybe it wouldn't end any better, but at least we'd be together for a little while.*

With his finger, he gently traced the lock of hair that had lay there on her pillow since the day Mary died.

I'm so lonely without you. I will see you again soon, but I'm not ready yet. I will love you always.

*****

It was late springtime then but didn't feel like it, and it had been a long, sad goodbye. Mary came home from her final round of treatments almost one year after she had first walked through the cancer center doors. She was a strong woman and had stretched six months into twelve but was now prepared to die in her own home and in her own bed, and sometime toward the end of the twenty-third night, she did just that.

On that quiet morning, Bryan had awakened to find her life had drained away. He had been asleep, dreaming his horrible dream, when death came to her, and the last thing he ever wanted was for Mary to have died alone. When he touched her, she was still soft and warm, and the guilt consumed him instantly as if his own life was escaping through every pore of his skin. Desperately, he tried to revive her, but there was nothing he could have done that would have brought her back. Everything that could have been done had already been done in the months leading up to that sad morning. The disease had ravaged through her bones and had finally run its course. Her time had come, and all he could do was hold on to her for a little while, to suspend the moment when he would have to let her go and accept that she was gone.

Bryan lay back down beside his wife one final time before he would let the paramedics take her lifeless body. As they

17

lifted her from the bed, he saw the lock of hair fall to the pillow, gently spiraling down through the dusty air in slowed motion, through the early sunlight that filled the room and then, for a brief moment, disappearing into her passing shadow as she was carried away. Five years had gone by since that morning, and it still rested where it had fallen. Of all her things that surrounded him, filling the rooms and closets of the old house with her memory, it was the single strand of hair that mattered to him most.

*****

Bryan wiped the tears from his face with the blanket before tossing it off and stood up; the tired floor boards creaked under his sudden weight. Reaching across the bed, he carefully lifted the pillow and returned it to the bottom of the dresser before he gently closed the drawer and turned off the light.

He found his house shoes below the night stand and slipped them on. As he shuffled across the room toward the door he paused in front of the wood stove, holding his hand out to check if it was still putting off heat from the log he had added sometime during the night. He whispered to the silhouette lying quietly on the rug beside it. "Come on, Molly; I know it's early, but we need to get up now. I have to get ready to leave later today, but you can stay with our friend Sophie down the road. She's such a good neighbor to us, and I know you like to visit her; I know you like to play with her little dogs. I promise this one will be just a short trip; I'll be back in a few days, and then we can go to the lake. How's that sound?" He opened the door and patted the front of his thigh to coax her up. "Walk with me girl; let's go outside."

The collie struggled to her feet and shook off the night; she followed him down the stairs and through the hallway to the kitchen. Trotting past him, she found her spot by the back door and patiently waited for him to open it.

Bryan pushed the button on the light above the stove and held it for a few seconds; it flickered and hummed as it came to life. He half-filled the reservoir of the coffee maker, then placed a paper filter and coffee in the basket before flipping on the switch. The bottle of aspirin was on the counter beside the sink where it always was, and he grabbed it without looking, counted four in his hand and then poured himself a glass of cloudy water.

"I hate to say it, old girl, but I should probably set the alarm to go off earlier. Her dream is coming sooner, and I really don't want to be asleep when it comes." Looking down at her gray, aging face, Bryan thought he saw just a trace of sadness in her eyes. "The nights are getting worse, aren't they Molly; pretty soon I won't be able to sleep at all and then what do we do?" He swallowed the pills with a long drink and emptied the rest in the sink. "You want to go outside, don't you?"

Her tail answered, slapping excitedly against the wall. She paced back and forth; her breathing accentuated with puffs of heavy panting that sounded like she wanted to bark but didn't want to make any noise. "Quiet now. Take it easy, girl; you don't want to get too worked up and hurt yourself." Molly backed away awkwardly as Bryan approached to let her outside, her arthritic hips now wobbling noticeably, struggling to keep her rear legs steady beneath her. He stroked her soft head and then down along the nape of her neck. "It's just you and me, little lady." Then he gave her a gentle pat on the rump before she disappeared through the open door.

Bryan followed her across the porch and down the few steps that led to the yard. A gibbous moon was slowly falling in the western sky but still glowed bright enough for them to see. They walked together for a while in a wide circle until Molly found a place to relieve herself. It was at the edge of the garden that ran along the garage and ended at the corner of Bryan's workshop. Neglected now, the raised beds had been overrun with wild rye and ragweed; blackberry bushes planted along the trellis now lay smothered below it, fallen over from seasons of unharvested weight. Around it, the fence had become a gray-green thicket of poison-hemlock; the umbel flowers now hanging dry, ready to drop before the approaching spring. It was Mary's garden, and the day she died, the garden died too.

When Molly stopped along the fence to pee, Bryan looked up, gazing up at the flawless canopy of night; the stars were clear and countless. Beneath his feet the grass was stiff and cold; a new dusting of snow lay on the sleeping ground like white lace. In the field behind the yard, the snow had settled into the furrows separating the ridges of soil and broken stalks of corn. The corrugations of earth, dormant in the long wait for longer days, ran from the edge of the yard into the waning night. They converged at an imaginary point somewhere on the horizon far beyond where he could yet see. Daylight was still two thousand miles away.

After Molly finished, she weakly clawed at the grass with her hind paws and then leaned her hips against Bryan as if she needed to rest from the effort. He reached down and scratched her behind the ears. "Good girl; let's go back inside. I'll make you some breakfast."

As they crossed the yard toward the steps, Bryan hesitated for a moment and became still. From the glow of the kitchen window, four squares of light stretched across the ground and fell just short of where the two of them stood, paused between the house and the barren farmland. Bryan looked up at the empty window centered above the porch, and Molly looked too. It was Emma's window.

Many years had gone by since his little girl had last stepped through her window onto the roof below. Mary said that Emma's fearlessness was Bryan's fault, for carrying her out there when she was hardly more than a baby, just so they could watch the sunrise together. When she had first climbed out by herself, Bryan was working on his tractor in the yard below, and it had both surprised and worried him; she was only four years old. He knew she would be careful, but he watched her for a long while to make sure she stayed near the window and away from the edge, just like he had taught her. Later, he grew easy with her presence above him, watching, being near him as he did his chores in the yard. She used to tell him that standing on the roof made her feel real tall—just like her daddy.

During afternoons when the weather was warm, Emma would sit up there and read her picture books in the cool shade of the house or gaze at the line of river bluffs to the east at the end of the day, watching them change from cream to milky orange with the sinking sun. On the weekends, she might watch Bryan ride his tractor back and forth across the field or glance up at him from her reading as he came and went through the big door in the side of his workshop, going about his projects. Oftentimes on weekdays in the summer when he stayed at his office past dark, she would be on the roof with her blanket and pillow, waiting there for him when he came home, her voice calling from above like a sweet breeze as he emerged from the garage, calling him to come upstairs and tuck her in bed. It was a cherished but painful memory from a lost lifetime, a time when Bryan was free to linger here in the yard just for the chance to see his little girl wave to him from the roof below the window of her room.

But the roof was now empty and the window barren, except for the draperies that hung loose and waved ever so slightly in the cold, falling air inside the glass. The sash and trim were blistered with peeling paint from the absence of repairs that had gone undone for too long. A loose board draped from the eave and clapped against the house when the wind blew; it had almost worked itself free. The gutter, split at the seam above the window, spilled water across the glass when it rained, and it too had been left unattended.

There was a time when Bryan would have easily fixed it all,

but now he chose not to. He had lost the will to climb out on Emma's roof, as if repairing these things might be an admission that he was moving on and letting her go—but he could never let her go.

Reaching down, he scratched Molly lightly between her ears again. "You remember her, don't you girl?" She pushed her head against his touch. "I remember her too."

He looked away from the house, back across the field into the darkness and reflected on the absence of color in the pre-dawn landscape. He spoke aloud in a tragic epiphany, "It's all gray, Molly, just like the night is now. The color is there, but I just don't see it anymore. Even during the day I can't see it, and even if I could, I really don't want to. It left with her—all of it. I know you loved Emma, everyone did, but she was my baby and my joy; she was my *color*."

Standing in the middle of the frozen yard, he faced the cold, gray emptiness of his life without color. "It all means nothing without her." He waved his hand through the air in front of him, speaking to Molly as if she could understand, but he was really just speaking to himself. "I'd do anything to have my little girl back again—*anything*. He let the morning tears fall freely down his face; they felt like razors against his skin. The traces of Emma's life beckoned his heart and stabbed at his soul.

*****

Bryan turned to walk back to the house but sensed a sudden change in the air as if the pressure was falling before bad weather, and he knew what it meant. His ears grew vacuous, receding to an anxious silence. He slammed his eyes closed and tried to think of Mary with him somewhere, anywhere in the other time, but it was no use; the sounds arrived anyway just as they did before. Slowly at first, the hissing began in his left ear and circled through his head to the right. Sewn within it, he could vaguely hear Emma crying to him repeatedly from someplace far away, a sad whisper that ripped at his heart: *please, daddy...,* but the clatter was rapidly gaining strength like the throttle of the van's diesel pulling away in his dream. And then the howling arrived and overpowered it all, like the wail of sirens that descended upon him every horrible night as he chased her empty bus.

Daddy, will you come with me?

He shook his head violently to listen, to break free of the clamor, but as soon as he could quiet his brain for a moment, it would begin all over again. Faster and faster the sounds cycled, *her voice, the diesel, the sirens...* they clicked rapidly between his ears, repeating over and over. He had to break the sequence of urges before they ransacked his mind; pulses of love, fear and rage anxiously beat from his chest, one after another. He fell to his knees, pushing the sides of his head to keep the painful pressure from exploding his skull. *Concentrate on my voice, Bryan,* he heard Mary suddenly call to him, somehow breaking through it all. *I'm here now, lover, just listen to me; concentrate on my voice, and I promise it will all go away.* And he did. And it did.

His ears grew quiet, and the pain receded; his thoughts became still. In the fog of exhaustion that followed appeared a glimpse of her window and roof as they once were; with it arose the sweet but impossible anticipation of Emma being there above him. Behind his closed eyes the color of a memory began to fill his mind like sweet wine, intoxicating him with the image of... *their pretty farmhouse surrounded by spring willow swaying in a light wind. Four white posts standing clean and straight, holding the roof above the shaded porch, dressed in a hedge of neatly trimmed evergreen. The roof rising gently away, resting below the sill of her open window, drapes breathing in the morning air, early sunshine mixing with shadows of departing clouds drifting in a silent song across the butter-colored wall.*

Her pillow and quilted blanket lying neatly in front of it, waiting for her to arrive, the corners curling slightly in the breeze. A lone hawk circling overhead through an eternity of blue sky spinning lazily above it all.

*****

When the imagery left him, Bryan didn't move, vainly hoping that it might return. He pulled a deep breath through his nose and felt the cold, cruel air of the present. Reluctantly, he opened his eyes to find what he knew would still be there. Everything had changed back to what it was, and the color had gone away too. He slowly struggled to his feet; it was time to go inside.

As he reached the porch, he paused to answer Emma's question, her question from the dream. To the empty roof and the billion stars still gathered above, he released his reply.

"I will come with you soon!"

His voice, a hard mixture of sadness and anger, shattered the quiet and thundered off the wall of the broken house, echoing back to him as if an affirmation to a promise.

Bryan shuffled into the house and closed the door, forgetting for a moment that he had left his old companion behind, alone in the yard.

*****

Molly looked up at the four dark squares of Emma's window and tried to stand still, as still as her fragile hips would allow. She had slept on the floor next to Emma's bed in the back bedroom on the second floor of the old house every night of every day of Emma's life and for a very long time after she was gone. Molly didn't know to be angry; she was just waiting for her little friend to come home.

*****

–5–

A SHORT ROSE

Some said the D stood for Death, but D-pod wasn't death-row. By design, the massive walls quelled escape but also silenced the intelligible transfer of a voice making even the most basic of human contact futile. Only the wailing, siren-screams from beyond sanity's edge held enough sound energy to pierce the monoliths and thick steel doors. 'D' was a vessel of hardness, gripping sound so tightly that even the calming effect of a passive silence was not possible. From the six concrete slabs that defined his existence, the echoes of a man's breath, like the incessant ticking of a clock, whispered to him and damned him even as he slept.

Left alone in his cell year after year a man became riddled mad by a contradiction: the physical confinement of one's body, and the freedom of one's mind to come and go. His comprehension of the self seesawed randomly between piercing acuity and a sensory wasteland. It wasn't death row, but it wasn't long before the men who were confined there wished that it were.

'D' was home and hell to forty-eight men, most of whom dwelled outside the limits of tolerant behavior in one of the harshest social environments imaginable. D-pod was maximum security isolation housing, sequestering the most vicious inmates to protect the rest, and for a repentant few, mercilessly preyed upon by the evil and strong, it was offered as a place of asylum, a chance to live out their sentence ironically within inches of the predators who would otherwise take pleasure in cutting their throats. Although compressing and cold, *Death Pod* was the only place in Rockville Federal Penitentiary where someone like a convicted pedophile could ever hope to survive.

*****

The watch officer canceled the locking mechanism on the door to D8, releasing it with a click, then triggered the pneumatic operator from his remote position in the pod control room. Thurman Goethe's attention had been focused on monitoring the first moments of the night's slow change from darkness to dawn through the four-inch tall window high on the back wall of his cell. If he got close enough and low enough he could look up and out to steal a thinly framed view of the emerging Colorado sky. This was Goethe's final morning at the end of thousands of mornings, and he afforded himself the pleasure of watching one last time. When he heard the lock pop open, he withdrew from the window immediately, crossing his cell in three long strides, and squeezed through the slowly widening passage.

Halfway into the opening, Goethe sensed the absence of something and paused.

Wicked thing,

This brain

Of mine

Piloting my way

Thoughts, like footprints

Washed by rain,

And time

Here I am

But where have I been?

"Carelessness," he said stepping backwards into the vacant cell. *That's what got you in here in the first place, Thurman.* He pulled his gym bag from the shelf above the bed and checked it for the few personal items he could claim as his own. From below his mattress he retrieved his journal and sat on the edge of the bunk for a moment. Thumbing through the pages of poetry, he admired the shear bulk of material he had written; it was all very good. He tore out the last page that he had scribbled on the night before and set it on the pillow for the next occupant to find. As he stood, he glanced down smiling at the few, concise words he had written before sliding the journal into the bottom of the bag.

a) Hide
b) Hunt
c) Submit
  Pick one, asshole, or DIE

Then Goethe turned happily away from a fourth of his existence and walked into the dayroom for the last time.

*****

Twenty feet in front of him the door to the secure corridor wouldn't wait. Nearly sprinting, he cleared the narrowing passage and stopped his forward momentum just a few feet from the curved concrete wall below the control room. The mirrored glass tilted just over his head and reflected him standing below it, warping his body into a distorted pose that made him appear like he was bending over backwards. He had always thought the room looked as if conceived in science fiction, like some shiny bullet-proof cocoon, a place made for cowards to hide. Behind the glass, he sensed the officer's eyes peering down on him, and he felt the spineless distain broiling behind those eyes as well.

Goethe calmly looked up, through his own reflection, into the unseen void beyond, and imagined the hairy little prick sitting naked in a chair—a fat, faceless head drooling and bobbing side to side, pushing lighted red and green buttons with

29

fat hairy little fingers as if in a railway switch yard, directing which tracks the box cars full of cattle would follow to the slaughter. Goethe stared motionless up into the glass and would have spit blood through it if he could. He would cut the prick too if he ever got the chance. *Perhaps someday soon; Thurman's not that particular anymore. He can find you.*

After savoring the urge for a moment, he turned away and casually followed the curved wall toward the interlock vestibule, trailing his hand along the cold, gritty surface as he did. Above, Goethe imagined the fat man turning slowly in his chair, tracking him to the secure door where he would be made to wait for as long as the hairy little prick pleased.

A long minute passed. "Be careful you don't blind yourself," Goethe mumbled through his clenched teeth. He was sure the son-of-a-bitch was playing with his pecker. *Go ahead, you fat little man; take your time; enjoy yourself. Thurman will see you soon enough. You have a lovely wife and little girl, don't you?* A buzz, then a click, and the door slid out of his path. He stepped into the vestibule, but the door remained idly open.

"You sure you don't want to change your mind, Thurman?" The coward's grating words came through the speaker above him, followed by phony laughter. "Don't worry; we'll save a spot for you. The short roses always come back."

Goethe ignored the taunting because he had to. It was just to agitate him—to add to his misery, but he wasn't miserable; that's only what they thought he was: a miserable man who had done wretched things, things he would soon reclaim. *You can do this, Thurman. Just a little longer like you promised me. Let them think their ignorant thoughts. They will never understand you; no one possibly could. You survived this rat hole, and you're much stronger now. They didn't make you miserable, Thurman; they made you stronger.* Then he thought of his last mistake and all the lost years it had cost him. *Of course, you do remember it was your weakness for that Blake boy that got you in here. I'll never let you be weak again!*

Another buzz, another click, and the door began to close. Goethe held his breath until he heard the lock engage. In front of him was another door and another wait, but he didn't mind now if he had to stand there all day. Without expression, he looked up into the camera and wondered how many assholes in this massive prison were looking back at him just then. He was finally free of Death Pod, and he wanted to smile at them all.

*****

Beyond the vestibule, a long corridor led to the master control station, another secure room raised above the floor but larger than the one he had just left behind. It was also wrapped in hardened glass although, instead of mirrored, this glass was only heavily tinted and clear enough to see through. The room was dark but backlit from the light in the corridor that continued beyond. Goethe could easily discern the shape of the guard who was standing rigidly inside but couldn't determine if the shape was turned toward him or away. Regardless, Goethe knew he was being watched from there. He looked back into the camera and then at the motionless silhouette in the control room and began to wonder if it was a real breathing man or just a cardboard cut-out. *What are you thinking about, Mr. Jail Boy? I bet it's hard to masturbate in there when people can see you. It's a shame they don't pipe nitrogen into this little room I'm standing in, now isn't it? I bet you wish you could gas Thurman right here and watch him die. How nice would that be?*

As if he had heard Goethe's thoughts, the officer picked up something from the console and held it in the air for him to see. It was a rose. With one hand he held the stem, with the other he grasped it just below the flower and snapped it in half but not quite all the way through. In slow arcs he waved it side to side above him, the heavy bloom swinging from the broken stem contrary to the sweep of his hand. He did this until the stem weakened enough to send it to the floor. He stood still for a few moments with his hand lingering over his head, holding the decapitated rose, then reached down to the console and released the lock.

Goethe heard the familiar click and moved closer to the door as it began to slide away. With a wide grin he smiled up at all the assholes behind the camera; he just couldn't help himself this time.

*****

Release processing went much quicker than he had expected, and other than a few torments from the Property Clerk, which he easily ignored, it had gone uneventfully. His gym bag was a little heavier now with the few items they had confiscated from him eight years ago. Most of it he wanted to throw away rather than carry with him but decided to deal with it later. After passing through one last secure vestibule, Goethe found himself standing outside in a wide green yard that buffered the prison from the state road and the small empty parking area on the other side. It was a brisk March morning, but he wasn't cold.

Grass. Goethe reached down and drew his hand across the manicured surface still stiff in the morning chill. The lawn stretched away from him for a hundred yards in both directions and he wondered how many trustees were whored into keeping it so lush in the cold, arid climate. *Bastards—every one.* He pulled up a handful and recalled its sweet smell; it had been a very long time. In front of him, a single walkway led through a pair of gates in the double fence line and ended at the gravel shoulder along the edge of the blacktop. A single car with its occupant idled at the curb, but it wasn't there for him.

Crossing the yard, he sensed the beginnings of a brilliant sky gathering above, but he deliberately avoided looking at it. He was also intensely aware of the low sun kissing the side of his face and ignored that too—for now. The moment wasn't yet right. There were still two rows of fence and coils of razor wire standing between Goethe and his freedom. He took a deep breath. *Just a few more steps, Thurman.*

As he approached the first gate it began to open. He was lured by the shimmering layers of steel mesh and wire as they fell in and out of alignment, creating an alternating pattern of metallic barrier—then electrified openness. And passing through the final gate, Goethe felt like he had finally been cut loose from his moorings, a mighty vessel liberated to head out to the deep, open sea.

Swiftly now this night,

I cut through all that rises

To my sharpened bow

Fail never, my might

I, gray prowler of the sea,

Am the Destroyer!

*****

Thurman Goethe stood outside the Rockville Federal Penitentiary a free man. The prison had arranged for transportation from a Canon City taxi company, but it was nowhere in sight. He glanced at his watch, 7:13 a.m. His ride was late, but he was in no hurry this morning and, right now, he really didn't care if the cab came at all. It was ten miles to town, and he could easily be there by noon. If the cab came, he could flag it down along the road, or he could hitch a ride from a passing car, but he decided he would do neither. He had all day—*his* beautiful, unbounded day—and he would make sure to enjoy every step.

Goethe turned east toward the sun, targeting a road sign three hundred yards down the pavement, beyond the end of the fence line. That's where he would stop and allow himself an unfettered view of his new sky; first he had to put some distance between him and his hell of the last eight years. The sun was only an hour old but had already begun to burn some of the chill off the morning. Behind him, to the west, the Rocky Mountains were painted gray and chalky blue; the lower foothills just hinting at the emerging pastels from a mild winter and an early spring. With each step he could feel a lifting sensation; a smile spread across his face. Starting today, everything was going to be alright.

Squinting against the bright, rising sun, Goethe strolled casually down the gravel shoulder of the two-lane blacktop. He liked the warmth on his face as he walked; there was a slight breeze from the north, and the fresh air tasted much better than he remembered. He turned around to admire the silent beauty of the mountains he hadn't seen in years and walked backwards for a while, taking awkward but confident steps knowing there would be no wall or fence to stop him now. Except for the penitentiary crowding the foreground, the imagery was nearly perfect.

He kicked something with his heel, almost stumbling, and looked down to find a small dog lying stiff at the side of the road. *Why hadn't you noticed it before, Thurman? This is not good.* The side of its belly gaped open and was hollowed from the feeding of scavenger birds helped by young flesh flies that now buzzed in and out of the hole in defiance of the cold air; they swarmed around Goethe's feet. He squatted over the carcass and poked at the broken ribs; his head took a tilt of curiosity. Feeling warmth growing inside him, he stroked the head of the crushed animal.

Treasures,

once alive

ride the tides

and wash to my feet.

Beauty is never made

But always something found

Standing, he glanced one more time at the dead creature, then continued down the road until he reached the end of the outer fence. The road sign was still a hundred yards away, but Goethe wanted to stop here, having decided that this exact spot marked the threshold to his new beginning. One step farther and the prison would be forever behind him.

*****

Fifty feet from the edge of the blacktop, an abandoned guard tower anchored the corner of the fence and rose above the clay ground like a medieval bastion. He left the pavement and walked toward it, circling around slightly toward the east to stay in the sun. The morning breeze pushed gently against its vacant massiveness but slipped unheeded through the broken windowpanes in the perch. High-resolution cameras were mounted to a mast rising above the roof and had replaced the humans once posted there. They peered diligently in all directions across the empty landscape.

Goethe stood near the base of the tower and spit at it, shy of hitting his target by several feet. He glanced at the mountains to the west and then back down the road to the car still waiting at the gate and to the years he could now leave behind. His long shadow reached across the red earth, through a narrow patch of scrub grass and climbed up the wall of the tower. He stepped forward so that the full silhouette of his torso was there on the concrete surface for him to study. In his stenciled image he saw that he was still lean, although his shoulders were perhaps not as square as they were when he first entered this place. Even so, he was more than satisfied. He ran his fingers across the stubble above his neck and felt the broad, bare dome of his baldness; it was his one physical change which he loathed.

It's time to look at your beautiful sky, Thurman. But something stopped him. He became keenly alert. It was a familiar but involuntary sensation, like the constant vigilance he had learned to keep within the walls that he now stood beyond. He sensed danger but couldn't identify the source and he was terrified to turn and face it. *That can't be; you're out here and they're still in there.* Danger turned to defiance. *Dammit— Thurman is free!*

A sharp pain burned through his hand. He dropped his bag, grabbing for the wound, and spun around instinctively toward the threat; just as he did another more violent pain exploded through his groin and buttocks. The far-off sound of the high-powered rifle reports came next, but Goethe never heard them. The force knocked him backwards, but he stayed on his feet staggering for a moment, then dropped to the ground with his legs folded under him. His back, neck and head arched in agony as he groped the warm wetness between his legs. He saw the tower wall inverted above him and became terrified by the wide splatter of blood. *Thurman's blood!* At the center of the red spray, a three-inch circle of concrete had shattered from dirty gray to white; a scarlet cloud of dust hung in the air and drifted up lazily in the light wind. Adrenalin charged his nervous system; instantly and inexplicably he was sitting up on bent knees looking down. He knelt with his head bowed forward looking into the dark, ragged mess of flesh and fabric where his crotch was just an instant before. Vomit spewed from his mouth as nausea overtook him, followed by fear. He swayed slightly, left to right, and then fell back again, his head hitting the dry, hard ground with a muffled thud. The moment stood still.

Goethe lay next to the prison with his lower legs hidden somewhere beneath him. Feeling nothing below his waist, he struggled to find them with his hands, certain that they too were gone. He grabbed the open gym bag next to him, spilling the contents across the ground; he slapped around blindly clearing away clothes and books until he felt the familiar leather cover of his journal. He brought it to his side clutching it tightly, weeping while his life, warm and red, emptied from him and flowed away in a widening crimson stain, filling the cracks in the clay and clotting with dried clumps of scrub grass, dirt and sand. In the slow march of minutes that followed, Goethe's mind fought the freezing darkness that was trying to invade him, searching for answers, reasons, understanding—*anything*, but his mind was empty.

A surprising calm followed the anger and fear, and within his fading consciousness he began to count slowly backwards from thirty-four. Each was a year of his life, and for each year uttered he combed his memory for a single image or thought, something that would carry him away and let him be somewhere else, somewhere away from the horrible prison, this evil place, this cold ground, but there was nothing. When his countdown reached ten he gave up; it hurt too much to go any further; it hurt even more than his wounds. Age ten marked the moment in time between what he could remember and what he chose not to. He reached into the wet hole between his thighs and raised his hand to see the blood, but his sight blurred and it made him afraid again. As he struggled to pull air into his lungs a simple, final truth came to visit him. *You are dying, Thurman.*

Then, in a tumultuous instant, his vision receded through a dark tunnel to the back of his skull, and from the edge of the sudden darkness, with perfect clarity, he saw his cerebral nakedness. And at the other side, far across the cavernous space of his mind, two round openings filled with brilliant blue pierced the black. As they grew smaller and farther away, Goethe thought he could see thin wisps of clouds cross an infinite sky— his sky. It was beautiful.

A brittle leaf clings

Postponing its solo journey,

Then yields to fall winds

He felt very cold.

*****

−6−

TOM RUSSELL

The light tapping on his study door told Tom Russell that Haden, his youngest boy, was probably hungry for some pancakes. It was Sunday morning, and Sunday morning meant pancakes. Last night he had promised Haden that he would play catch with him after breakfast, but only if he was able to get a little paperwork done first. Katie, the middle child, was next door at her friend's house and would be home soon; she would need help on her fourth-grade social studies project. Rob, the fifteen-year-old, hadn't asked for anything but was already out in the garage trying to get his dirt bike running again, and he would probably need some help before the job was finished. The every-other weekend he got to spend with his kids just wasn't long enough, especially since he kept letting his work interfere with their time together. Somehow he couldn't find enough time to spend with them while he was still living under the same roof; he wondered how he was supposed to find the time now that he no longer did.

Tom closed the case file he had been laboring over since before dawn and scribbled a thought on a post-it that he stuck inside the cover before tossing it on the pile of active FBI cases filling the corner of his desk. He picked up the thick red accordion folder from the floor and returned it to the top of the stack where he kept it to remind him not to make the same mistakes with his kids that he had made with their mother. Between each of the hundreds of pages of research, records and photographs inside the red folder is where the book of Tom's ruined marriage was written, and he left it there on top, as a sledgehammer, a visual encouragement to put down his work for a few days a month and spend a little more time with his kids. Had he found that discipline while working that particular case, he'd probably be in his bathrobe right now helping his ex-wife Nicole make pancakes for their three children in the kitchen of his old house on the other side of Arlington. He grabbed the folder back off the pile and set it on his lap. The edges were worn thin from thousands of hours of study and were irreverently held together with gray duct tape where they had separated. The title had long ago faded illegible.

*****

The case had begun more than four years ago with the intense search for a child predator that had been plaguing the South County neighborhoods of St. Louis through early that spring and into late summer. The perpetrator abducted his victims by luring them into believing their mother had been hurt, and he was sent to bring the child to the hospital where she was taken. Once in his car, he would offer a soda or candy heavily laced with zolpidem or benzodiazepine, both widely distributed sleep prescriptions. When he had completed his business, he would shave a three-inch sampling of hair from the back of their head before leaving them in the middle of the night wrapped in a blanket, drugged but alive, at remote spots along the service roads that paralleled the several highways leading in and out of the city.

At the time, Tom had been sent from Washington to work with the joint-agency task force set up between the local FBI resident office and St. Louis County law enforcement. The County had been under heavy media criticism for making little progress in the investigation and approached the FBI for assistance. It was turning into a long summer, and the community demanded that the nightmare come quickly to an end. After weeks of pushing the limits of every resource involved in the case, Tom narrowed the investigation's focus to a single person of interest: a registered child sex offender by the name of Greg Levy.

*****

Levy had settled into a south city apartment soon after his release from the state prison in Sedalia after serving three years on a Class-C felony for child enticement, and he had been out on parole for almost a year when the abductions first began. His history seemed to vaguely fit the crimes: the hospital ruse, the drugs, the blankets were somewhat similar to his prior known methods, but they also clearly indicated an escalation in the severity of his engagement with minor children. Regardless, Tom saw a pattern and was convinced that there was a connection. In his mind everything seemed to fit, everything except for the shaving of the hair. That radical detail had never been associated with any of Levy's prior offenses. It bothered Tom because he knew it was extremely rare for a serial predator to change their behavioral pathway that significantly and abruptly.

It was decided not to bring Levy in for questioning. They had no hard evidence, and if he fooled their interrogations, he would likely go quiet for as long as necessary to avoid capture— pedophiles liked to be with children, but they liked their *freedom* to be with children even more. Instead, a covert 24/7 surveillance was set up to shadow Levy with the intent of catching him when he attempted to take the next child. The pattern of abductions was repeating about every nine days, and Tom knew it would be just a matter of time before Levy's urges would kick in again.

Four days into the first week of the operation Levy went missing, and seventy-two hours later his dead body was recovered, badly mutilated, from a construction dumpster in a remote corner of Jefferson Barracks Park, not far from the apartment building where he lived. If he had not already been under investigation for the sexual assault of children, Levy's murder would have otherwise looked like a gang-related south-city homicide; that and the disturbing fact that his body had been shaved, or more specifically, cut hairless, and covered in quicklime before being stuffed in a plywood crate four-feet long and twenty inches square. Had the trash hauler not eyed the plywood to take home to use for shelving in his garage, Levy would still be missing and forever entombed somewhere deep in the county landfill.

The only witness had been one of Levy's elderly neighbors who was entering her apartment across the hall from his and saw a large man knocking on Levy's door the evening before he disappeared. She hadn't gotten a very good look at the man, but she was able to provide a good enough description for the sketch artist to draw a simple illustration indicating his height and build but not much more.

She remembered that he was a white man and big, almost filling the frame of Levy's doorway, but because he had worn a loose-fitting jacket and ball cap, she couldn't really guess his weight or recall any features of his face or hair; she thought he may have had a beard, but maybe not. She said she hadn't felt afraid of the visitor and entered her apartment before Levy answered the door. She couldn't really recall if he actually had. After the neighbor had gone inside, she didn't remember hearing anything at all that would have suggested a struggle, but she did admit that her hearing was poor and she always kept the volume turned up when watching the TV. Until Tom knocked on her door a few days later, she had forgotten all about the strange man she had seen in the hallway. She had also failed to remember the plywood crate and furniture dolly she walked by when she had gotten off the elevator that evening. Since they were both gone the next morning when she left to go to her doctor's appointment, she had forgotten all about them too.

Even though Tom's team had run a tight surveillance on the

apartment building, they had only been interested in the comings and goings of Greg Levy in 4E. They didn't pay much attention to the other eighty occupants or, for that matter, anyone who looked like they were moving their belongings in or out of the building, such as someone pushing a dolly and a plywood crate through the rear service door. People moved in and out of apartments all the time.

The sketch artist had drawn a large, mysterious figure with the brim of his ball cap pulled low, the uncommitted features of his face obscured within the long shadow. The pose showed him broadly from the back, with square set shoulders and well over six feet tall; his face was turned to the side but not quite in profile. Except for his size and build, indicated by the one-foot grid printed across the paper, almost nothing about the drawing indicated any other significant characteristic of the man for whom Tom Russell would inexplicably destroy his marriage over the next ten months trying to find, nothing except for the gesture of his one large hand held open toward the elderly neighbor as if to suggest that he meant her no harm. Just as she had insisted, the drawing didn't make the man look dangerous at all; it was simply the image of an undefined stranger captured in lead pencil standing alone in a hallway, posed as if he was patiently waiting for a closed door to open and the chance to brutally kill Greg Levy.

*****

To everyone involved in the investigation, the most gripping aspect of the murder was that the body had been completely shaved, and it was obvious that the man in the hall, if he was the killer, had not been gentle going about it. The application of caustic quicklime to the multitude of coarse lacerations suggested that pain was the killer's primary objective in doing so. The medical examiner concluded that Levy was alive at the time and had probably endured quite a bit of it. Tom knew a little about quicklime, or 'burnt' lime as they called it at the concrete batch plant he worked one summer in college. When mixed with water, it could cause severe corrosive damage to unprotected skin similar to second-degree burns. He remembered how it felt the first time he accidently spilled some on his sweaty arms—he couldn't rinse it off fast enough.

Levy's mouth was packed full of the lime and concealed a piece of jagged red glass that analysis confirmed to be the implement used to remove Levy's hair and a fair amount of his skin as well. The cause of death was determined to be asphyxia in the form of suffocation as a result of the lime hydrating in his mouth rapidly, heating and expanding from contact with his saliva and the moisture in his throat and nasal cavities. The shaving of the hair and particularly the near scalping of a patch at the back of his skull meant that the kill was clearly in retaliation for the crimes that Levy was suspected of committing.

Most of the investigative team believed there was a correlation between Levy's death and two similar murders that occurred within a few hours of St. Louis earlier that year, but Tom wasn't convinced at all. The first two kills: Michael Chapman in Columbia, Missouri, and Allen Randall in Paducah, Kentucky, were similar to Levy in that they were also convicted child predators; that fact was obvious and impossible to ignore. But other than the victim's sexual tendencies, the murders had very little in common, particularly the level of violence exhibited in the method of Levy's death compared to the others, as well as the manner in which Levy's body was disposed—*like so much trash.*

Tom argued that the escalation of violence was too sudden and *way too* severe. He had seen the pattern before: the killer gets comfortable in his craft, develops a taste for it, then ratchets up the game, but the vicious nature of Levy's death was orders of magnitude more violent than the prior two and not a gradual progression at all. Besides, there had been no effort to conceal the bodies of Chapman or Randall. In clear contrast, the killer had intended Levy to completely disappear, buried under a mountain of St. Louis garbage. The fragment of glass in Levy's mouth also separated the cases. Tom knew it to be a significant element of the killer's method, but no glass was associated with the first two murders, and it was simply one more reason to challenge the connection. Then Tom discovered the hidden pattern.

*****

Michael Chapman, the first victim, was found dead in his Columbia apartment bathtub with a lethal level of Rohypnol in his system, the popular date-rape drug readily available on the nearby university campus. He died of a heart attack before he entered the water. When Tom dug into Chapman's criminal history, he discovered that three years previously Chapman had taken in a young runaway from New York City who was working at a local strip club and living in her car; she was barely sixteen years old. One night they took to partying and consuming too many cocktails laced with ample amounts of the same drug that would cause Chapman's death three years later. There was no evidence that the girl was raped, but she did drown in the bathtub sometime later that evening. Chapman admitted at trial that he provided the alcohol, but *she* must have laced the drinks with the drug; after all, the girl did work in a strip club. He testified that she had to have died after he passed out on the kitchen floor. The last thing he remembered was her crawling away from him, wanting to take a cool bath. Because of the contribution of the alcohol to the girl's death, Chapman was charged with a felony offense for supplying an intoxicant to a minor and was remanded to the state prison for thirty months.

The second victim, Allen Randall, was a middle school photography teacher who had coaxed some of his more gullible students to take rides with him in the Kentucky countryside where he would pay them to undress in front of his camera for a 'special' exhibit he was working on for a big art gallery in Memphis. To convince them that their identity would remain anonymous, he would have them pose with a black latex hood stretched over their head. Later, he would add their images to the collage of child nudity he kept in a locked room in his basement where he liked to watch his pornography. Shortly after he was released from the county jail, Randall was discovered strangled and naked on the floor in the motel where he was staying. His body had multiple ligature marks, but no bindings had been found by the police.

After what Tom had learned about Michael Chapman's death, he re-read the police report more carefully and studied the crime scene photographs for some detail he was sure had been missed. What caught his attention was the cheap motel print screwed to the wall above Randall's body. In one of the pictures that showed the frame clearly, the bottom screw appeared to be missing. When he went to the motel and removed the print, he found a series of photographs taped to the wall capturing several views of Randall's bound and naked body. His head was covered with a black latex hood.

Then, after Levy was killed, the murders stopped and the investigation was shut down ten months later. Several agents on the team thought that the spree, if it was one, may have simply run its course, but Tom knew otherwise. He didn't know why the killing stopped, but he knew it hadn't ended—something had changed; something was distracting the killer. The horrific nature of Levy's murder meant that a significant shift had occurred; a stressor had been introduced that had manifested in the extreme violence. The unknown subject, or UNSUB, wasn't done. With Levy, he had found his voice and was just getting started.

Before returning to Washington, Tom held a final press conference to announce that the killings had evidently ceased, and the unsolved cases were now considered cold. During the briefing, Tom offered a politically incorrect response to a reporter's question on public safety by casually stating that the killer *only* targeted child predators, referring to them derisively as 'short roses'. He then added that he was confident the general population was not and had not been in any real danger at any time.

The next morning the front page story in the St. Louis Post Dispatch suggested that Special Agent Russell's remarks had been openly callous toward the rights of misunderstood members of the community who were victims themselves and could not be held responsible for the urges that they struggled to control every day. The reporter had done her research and made sure to explain that *'short rose'* was prison jargon for convicted pedophiles. She then cited some disturbing statistics illuminating just how short their life expectancy was on the inside. The headline shouted across the top of the page:

'FBI Punts on the Short Rose Killer'.

*****

Now four years later, Tom still couldn't completely let go of the case; it was never far from his thoughts. He had been obsessed with the events in St. Louis and was still plagued by a single, simple question: *how was it that the killer could peg Levy for the crimes of that spring and summer, but it had taken a team of law enforcement and months of investigation to arrive at the same conclusion?* At first, he thought the killer must have known Levy or known about him, but that theory grew weak as soon as he tied Levy to the murder in Columbia, and when he locked down the connection to the Paducah killing, it evaporated completely.

Tom looked at the drawing of the big, faceless man standing in the hallway and rubbed his tired eyes. *The Short Rose Killer—SRK.* The name in the headline had stuck with him; it was perfect. *Why hadn't I thought of it?* He lingered on the drawing for a moment longer, then returned it to the plastic sleeve and slipped it into the front pocket of the red folder before tossing it back on the top of the pile. The rest of his work would have to wait until this evening after he dropped the kids off with his ex-wife at his old house on the other side of town. He brought his attention back to the tapping on the door.

"Yes, Haden."

The six-year-old poked his head into the room. "Dad! How did you know it was me?"

"Well, let's see," Tom answered analytically. "First, the knock was low on the door; that meant it was probably you, or it could have been Katie. I also heard a sniffle, just barely, but it was a definite sniffle. I remembered you were getting over a cold, Haden."

"Katie could have got a cold from me or one of her creepy friends; you never know." Haden was trying.

"Yes, but Katie's not here. She had a sleep-over next door with her friend, you know, one of the creepy ones. Besides, I know it was you; the dog gave you up," Tom said conclusively.

"Dad!?" Haden looked confounded. "How? Jake couldn't give me up; he's outside. I let him out myself!"

"Exactly, I know he's outside; I saw him through the window. Look." Tom pointed out the window. "He's sitting at the back door with *your* baseball in his mouth. He's not waiting for Katie; we've already established that she's next door. He's waiting on you or Robbie, and Jake doesn't play catch with Robbie; he plays catch with you. That puts you in the hall knocking on my door."

"But sometimes Robbie plays catch with Jake, dad; I've seen him before."

"Nope, Rob's out in the garage working on his dirt bike. I

saw him out there when I came downstairs. He's trying to get it going, so he can go riding later today before I have to take you guys back to your mom's."

"What if Rob came in to go to the bathroom? He might have knocked on the door." Haden was pretty sharp and liked to try to outsmart his dad.

"Sure, he could have, but I heard him go to the toilet less than five minutes ago; I heard him on the other side of this wall." Tom tapped on the paneling behind him.

Haden pressed the cross examination. "How did you know that wasn't me going to the bathroom before?"

"Easy—he flushed the toilet."

"But I flush the toilet sometimes!"

"Let's just say Rob's faucet is a little louder than yours," Tom slapped his thighs, "and maybe I'm a pretty good detective."

"Okay, dad," Haden confessed, "you got me."

Tom smiled. "So, good morning young man; what brings you knocking on my door? Are you hungry?"

"What did the fish say when he bumped into the wall?" Haden asked.

It was the same joke Haden asked him a month ago, but Tom couldn't get irritated. "Is that why you came in here, to tell me a joke?"

"Dad! What did he say?"

"I could guess, but I'd rather you tell me." Tom smiled as he waited for the punch line.

"Dam!"

Tom let out a chuckle. The same joke still sounded cute coming from his little kid. "Very funny Haden. Should I wash your mouth out with soap now, or should I wait until after breakfast?"

"Dad, you know! The thing that holds the water back!"

Tom laughed again. "I know, silly." He wrapped his arm around his son and scrambled his thick head of sandy-brown hair, then tickled him under his arms."

Haden started giggling uncontrollably and tried to get away. "Dad, don't do that; I hate it when you do that!"

"Okay, Haden," Tom let him escape, "since you fooled me with your little fish joke, how about some pancakes?"

"We better let Jake inside first; he needs to eat too. Will you play catch with us after breakfast? You promised."

Tom rubbed his eyes again and turned off the desk lamp. He was tired of reviewing his case files and needed a break anyway. It was supposed to be a long, quality weekend with his kids, but he had already spent most of the morning locked in his study.

"I'm in like a glass eye, buddy." Tom popped out of his chair, snatching up his son in one swift, effortless move. Like a sack of grain, he tossed Haden across his shoulder and carried him through the house and into the back yard where Jake was waiting eagerly for him to return. The retriever let the ball drop from his mouth and barked excitedly.

Tom set Haden down next to Jake and turned to go back inside, but Rob was standing in his way. He had Tom's cell phone loosely wrapped in a shop rag. There was more grease on his face than he had on his hands, and his face didn't look very happy at all.

"I can't believe they're calling you again on the weekend, dad, *our* weekend! Is there no other hot-shot in that fancy place you work who knows what to do, or are you the only one or something?" He dropped the phone in Tom's open hand. "And tell whoever it is that you *promised* to help me get my bike running this weekend, or did you forget that too? I could really use your help if you have a moment, you know, whenever you get done with saving the rest of the world."

"I'm sorry, Rob; I'll be out in the garage as soon as I finish this call. Haden, we'll make pancakes right after I help Rob." Tom could only smile weakly at his boys before going back into the house. He put the phone to his ear. "Yes?"

"Tom, this is Charlie; gotta a few minutes?"

Charlie Grainger had been Tom's first boss at the Behavioral Analysis Unit in Quantico, Virginia, before Grainger was promoted to Assistant Director over the entire Critical Incidence Response Group. That put him above the day-to-day investigative fray, managing a lot more resources and pushing a lot more paper than he cared to admit. Charlie had offered Tom his old job running the unit, but he turned down the offer along with the healthy bump in pay, arguing that he was built for field work and nailing the bad guys rather than driving a government desk. They hadn't talked in months, but Tom suspected Charlie kept his eye on him from his fancy eighth-floor office. They went back a long way and shared a lot of history, including SRK. Tom knew a call from Charlie on a Sunday morning would have to be important.

"Sure Charlie, it's been a while. What can I do for you?" Tom was sincere.

"Well, first, how are the kids? Rob's a junior now, isn't he? I bet Haden's getting big. How's that sweet little girl of mine?"

"Yeah, Charlie, the kids are good, I'm good, the dog is good, everyone's good; I appreciate you asking but shouldn't you be in church or something? I know you didn't call me just now to ask about the kids."

"That's correct, Tom."

Tom noticed the immediate shift in the tone of Grainger's

voice. He knew it meant the pleasantries were over, and Grainger was about to drop something significant on him. His old boss always changed his tone to get your attention; it was something he did just before he was about to tell you some information usually worth hearing.

"You remember the abduction of that couple out in Moline late last year? Their name was Lowen; uh, hold on a second..." Charlie's voice trailed off for a moment. "Bart and Alice. It sure smelled like your guy's handiwork, but the husband and wife thing didn't quite square up with the profile. Besides, you were spread pretty thin at the time and tied up with the 'Butcher' case, as I recall. You convinced me to let the boys in Unit Four handle it until they could come up with a body or two— otherwise you were too busy and didn't have the head space. I believe you had me promise to give you a call when they found the happy couple." Grainger paused to clear his throat. "Well Tom, they found the couple, and it's pretty safe to say they weren't very happy. This is me making good on my promise."

Tom's heart leapt. "How, Charlie? Where? When?"

"Some hunter up in Iowa got stuck out in the woods during a late winter storm a couple of weeks ago and found one of the bodies, or what was left of it—that would be Bart. Part of Alice was there too, but the hunter didn't know about her; he was probably too busy pissing his pants to look around much. When the sheriff showed up, the one corpse was obvious, but they also found the bones of a full leg and foot buried in the snow a few feet away; it still had a shoe on it, ladies' tennis—size nine. Since Bart's remains included one leg and most of the other, the extra one kind of threw off the body-part count. Their ankles were shackled together, and both were chained to a steel stake driven five feet in the ground. " Grainger stopped talking for a moment while it sank in, "Yeah, I figured that little nugget might get your attention, but there's more. It would be a lot better if we could talk in person."

Tom struggled to mask his enthusiasm for what Grainger was telling him. "Charlie, that's great news but shitty timing, as usual; it's my weekend with the kids, and you of all people should know what that means." He paused to muster all the self-control he could possibly summon. The best thing he could conceivably hear today was that Bart and Alice Lowen had been found dead and not by natural causes. The responsible father part of Tom hoped that Grainger would graciously apologize for the call and insist on phoning back later when the kids were gone or, better still, tomorrow morning. He still had plenty of work to do that he needed to finish tonight but had just come to the realization that focusing on anything else today was now going to be next to impossible. The other part of Tom wanted to run circles around the yard and dance with the dog. He bit his lip because he knew he would immediately regret what he was about to say; so much so that he had to force the words out of his mouth. "Can't this wait, Charlie? You know there is no way that I can come in right now."

"Not really, and you don't have to. I'm standing on your porch."

*****

Tom greeted Charlie warmly in the front hall and then walked him back to the study where they could talk openly behind the closed door; it had been a long time since Charlie had met with Tom in his home. The Van Gogh print over the mantle was still crooked and gathering more dust, the bottom half still hidden by stacks of well-used psychology textbooks and dog-eared operational journals. Rows of brown file boxes were still loosely piled along one wall and halfway down another and they made it look like Tom was either moving in or moving out—just like the last time Grainger was here.

Tom stood by the window and checked on Haden in the back yard. Rob had stayed outside and was playing catch with him.

Great kids. He turned to face his old colleague who obviously looked uncomfortable in his wool suit. Tom liked to keep the room a bit warm; it helped him relax, and that helped him think. "You didn't have to dress up for me, Charlie."

Grainger set his briefcase on the floor and settled on the arm of the leather couch; he was wiping a bead of sweat off his over-sized forehead with a handkerchief. "I can't help it, old school. You know me, Tom; leisure clothes make for leisure minds."

"I do know you, Charles, so how about *you're never too old to be stupid?*" Tom smiled. "Now take off your coat, you idiot; you're making me uncomfortable."

"Sure Tom, you're right; I believe I'm still among friends." Charlie tossed his coat across the back of the couch.

"Yes, you are Charlie, but that's about to change," Tom said. "Now it's really good to see you and I mean it, but you're making some angry boys out back; I can only keep the wolves at bay for so long." He pointed out the window. "Now, tell me everything before I'm forced to beat it out of you, or maybe I should just let them do it." He tapped on the glass.

"We think it's him, Tom. He's back."

The words hit Tom like a bomb blast; he knew exactly who Charlie meant, but he didn't understand his statement. If Grainger was right, the couple's bodies found in the Iowa woods meant that the Short Rose Killer had claimed two more victims after lying silent for a very long time, but these kills happened a year ago. That meant that SRK wasn't back from anywhere, at least not recently, and it also meant that the crime scene wasn't going to give up much in the way of usable forensics. Tom sat on the edge of his desk and, without realizing it, placed his hand on the red folder. "The Lowen's case was a year ago, Charlie; how can you say he's back? Do you mean—as in right now?"

"When I get done blabbering, I think you'll have the answer to your questions, so hear me out." Charlie loosened his tie.

"The circumstances around the Lowen's death strongly suggest it was him; then something went down yesterday and, well, that's the other part I didn't tell you on the phone, but I'll get to that in a minute. Tom, I came to you this morning because you're the best; you're the only one who can figure out all this crap."

Tom had held a blank expression on his face, waiting for his thoughts to coalesce and give it some kind of form, but a weak and marginally fake frown was all he could do. "As much as I'd like to believe it, how can you be sure that the Lowens were even him? There has to be something more to it, and don't stop at the foreplay. I need more information, Charles; some details would help me to think this through."

Charlie pulled off his tie and undid his top shirt button before loosening his collar. "Okay Tom, from the beginning. As I said, the Bart half of the pair was discovered by the hunter a couple of weeks ago in some dense woods not far from the Minnesota state line, about a hundred and fifty miles from Moline, where the Lowens went missing—pretty much between North and South Nowhere, I'd say. Apparently the hunter got stuck out there in some freak snow storm and was wandering around in the dark looking for firewood when he found what was left of the husband. The local sheriff got spooked by the extra leg thing and all the dungeon hardware, so he brought us in when he realized what they were dealing with. It's a good thing they called us when they did before messing things up too much; luckily they didn't touch or move anything and waited until we could get our anthropology team out there to process the site.

We're guessing if it was like the others, they were killed not too long after they disappeared, and that puts the bodies out in the weather for almost a year. We've brought the remains back to Quantico just last week and moved them up to the front of the line. Odontology was able to match up the teeth with Bart's records, but unfortunately there wasn't much else left for the lab to analyze. For now, we're just going to assume that the leg belongs to Alice; DNA says it's female, and we should be able to match it up with hers in a day or two. Skeletonization was pretty advanced, so I doubt we'll get anything to establish how they were killed. From what we can tell, there weren't any holes where there shouldn't be and no broken bones. The remaining fragments of the clothes we found might tell us something, but most, if not all, of the trace will be long gone. The important thing we know right now is that the Lowens were taken out there in the woods alive and killed later; the fact that they were chained to the ground kind of makes it obvious, don't you think? I wonder how long he kept them out there before he finished them off."

"Hold that thought." Tom started thumbing through the pocket at the back of the red folder; he remembered reading something about the Lowens that Charlie had emailed him back when they first went missing. When he found what he was looking for, he pulled the file and opened it on the desk, scanning through the pages quickly. "Charlie, they weren't taken out to the woods to *be killed*." He had already caught up to Grainger's thinking and was several steps ahead. "They were taken out in the woods and *left to die*. There's a big difference, and it's a critical distinction, particularly if we're talking about SRK." Tom pulled a page from the file and handed it to Charlie. "Right there—halfway down, read it. The Lowens were arrested for almost starving her three children; Bart was just the deadbeat stepdad; don't you remember? It made national news. Social Services took the kids away when they found out they were feeding them dog food and water. At first the couple thing didn't fit what we knew about SRK, but now I get it. It seems that our old friend chained the Lowens to the ground and left them out there so they would know how it feels to starve to death. *That,* Charlie, follows his M.O. to a tee."

"And that is why they promoted me upstairs, Tom." Grainger chuckled, "they figured they needed to get me out of the way of the sharp brains like yours. There are a couple of other little details that you might be interested in; let's say they're the icing on the cake. First, Bart did his time in the big house at Joliet and Alice did hers in Decatur. I know it's minor, but the inmate thing squares up with the other kills. Second, Bart was still wearing his leather coat and, this is the good part, lying in the bottom of his empty rib cage we found a small piece of red glass."

"This is great, Charlie! I apologize; thanks for coming by this morning—I mean it. You're right; he is back! The first kills were so long ago I figured by now we'd seen the last of him; four years is a long time to go quiet—well three years actually. This Iowa find could mean that he's re-opened for business but not yet up to full production. It doesn't help us much that the Lowens died in those woods a year ago; but the crime wasn't cold enough to destroy the two most important elements we know about SRK: his victimology and his method. The Lowen's child abuse history and the Edgar Allen Poe crime scene confirm both, and he was kind enough to leave us his signature in Bart's belly. He probably fed it to him as a last meal. Charlie, how he kills has a direct correlation to why he kills; he takes the eye-for-an-eye type approach—that's our guy. I shouldn't get too hopeful but I… what is it?" Tom looked at Grainger's face; it had a big grin across it. "What's so damn funny?"

"I'm glad you said that; let me show you something." Charlie opened his briefcase and pulled out a thumb drive; he handed it to Tom. "Stick this in your laptop and Merry Christmas. I'm going to find a pot of coffee. You're awake, so I assume there has to be one around here somewhere."

*****

Tom dragged the .avi file from the drive to his desktop and double-clicked the icon; it immediately filled the screen. The date and time stamp in the lower corner showed that it was taken early yesterday morning. It was high-resolution security footage from three stationary cameras mounted high above the ground. The video captured a ten-minute timeframe cycling through three different views about every fifteen seconds; each appearing to be from the same position but looking in different directions a little less than ninety degrees apart. There was an overlap between each field of view so the surveillance of the area caught by the cameras appeared to be uninterrupted. Tom watched the video run to the end and hit pause just as Charlie walked back in from the kitchen with two cups of coffee.

"I found a little brandy and spiced them up a bit." Charlie handed one cup to Tom. "I hope you don't mind. It's almost noon and I think we've earned it. Whaddya think of the video?"

"Yeah thanks, no worries. Okay Charlie, I see a man approaching the first camera from a little ways off until we lose him at the bottom of the frame at about seven minutes in. It looks like he's walking along the shoulder of a two-lane road. He stops once to check out something on the ground, but I can't make out what it is, probably road-kill. There's a high-security fence line about fifty feet from the shoulder and what looks like a corrections facility just at the right edge of the frame. The mountains in the background tell me it's somewhere out west, I'm guessing along the Front Range. It looks dated; I don't recognize it. The fencing returns to the wall before it gets to the corner of the building. That seems odd—not sure what their security guy was thinking. Anyway, we pick up the walker at the right side of camera two; when he gets to mid-frame he leaves the shoulder, walks toward the building and drops out of the field of view.

Camera three shows the road now at the right edge of the screen, looking the other direction; I'd say east based on the timestamp, glare and shadow directions. There's no security fence in this view, and the building is now on the left side of the screen. So the cameras are posted high at the corner of a secure facility and cover a two hundred seventy-degree field of view."

Tom re-started the video at the seven minute mark where the walker disappears from camera one and gets picked up by camera two. "Look, Charlie, he walks out of camera two but never makes it to camera three. He drops from the coverage and stops between the two, between the road and the building, at least for the duration of this footage. There were no cars, so he wasn't picked up. He's standing down there somewhere below the cameras and out-of-view. We have camera number two looking across the road into the countryside; we have some hills, low vegetation and no trees; nothing—" Tom's face broadened with a big grin, "*but there it is.*" He glanced at Charlie, who was looking right at him.

"You saw it, didn't you, Tom? I knew you wouldn't miss it; I had to watch the damn thing five times before I saw it, and I knew what I was looking for." Grainger was smiling too. "You're the best there is!"

"I missed it the first time through, but yeah, I just saw it." Tom moved the cursor back to the eight-minute mark and hit play. Twenty-two seconds later he hit pause. "Right there Charlie—on that knoll." He pointed at a tiny bright spot in the middle of the screen. "That's it right there; very interesting."

"Keep going, there's a second shot a few seconds later," Grainger added.

Tom let the video play for another ten seconds before pausing it again. "Okay, you're here in my study on a Sunday morning, so someone must be dead; that means when you say 'shot', you're talking about a rifle." Tom replayed the video and let it cycle through the events one more time. "At first I thought it was muzzle-flash, but it lacks the intensity, so we can assume he used a suppressor. If he was concerned about sound, he'd make sure his gear was blacked out also—no one polishes a rifle barrel before sniping someone. The flashes were bright but focused; more like a glint from the sun reflecting off, say, maybe a watch face? He was probably working the bolt after each shot;

that he'd chamber a round after the second one is telling; it also makes him right-handed in my book. We can assume the walker was the target since I didn't see a herd of elk or bison roaming around."

Grainger frowned at Tom's lame attempt at humor. "On that we can agree."

"So, Mr. Assistant Director, how's this tie back to SRK?"

Charlie pulled a folder from his briefcase and handed it to Tom. "The walker is Thurman Goethe. He was just released after doing eight at the Rockville Federal Pen for fondling a twelve-year-old boy."

"Got it, Charlie; he did time; that's a little obvious, don't you think?"

Grainger just smiled. "Prior to going in, we had been watching Goethe for child trafficking, but we were never able to close the deal, and he was moving around a lot. So when we got the chance, we sent him away on the assault charge just to get him off the street. He did most of his time sequestered from general pop; you know the short-rose thing. I've heard traffickers are even lower on the food chain, if that's even possible. Goethe wasn't on the outside much longer than the duration of that video before he was gunned down by the shooter you just saw in camera two."

"Okay, Goethe did bad stuff to kids, so that would get him on SRK's radar; and as for being a slammer alumni like the rest, well, we still have to figure that one out, but a long-distance rifle shot? It doesn't fit, not even remotely. He's an up-close kind of guy; forget about Randall and Chapman; that was him just getting warmed up. Look at Levy and the Lowens; they were abducted, then died a short while later in a very personal, cruelly individualized way. That's his method, Charlie. Death by a sniper shot is not how SRK would do it; there has to be a strong correlation to his prey, remember?"

"Exactly; on this we can also agree." Charlie handed Tom another folder with a single page ViCAP brief inside. "Read it."

When Tom was finished, he looked up with a stunned expression. Charlie continued, "Every four days some poor kid gets abducted by a complete stranger—half are horribly abused and half of them don't make it home alive. The survivors are scarred for life. Apparently your old friend has come out of retirement to do something about it."

Tom leaned back in his chair and rubbed his eyes. "It would appear so. Do you have any photos from the shooting?"

Grainger gave the last folder to Tom; his briefcase was now empty. "One shot blew through his hand, and the other was the money-shot to his crotch. My guess is the hand was a miss. Incredibly, Goethe lived; that's why you see all the EMT action in the photos. They were trying to get him stabilized for transport. I should have a report from the hospital later today; I'll email it to you when I get it. You should be able to talk to him in a day or two if he pulls through. I put you on the 10:15 American flight out of Reagan tonight. I've arranged for someone to pick you up at the airport in Denver and you'll want to bring your kit. I know you're particular, and I doubt the local resident office will have exactly what you'd want. I'm sorry that you have to fly through Dallas; there wasn't anything direct on a Sunday night. I trust you'll be on it?"

"Charlie, I'm in shock."

"That will pass, my friend. One more thing, Tom; you'll be meeting a young agent out of the Oklahoma City Resident office. She said she's met you before but agreed to work with you anyway, if you can believe that. She's done real well, so we're looking to move her up to the big leagues, and I'd like her advanced training to be with the very best. That means you two are going to have to figure this damn thing out together. I know you usually like to work alone, but I think this time you'll be glad to make an exception. You can thank me later."

*****

-7-

ROCKVILLE

Tom stared into the airplane window as if it could be a portal to some other place or time, but found only empty darkness. Above him, he knew there would be stars, but he couldn't see them through his reflection in the glass. He closed his tired eyes to block out the harsh reading light from overhead and massaged them with a light touch; he reached up and turned off the switch. The pulse he felt against the back of his eyelids reminded him again why they called these late flights red-eyes. He thought s*leep-deprivation* would be a more accurate term but didn't have quite the same graphic appeal. It had been some time since he had to take a commercial airline while working an investigation, and particularly one in the middle of the night. At least he was in first class.

His first plane had left Reagan International a quarter-past ten, but the connection through Dallas was delayed by weather and hadn't gotten off the ground until a little after 1:00 a.m. Central Time. Neither flight had been long enough to gain any restful sleep. In the empty seat next to him lay the material he had pulled together earlier in the day, including the brief Grainger had given him on the Colorado shooting, Goethe's criminal record, the updated Lowen file and the red folder he kept on his desk. He also had a one-page bio on Ms. Kate Morrow, his shiny new protégé, but had barely even looked at it. A late email from Charlie was waiting for him on his tablet that included an attachment of some additional video taken from a camera above the intake-release area where Goethe had first set foot outside the prison. He would check his email again during the drive out to the scene of the shooting.

Rather than sleep, Tom had read through the short brief a half-dozen times and added notes in the margins and on the back of the pages while working through some of his preliminary thoughts on the attack. It was early in the case, and, as he expected, the available information was still pretty thin. The lack of close physical interaction between the offender and Goethe really troubled him. In all his prior attacks SRK had first abducted his victims, then physically assaulted them with his hands or with some weapon in close contact prior to or during the actual act of murder. His method of operation was always face-to-face and personal, not from a thousand yards away.

As part of SRK's killing technique it was important that he graphically enhance a particular detail of his target's crimes. Tom referred to it as an *echo*. Levy had shaved a sample of hair from each of his victims, so he, in turn, was violently shaved head to toe prior to being suffocated; the Lowens had deprived her children of decent human food, so the couple was chained to the ground for a first-hand experience of what death by starvation would feel like. Tom had no doubt that SRK had stayed with Bart and Alice Lowen in the woods long enough to watch it happen.

Among the commonalities evident between each crime, it was the personal nature of the assaults that was the most telling, and anger was always the underlying factor. In this particular instance, both of those critical attributes appeared to be absent and that's what was confounding Tom. When serial offenders changed their methods, it was usually to throw off the progress of an investigation—this one was just getting started.

*****

The stewardess' voice came through the speaker over his head and announced that they had started their initial decent into Denver. Tom turned back on the reading light and opened the file to sift through Goethe's criminal record one last time before the plane landed. After scanning through the early juvenile arrests, he skipped ahead to the page that Charlie had handed him that morning in his study and read it again. Clearly making his point, the page was a ViCAP bulletin from nine years ago listing Goethe as a suspected mule in the child sex trade rumored to have forced his captives into sexual surrender by tying them to a tree and firing a few rounds between their open legs, just below their genitals. At the bottom of the bulletin one of his probable known aliases was given as 'Zielmacher', the *'target maker'*.

Grainger was convinced that the target practice aspect put the attempted Colorado kill squarely in SRK's column. That alleged tidbit, Tom thought, was compelling enough if true and would certainly classify the shooting as an 'echo' of Goethe's crimes, but it still didn't fully explain the uncharacteristic distance between the killer and his victim. And if it was true, *how would SRK have gotten that kind of information in the first place?* Yet, he had to admit that the victimology was undeniable, and the organizational element of the crime was definitely consistent with the five prior kills. Still, he remained bothered. *Where was the anger in looking through a rifle scope and pulling a trigger?* There had to be some other intrinsic reason for the physical separation in this particular assault. Without knowing what it was, Tom couldn't really be sure that this was the handiwork of SRK. He started to think that it was just as likely, if not more so, that one of Goethe's ex-colleagues or employers had shown up to make good on some old score. The sex trade was serious business. He scratched a note in the margin; it would be a priority lead to follow. Tom rubbed his temples in frustration; he hated dead-ends and this was starting to feel like one.

According to the report on the shooting, the EMT's arrived well before the local sheriff, but when they realized how serious the victim's wounds were, they decided not to wait around and take the chance that Goethe would expire before they could get him to the emergency room twelve miles away. There wasn't any methodical photographic record of his wounds, position on the ground or other critical information that law enforcement would have routinely captured had they gotten to the scene before the ambulance as they should have. The only first-respondent information Tom had to go by were the few photos that Charlie had shown him taken on one of the prison staff's cell phones and the poorly written report attached to the back of the FBI brief.

The two pages of the report were penned by the Fremont County Deputy Sheriff who had been sent out to cooperate with prison security to contain the scene and record his observations. Tom sensed that the deputy felt he had better things to do with his Saturday morning than spend it out in the cold helping the Bureau of Corrections clean up their own mess. It was fairly apparent from the lack of thoroughness in his comments and the small number of photos he had taken of the crime scene that he had already yielded any jurisdictional interest in the case and was waiting for the Feds from Denver to show up. An attempted murder investigation was going to eat up a lot of time and resources that the Sheriff's Department didn't have, and since the victim happened to still be on federal property when the shooting occurred, *why not let the government deal with it*?

By mid-morning Saturday, the Denver Field Office would have already set up a perimeter, but the effect of the wind, rain, vehicles and even animals could alter the forensic yield of the scene significantly. Tom wasn't concerned so much with the scene at the guard tower; that was the victim's end of the attack and would only provide tertiary information primarily as it related to Goethe. Tom was infinitely more concerned with the preservation of evidence on the knoll and the immediate vicinity; he hoped the last nineteen hours hadn't erased something important. He picked up the folder and made a note on the cover to get some additional data on the weather, wind direction, speed and sun angle at the time the shots were fired. The report went on to say that at approximately 7:33 a.m. Goethe had taken a bullet through the inguinal area of his lower abdomen doing significant irreparable damage, and a different shot passed through the center of the palm in his left hand. He was first stabilized at the small hospital in Canon City and then taken to Memorial North in Colorado Springs, where he was still in critical condition after a complicated eight-hour surgery. Tom wanted to talk to Goethe as soon as possible; the groin wound was extremely serious, and he had lost a lot of blood. Grainger's brief gave him less than a twenty percent chance of surviving.

*****

As soon as the plane arrived at the gate, Tom grabbed his carry-on bag and field case from the overhead compartment and moved quickly to get off the plane. Not surprisingly, the concourse was empty except for a couple of cleaning crews and a few stranded travelers sprawled uncomfortably across the airport chairs. The clock above the arrival-departure monitors indicated 2:47 a.m., but his body was still on Washington time and told him it was two hours later.

After the tram ride to the main terminal, Tom made his way past the baggage claim and car rental counters to the exit marked for ground transportation. As he passed through the sliding doors, the cold mountain air hit him squarely in the face; reflexively he pulled his coat collar up and across his chin. Virginia was enjoying a mild March; this was quite a bit different. He hoped the local weather forecast was correct, and the warm front would arrive by early morning as predicted. Before he could approach his ride idling at the curb, the young agent leaning against the fender stepped forward pulling off his glove. He extended his open hand to Tom.

"S.A.C. Russell? Field Agent Stacey sir, Denver office; first name Alex. I recognized you from the photo in your bio."

"Agent Stacey, thanks for the ride and thanks for wearing the

FBI cap. I'm not sure I would have spotted you otherwise."
Tom gave an exaggerated nod toward the big black SUV.
"Please call me Tom."

"Uh, yes sir; not a problem." The agent shook Tom's hand
and with the other reached through the open passenger window
and pulled out a stainless-steel Thermos. "Coffee, Agent
Russell? Uh, sorry, Tom; I'll get to work on that." Without
waiting for a response, he screwed off the cap and poured a cup
for Tom, careful not to spill any as he handed it to him. "It's
probably still pretty hot; I bought it fresh an hour ago on the way
here. It might be just a bit strong, but I figured you could use a
little goose. It's late or early depending on how you want to
think about it, and I suppose you've had a long flight. From
what I know from the scene and heard around the office, I'm
pretty sure you're about to have a very long day too."

Tom smiled. The coffee was a thoughtful but completely
necessary gesture after the crappy flights and no sleep. He
pulled himself up into the SUV and pushed the window button to
close it; next he found the control for the seat heater and set it on
high. "Thanks for the brew, Alex. I really needed it; I think I'll
recommend you for a promotion. Now, if you don't mind, let's
get up to Rockville."

"Yes sir." Agent Stacey rounded the vehicle with a big grin
and climbed behind the wheel. "Canon City is about a two-and-
a-half hour drive from here, sir, and the prison is another fifteen
minutes the other side of town. It'll be smooth going this time of
night, and we'll easily get there well before daylight as you had
requested. Colorado Springs would have been a lot closer to
bring you in, but since you had to fly commercial, the first
available flight didn't get in until much later this morning.
Besides, the long drive should give me some time to answer any
questions you might have if I can, or maybe you'll want to check
out for a while. I was at the scene most of the day yesterday, but
they had already moved the victim to the Canon City E.R. long

before I arrived; they had no choice, or he wouldn't have made it. Sir, we have some new information that came in late last night and didn't make it into your file. I'll fill you in on the way up the mountain when you're ready. Have you eaten anything?"

"Glad you asked," Tom hadn't realized how hungry he was until agent Stacey mentioned food. "I had a snack during the layover in Dallas, but it's long gone now. I should probably try to eat something before we get there since it sounds like we have a little extra time. Pull over anywhere, and I'll grab a donut, maybe two. Once I start working the scene, it might be pretty late tonight or tomorrow morning before I can ease up and take a break."

"I thought you might say that, sir." The agent stretched his arm over the back of his seat to retrieve a small paper bag and handed it to Tom. "I picked it up at the gas station when I stopped for the coffee. Unfortunately, it's not donuts. The package said it was made fresh yesterday, but I wouldn't count on it. Sorry, sir, there's not much open this time of night but I'm happy to stop anywhere you want; just let me know."

"Thanks, no worries." Tom pulled a stiff turkey sandwich from the bag and peeled off the plastic wrapping letting it drop to the floor. He figured the food was going to taste about as bad as the coffee but took a quick bite anyway to calm the hunger rattling around in his empty stomach. He ate in silence while they drove away from the terminal toward the glowing cloud cover hanging above Denver. To their left, the approaching sunrise was still over three hours away.

*****

As they climbed the on-ramp to I-70 west, Tom washed down the last bite of sandwich with the remnants of his now cold coffee and looked out his window. Without turning to the agent he asked, "How long have you been assigned to Denver? You guys cover, what, thirty-two counties?" Tom knew, of course, about Denver's jurisdictional reach; what he didn't know was the practical experience of Field Agent Alex Stacey.

"Came here right out of Quantico about five years ago, sir. The wife's family lives between Broomfield and Boulder, and it's been good for her to have them around since I'm not home much with work, but I suppose you know how that goes."

Tom knew well. He wondered if Nicole had had some of her family around during those earlier years, they still might be together.

"What about you, sir?" Agent Stacey added. "I saw in your bio that you've been with the Bureau for nineteen years, first in your class at Quantico and the youngest graduate in the Academy's history at twenty-three. You started right out of the chute doing behavioral analysis for Violent Crime at CIRG for the first fifteen years, did a stint in St. Louis, and then back to DC where you've been ever since."

"Actually, I've been assigned to DC the whole time; I worked back-and-forth between DC and St. Louis on a case for a little over a year." Tom stopped short of mentioning SRK. He figured it would generate a lot of unproductive chatter with the young agent and didn't know if Stacey was even aware of the potential connection between then and now. Depending on what he found out at the crime scene, there would be plenty of time to discuss the case history with Stacey and his Denver colleagues over the next few days. Besides, at this point it would be a lot more valuable for agent Stacey to spend a little more energy focused on Thurman Goethe than the history between Tom Russell and SRK. He re-directed the conversation back to the shooting investigation, "I assume Warden Baggett will be meeting us up there?"

"Uh, yes sir. He's quite the character though, and comes with a little bit of a Napoleon complex; you'll see what I mean when you meet the guy—all five-foot-nothing of him. We met for the first time yesterday; Baggett's a little on the bossy side, and I think he's full of it when he says he'd like to help the investigation. I don't think he actually intends to do anything except stay the hell out of our way; then take some bows for the cameras when we wrap things up."

Tom stared out the window as they turned south on I-25; the scene slowly changed from a dotted net of street lamps crisscrossing the sleeping suburbs of Denver to dark open countryside, interrupted by an occasional light pole casting blue shadows into the black. The cloud cover had loosened enough to reveal a full moon lighting up a veil of late winter snow lying on the foothills off to the west. He always liked Colorado.

Years ago, he and Nicole had visited Estes Park during that first October after their wedding. They had rented a remote little place on Prospect Mountain but rarely left the cabin to enjoy the surrounding scenery; they had plenty of firewood, wine, and food and found enough to do to keep them entertained without having to go outside. Tom shook the memory out of his mind; it would be better for him to focus on the case as well. Besides, the recollection only reminded him of his inability to make the rare but perfect moments, like the days in that little cabin, carry his marriage through the tougher spots. He well knew what fueled the failures in their relationship and still carried around the guilt for having made little effort to salvage it. Toward the end, when Tom honestly allocated the blame for why it had all unraveled, for why his wife strayed from him, it became obviously clear that Nicole had been right all along. His killers always came first.

*****

Tom turned on the map light under the visor and pulled out the case file from his bag. They continued along in silence for a while as he studied the few available photographs he had of Goethe lying on the ground at the scene. *Thank God someone had the sense to take some pictures.* The tower camera had shown two shots fired about one or two seconds apart. One shot was a bulls-eye to the groin, that was obvious from the photos, but the hand wound still bothered him. The bullet went through the front of his palm and out the back of the hand, but the crotch shot was clearly frontal or nearly so. The Sheriff's report speculated that the hand shot was intended for Goethe's head but had missed and hit his hand as he held it in the air over his eyes to shield them from the bright, rising sun. *What if the report has it wrong?* He would ask the doctor about the wound to the hand. Then he turned the photo over and scribbled a note across the back. *Which shot came first?* He found the button along the side of his seat and reclined it back slightly as he closed his eyes. "You mentioned you had some new information, Agent Stacey?"

"Uh, yes sir," Stacey cleared his throat. After glancing in his mirrors, he switched lanes to pass a slow-moving truck. "First, we checked on the cab company that was supposed to show up and take Goethe to the bus station in town. Rockville made the arrangements like they do for all the parolees who don't have their own transportation. Well, it appears that someone identifying himself as a prison staffer called late Friday night to cancel the ride. That's why they didn't show up."

"Interesting." Tom thought about the information in the nine-year-old ViCAP bulletin on Goethe that he had read again on the plane. *The shooter knew about that, and now he knows enough about the details of the release process to cancel a cab ride. How could he possibly know that Goethe would need a ride?*

Agent Stacey continued, "Also, per your instructions, we checked all the airlines between Cheyenne and Santa Fe for incoming passengers who checked hunting rifles, or anything along those lines over the last two weeks; we didn't worry any about handguns, of course.

We have twenty-seven non-officials on the list and probably

a few more we don't know about that were missed through airline paperwork errors; of course we're not in any kind of hunting season this time of year. Most of them were probably guys returning home from cougar and sheep hunts down south in New Mexico. If this was November and at the front end of Late Elk season, that number would be ten times that amount. Late Elk brings in a lot of out-of-state hunters, especially the ones heading to private lands. They're pricey, but the P.L. operators have a much higher harvest rate," Agent Stacey paused. "Sorry sir, I'm sure you don't care any about that, but if you want to come back in about six months I'd be glad to set you up."

"No thanks. I don't hunt elk." Tom still had his eyes closed. "It's a long shot anyway. If the offender came in from out-of-state, you'd like to think he'd be smart enough to drive in to avoid taking a rifle on a commercial flight. He can't take it in his carry-on, and he's not going to check a rifle without reporting it to the airline. They scan every piece of luggage, and an unexpected gun popping up on the X-ray would draw a bunch of attention. The T.S.A. would have yanked him off the plane, and Goethe would now be on a bus heading who-knows-where instead of on life-support in the I.C.U. So, if he flew in and followed the rules, he'll be pretty easy to track down. Twenty-something subjects won't take much to ferret out; it's just time and resources at this point. Unfortunately you'll need to check them all; if he did fly in, he'd likely break up his travel on separate flights through a decoy city or two. For grins, you can start with the inbound flights that originated from airports about a four-hour radius from St. Louis; also include both Chicago airports in that list. You never know, Agent Stacy; we might get lucky."

"So you believe he'll be from out-of-state?"

"Well, what I do believe is that I don't know what I believe at this point; if that makes any sense. But we do think this attack may be related to a series of fairly recent kills we've been tracking back in the Midwest." Tom opened his mouth wide and yawned; the pull of sleep was overwhelming.

"Sir, why don't you check out for a few minutes?" Stacey asked. "I got this. We're still about an hour-and-a-half out, and, don't worry, I won't let you sleep through the good stuff."

Tom yawned again, "Good idea." He reclined his seat a little more to about half-way. "If it is our Midwest boy, he'll be from somewhere around St. Louis; and, if he didn't fly, that would make for a healthy drive to get out here, but he could easily do it in a long day. People do it all the time. If it's not him, then I really don't have a clue."

*****

When Tom woke up, he could tell that they had left the highway from the change in the sound of the tires on the pavement. He glanced at the clock on the dashboard. *Seventy-five minutes—must be a new record for me.* The sun hadn't come up yet, but surprisingly, he felt fairly refreshed. He was glad that the sky had not yet started to brighten. *One thing at a time.*

Agent Stacey handed him the Thermos. "There should be a bit left; it might still be warm, but I can't guarantee it. I have a mind to lose this one and replace it with a Yeti, but the wife bought it for me as a gift, and losing it might be a critical error in judgment."

"You're probably right." Tom refilled his cup and set it in the console after taking a sip; he straightened up his seat and looked out the windshield at the approaching landscape. The night sky was now clear, and in the thin high-altitude air, the moonlight was strong enough that he could differentiate between treeless countryside and the wooded foothills rising above it in the distance ahead. What few buildings they passed were far from the road and looked like floating specs on a vast rolling sea of snow and moonlit prairie grass.

Tom remembered that he needed to check his email. He pulled the tablet from his bag and turned it on, then navigated to his inbox. Grainger's mail was at the top of the list; the subject line identified it as video footage taken from the Rockville release gate. He opened it to read the content, but there was nothing serious, just Charlie's poor attempt at humor that he probably lifted from the title of one of his grandkids' storybooks: *"Thurman has a bad day..."*

Tom chuckled to himself; he missed working with his old boss. He double-clicked on the attached .avi file, and it filled the screen. A few seconds in, Goethe appeared from the bottom of the image and walked along the sidewalk away from the camera and toward the pair of gates in the double fence line, his gym bag swinging from his left hand. Tom paused the video; he had noted that Goethe held the bag in his right hand in the tower footage that Grainger showed him earlier. He thought the detail was important but didn't yet know why; he pushed *play*. Goethe's back was to the camera, but the lightness of his body language showed him to be in a buoyant mood. When he got through the gates, he appeared to check his watch, then briefly looked right and left down the road. There was a car sitting at the curb, but no interaction occurred between Goethe and the driver. About twenty seconds later, he began walking east in the direction of the guard tower that could be seen in the distance in contrast to the brightness of the low sun. The camera at the release gate must have had pan-tilt-zoom capabilities and followed him down the road; the focus of the image worsening as he grew smaller and smaller and then disappeared behind the tower wall. The time stamp at the bottom of the frame showed it to be a little after seven-thirty-two; the camera stayed locked in that position waiting for him to reappear, but he never did. According to the report, that's when security was called to go out to the tower and investigate. A minute or so later Goethe would be gunned down, just thirty seconds before they arrived.

After watching it through, Tom re-played the video one more time, but there was nothing of value that he could immediately see. He had hoped it would have helped to confirm the location of the bright spots he saw on the knoll in the video footage from the tower, but the clarity of the distant image was disappointing, and the sun angle would likely be wrong anyway. He decided to watch it again later.

They passed an official-looking sign reading: 'Rockville Federal Corrections Center-Federal Bureau of Prisons', but no buildings were yet in sight. "It'll be just over this next rise;" said Agent Stacey, "the sky's starting to lighten a bit. For the record, sunrise is officially six-seventeen, and you'll run out of workable daylight by six-o-four tonight."

Then I should be asleep by six-fifteen.

A minute later Tom could see the abandoned east guard tower come into view, at first as a silhouette against the emerging sky and the bright lights of the complex, then a little more defined in the fringe of the headlights as they approached. He could barely see the three cameras mounted to the mast above the roof. Stacey slowed the SUV to a crawl and moved into the oncoming lane. A prison security vehicle was idling at the side of the road with its headlights grazing across the ground in the direction of the tower; police tape stretched between four orange stakes fluttered in a light breeze and marked the boundaries of the crime scene. The occupant seemed to be busy talking on his cell phone but looked up and waved as they slowly drove by. Tom glanced over his shoulder toward where the shots had come from, but it was still too dark to see anything other than the shape of the land.

*****

Agent Stacey turned into the parking area across from the release gate and pulled next to the only other car in the lot. "The warden's expecting to meet us just inside a little after six; mostly for a handshake and *'whatever we can do for you'* type platitudes, but don't believe him. At least he'll have us some fresh coffee and donuts. The rest of my team should be on their way; we're staying at a hotel over in Canon City. I believe you and the young lady from Oklahoma are booked there also. It's not great, but it's clean and does have a pretty nice restaurant and bar downstairs. She was supposed to have checked in late last night; I understand she's not too hard on the eyes, by the way."

Great, that should help. Tom grunted to himself as he climbed slowly out of the SUV, feeling the effects of a long night of travel in the rigidity of his legs. The air felt quite a bit warmer than it had at the airport, so he didn't bother to button up his coat. The warm front had arrived on schedule.

He left his field kit on the back seat and followed Stacey across the road toward the man-gates in the double fence line. A little farther down, Tom could see the entry to the vehicle sally port; an empty corrections bus with bars welded along the windows was parked outside with its lights on and engine running waiting to be admitted to the prison. After showing their I.D. to the camera, they passed through the pair of gates, then followed the sidewalk to the security vestibule where both doors were standing open, and entered the inmate release area. It took a moment to adjust to the harsh lighting.

The release lobby was a large room with two rows of steel waiting chairs filling the center of the space; they were bolted to the floor and arranged on an angle to face the television mounted from the ceiling in the corner. A guard station was recessed into one wall and separated from the room with a layer of wire glass; a single walk-up counter and transaction window was along another. Above it, the sign read in bold letters: 'Do Not Approach Until Your Name Is Called'. Someone had hand-written *'asshole'* at the end, but it had since been scrubbed nearly illegible. Beside it, a property transfer drawer projected from the wall sagging slightly between its guides. There was no one in the lobby since the first inmate processing wouldn't begin until seven, but Tom could hear a conversation coming from the open doorway a few feet from the window. He stuck his head in the room while lightly tapping on the door.

The warden was sitting behind a cup of coffee at the end of a small conference table; across from him a much younger, professional-looking woman was leaning against the wall with her hands buried deep in her coat pockets. Her long brown hair was pulled up in what looked like a hasty manner and framed the focused but attractive features of her face. She stopped talking when Tom entered the room; Agent Stacey followed closely behind. "Warden Baggett? S.A.C. Russell, but please call me Tom. I believe you've already met my colleague, Alex."

The warden stood to shake Tom's hand. Stacey was right, he *was* five-foot-nothing, maybe even a little less. Under his coat, Tom bent his knees slightly to appear not to tower over him as much as he did, but his eyes were still a good foot above the warden's head. Rather than wait until the introductions were complete, Baggett cleared his throat and immediately began to talk. His voice was surprisingly gruff and a little hostile.

"First off, as I was telling this fine young lady, everyone's welcome at my prison. I don't care which side of the bars you happen to be on, and I do appreciate you coming all the way out here from Washington on such short notice, but, that said, this here is a genuine five-alarm cluster if I ever saw one. So I'm going to trust that you and the rest of your fancy entourage with your high-dollar gizmos will get this mess cleaned up before I'm ready to sit down and carve my Easter ham. I don't think that's unreasonable, do you?" Baggett took a breath but didn't wait for a response.

"Yes, well, and I'll be glad to help your crew all I can, but my job ends at that fence line I just permitted you gentlemen to walk through. And, by the way," Baggett banged the tips of his fingers on the conference table, "I was just talking with the pretty Ms. Morrow here about my release procedures and how that cab ride could have possibly been canceled by some unknown person. Well, I've already started the process of interviewing my staff, but I doubt they'll say too much. Most of my people are good folk, and they know if they want to continue to work at my prison they have to follow my security protocols to the tee, but some of 'em might be prone to blabber a little when they're off-duty and trying to make themselves sound important, particularly if they get a few beers down their gullet. It is possible that one of 'em gave out the information to someone they shouldn't have, but considering the bloody mess that resulted all over my tower, I don't think anyone's going to step forward and risk losing their job over it. Would you?"

"Excuse me for interrupting, Warden;" Agent Stacey glanced up at Tom from his phone, his expression looking decidedly detached from the one-man conversation, "I just got a text that the team is on property. It should be light enough now that they can get back to combing the knoll; they're heading up there now. I've asked that a couple of men stay behind with you at the scene in case you need something for them to do. I'll get the car and meet you and Agent Morrow outside."

After Stacey left the room, Warden Baggett continued, "As far as the victim's release schedule, that information was published in the Canon City paper days ago, just like the rest of 'em was. I've been doing that going on five years now, ever since that rancher from Coal Creek offered a hitch-hiker a ride to town and got a pretty bad beating right before the guy stole his pickup. Mr. Dumb-shit Carjacker had just got out of my place on parole and apparently wasn't real smart about what's generally required in order to stay out. That's why I put all of 'em all in cabs and cruisers now. It really ain't my job to get 'em to the bus station, and it sure as hell ain't my job to buy 'em a ticket to Denver either, but I do it anyway so as to, uh, avoid any unnecessary PR complications, if you know what I mean. I'm the biggest employer in three counties, but for some reason I'm still not real popular with some of the folk who live around here, and, by the way, I officially don't give a shit if you really want to know, but apparently some people think I should pretend to."

Tom politely smiled as the warden finished his rant, then helped himself to some coffee from the carafe sitting on the cart in the corner of the room. He opened the box of donuts and looked over each one critically; the lone chocolate cruller was really tempting, but he decided to pass. *See tough guy; the pretty lady is already affecting your behavior.* He extended his empty hand across the conference table. "Please excuse my rudeness miss; they try not to let me out much." Tom thought he sounded like a stupid freshman but pressed on anyway, "I'm S.A.C. Tom Russell. That would make you Special-Agent Kate Morrow. I have a Katie back home in Virginia; well, actually she lives with her mother. Grainger has said some good things about you; said you two had a very nice visit down in Oklahoma City a few weeks back, and he's considering you for a spot at the Hoover building in D.C. Charlie asked me to assist with your advanced field training, maybe teach you a thing or two and otherwise help in whatever way I can."

Agent Morrow's face mildly brightened but with a practiced, professional-looking smile; she looked directly into Tom's eyes. When she offered him her hand, it mostly disappeared in his; even so, he couldn't help but notice that her fingers were long and their grip quite firm. When he released his grasp, her hand quickly returned to her coat pocket like she was holstering a sidearm. Still, her eyes remained locked on his, not so much exuding confidence, which they certainly did, but as if she was reading his thoughts behind them. "Yes, that's right, Kate Morrow, and don't call me *Katie*; ever since grade school my dad is the only one who gets to call me that. Please thank Charlie for offering your help, Tom. You can start by passing me that chocolate donut."

*****

Special Agent Morrow jumped out of the SUV before it came to a complete stop along the side of the road, about a hundred feet short of the crime scene at the base of the abandoned guard tower.

"How's that for youthful ambition?" Agent Stacey almost laughed as they rolled to a stop. He shifted into park and turned off the ignition.

Well, nothing comes from doing nothing. Tom got out onto the shoulder and stretched his arms above his head; already feeling a little off, he slapped his hands on the roof in a poorly attempted drum roll, then opened the back door to grab his case. As he leaned across the seat to reach it, he spoke to Alex who was still behind the wheel. "I prefer to pace myself, young man. This one's going to be a marathon—not a sprint."

Two FBI agents were talking to the officer in the security vehicle and stepped away when they saw Kate walking briskly toward them. They intercepted her just before she could reach the yellow police tape. Tom smiled when he saw her have to pull out her credentials and present them to the men. *And so it begins.*

A half-dozen other agents were climbing the gentle rise to the east, their blue FBI coats swinging open in the mild morning air; each had a forensic case in one hand, two carried shovels in the other. Tom introduced himself with a handshake and exchanged names with the two agents standing either side of Ms. Morrow; she didn't look very happy when neither bothered to ask Tom for his credentials.

"Okay Kate, first let's do a walk-around at the perimeter and then work our way in. Agent Bronowski and Jones, you'll need to give us a little time to get acquainted with the scene. I assume everything has been thoroughly documented by now?" Jones nodded his head yes as he lit up an unfiltered cigarette. "Good," Tom said, then ducked under the police tape, holding it up behind him so Kate could follow. She immediately split off to look at the bullet holes in the tower wall.

Tom walked studiously around the fringes of the scene; he wasn't too concerned about disturbing anything now that the specifics had been thoroughly recorded. Other than the ballistics from the slugs pulled from the wall, there was nothing here that was going to lead them to S.R.K., but that didn't mean there was nothing to learn. Tom knelt over the gym bag and the loose pile of books and clothes that were sprawled across the ground. Traces of Goethe's blood were evident on the bag and the covers of several volumes; one in particular had a significant amount of blood on the binding. Tom remembered seeing him clutching a book in one of the photos; he pulled some blue nitrile gloves from his coat pocket and put them on, then reached down and picked it up. By then Kate was standing next to him, looking curious about the contents of the journal in his hand. Tom thumbed through it, stopping arbitrarily to glance at a word or two of the poems that filled the front and back of every page.

"Creepy stuff." He flipped to the end. "The final entry is dated day before yesterday. Interesting how he seems to have run out of paper pretty much on the same day he ran out of his sentence—good planning." Tom closed the journal and re-opened it at random. "Okay, here's one for you, Agent Morrow:

"A prison rat danced on a razor blade,

His severed balls bounced on the floor

He should have been a good little rodent,

Instead of spreading his legs like a whore"

Kate raised her eyebrows, "My, what lovely talent. Oxford graduate I assume?"

"I'm not sure." Tom knew she was joking, but he wasn't in a joking mood, at least not any more. He handed the journal to Jones, who was standing nearby, just on the other side of the police tape. Jones placed it in a large evidence bag and set it down next to him. Tom scanned the titles of the other books on the ground, but there was nothing especially interesting; Goethe was slime, and slime was what he read. He saw Kate kneeling over the blood stain a couple of feet away. "See anything?"

"Just a large concentration here, I assume under his mid-section; there's some pretty serious blood loss. You can still see the imprint of the top of his shoes there; it looks like he had his legs folded under him. The smaller stain next to your foot is likely where his hand came to rest with the journal. Good thing the shooter was remote and we're not looking for any evidence he would have left here; the EMT's sure made a mess of this place."

Tom checked his watch; 7:31. The sun would be in the same position in a couple of minutes. He took a few steps away downwind and picked up a handful of powdery dirt; he released it slowly through his fingers, observing the strength and direction of the breeze, then dusted off his hands. *Similar conditions to yesterday morning.* He would remember to confirm his thought later. Agent Morrow approached but seemed careful to keep a few feet of distance between them. She checked her watch also and then nodded at Tom. For some reason he liked how she did that.

At 7:33 Tom positioned himself facing the base of the tower and about ten feet away, standing slightly to the side and keeping downwind of where Goethe had been found so as not to disturb anything unnecessarily. He rotated to his left, calculating a three-quarter turn to face south of east in the direction of where the shots had been fired. He checked back at the bullet holes in the tower wall and the array of dried blood splatter, then back to the rolling landscape. The first rise in the land was about three hundred yards away, and the rise beyond was just slightly higher and directly aligned with the first, perhaps another four or five hundred yards farther from where he stood. *About a half-mile.* Tom roughly calculated in his mind. *Impressive.* The team of a half-dozen agents could be seen working the ground on the closer knoll. With the sun aligned almost directly behind them, just a few degrees above the horizon, it was difficult to look long in that direction. *That's where I'd do it.*

Next Tom began a slow-motion reenactment of Goethe's projected sequence of movements during the shooting as outlined in the Deputy Sheriff's report. The report speculated that the first shot was meant for Goethe's head but missed, hitting his left hand as he held it above his face looking toward the hill and into the sun. Considering Goethe's history, the groin wound should have been considered premeditated, but according to the report, the target of the second shot was uncertain, taking into account that the shooter may have over-compensated for the first attempt hitting his victim too high. Apparently the Deputy was not aware of Goethe's history. The report tried to square up the fact that a clean bullet hole was to the right side of the blood spatter on the wall, but the victim had been shot through the palm of his left hand. If Goethe had been facing the knoll with his arm at his side, the bullet would have gone through the back of his hand between his thumb and forefinger unless he had it unnaturally turned or raised with the palm toward the knoll. The report claimed that Goethe was facing the knoll since the groin shot came from the front. Tom didn't like the narrow-minded thinking evident in the Deputy's conclusions.

He looked to the agents working on the hill and raised his left hand in front of him high enough above his eyes to block the sun, just above the top of his forehead. Accounting for his offset relative to where Goethe had been standing, he looked back at the tower, projecting the path of a bullet from the hill through his hand to the wall. The bullet hole to the right of the splatter was way too low. He knew the trajectory of a high-powered round wouldn't deflect that much going through the small bones of the hand. A bullet moving that fast would exert four thousand pounds of force concentrated in an area the size of a pencil. And if it had deflected, it would have passed through Goethe's skull in order to hit the wall as low as it did. Next, he tried doubling over so that his torso was about forty-five degrees to his waist, this time assuming the first shot hit the groin. With his right hand he pretended to release the gym bag. He looked toward the hill and again raised his left hand to block the glare, then moved it back over his shoulder from the force of the imaginary bullet. He dropped to his knees, then fell to his back looking up at the sky. As he sat up, he looked over at the array of clothes and books on the ground, again accounting for the offset of where he was compared to where Goethe was found, and shook his head. He looked up at the hole in the tower wall. *Correct side for the bullet, but my hand position felt forced, and the hole is still too low on the wall. The books are on the wrong side; I would have to have the gym bag in my left hand for them to end up there, but the tower camera showed the bag in Goethe's right hand. Maybe he had set it down before the shooting started?*

Something wasn't right; he got on his knees and doubled over again, but this time he was tight to the ground. He strained to raise his left hand above his eyes, figuring it to be about three-and-a-half feet off the ground, and looked back at the hole. *The hand is all wrong and the hole is still too low;* he shook his head one more time as he stood. There was no way that Goethe had his hand that low when the bullet went through it. Tom figured he'd have to be almost lying on the ground. The geometry was all jacked up, and the gym bag was still on the wrong side if it had, in fact, stayed in his right hand as the camera showed. *Dammit—the report missed something.* He started to begin one more time, but Kate stepped in.

She faced the tower wall, again about ten feet away just as Tom had, and took off her coat spreading it out on the ground next to her. She didn't turn to face the knoll just yet; instead, she swung her left hand toward the wall as if it had just been shot. Then she opened her right hand dropping an imaginary gym bag to the ground and grabbed her wounded left hand with it. Next she spun around on the ball of her left foot twisting her shoulders until she could look directly at the knoll, but having swung her right foot only about three-fourths through her upper body rotation. When she reached a reasonable position based on the groin entry wound, her right leg was trailing behind her hip. Through the rotation, her body had moved about two feet to the left of where she had first stood.

Tom watched her movements but avoided dwelling on the curves of her body pressing against her thin blouse as she turned. Kate looked back at the tower, at the location of the two bullet marks, and then at Tom who was now smiling. "That would support the location of the exit wound in Mr. Goethe's lower right buttocks Special Agent Morrow, as well as how a shot through his left hand ended up to the right of the blood splatter."

"Correct." Kate continued with the final sequence of movements. She cupped her hands over her mid-section, slowly dropped to her knees on top of her coat and leaned forward. Tom watched her strain to look up toward the knoll and then look to each side. Lastly, she settled her gaze on her midsection.

If I was Goethe, that's where I'd be looking about now. Tom shook off a chill. *I'd be checking if my package was still there.*

Kate then fell on her back so that she was facing up, keeping her twisted legs folded beneath her like the shoe imprints had suggested. She stretched her left arm out from where she lay and marked an arc in the dirt with her fingertips to record her reach. She bounced to her feet and dusted off the back of her skirt. Tom picked up her coat and shook it out before helping her put it back on. Kate was smiling now too. "Well, whaddya know, Mr. Special Agent-In-Charge Russell; how's that for my first week out of the Academy?"

"Nicely done." Tom said it sincerely; he thought he knew

exactly what she was suggesting in the sequence of movements displayed in her reenactment. "That also explains the location of the bag, books and clothes. Goethe was grabbing for his poetry with his wounded hand. If he was facing the knoll when he got shot in the left hand, he would have dropped the bag on his other side which contradicts everything we see. Got time for a walk?"

*****

They ducked under the police tape and crossed the road, walking down a gentle bank and across a low, dry swale in the direction of the first knoll. It didn't occur to Tom that he needed to talk, so he didn't. If he got an itch to socialize with Ms. Morrow, he would do it later when they were off the clock. In his now-racing mind, it was better that he used the time to think about the business of SRK. Considering the rough footing, they kept a brisk pace and in less than ten minutes they approached the crest of the first knoll and stopped. Kate was the first to break the silence. "Okay Agent Russell, why the interest in the wind?"

"Why not?" Tom paused for a second and decided to be more cooperative with the somewhat overly-confident, but pretty, young agent assigned to him. There was no sense wasting any time fighting it; Grainger said they were supposed to work together as a team, and, like it or not, he'd better start getting used to her company. Besides, right now he couldn't imagine a more entertaining partner, and this could turn out to be one of those long, drawn-out investigations. Nonetheless, the sudden check on his attitude fell short of preventing him from engaging in a little harmless and playful banter. "I know you've trained with a high-powered sniper rifle or two. You would have had to at the Q-Co range before they let you graduate *last week*." He winked at Kate.

"Yes, last Tuesday in fact." Kate bantered right along. "A pretty pink Remington Model 700 as I recall. And on

Wednesday, all the good girls got to shoot a Parker-Hale M-85. It was *sooooo* big!"

"Alright; fair enough." Tom returned a broad smile but brought it quickly back around to trying to make his point. "How far did you shoot?"

"A hundred yards—the same as everyone else," Kate said. "I don't like the big bores. They can mess up my shoulder for days. When we switched to the SR-25 platforms, I held a tight pattern at that distance, three inches on average for a full magazine in semi-automatic mode. In the field I prefer to stick with my nine-millimeter Glock." She patted the sidearm holstered at her hip. "I do recall that the XM 110 and Mark 11 are precise to about nine hundred yards, but I understand some of the pros prefer the old bolt-action M24 for long-range accuracy. All three have the quick-mount silencer which, of course, completely eliminates muzzle-flash for position concealment."

Tom eyes had followed her hand to the curve of her hip but looked immediately away at the agents combing the hillside just ahead and then turned back toward the abandoned guard tower. Kate turned also.

"Yeah, I read that chapter too. Okay, Kate, consider the following example: at this range and altitude, a 220 grain, 300 WIN-MAG round will travel at more than three thousand feet per second in clean air and is accurate to maybe an inch or two for someone who can dial in the scope properly and really knows how to shoot. Factor in a little breeze and it gets real difficult to hit a basketball at this range, let alone a pair of testicles. But the next thing you know, Goethe is singing like a choir girl; that's some good marksmanship. Now add in a little breeze and we're at Olympic-level shooting. You don't account for the wind; you don't hit diddly-squat. Anyway, to say I'm impressed is an understatement; that's why I'm interested in the wind. It tells us how good this guy really is. And that, Agent Morrow, speaks of discipline, practice and patience. It also means he's most likely to have some shooting history, military or otherwise, and that bit of information should prove very useful."

"I get it. So the guy's a good shot; that much we know already," Kate said. "Just ask Goethe."

Tom continued, "But the detail that's really bugging me now, Ms. Morrow, is the shooter didn't know Goethe was going to stop at that tower. He had Goethe in his scope from the moment he walked out that gate to when he stood by that wall. There were plenty of chances to take his shot as his target walked down that road; he was walking right toward him." Tom paused for a moment, then looked at Kate. "On second thought, I think the plan was to kill Goethe about when he reached that spot along the road; the fact that he stopped at the tower only required a minor adjustment; but why that *particular* spot?"

"With all due respect S.A.C. Russell, it may have been without any basis, you know, in accordance with *Random's Law.*"

"Yeah, well I've always had a problem with randomness when it comes to crimes like these," Tom responded, "particularly when everything suggests that the offender is otherwise quite well organized."

"I have another thought, Agent Russell, if I may. This hillside roughly follows parallel to the road; maybe the shooter was front and center down there when Goethe came through the gate. He could have stalked Goethe from there to here, keeping on the south side of the rise, just out of view. He tracked Goethe until he felt like taking his shot; maybe there was nothing really scientific about it. When Goethe stopped at that tower, for whatever reason, the shooter just decided the moment felt right. He had some time and set up his gear and then took his shot. You might be over-thinking this."

Tom took his time responding; working with this young woman was going to take a little more humility than he thought.

He answered with a wry smile. "Nope, everything tells me that this deal was completely planned. What you suggest is possible, but setting up his shot would have taken more time than a couple of minutes while Goethe stood around picking his nose at the tower, and walking cross-country leaves unnecessary evidence; it compounds the risk unnecessarily. Besides, he was waiting on a cab to take him to town; he didn't know that the ride got canceled. If he goes on a walk-about, he's going to walk in the direction that the cab is supposed to come from. So that we don't *over-think* this, Miss Morrow, try this: which way is Canon City?"

Without having to think, Kate pointed east down the two-lane blacktop.

"Correct," Tom answered. "Forget about the cab for a moment. You've just spent eight years in a seven-foot-by-ten-foot concrete box, and you just got your Get-Out-of-Jail-Free card. You own nothing but a couple hundred bucks in your pocket and what's in your sorry little gym bag. It's a nice sunny day in a brand new world; your ride is late, so you decide to take a walk; are you going to walk up into the mountains, or are you going to walk toward town where you can get a side of beef and a couple of beers?"

"Fine—that makes total sense." Kate surrendered the point. "I'll agree; the shooter was counting on that exact outcome and Goethe stopping at the tower was just a wrinkle in the execution of his plan. And you're right; the guy is organized; he set the whole thing in motion by cancelling the call for the cab. He probably also had a Plan-B if his target decided to hang around at the gate for the cab and wasn't able to make the shot from this knoll."

Tom continued. "Yeah, maybe, but he didn't shoot Goethe from here." He waved toward where the agents were working just a little farther up the rise. "He shot from there." Tom pointed at the next higher knoll more than twice the distance to the guard tower from where they stood.

"How do you know that?" Kate was trying to catch up with Tom's brain. "You haven't even seen the top of the first hill!"

"Google Earth."

"Excuse me?" She cleared a strand of hair from the corner of her mouth. Tom didn't hear her question and had already started walking quickly toward the second knoll; his breathing a little measured from the brisk pace.

"After I saw the security footage, that was the first thing I checked," Tom called over his shoulder. "In the video, I couldn't tell from exactly where the glints of light came from. Both knolls align perfectly with the tower and the sun's position at the time the shots were fired; that second knoll is just a bit taller and overlooks the first."

"Okay, so why make it exponentially more challenging by setting up your position on the hill farthest from your target?" In spite of his longer gait, Kate had no trouble following just a few feet behind Tom.

"That's what Google Earth showed me." Tom reached the top of the first hill and walked right through the middle of where the other agents had been combing for clues, knocking over evidence markers and nearly tripping on the leg of a camera tripod. The agents immediately ceased what they were doing, frozen in complete astonishment.

Agent Stacey was tediously picking through a shovel full of dirt that he had carefully spread out on a white plastic sheet. When he heard all the commotion, he quit what he was doing and looked up just as Tom rushed by. "Um, S.A.C. Russell, is there a problem?"

Tom paused briefly and turned around, holding up his index finger. "I'll be with you in a minute, Alex." He continued for another twenty-five feet and stopped, waiting for Kate to catch up with him; she had taken the long way around the area where the other agents were working instead of following Tom through it. When she reached him she didn't look very happy, but he didn't expect her to be. He put down his case and waved his hand at where the back side of the first hill should have been, but there wasn't one; he took a deep breath.

"See Kate, it's a bench—not a saddle; there's no place to conceal a vehicle; it would have been in full view of the tower camera the whole time. The closest place he could have hidden his ride is behind that next hill. Assuming he's in decent shape, with gear he can probably move along at about seven or eight miles-per-hour; that means he could cover around a hundred meters in thirty seconds. To get from here to there would have cost him at least two, more likely three additional minutes of getaway time, not to mention yielding us a lot more camera footage. That's an eternity of time if you think anyone may have witnessed your shots or saw your target go down. Remember, thirty seconds after Goethe disappeared under camera number two, prison security dispatched two officers to check it out. I don't know if you noticed, but they drive four-wheel-drive SUV's. If their cameras or officers had spotted the shooter running up that hill, don't you think they would have followed in pursuit? They would have been all over him before he ever made it to his vehicle; he wasn't about to take that chance."

Kate loosened the zipper on her coat, but Tom didn't notice. "Well played, Agent Russell. It looks like Charlie Grainger was right; I may learn a thing or two from you after all."

Agent Stacey walked up to Tom. "What's going on, sir?"

"Alex, I wish I had better news for you, buddy, but you're working the wrong hill. We'll write this little exercise off as good practice for your crew; S.A. Morrow will fill you in later. We'll need a half-hour up there before you move everything;" Tom motioned to the second knoll, "it won't take us long."

*****

Tom and Kate left Agent Stacey with his arms crossed and eyes closed, shaking his head. Ten minutes later they were nearing the crest of the higher rise. Tom set down his case and opened it to expose a short tripod and rifle scope. He pointed to a rocky area about twenty feet away that had a slight incline sloping away from the prison. "That's the spot; that juniper and those rocks would have provided good concealment from the cameras."

"Shouldn't we go have a look?"

Tom responded by turning away in the opposite direction. "We'll get to that shortly; I need to be in the mood first." He picked up a small rock and tossed it back and forth between his hands like a baseball. "Remember, Locard's Principle applies to more than just physical contact with the scene."

"You mean the *'every contact leaves a trace'* Locard?"

"Yeah, that's the one. I understand he was a big fan of Sherlock Holmes. Well, he was a fan of the author anyway," Tom clarified. "I submit to you Russell's Corollary to Locard's Principle which says: *'a heightened emotional state leaves kinetic residue.'* Kinetic energy is energy passed from one object to another or, in this case, from our shooter to this hilltop. The place is glowing with it."

*****

Tom attached the scope to the tripod and set it on the ground facing south, away from the prison. Before Kate could ask, he had his coat off and was lying on it looking through the eye-piece; the empty half was spread out next to him. He spent a minute slowly panning across the landscape through a narrow arc. "Right there, you can still barely see the tire tracks on the other side of that draw at about two o'clock; he must have lost traction climbing that slope." Tom felt the sun warm his back as Kate lay down beside him, blocking some of the breeze; it was a little stronger compared to what had been at the tower, but he stopped thinking about the wind when he sensed her closeness. He hadn't been nervous with a woman in twenty years, and all of a sudden that's exactly how he felt. There was only one way he knew to get rid of uncomfortable feelings: say something brainy. "Ground's heating up; the pressure must be dropping a bit." He rolled to his side away from Kate so she could slide behind the scope. After he watched her wiggle into position, he rolled his eyes back in his head. *You're an idiot, Tom.*

"Okay, what are we looking at?" Kate put her eye to the lens.

"About five hundred meters down slope, the horizontal crosshair should be aligned with a dry river bed; that's Cottonmouth Creek. Right of center you should see a good-size boulder; look just right of that; there are a couple of deep ruts. The clay is darker red—they look fresh. Can you see them?"

"Got it." Kate scooted slightly toward Tom to get more directly behind the scope, her hip pressed lightly against his.

"Now pan left, that's Bluegrass Road. It connects back with Highway 9 about a half-mile east of here. I can't guarantee those tracks were made by the shooter, but I'd put money on it. Alex and the others should be able to figure it out pretty quick. Let's move on to the main event. Shall we?"

Tom sat up and carefully removed the scope from in front of Kate's eye. He set it up on the other end of his coat and lay back down facing the prison; Kate did the same. She was first to look through the scope and adjusted the aim and focus so that the blood stain on the tower was in the crosshairs. "Amazing clarity."

"Yeah, it's a Zeiss-Hensoldt—British military issue; I've used that one for years. Charlie got it for me as a gift. The optics are exceptional, extremely bright; notice the steps on the reticle. The space between each pair of lines represents a one meter tall target at a particular range; take the number below the line and add two zeros. So the mark over the ten is a one meter tall target one thousand meters away."

"Incredible. I'd like to try this on a Lapua .338. I think I could hit a button at a half a mile." Kate slid to the side so Tom could get behind the lens; his broad shoulder pressed against hers, but she didn't move away.

"Or how about the palm of a hand?" Tom clicked his finger as if pulling a trigger and whispered the sound of a gunshot between his lips. "And there you have it." He rolled to his side resting on his elbow and looked at Kate who was now on her side looking at him.

"Exactly what do I *have*, Agent Russell?"

"*The answer.*" Tom sat up and turned toward the tower; the agents on the lower knoll were packing their gear, but he wasn't watching them. Kate was still lying on the coat and rolled onto her back impassively gazing up at the sky, chewing on a fingernail. She crossed her legs and then sunk her hands in her coat pockets.

Tom continued, "As you brilliantly suggested in your little demonstration at the tower, the shooter clipped Goethe's wing to get him to turn around so that he could squeeze off the money-shot a second or so later. The gunman wanted Goethe facing him."

"Is *that* what I was suggesting?" Kate sat up now, looking puzzled. "I was *suggesting* that the first shot missed its intended target, *that's all*. The shooter was trying to blow away Goethe's privates; he had the rear entrance to the theme park dialed into his scope and squeezed off a round. From the back, front, side, it didn't matter to him; they would have splattered all over that guard tower just the same; he just missed shot number one.

Goethe turning an about-face explains the position of the bullet holes, the gym bag, the blood, everything, but that's all it does. I agree that the sheriff's report was a bit myopic; he couldn't visualize that Goethe might have initially been facing the tower, but the sexy new Super-Girl could, okay? *I know—it's a curse.*" Kate batted her eyelids playfully at Tom, but he wasn't biting. "Look, the average male hand hangs, what, a little below the *boys* and about a foot to the side right? Given that, it's reasonable to think that the first shot just missed its target and Goethe was reflexively turning around as the second, corrective shot was delivered and—there you have it; the park is officially closed. However, I am interested in your version as well, Agent Russell; would you care to try and convince me?"

"Yes, he was going for the *boys* as you say; on that we can agree. But he wanted Goethe to face him. No, it was stronger than a want; he *had* to have Goethe facing him. A groin shot won't kill a man instantly, and the shooter was counting on it. He was talking to Goethe through the scope of his rifle." Tom removed the Zeiss-Hensoldt from the tripod and peered into the lens as if he was the shooter. "He was saying: *Thurman, I'm not just killing you; I'm killing you in the way you deserve to be killed, and I'm making sure you know it.*" Tom lowered his voice. "Look, after Goethe got out of prison, the shooter could have picked any place and any time to come after him, but he chose yesterday, the exact day—no, the exact *hour* of his release. Think about it; Goethe is undoubtedly having the best morning he's had in over eight years, maybe even his entire life, and the shooter picked that morning specifically so he could spoil the big party. How's that for maximum dramatic impact?"

"Okay, Tom, I'm almost convinced. Keep going."

"Look, the shooter wanted a front row seat to watch the sudden panic, the fear and surrender spread across Goethe's face like gasoline caught fire; his intention was to transform Goethe's most special of special days into a scorched-earth type nightmare, and it looks like he may have succeeded. That also means he had to be facing Goethe when he pulled the trigger, and that says to me this was extremely, and I do mean *extremely,* personal." Tom smiled to himself. *Apparently Charlie was right after all.*

"Are you keeping something from me Agent Russell? You sure do seem to have a commanding grip on the shooter's profile, and I might add in record time."

"How about I tell you over dinner tonight?" Tom just blurted it out. He had purposely kept SRK off the table and told Grainger he would do so to see how Agent Morrow worked with a blank sheet of paper. From what he saw at the tower, she had done exceptionally well. Now he needed to come clean and dinner in public seemed like the best place in case she had an inclination to get upset with him for whatever reason. Tom knew he may not understand much about the workings of a woman's brain, but he did know that they didn't like secrets kept from them. Besides, Kate did have a feisty personality, and that swing swung both ways. "It goes a bit deep and will make for some good conversation over drinks; there's some ancient history I need to get into as well. I need to walk you through it step by step and..." Tom knew the bell couldn't be un-rung, but he rang it anyway, "it's the best excuse I can think of to get you to have dinner with me."

"Okay, it's a date, Agent Russell, but I must warn you, I've been known to run up a serious bar tab."

"Roger that." Tom wasn't sure what response he had expected, but that wasn't it.

*****

−8−

THE PATIENT

S ally Roberts didn't like the patient in room nine. She had worked the surgical I.C.U. at Memorial North for the last ten years and couldn't remember ever not liking one of her patients. Motherly by nature, she instinctively took to nurturing the sick or injured and was particularly compassionate with the children that ended up in her care. Sally didn't like the patient in room nine, not because he said any unkind words to her or made any unpleasant gestures; he had not yet regained consciousness. It was because of what the police officer stationed outside his door had said before she first entered the room:

"It's just a precaution ma'am. Someone tried to murder him, and we just want to make sure nobody shows up here to finish what they started; but don't worry, we don't really anticipate any trouble. You might want to know that the guy's no patron saint; he just got out from doing a little time up at Rockville. They say he sodomized a teenage boy. Can you believe anyone could do something like that? I have a young one at home, so, if you ask me, the man got what was coming to him. That's probably why I should stay out here; if I go in there I might trip and accidently pull a plug out of the wall or something."

Sally didn't like the patient in room nine because he had sodomized a teenage boy.

Her twelve-hour shift began at 7:00 P.M., and by then the character of the floor had usually changed over from the unpredictable bustle of the day to the relatively quiet routine of the night, tedium mostly consuming the long hours until morning. The unit was nearly half-empty, and after checking the condition of her other patients, Sally didn't expect any serious challenges to develop on her shift. Earlier, the charge nurse had said the remaining surgeries on the floor were also in fairly stable condition; they would probably make it through the night without any major incidents as well. The doctor hadn't left any special instructions either, so Sally figured she was in for a somewhat relaxed and hopefully uneventful shift. She hadn't yet checked on the patient in room nine.

The man had arrived yesterday afternoon from the O.R. after undergoing several operations for gunshot wounds and was still in serious condition at the time she began her shift a few hours later. Fortunately for her, they had assigned an additional critical care nurse and patient assistant to help tend to him through the first crucial night. If he was going to code, they expected it would happen within the first twenty-four hours.

Room nine was behind a closed sliding glass door at the end of the unit, away from the nursing station and away from the other patients. The same officer who was on duty last night was thumbing through an issue of Sports Illustrated while tilted back in his chair; his shoulders were propped against the corridor wall. He looked up when Sally approached, "Good evening, Miss Roberts; let me know if you want me in the room with you. Our friend's been real quiet since I got here at six." He tapped on the glass, "I'll be right outside." She greeted him with a polite smile, then turned away to rub a little peppermint oil under her nose from a bottle she kept in her pocket. Reluctantly, she slid open the door and entered the room.

The privacy curtain was gathered along one side of the bed and kept the patient shadowed from the bright glow of the parking lot outside. The light pushed through the half-opened blinds and cut like yellow spears through the thick air, acrid and heavy with the unmistakable stench of G.I. bleed and black blood. From the foulness in the room, the respirator drew its hollow breath and clicked each time the bellows filled, a slow mechanical rhythm steadily keeping death at bay. Tangled wires emerged from somewhere beneath the layers of bed sheets and spilled over the side, crisscrossing the floor until they reached up into the cluster of flashing monitors and beeping machines. The room seemed more alive than the man lying in the middle of it.

Sally anxiously approached the patient. She typed her username and password into the mobile computer at the foot of the bed and double-clicked on the file she needed to review. She noted that there had been no improvement to his condition during the past twelve hours; the records of his vitals did not look good. She knew his wounds were grave because she could smell them, but she also heard that the surgeons who had worked on the patient in room nine doubted that he was going to survive.

The file said nothing of the man regaining consciousness that day, but she could see a notepad in his left hand and his right hand held a pen. Carefully, she pulled the pad from his loose grasp and took it to the window. She glanced out through the blinds at the light snow that had begun to fall and then back toward the patient lying motionless on the bed. The writing was scratchy but legible and after reading it once, disgust was the only thing she could feel. She forced herself to read it again:

Beneath the steaming caldera

Thurman sleeps

A vast scar's slowly healing, as

His fire keeps

Deep from black wounds, hot fissures spew

Hell's sweet breath

A rancid wind will bring to you

Your horrid death!

Sally stood frozen in disbelief. *Why were they saving this terrible man?* She could feel the nausea from the awful smell filling her throat. A suffocating panic began to overwhelm her; she needed to leave. Hurriedly, she reached over him to replace the notepad where she had found it; her hand shook visibly from the invading tremors. She felt aware of another presence in the room and looked up, but there was no one else. Now frightened, she pulled the curtain cautiously to the wall so that the light from the window would help her better see.

Then, for the first time in Sally's life, she saw evil, and it appeared in the grotesque aberration of the patient's face. Thin bands of yellow light cut across his bruised and jaundiced features; his eyes were now wide open and red, their rage fixed upon her. A foaming mixture of blood and spit boiled up from around the tube in his mouth and pooled in the deep cleft of his chin. Sally gasped; she couldn't swallow, and she couldn't breathe. She couldn't allow *his air* to be inside her lungs. The notepad dropped to the floor as she ran, vomiting, from the room.

*****

–9–

BULLDOGS BARKING

K ate was already sitting in a corner booth when Tom walked into the restaurant. She was typing on her laptop and pretended not to notice him until he was sitting across from her.

"Not exactly what I had in mind, Kate;" Tom spoke over the country music playing in the background; it wasn't so loud that he had to raise his voice, "but thanks for meeting me here. Alex said one of his crew was celebrating her promotion, so they'll be doing it up at the hotel sports bar; I thought it would be better if we met someplace other than there. The hotel manager did say this place has great food and cheap drinks."

"Check and double-check; so what's not to like?"

Tom grinned as he set his coat and the red SRK folder on the seat next to him. "I know it's a bit late to be eating, but I thought I better fill you in, so you can start from a fresh perspective in the morning. I apologize for running late; I may have fallen asleep in the shower."

"You *may have* fallen asleep?" Kate slid her computer to the side and put on a compassionate smile, "Long day?"

"Yeah, it was, and the time change hasn't helped either; I'm sure I'll feel better after a beverage or two. What would you like from the bar? I'll fetch us something."

Kate glanced at her glass to see if it needed freshening. She was drinking sparkling water as a follow-up to the Absolut and cranberry juice she had earlier from the mini bar in her room; she knew she should pace herself, at least until after they got done talking business. She was interested in getting to know Tom *the man,* but was more interested right now in what Tom *the agent* was going to tell her about the history behind the shooting at the prison.

"I'll tell you what, Tom, I'll take another orange LaCroix in a big glass with ice." Kate paused a moment to reconsider. "But since you're making the trip, you may as well bring me a shot of flavored vodka, peach if they have it, Grey Goose if they don't. I can mix them together and nurse on it for a while until I get a little food in my belly. I might be starving."

"Might be?" Tom chuckled. He put the folder on the table and pushed it toward Kate.

"Have a look; I'll be right back."

Kate opened the flap and took stock of the volume of material as Tom slid out of the booth. "You can take your time at the bar, Mr. Russell; it looks like you'll need to stay there a week or two if you expect me to get through all of this before you come back."

"Oops; sorry." Tom leaned over the table and reached into the folder. Kate looked straight into his eyes without blinking; she already liked him enough to let him know it, but he didn't return her gaze. He pulled out a four-page synopsis from the front pocket and handed it to her; his hand was shaking enough that Kate noticed it. "This should suffice for now. Grainger had me work it up last night before I got on the plane; he wanted me to bring you up to speed without overwhelming you all at once." Tom winked at Kate and left to get the drinks. When he got back a few minutes later, she was typing on her computer while speaking the letters out loud: "V-I-N-E."

"What's that?" He set their glasses on the table.

"Victim Information and Notification Everyday: *V-I-N-E.*" She turned the laptop toward him so he could see the website home page.

"I know what it is, Kate; what are you thinking?" Tom slid back into the booth. He scooted around on the seat where they could both see the screen together.

"V.I.N.E. could explain how the shooter knew Goethe was being released." Her tone changed abruptly, "And while we're on the subject, Thomas, when were you going to tell me about the Short Rose Killer?"

"Uh, what day is it?" Tom stirred his whiskey sour and took a long pull.

"Are you serious? It's Monday." Kate lifted her hands from the keyboard and folded her arms across her chest.

"Grainger said wait until Tuesday; I'm a day ahead of schedule." Tom folded his arms across his chest too and added a clumsy, boyish grin on his face. Kate didn't know if he was trying to be cute or a smart-ass.

"I don't know about this Grainger guy anymore;" Kate exhaled, "he seemed straight-up when we met in OKC. Why would he want you to withhold this information from me? I can't help the case if the Bureau clips my wings." She threw back the peach vodka without mixing it with the LaCroix and set the shot glass upside down on the table and not too gently.

"Charlie wanted to see how you performed in the dark and, by the way, you did exceptionally well today. That's why I couldn't wait until Tuesday; I got a pretty good idea of what he sees in your capabilities. I'm very impressed; he's smart to move you to D.C. We could always use someone with your talents." Tom took another pull.

"Well shit." Kate sat up and closed her laptop. "You had me thinking you were David Copperfield or something out there on that hill today, and all the time you were sitting on a three-inch thick folder tracking a four-year-old investigation?"

"It was closer to five; and it cost me my marriage."

Kate was mad and didn't like Tom working the sympathy angle, but she wasn't in the mood for an argument. "Alright; I'm sorry. Why?" Kate calmed down quickly. She was just getting started in the FBI but already knew from her childhood how a case could destroy a marriage. Her dad was a Tulsa police detective, and she remembered the long hours he worked and the long fights with her mom that followed. His career kept him away from his family like a bad addiction. "A major investigation was a narcotic," he had said. You couldn't stop and you always wanted more. Kate was already hooked by what she saw today up at Rockville.

"We didn't have V.I.N.E. when I was working the first three murders in St. Louis," Tom began. "You couldn't just enter a convict's name on a website and get a notification of his release date; besides the first five victims had been out of prison for months before they were killed. Even if V.I.N.E. existed then, the site stops tracking parolees ten days after their release. We figured SRK was somehow tapped into the sex offender registry, but that didn't explain how he knew specific details of the cases, Levy's in particular, that weren't disclosed to the public."

"Then he would have to be somehow connected to law enforcement or justice," Kate said. She glanced up and saw the waiter standing patiently next to the table and wondered how long he had been there waiting for a break in their conversation. *I bet his ears perked up when he heard Tom say 'sex offender'.*

"Are you ready to order, or would you like a little more time?" The waiter talked with a thick eastern European accent.

"Oh, we're so sorry; we haven't even looked at the menus. Can you give us a minute please?"

"Yes ma'am." The waiter bowed almost imperceptibly and hurried across the room.

Kate slipped off her shoes and folded her legs on the seat as she opened the menu. She didn't bother to fix her skirt; she wanted to see if a little thigh might catch Tom's attention; he was sitting close enough that the leg was definitely in play. "I'm calling a time-out Tom, can we back this bus up a little? First we'll decide what we want to eat, then you may continue with whatever you were talking about. "I'm getting a little vodka fog and would really like to wake up tomorrow knowing what the hell is going on."

"Alright, good plan, Agent Morrow."

When the waiter returned, Kate still didn't know what she wanted. She closed her menu and set it on the table. "I'm from Oklahoma, so that means I like meat. What are your dead-cow specials?"

It looked like the waiter was trying hard not to laugh. "We have an excellent eight-ounce ribeye served with a twice-baked potato and mixed vegetables for $19.99."

"Say no more, comrade—that works for me. I'll also have a Colorado Bulldog when you get a minute, and put it in the biggest glass you can find." Kate hadn't had a Bulldog in a while, but the glossy picture on the back of the menu looked enticing.

"Make that two specials; skip the Bulldog for me; I'll stick with whiskey." Tom finished his drink.

"Yes sir." The waiter collected the menus and tucked them under his arm as he walked away.

"I lied, Tom; I know what you were telling me just before we ordered. You said you lost your marriage and that sucks, right? I apologize for that. Now would you care to continue, or does Grainger have a schedule for when you can share that information with me too?"

"Very funny." Tom then added in a whisper, "I might remind you that you are in training; I work for Charlie; and he still calls the shots."

"Fine;" Kate whispered back, "I got it—*the juicy marriage stuff please?*"

"Okay, if you'll be patient, I'll get to that part eventually." Tom slid the red folder off the table and set it between them. He cupped his hands around his empty glass and turned toward Kate. "When Levy was killed, we flagged two other murders that occurred in the area during the prior twelve months: Michael Chapman and Allen Randall—I included them in your brief. At first, there appeared to be really nothing at all similar between the three except for the victims' apparent shared appetite for children. But when I really dug into their criminal histories, I discovered that the killer was emulating, or *echoing*, some aspect of each victim's past predatory behavior and then made sure they died by it or at least got a stroll down memory lane before they were killed.

When I came across the copy-cat pattern, I needed to know how he was getting his information. I could chase it down for Chapman and Randall to old news reports and public records of their trial proceedings. It was a lot of work to find the information, but it was there if you were willing to look. In the case of Levy, the shaving of the hair on the back of his victim's neck didn't show up in any of his priors, and we were keeping a tight lid on that little nugget of information as a hedge while we investigated the abductions that summer. Family members and friends of the victims would have known about that detail, but we checked out everyone there was to find and got nothing. Do you know where the shaving thing showed up?"

"How about you just tell me?" Kate was interested but didn't feel like working for it. She preferred to let Tom talk while she decided how the rest of the evening was going to go. *All that time in the gym and the man still hasn't looked at my legs.*

"We found it in the sealed record of a physical examination of Levy's son. The kid was ten, as I recall, and had nothing to do with why Levy went to prison. But when his father was hauled off for child enticement, Social Services ordered a routine exam to see if the boy had been abused. They found significant scar tissue from the base of his neck to half-way up the back of his head. Eventually, the boy admitted that his dad roughly shaved that patch of hair as punishment every time he did something wrong; apparently it was an '*I*' for '*Idiot*' and was meant to embarrass the boy in front of his friends like a modern-day Scarlett Letter, I suppose. How jacked up is that?" Tom rubbed his eyes for a moment with the palms of his hands. "Shortly after I joined the investigation, I was thrown by the sudden shaving thing; it appeared that Levy's M.O. had significantly and inexplicably deviated from the first couple of abductions, but as I later discovered, he apparently just decided to start acting out what he routinely did to his own poor kid. I guess we'll never know why.

That's when we decided SRK would have to have a source of information beyond CNN, the Internet, and the public record. So, as you correctly suggested, Kate, we figured he would have to have a connection with law enforcement or the justice department or even corrections. Do you know how many potential suspects that generated?"

Tom paused as the waiter returned with their drinks; he downed half his whiskey before he continued. "One million plus. The DOJ alone has a permanent workforce of over one hundred thousand, Bureau of Prisons: forty thousand; law enforcement: nine hundred thousand. Of course we filtered that list with anyone who had been a victim of a sex crime as a child or who had a young family member as a victim and who also had recent connections to the St. Louis area. Right or wrong, we focused on St. Louis since, at the time, it was roughly in the middle of all the killing. Now with Mr. Goethe in the mix, that doesn't appear to be true anymore. On top of all that, we had to look through a thirty-year window; that meant we had to tap into juvenile records wherever they still existed. What we did find was thirty years has a way of erasing history that was never meant to be seen." Tom finished his drink. "Believe it or not, and sadly, that got the number on our victim-suspect list, a very incomplete list, down to just under forty-five hundred. There are a lot of people out there with ugly childhoods."

"Why the thirty-year window?"

"Think about it Kate; you're sexually molested as a kid and you eventually grow up to struggle in an unkind world where you don't seem to fit in anywhere; you're messed up. There's no other way to describe it. One day, you decide you're going to try to fix your life, or maybe something happens that triggers the pent-up rage you've been harboring—either way you direct your anger at the particular group you hold responsible for all your problems, right? How do you put an expiration date on that?

Now process this thought: a thirty-year window means the killer could have been from anywhere before he got to the St. Louis area, and that's how we got to the forty-five hundred suspects. Think about all the municipalities involved in our search for juvenile victims and the potential for lost or destroyed records. Logistically it was overwhelming; even with our Bureau resources, we probably only barely scratched the surface. The numbers alone were just staggering and, as I said, very incomplete, which also means they were unreliable."

Tom emptied what was left of the ice melting in his glass into his mouth, then continued, "We looked for patterns beyond what we already knew but found nothing. SRK starts in Columbia, Missouri, then moves on to Paducah, Kentucky, four-and-a-half hours away. He brutally kills Levy in south St. Louis and goes dormant for three years. Then a year ago he starves a husband and wife team from Moline, Illinois, but does the deed a couple of hours away in Iowa. Now Goethe gets gunned down in Colorado, clear out in another time zone. I don't see a pattern, Kate; I see randomness." Tom cleared his throat. "I used to think St. Louis might have been his home base, but I'm not so sure anymore or if it's even important. Maybe he just lives there; I suppose even serial killers have to live somewhere, but this one sure likes to commute. It seems like he's just randomly shooting fish in a barrel, and the barrel just keeps getting bigger. Who knows how many undiscovered bodies are still out there? It's just dumb luck that we found Levy and the Lowens because they were never intended to be found."

Tom stared at his empty glass. "Okay, now you can forget about everything I just said. What SRK does before, during, and after he kills is secondary. It comes down to this: if we can figure *how* or *why* he's selecting his particular victims, the fish in his barrel so to speak, we'll be able to figure out who he is. You solve that mystery and you win the prize. And that little enigma, Kate, is what cost me my marriage."

"Woah," Kate felt a little lost; the first Bulldog had kicked in on top of the vodka and she had just waved to the waiter to bring another, "this whole time I thought you were going to tell me you fell for some hot young partner like me." She batted her eyes at Tom.

"Nope, my ex-wife dumped me for some guy who evidently made an effort to spend a little time with her; apparently I was too busy to notice. I could sit here and blame SRK, but that would make me a coward."

Kate really didn't care about his failed marriage, but she was beginning to wonder if Tom could even read a hint from a woman. *Is he always this serious?*

"Okay, let's shift gears and talk about the glass, Tommy. Levy had it in his mouth, right? And..." Kate scanned through the synopsis in front of her, "oh yeah, it looks like Bart ingested his; both fragments were red—that's important. What about Randall and the Chipmunk guy?"

"Chapman."

"Isn't that what I just said?" Kate was a little drunk and

trying to get Tom to lighten up, but the man just wasn't playing along.

"Nada. After we made the connection between the first three, we went back and re-checked everything and turned up zip. So now that Goethe has entered the equation with his junk splattered all over the prison wall, we'll have to go back and question everything we thought we already knew. We won't find any glass this time either unless SRK mailed it to him in prison with a bow on it. It will just be another dead end. Did I mention I hate dead ends?"

Kate giggled at a snarky thought that had entered her head. "Wow; a Super Unpredictable Vigilante! I bet that's never happened before! Maybe we should call him SUV?!"

"Very funny, Kate; are you ready for another drink, or perhaps we should go with water this time?"

"Too late; I already ordered us another round. And the glass fragments?"

"Yes, the glass. Levy's piece was about a hundred years old, give or take. We're still waiting on the test to get back on Bart's sample; I suspect it will be a match. I thought the glass would turn out to be a significant lead, but since Goethe's attack seems to deviate from the pattern, as with pretty much everything else, we're back to square—"

Kate waved her hand for Tom to stop talking. "Okay Thomas, let's cut to the chase. By the way, Super Special Agent Russell, what does '*cut to the chase*' even mean? Never mind." She waved her hand again. "You probably know, and I really don't want to, so here's my take-away from all this so far." She cleared her throat with an exaggerated '*ahem*'. "We have a large, white male, mid-thirties to mid-forties, prior victim of abuse or the abuse of a loved one; he's a really good shot with a rifle and maybe lives in St. Louis or maybe not. He usually kills up close but maybe not, has a confused method of operation *or*

'M.O.' as your best-buddy Charlie would say, and apparently just hasn't yet figured out how he wants to do all this. He's killed five already and botched one, but Goethe could still move over to the dead column, and he viciously murdered one marriage that we know of. How am I doing so far?"

"You're doing fine, Kate, but can we try to be a little serious about all this?" Tom's smile was on the fence, but Kate and her bulldog were having too good of a time.

She continued, "We have maybe two pieces of one hundred year old glass, but they've shown up in just under half of the crimes which is usually not good unless that's your batting average. He has some kind of magic source of information, blonde hair and prone to terminate his prey quite violently. On the plus side, he's doing the world a huge favor by getting these child predators off the street because apparently the rest of us suck at it. Oh, by the way, I made up the blonde hair part just for fun and," Kate covered her legs with her skirt and leaned into Tom, "I will get serious, but it will have to wait until Tuesday."

*****

The air outside had turned cold again but was still tolerable. Tom walked beside Kate quietly; he had done enough talking tonight and hadn't yet decided if it had been a waste of time— still, he had enjoyed watching the pretty young agent get a little drunk. He listened to his shoes crunch across the packed snow on the sidewalk.

Kate had been quiet too but spoke first. "Thanks for walking with me, Tom; obviously I needed some fresh air. I acted like a jerk over dinner, didn't I?"

"That would be the bulldogs barking."

"No, that was me," Kate confessed. "Grainger's little stunt kind of put me in an odd mood. My dad taught me to drive hard wherever I'm going, so I don't like sitting in the back seat. Grainger had me riding in the trunk." She stopped and grabbed Tom's coat sleeve. "You don't get out too much, do you? You seem a little stiff. Since it appears we'll be working together for a while, it would help if you could get comfortable with me."

"It takes me a little while to loosen up I guess, socially, I mean. I was married to the same woman for half my life; it's been a difficult adjustment the past few years; you know—all work and no play. I guess it's always been that way with me." Tom paused. "Have you always been this direct, Kate?" He decided that maybe it was time to drop his guard just a little, "You know, it is refreshing; I actually like it."

"Good; get used to it."

"Tell me about growing up in Oklahoma." Tom wanted to point the conversation away from him.

"I don't remember too much about it when I was real young," Kate began. "It wasn't like we lived out on the prairie or anything; we were just city folk. We had a cozy little house in Brookside just east of downtown Tulsa, no siblings, just mom, dad and me. There was a fenced back yard, so they always made sure I had a dog or two to keep me company. My favorite was Sweetie-Pie, a little Boston terrier, but he died—they all died."

Kate stopped and shook her head at the sidewalk, "No, that's not right. Sorry Tom; that was a tad grim. I get that from my mom; she's kind of a Debbie-Downer, although she did give me my stunning good looks, along with a dry sense of humor. The brains come from my dad's side, that and my overly high-achieving ambition. He's been a Tulsa detective for almost twenty-five years and before that a beat cop for another fifteen. Dad just recently took a deputy chief position for a small town on the Pacific coast just north of Seattle. The pay sucks but he'll get to fish as much as he wants. He says he's going to play Andy Griffith for a while until he's ready to retire, but I don't think he ever will. It would probably kill him—unless my mom takes care of that first."

"Have you been out to see them yet?"

"No, but I need to—maybe after we finish this case." Kate made a funny sound like she stopped herself from laughing; it sounded almost like a snort. "When I was in my early teens, he would take me with him to the police station after dinner so I could pretend to help him go over the evidence of some big case pinned to the wall in his office. It was amazing to watch him organize and connect seemingly unconnected events, crime scenes and victims, looking for the pattern that might weave them all together. I can still see him sitting in his squeaky old chair with his hands folded behind his head, staring at the clutter on his wall. He used to say to me, '*Katie, I may not know when I'm done, but I damn sure know when I'm not finished.*' To this day, I still don't know what that means. Then he'd add, '*this is dangerous work; it's no place for a girl,*' and he would point to some gruesome image and I'd get some variation of his usual lecture on the darkness of mankind followed by the pep talk about how I should go after what I want with apologies to no one. Detective Hank Morrow's little daughter needed to push herself to be her absolute best so she could go anywhere and do anything she wanted and—well, you know, *blah-blah-blah.*

Usually by nine my mom would call to break up the party and make dad bring me home so I could get to bed—some nonsense about the importance of school and a good night's sleep. You can imagine that she wasn't a big fan of my police department visits. I guess she figured that solving rape cases and murders was not a healthy evening pastime for a middle-school kid. Then as I got older and interested in normal teenage girl stuff, dad started coming home for dinner less and less, and my crime-stopper days sadly came to a close."

Kate stopped talking for a moment and looked at the ground. "You know, I think he was just trying to spend some time with me, and that was the only way he knew how to connect.

Anyway, I don't know if he had surrendered to his work or was just avoiding my mom; I think it was a little of both. One's no good without the other, you know."

"I do know," Tom reflected for a moment on his own childhood. "Dinner at my house, when we had it, was usually not too pleasant. My dad and I never actually got as far as a fist fight, but there were times when we got pretty deep in the weeds. Do you know when someone just won't let go of an argument, no matter how pointless it is? Well that was my dad—he always had to win, no matter what the cost."

Kate stayed quiet while they crossed the street under a flashing yellow light; they could see the hotel at the other end of the block. "Wow, Tom, we got here quickly. What should we do about our cars? We left them at the restaurant."

"I'll fetch my rental in the morning, then pick you up and give you a ride to get yours, or you can ride along with me to the hospital in Colorado Springs. I do want to go back up to Rockville one more time before we fly out, but right now I'd like to hear the rest of the Kate Morrow story. How does it end?"

"Well there's not much left to say. Let's see. I was a bit of a loner in high school and, I'm sure you'll be surprised to hear, not particularly popular; you know, the acne, glasses and braces thing. I didn't blossom until I was a junior at college. Besides, I was always real smart in school, and most boys don't like the ladies to be smarter than they are. Would you agree?"

Tom heard the question but couldn't think of anything clever to say. He thought the best response was no response at all.

Kate continued, "I did my under-graduate studies in criminal science at OU in Norman and went to Penn State for my masters' work in Methodology and Advanced Criminological Theory. I finished at the top of my class, by the way. I saw you give that lecture on your book: *Psychopathology—Inside the Criminal Mind.* That brainy manuscript made you a rock star in our little department. I doubt you remember, but afterward you signed a copy of it for me. I still have it and open it from time-to-time when I can't get to sleep." Kate smiled. "I think I had a crush on you back then."

Tom didn't know how to respond. "Um, yeah, Penn State. I saw it in your bio; it's a great program, very competitive, and a free-ride deal if you can get in." *Relax, Tom; just talk to the woman.* "I understand it's limited to five or six of the very top applicants, so I guess that would make you the best of the best." Tom paused to retrieve another thought he had lost in his discomfort. "Oh yeah, happy belated birthday. If I recall the date right, you reached the crest of the hill last Thursday—*thirty big ones.* Welcome to the other side, where gravity takes over."

"Not according to Kate's Law."

"Which is?"

"There's a fix for everything; just insert money."

"Yeah, sure; we work at the FBI, remember? I don't know what deal you cut with Charlie, but I've been with the Bureau for almost twenty years and there still aren't enough digits in my monthly paycheck to make a phone number."

"What? I'm not sure I understand, Tom." Kate twisted her face. "You must be the oldest nerd I've ever met."

"Thanks, Kate. You're probably right."

*****

They walked around the back of the hotel to the rear entrance from the parking lot. Tom didn't explain why, but suggested that it might be awkward to come through the lobby together and run into Alex or any of the other agents who were probably still celebrating at the bar. They paused outside the door while Tom fished through his pockets for his room key.

"The walk was nice. Thank you, Tom. The cold air felt refreshing; it helped clear my head. I hope I didn't blabber on too much about myself, and I'm real sorry for how I acted at dinner. Grainger's little game gave me the cramps. Can we start over?"

"Sure, and I can't say as I blame you. We'll figure out some way to get back at Charlie. His sense of humor is less than mine, if you can believe that. It should be fun."

"Tom, I need to say something but don't get all weirdo on me."

"Okay. That might be hard for me, but I'll try." He winked at Kate.

"At the restaurant, you hardly noticed I was in the room. I don't think I could have been more obviously interested in you, and it wasn't the alcohol." Kate stopped Tom from swiping his key in the door. "Look, I know you might think it unprofessional, but we were off the clock at dinner and still are. I need to say what I am about to say and since you said you like me to be straight-forward, well, here it goes... You and I are going to be spending a lot of time together; if you're attracted to me, I'd rather know it now than later. Life is too short to share with regret."

Tom put the key back in his pocket and turned so that he was facing directly at Kate. He raised his chin and rubbed it studiously as if he was forming a thought; a wry smile appeared across his lips.

"Let's see; where to start? You have a small red mark on your left breast that revealed itself when you crossed your arms at the table and nudged your cleavage toward me—*thank you very much*. The scratch likely happened when you were buttoning your blouse and nicked your skin with your thumb nail. The nail has a sharp snag on it, probably from chewing it on the knoll today when you were lying next to me on my coat.

118

You didn't take the time to file it smooth because you were in a hurry and wanted to get to the restaurant before I did so you could pick our table. You selected the back corner booth so you could control the room; from there you could see me come through the front door before I would see you. You then appeared to be distracted by your work, so I might study you uninterrupted as I approached. You knew I was coming toward you, but you didn't look up. Instead, you stared at your computer and twisted your necklace as if deep in thought, but you really just wanted me to watch your long fingers turning gracefully at the nape of your neck. You have stunning green eyes, but you're only wearing a contact in the right one. I saw it when I handed you the case folder. You must have lost the left lens because I saw you wearing it when you looked through my scope on the knoll. You're self-conscious about a barely perceptible flat spot you have just above your hairline, so much so that you frequently fidget with your hair to conceal it, but you shouldn't. You have a little tattoo of a sledge hammer low on the outside of your left heel; below it the inscription says '*make no little plans.*' It's from my favorite Daniel Burnham quote that finishes: '*...they have no magic to stir men's blood.*' The tattoo was well hidden and I didn't see it until you took off your shoes at the table. You're not wearing stockings and, by the way, your legs have perfect muscle tone, in my opinion. Shall I continue?"

"At your peril." Kate rose up on her tip-toes and kissed Tom's mouth, then stepped back gracefully with her eyes closed.

Tom placed his hand lightly under her chin and raised it gently as her eyes reopened; he looked directly into them and didn't blink, "I'm sorry if you thought I didn't notice you, Kate; I could do nothing but. You might say I haven't wandered into the ladies department in quite a while. I may be a little lost."

Kate pressed her body between his hips, "Mmm, I think you know exactly where you are."

"I have three kids."

"So?"

"I'm half-again older than you."

"Then let's not waste any more time."

Tom swiped his room key in the lock and opened the door for Kate. He followed her to the second floor landing and stopped. She was already several steps above him and turned around.

"This is my floor, Kate." He moved slowly toward her and she descended toward him; he put his hands around her waist when she reached the bottom step; their lips were perfectly aligned. He leaned in to kiss her again and she received him warmly, then lowered her head as if in surrender. Tom combed his lips tenderly through her hair until he found the little flat spot and kissed it too. "At least now I know you'll never go all commando on me and shave your head."

"Don't be so sure; I might just try the G.I. Jane thing—it could be fun." Kate nibbled at his chin playfully. "Well, Special-Agent-In-Charge Russell, will you be coming with me?"

Tom didn't know if he was ready to go any further right now or if he should at all. For the first time in a long time he was thinking about what he wanted, not his caseload, not the Bureau, not his kids, and it felt wonderful but terrifying; he felt young and old all at the same time. He wasn't afraid of being with Kate tonight; he was afraid of all the mistakes he would make tomorrow and the days after that. His private life was simple and uncomplicated and dull just the same, but he liked it fine the way it was, humdrum and all. Kate Morrow was crazy beautiful; she was also smart, bright, fun, complicated and anything but predictable.

She was a firefly.

Tom wasn't sure he needed any more unpredictability in his life right now; after all, he had a *Super Unpredictable Vigilante* on the loose. Her words were clever, and the acronym had made him smile. *If we get involved, will it help or hamper me from finding SRK?* Tom was still thinking about what he wanted but not in the way he probably should. *Don't be a fool Tom; whom do you want more?*

"I think perhaps I should say goodnight, Kate." He started to pull away.

"I think not, Thomas—you know *you can have us both.*" Somehow Kate knew exactly what he was thinking. "This is my spare key, room three-one-three." She slid the plastic card into his hand and kissed him again. "I'll be waiting for you in the shower. I promise not to let you fall asleep."

*****

−10−

FIRST LETTER

Tom held the door open while Kate slipped into the car; he was on his cell phone and waiting for Grainger's assistant Pam to connect the call. The sky was clear and the new sun was already melting the dusting of snow that had greeted them outside their hotel in Canon City an hour earlier.

"I have the Assistant Director for you, Tom."

"Good morning, Charlie; we're just leaving the hospital now. Goethe's still breathing but not even close to coherent; in fact he's barely conscious. They're keeping him pretty sedated. They have him scheduled for a colostomy later today, most likely irreversible according to his doc, so I guess he'll be wearing a bag for the rest of his life. Nothing like having to empty your own feces a couple times a day to keep you in a cheery mood." Tom chuckled. "It looks like he'll be unavailable for another day or two, so we're on our way back up to Rockville." He waited while Grainger responded. "Hold on—let me put you on speaker." Tom got in the car and set the phone on the dash. "Go ahead, Charlie; Kate's sitting right here next to me."

"Good morning, Kate; is Tom taking good care of you?" She looked over at Tom with a goofy smile and crossed eyes; her tongue was poking through the corner of her mouth. Grainger didn't wait for her to answer but kept talking. "I want you to put Goethe on the rear burner for now; I'm not sure he'll end up giving us anything we can use, but you can circle back around to him later. It sounds like he's not going anywhere soon. Listen, we just got a piece of evidence that the two of you will be very interested in. It's a letter that came in late yesterday; we had it couriered to Quantico overnight so we could get it to Lab Services first thing this morning. We're running it through Trace, Latent and Chemistry for workups and sent a copy to the document nerds at QDC so they can have their fun with it; they'll get the original later." They could hear Charlie cough over the phone. "Sorry, I choked on my coffee; must be the excitement; give me a second." He coughed again and cleared his throat. "I know it had to be a long day yesterday, so I figured I'd give you the benefit of the time difference and let you two sleep-in for a while before I sprung this on you."

Kate shot another look at Tom while cupping her hand briefly over the phone. She whispered, "He knows?"

"Of course not, Kate." Tom didn't bother to lower his voice.

"What's that, Tom? I missed it."

"Nothing, Charlie, so what's so important about this letter?"

"Well, would it mean anything if I told you it was accompanied by a small piece of red glass?"

Kate grabbed the phone and turned up the volume; Tom gripped the wheel even though they weren't moving. "Okay, now you have our attention."

Charlie continued, "A middle-age couple from Roswell, Georgia, turned it in; name is Hoffman. Unfortunately they've been sitting on it for a while, so they'll have buggered up any trace evidence by now. It's post-marked February 3rd from Ellis Grove, Illinois, and they got it a few days later—no return address. Apparently they struggled with what to do about it; I guess their Christian conscience won out. The letter is a blatant, but anonymous, offer to snuff the man who took some liberties with their autistic son almost nine years ago; the guy's already out on probation, believe it or not. I guess they needed his cell. In case you're interested, the creep tied the poor kid to his bed and made him watch while he masturbated all over him. He cleaned up after his little party, but the idiot didn't know about the nanny-cam." Charlie cleared his throat again. "The letter doesn't mention his name, but we know it's Bobby Mayfield, and he did his time, what little there was of it, in my humble opinion, at Dooly State Prison, also in Georgia, for sexual battery of a minor. It was his first offense according to his sheet, so I guess they let him off easy. You gotta love the Georgia courts. Mayfield had just started working for a home health service as the boy's caregiver, so the parents could work during the day—hold on."

Charlie's assistant must have walked into his office; they could hear him say something to her in the background. "We checked on Bobby, and he's still residing on the green side of the grass, so it looks like the author of the letter apparently didn't get what he needed. I sent a plane to the Fremont County Airport outside Canon City this morning; it should be on the ground by the time you get there. I'll have a car waiting for you in Atlanta to take you up to Roswell; the pilots have been instructed to fly you back here when you're done. As soon as I get off the phone, I'll email you the letter; there are a couple of hard copies on the plane. I'll be curious to hear what the two of you think. Talk to the Hoffmans, have a look around, then meet me in my office tonight about six so we can go over the letter and everything else we have. I don't want either of you doing any of the canvassing work; we'll leave that to the Atlanta Resident Office. Your time is too important to waste interviewing the neighbors about what they might have seen six weeks ago. I want your plump, juicy brains up here in DC. I'll have Pam book a nice room for Kate at the Grand Hyatt down the street. Tom, I really need you to dust this SRK case off for me, so bring that fat red folder of yours. I can't keep my facts straight anymore, and it looks like it's starting to boil up again. I need to be able to keep the Director informed. I'll see you both tonight unless you get held up in Roswell for some reason. Let me know if you do." Charlie hung up.

Tom and Kate sat silently in the car for almost a full minute. Kate spoke first. "SRK needs *permission to kill?*"

"I'm stunned." Tom leaned his forehead on the steering wheel and started the car. "You know, after last night I thought today was going to be rather dull, comparatively speaking." He pulled out of the hospital parking lot and headed in the direction of Canon City. "We'll need to fetch our gear; you can leave your car keys with the front desk and call the rental company to have them pick it up at the restaurant."

Kate wiggled in her seat like she was suddenly chilled, "This is exciting!" She slid her hand up the inside of Tom's thigh. "Have I told you this morning how much I liked your scope?"

"You mean my Zeiss-Hensoldt?"

"If that's what you want to call it—sure."

Tom glanced over at Kate with a timid smile while he tried to push the image of her nakedness out of his head; he would have to savor that thought some other time. "I really enjoyed last night Kate, I mean *I really enjoyed it*, but this letter could be a tectonic shift in the case, and we need to be thinking clearly."

Just as he said it, Tom blew through a red light without even slowing down; he didn't see the signal until it was too late. Kate stole a breath as she braced her hands on the dash for an impact that didn't happen. When they cleared the intersection they both checked their side mirrors for the police, but none appeared.

"Sorry, Kate; that would be the clear thinking thing I was talking about. I'll tell you what," Tom checked his mirrors again, "how about you cancel the room at the Hyatt and come home with me tonight instead? I can think better now if I know we can be together later. We'll pick up a little wine, and I'll make us a salad; I have some amazing home-made crab cakes I've been saving in the freezer. I'm actually a pretty good cook when I bother to take the time. We'll have a romantic dinner in front of the fire and then, uh… *you know.*"

"I do." Kate puckered up and blew him a kiss. "I would like that very much, Tommy, but for now let's get to the hotel in one piece so we can get our stuff, and don't forget your Zeissy-Hensy thing."

Tom couldn't stop the smile from spreading across his face; he wasn't sure if it was from the thought of Kate's naked body entangled with his or if it was the letter and the red piece of glass. Maybe it was both. Either way, it didn't matter; the day was shaping up to be anything but dull.

*****

Tom looked through the round window at the mountains receding rapidly below. He thought he saw the Rockville complex just before they broke into the clouds; the FBI jet was climbing fast. Kate had her head down, reading the Roswell letter on her smart pad. A hard copy lay on the seat in front of Tom facing him. He leaned forward with his hands folded and his elbows resting on his knees; he scanned over the page as if he was studying the label of an expensive bottle of champagne before opening it. There was nothing extraordinary about the presentation of the words on the white sheet of paper, but there were some things he could know without reading them. *Left alignment, double spaced and no bolded type; he's confident in what he's saying but wants it to be consumed slowly. Rage Italics Font—how fitting. He needs it to appear personal without committing to it in his own hand.* Tom was curious about the weight of paper the original was printed on and if it had any trace marks from the printer that was used. The Lab would find them if they were there. Kate reached across the aisle and tapped his shoulder. "So what do you think?"

"I haven't read it yet." Tom didn't look up.

"Okay, whenever you're ready. I'm going forward to get a bottle of water; do you want one?"

127

"Sure, that'd be great."

Tom wanted to absorb each word, their meaning fused to the paper like musical notes heavy with significance beyond the shape of the ink. Almost five years had passed, and he would finally hear SRK speak; not in the language of death he had brought upon his victims, but in the language of SRK's own words:

'Dear Christopher's Mother,'

Telling; Tom considered the singular salutation, *it's addressed to the boy's mother.*

'If you could go back to that day; if you could walk into the room where Christopher slept and find Bobby Mayfield on top of him, what would you do?'

Tom thought about Haden. Without any moral hesitation whatsoever, he knew exactly what he would do.

'Do not let time erase your anger, for the Predators dwell among our children freely, taking, touching, hurting what they will. What is taken does not come back.'

"Bingo." Tom looked up for Kate, but she was leaning into the cockpit chatting with the pilots.

'Bobby Mayfield is a Demon, and the Demon hurt Christopher, the most vulnerable of all God's children. It will hurt others too. It has to pay the price in blood for the pain it has brought into your home.'

You're talking about your pain, aren't you, SRK? Tom re-read the first few lines looking for a 'he' or 'him' in reference to

Bobby Mayfield, but they weren't there. *Why do you dehumanize your prey?*

'Our children see the world through a special window. It is pure like crystal and somehow filters out the evil on the other side; it separates them from it and shields them from harm. But for too many innocents, like yours and like mine, the glass is shattered, and the evil slithers through.

I have given you a small piece of this special glass; it will not break in the face of evil. If you want to send Christopher's Demon back to Hell, hang this where it can be seen from the street.

You will know when it is done.'

Tom flipped the letter over to the photo of the piece of red glass stapled behind it. The ruler pictured with it showed the glass to be about an inch wide and a little less than two inches long. It was shaped roughly like a tear drop and had a hole drilled through the smaller end with a piece of monofilament threaded through it in the shape of a loop. *A pendant.* Tom leaned back in his seat. *Damn.*

*****

"How'd it go in Roswell?" Grainger was sitting on the edge of his desk when Kate and Tom entered his office; he looked up from the fishing magazine he had been thumbing through before setting it aside.

"If you're busy, Charlie, we can come back later." Tom smiled at him and set the red folder on the small conference table next to the window. "You're thinking about taking *Lady Luck* out to chase some Stripers on the Chesapeake this spring, aren't you? Peak season is getting close, and you're getting the itch; I can see it in your face. If you're going, you're taking me with you—same deal as always; I'll bring the beer and hoagies, and you find the Bass."

"I'm thinking about selling the boat is what I'm really thinking. I hardly get to go out on her anymore, and the marina fees are killing me. I should just sell the old girl and charter something whenever I have the time—*which turns out to be never.* If we do go out, we're leaving the cell phones in the car. I don't want a repeat of last year; there's nothing worse than hitting a run of hungry Stripers just as the Director decides he wants to have a Saturday morning meeting upstairs."

"Agreed."

"Count me in too." Kate tossed her jacket across the arm of one of the conference chairs. "Back in Oklahoma, Dad taught me how to do two things well: catch criminals and catch fish." She combed her fingers through the back of her hair and pulled out a cherry blossom; she set it on top of the folder. "It's just a little too windy out there, but I'm happy to report that your pilots seem to know what they're doing. That sure was a fun landing."

"Those two are the best. Kelly, the short stocky one, was a carrier pilot in the first Gulf War, so he can be a little rough on the landings. I keep telling him it's okay to use the whole runway." Charlie got off his desk and sat down at the conference table; he pushed the red folder out in front of him and moved his hands away quickly like the contents were radioactive. "Okay, let's start with Roswell."

Tom was standing at the window looking down at the traffic stacked up along Pennsylvania Avenue. The sun was falling low in the sky and cast deep shadows from the building across the street. He turned toward Grainger and then Kate, who was now sitting at the table next to him. "There's not a lot to tell, Charlie.

The Hoffmans seemed like a nice couple, lived in a modest but well-kept home in a quiet neighborhood. Their son is nineteen now, and he stayed in the other room watching TV while we talked to his parents. Kate was able to spend a little time with him while the father took me outside to let me look around. I was interested in how SRK might confirm the presence or absence of the glass pendant; if he would have to approach the house or if he could see it from the street. There's a pretty good view of the front door from the curb, but he may have come in for a closer look when he didn't find what he was looking for.

The couple said they never hung the pendant, but for two weeks after the letter arrived, they kept a vigilant eye out for any strangers mulling about or someone coming to the door that they didn't recognize. They claimed there was nothing out of the ordinary. We pressed them on it pretty hard but they were adamant about what they saw, or didn't see. They were also very apologetic for not turning in the letter sooner; apparently they had a standing disagreement about what to do with it. The wife wanted to go to the police immediately, but the husband would have been happy if Bobby Mayfield ended up floating face down in the Roswell sewage treatment plant. Obviously he doesn't know anything about the Short Rose Killer, but he did keep referring to the author of the letter as 'Malachi,' which, as he explained, means God's messenger." Tom stepped to the credenza and poured himself a cup of coffee. "Anyone need some?"

"None for me, thanks," Kate chimed in while Tom took a sip and sat down across from her. "The boy, Christopher, was sitting on the floor with his legs crossed in front of the T.V. The room was fairly dark, and he didn't seem to notice when I came in; he was pretty engrossed in his show and didn't seem to want to talk. I'm no expert on the new DSM-5 designations, but I'd say he's between a level one and level two on the spectrum; I think his parents will most likely have to care for him as long as they're around. I asked Christopher if he had seen any strangers in front of his house recently, but he wouldn't answer me and I didn't pursue it. He did say that his dad was going to take him to the zoo next week, and he especially wanted to see the monkeys. I felt really bad for him and his parents. I can't imagine what it was like for him when Mayfield came into his room. I understood why his dad wanted to take 'Malachi' up on his offer."

"So what has the letter changed for us in the last twenty-four hours?" Charlie asked.

"Well, for starters," Tom answered, "we now know that SRK wasn't assaulted as a juvenile—at least that's what his letter seems to suggest. He uses the terms 'children' and 'innocents' interchangeably and in a possessive sense; he's referencing *his* child. Kate, would you agree?"

Kate nodded yes.

Tom continued, "That should help reduce our victim-suspect list quite a bit. Instead of looking for someone who was a victim or is related to a victim, we're now just looking for the latter, but we're still looking at a very large group of people. As I've said, Justice, Law Enforcement and Corrections are our most likely sources for candidates; let's call them our likely suspect 'pool'. How else would SRK know about young Christopher's bedroom ordeal, Levy's abuse of his own kid, and Goethe's history of gun practice with live targets? The Hoffman boy was a juvenile victim; privacy statutes would keep his records off limits to the public, so someone has to be inside the system to harvest that kind of information. What that involves, I don't yet know, but there are a lot of positions with easy access to police and court records."

Tom tapped his fingers nervously on the table. "This new information also shortens our search window by twenty years. We're no longer looking for a sexual assault that created the future SRK thirty years before he started killing; we're looking for a more current victim—*his own child*. To be safe, we should consider a ten-year timeframe prior to the Randal, Chapman and Levy murders. My guess is, at a minimum, the assault on SRK's kid was pretty traumatic, and he wasn't happy with the outcome in the courts, or maybe the perp was never caught; either way he's hunting down anyone that falls into his 'slithering' demon profile." Tom took a drink of coffee. "Our first priority should be to look at abductions where a child was taken by a stranger and killed, or the child was never found; that would get my blood boiling too. Next in line would be any abduction-murder cases that were resolved. We see a little over a hundred of these types of cases every year at the national level, so ten years would net us eleven to twelve hundred possible cases to comb through if we include them all. But we can't ignore abductions where the child was sexually assaulted but later returned home. That's a big number all by itself, probably sixty-thousand-plus. So how wide do we cast our net?"

"Good question, Tom," Charlie glanced at Kate, who was looking uncomfortable in her chair, "but let's not be too narrow in our search; there's no reason not to start with the full line-up. Since we're cross-referencing those case histories against surnames in your victim-suspect pool, we should be able to whittle it down fairly quickly. The resultant list can't be very long. The bigger question is, what's the geographic footprint of the pool? Numerically speaking, if I drew a line around all the kill sites we're aware of, including Goethe in Colorado and—hold on a minute." Charlie went to his desk and retrieved a scrap of paper he had scribbled some notes on. "Let's see, we'd want to include Gulfport, Mississippi, where Mayfield currently resides; so we're looking at a footprint that probably contains twenty-five percent of the U.S. population. St. Louis seems to be roughly in the middle of it, but I could say almost the same for a half-dozen other major cities. Depending on where he kills next, the center point could easily shift to Kansas City, Little Rock, Memphis—you get my point. Who's to say our guy even lives in any of them? For all we know, he could be working out of a Winnebago with a WIFI hotspot." Charlie sat back down and folded his hands behind his head, looking a little frustrated. "Let me change gears for a second. What about setting up a stakeout at the Hoffman's?"

Kate shook her head no. "Look, they received the letter on February 6th; we're almost through March. SRK would have likely come and gone within the first week. Operationally, it's going to tie up a lot of resources to monitor their home on the next-to-zero chance that he's going to show up now looking for the piece of glass, and if we did stake it out, how long would we sit and wait?

I think he moved on fairly quickly to satisfy his appetite, and it appears that Goethe was next in line; SRK sure didn't waste a lot of time getting to him, and he probably already had it set up. There is no way he could have thrown together what we saw out at Rockville. There will be more letters floating around out there already and more to come. Now that we know they exist, we can go back to the early kills and interview family members, particularly the mothers. If each of the first six attacks was triggered by the display of a piece of glass outside someone's home, we're going to have some interesting discussions with some very nervous people."

"The glass is still a puzzle." Tom took another turn. "Did you notice how SRK spoke as if *he* was this magic glass shield that he refers to?" Tom pulled the letter out of the front of the red folder. "Our elusive friend says, '*it will not break in the face of evil.*' I think he's talking about himself, metaphorically."

"I thought the same thing," Charlie said. "We're checking the refractive index, density and chemical makeup now. Hopefully we'll get a match with the samples we have from Levy and Bart Lowen. What about the Illinois post mark? It falls within SRK's little kingdom." Grainger was prone to change topics quickly. In his position, his view had to be from five thousand feet, not down in the weeds.

"I don't know yet if the postmark location is significant, but we'll check it out," Tom offered back. "Until we get another letter to compare, or SRK sends us a Christmas card, it could be just the place where he decided to drop it in the mail. That's good strategy if you're trying to avoid capture. The fact that it showed up in Roswell, Georgia, does tell us his hunting grounds just keep getting bigger."

"Agreed." Charlie got up again and headed toward his desk. He pulled a flask of bourbon from the bottom drawer and a paper cup. "Anyone else?"

"Maybe later." Tom went back to the window to watch the sun drop behind the capital city. Even in the weak light, he could still recognize the South Lawn of the White House where Pennsylvania Avenue turned west. His mind was getting bogged down by the numbers again; it was like they were looking for one man out of the entire population of Montana, and he didn't like the odds.

Kate had been mostly quiet but was about to offer a sober suggestion. "I know I'm the new guy at the table," she began, "and I know we need to do the investigative grunt work that comes with the job, but we also need an operational strategy. As Tom explained over dinner last night, there are just too many individuals in our victim-suspect pool to be able to check them all, and who's to say that SRK doesn't have a sympathetic friend feeding him inside information? Here's a radical thought: *SRK might not even be in the pool at all.* We can't yet know where he lives, but we do know where he works and that's all over, and his turf appears to be growing. But for now he seems to be primarily focused across the Midwest with a couple of notable exceptions. I agree we should start by sifting through the thousand or so abduction-murder records to see if we get a victim's name that shows up in the pool, however big we decide it is, but his pace is picking up, and he'll probably kill again before we get through the first fifty cases. We know his motive, and we now know his method; any egghead at Quantico would tell you that puts us at a huge advantage. I think SRK is overly confident that his letters are having the desired effect. To borrow Charlie's term, SRK's *kingdom* happens to include the Bible belt where a lot of people actually have a problem with sanctifying murder. It won't be long before he sends a letter to another Mrs. Hoffman out there who won't wait six weeks to turn it in, and when she does, couldn't we just let SRK come to us?

"Kate's making some sense;" Charlie added a little more bourbon to his coffee, "which makes me wonder why in the world she would ever want to get into a relationship with you, Tom?"

"It shows?" Kate was dumbfounded.

Charlie flashed his wide grin, "Only when you look at each other."

*****

–11–

HELL BOUND

Peter ran through the house and burst into the kitchen. He handed the loose stack of envelopes to his mother, "Look mom—I brought you the mail!"

Karen Fischer glanced up from her morning reading and shot her young son a look of alarm and relief. He had left the safety of their house without her protection but had returned unharmed and was standing before her with love radiating from his handsome young face.

"How many times have I told you not to leave this house without letting me know?!" Karen was only partly successful veiling her anger. It wasn't with Peter; it was with everything in the world around him, and that made the anger nearly impossible to control. She knew he was careful to avoid certain interactions with strange men like she had taught him, but it was wrong that he had to. Karen's anger was rooted in fear, in the seed of her darkest, innermost suffering, and she planted it where it didn't belong.

She forced a smile and opened her arms wide. Peter eagerly stepped into them and kissed the tear from his mother's cheek. "I'm sorry mom. I just saw the mailman come and wanted to surprise you. I waited until he was gone like you told me to."

Her heart melted. Peter made so many little efforts to try to fill what couldn't be filled. "I'm sorry sweetie; I'm so proud of how you like to help. You're my big little man. I like your surprises, but sometimes your surprises scare me." She handed him a cookie from the big jar on the kitchen table and kissed his forehead.

"Thanks, mom." Peter spun around on his heel and smiled. Everything was better now.

Karen thumbed through the short stack of bills and junk mail. Near the bottom a small padded envelope caught her attention; it bulged slightly across the middle. She set the rest of the mail on the table and held the curious package up to the light. A little heavy for its size, it had taken three stamps to post. Her name and address were neatly written; beautiful fluid letters flowed across the envelope in a loose but confident way. She checked the front and back, but there was no return address. *Who is it from?* She studied the postmark for a moment but was certain that she didn't know anyone from Ellis Grove, Illinois. There was her younger brother, Mark Jr., who went to school in Carbondale, but he left the state right after college and never went back. "Who do we know from Illinois, Peter?"

"Nobody, mom. Hurry and open it; maybe it's the good kind of surprise that won't scare you!" He knelt on his chair and reached across the table for the big jar and another cookie.

Karen removed the contents and placed the empty envelope with the rest of the unopened mail. There was another small envelope inside like a jeweler would have and contained whatever had given the package its weight. There was also a letter, neatly folded, and a yellowed news clipping cut from an older issue of the local paper. As Peter waited, she set everything aside except for the headline and then opened it.

The words revealed themselves like hammers to her chest, breaking the rhythm of her fragile heart. Bitterness swelled from her gut and rushed its poison to every cell in her body. "Peter, go upstairs!"

"But Mom, I want to see what's inside the little envelope!" He reached for it, but she slapped his hand away.

"I said upstairs, Peter; you mind me, young man, when I tell you to do something. Now go to your room!" It was that *'I mean it, tone'* that always brought him into line.

Confused and hurt, Peter shuffled from the kitchen. The door to the dining room swept closed behind him and brushed back and forth a few times before coming to rest. The air grew still except for the annoying hum of the refrigerator, but Karen didn't hear it. In the emptiness of the room she felt crowded by the words that now raced uncontrollably through her head, *over and over and over.* She hadn't needed to read the whole headline; after just glimpsing the date, her memory had completed it for her.

Child Rapist Walks after Serving 1/3 Sentence

Karen crushed the awful piece of paper in her hand and let it drop to the floor. Her head swam with disconnected thoughts; her pulse pounded against her temples while waves of emotion swelled in her chest. Vainly, she fought the rage consuming her and began to cry. *Is this someone's idea of a sick joke?*

She jumped up from her chair, knocking it to the floor, and ran to the sink. She turned on the faucet, filling her cupped hands full of water and drank in gulps until she began to choke. Grabbing the sides of the sink, she propped the heaviness of her body with locked elbows and vomited the clear liquid; the inverted distortion of her retching glared at her from the end of the chrome spigot. *Why wasn't I able to help her when she needed me? My sweet Lindsey!*

The guilt that time had softened returned to overtake her. She tried to focus on something real and now: the kitchen, the sink, the water rushing into the drain. She forced herself to concentrate on the spiraling flow disappearing into the hole, but it made her incredibly dizzy. Her legs, suddenly soft and weak, failed beneath her, and the world went black; her mind raced to take her someplace safe.

*****

She was in her childhood kitchen. The smell of sugar cookies warming in the old oven sweetened the air. Fresh cut flowers from grandmother's garden were neatly arranged in the vase perched on the sill above the sink. Lace curtains framing the open window stirred to a light breeze.

Karen went outside. The rickety screen door slapped shut behind her with its familiar clap as she danced into the sunshine reaching across the porch. Down the steps, her feet glided above the crooked boards and along the gravel path, through the gate and around to the front of her house. She paused to admire the thick carpet of bluegrass trimmed in the summer light and knelt briefly to caress its cool softness.

At the street, chrome-laden automobiles snuggled tightly to the curb, resting beneath a canopy of great American elm. The trees stood, soldier-like, one after another in proper rows up and down the peaceful avenue. Her first bicycle was there too, parked on the walk for all her friends to see; pink and white streamers fluttered from the end of shiny handlebars in the hesitant air.

Next door, a sprinkler waved water at the sky. The rhythm of its rain came and went as it washed the leafy arms of a young apple tree. Through the hedge between the yards, a stream of water collected, peppered black and red-brown with the soil it had stolen away. It wandered along the cobbled stones at the edge of the walk, searching for an easy path to the street. A solitary acorn bumped and twirled between the stone and grassy banks of the miniature river. It bobbed past eddies, spinning nowhere, and tumbled in circles, hastened along by a breach in the cobbles, then settled in a crack cutting across the sidewalk, taken on a torrent of black water rushing home.

Karen squatted over the concrete canal. The imagined boat passed between her young legs and disappeared over the curb. She raced to the gutter just in time to see the little oak seed cross the edge of the iron grating and drop down into the siphoning dark hole.

*****

The imagery faded away; slowly, Karen's consciousness returned, pulling her back to this morning.

She sat slumped on the floor with her back propped against the cabinet below the sink. For a moment she felt oddly happy, but it wasn't real; it wasn't now, and it wasn't here. It had been another place, a distant time, a forgotten feeling summoned from a sweet, long-ago childhood memory—her mind's reply to the shock and confusion of this moment. It was as if she had engaged the comfort of her youthful innocence to ward off a dangerous, threatening infection. Then as sudden as it had come, the happiness was gone.

She struggled to her knees and slowly stood at the sink again. She felt drained. All around the cluttered kitchen were her things, breadcrumbs collected from a different life, but they seemed less familiar now. She turned off the running water. At the table she righted her chair and sat back down, trying to orient herself to the present. The letter lay where she had left it. For what seemed like a long time, she stared at it and through it, wanting to understand. Then, holding her breath, she unfolded the foreboding piece of paper.

'Dear Lindsey's Mother,

I know your pain.'

Karen pinched the bridge of her nose and struggled to hold back the tears; ink blurred as they fell across the words. She forced herself to continue.

'I share your wounds. I know that your Lindsey

never recovered from the horror that this monster put her through. I suspect the fears she found in this world drove her to find her peace in the next.

Our children see the world through a special window. It is crystal clear and pure, and it somehow filters out the evil on the other side. Through the pane of glass their light is purified.

As they grow, their vision becomes less pure. They begin to see the awful and know of it, but the glass still separates them from it and shields them from harm. But for our children the glass was broken, and the evil slithered through. It took my little girl, too.

When they found her body, I wanted to hold her again, just one more time. She was hurt very badly; her body wasn't soft anymore. I wanted to tell her that I love her; I wanted to say goodbye.

I pray she didn't suffer long, but I know she is safe now with Lindsey, and all the others.

She still comes to me in my sleep and cries out for my help, but I'm a just prisoner to my own nightmare of guilt. I couldn't help her when she needed me then, but I do know how to help her now. When I find the demon that took my little girl, I will send it to Hell—very slowly. I will never stop searching, and one day _I will find it_.

But I do know, we know, who took Lindsey from you. And I know where it is hiding.

I will help you, if you will help me. Ask Lindsey to tell my little girl that her daddy is coming to see her soon. Lindsey will know her by her special hair; the way that it grows. Tell her it is straight and light brown and grows from two beautifully shaped spiral crowns. God made her special. Lindsey can find her; she will know her, I am sure of it.

If you do this small thing for me, I will gladly destroy the demon who took Lindsey from you. Those who prey on the innocents must burn eternally for what they do.

If you want your demon in Hell, hang this where it can be seen from the street. You will know when it is done.

*****

Karen calmly laid the letter on the table as she reread the last lines. She opened the small jeweler's envelope and shook the contents into her open palm. A twelve-inch loop of thin fishing line was threaded through a hole drilled through a little piece of red glass. The edges were crudely cut but smooth to the touch; it was made in the shape of a teardrop. She held it up to the sunlight streaming through her kitchen window. As it dangled from her fingers, the glass twisted back and forth. Red patches of color danced on the tablecloth, overlapping with the hues of green, orange and purple. *Through the pane of glass their light is purified.*

Without pause, Karen got up from the table and walked calmly through the dining room to the front entry hall. She stopped to study the photos hanging on the wall opposite the stair. From left to right were the special moments, frozen across the years, from the life of a once-happy family: Karen with her new groom, polished and handsome, she was so pretty then, too; hours-old Lindsey asleep in the arms of her tired daddy, propped in the chair by the hospital bed, pride radiating from his face; her first Easter egg hunt in the backyard; Lindsey posed with a big smile on her bicycle, the training wheels freshly discarded; daddy, mommy and Lindsey on the hood of their new Ford; Lindsey on a brown and white pony at her seventh birthday party; Lindsey at nine and Lindsey at ten. Then off to the right and all alone was the last picture of her little girl, taken just days before she ended her own life. Her father had coaxed the first real smile from her hollow face with a new kitten and had captured the miracle here. It had been her first smile since she was found brutalized almost two years before.

*****

Lindsey Fischer was abducted and raped when she was twelve years old. For the long months that followed, she had fallen deeper and deeper into a paralyzing depression. She could never talk of the horrible day; the psychologists could only get her to shake her head yes or no when asked about her ordeal. The results of the assault were obvious, but the details were never fully known. She could never give testimony. The man who had taken Lindsey from the park near their home had her for seventeen hours before he left her for dead in a wooded area twenty miles away. Her memory of the license number of the car was all that the police had needed to make the arrest.

The rapist's name was Boyd Duncan. He had been

144

sentenced to fifteen years at the Ohio State Penitentiary but was released on 'good behavior' after serving only five of the fifteen. Karen was told that room was needed at the prison for the more dangerous criminals. Lindsey took her own life just one week later.

Not long after Lindsey's suicide, Karen's husband left for work one morning and never came home. She hated him for it, for selfishly abandoning his family, but she really couldn't blame him. Like a tumor, his pain grew every day until all that remained was the shell of a man, a man she no longer knew. The loss of his daughter had killed him inside. Karen never saw him again.

*****

She took the photo from the wall and traced her finger around the edge of the frame; she held it gently to her chest. The tears flowed freely now. Her whole world had come apart by the single, violent act of an evil stranger. Karen's daughter was dead; her family was destroyed, her once-loving husband was gone. The only thing that could keep her going was Peter. *Sweet little Peter; he tries so hard to be a big boy. It's not his fault!*

She became furious again, furious at herself for not being there to protect her girl, to save her from the abduction by *the demon.* She was furious with her husband who had not found the strength somehow, somewhere, to save whatever it was that they had worth saving, for leaving her to cope all alone. She was furious—no *murderous,* with the monster that had caused her all this pain. Hell was *exactly* where she wanted him!

Karen kissed the tip of the finger that still held her wedding band then gently touched the worn corner of wood that framed the last happy memory she had of her little girl and stepped outside onto the front porch. There was new hope in the air; it was a beautiful spring day. Pink fuchsia overflowed from a hanging basket mounted on the center post. She knew they were in clear view from the street because she sometimes admired them as she walked from her car parked at the curb. Early on summer mornings, she would sometimes sit on the porch swing and watch the humming birds dance in and out of the sweet wells formed by the perfect flowers.

Karen Fischer placed her daughter's photograph on the railing and looked out to the empty street. She wondered how long it would be before he would come. On tip-toe she removed the heavy basket and lowered it to the floor. She pulled the pendant from her apron pocket and reached up to place it over the hook before setting it spinning with a tap of her finger.

There was great power in this little gift. Sparkles of red light glittered in her eyes. She closed them tightly and silently wished this small piece of glass could magically turn back time.

*****

–12–

THE VISITOR

B ryan shrunk low in his seat and avoided making eye contact with the other passengers; it was best if he didn't draw any attention to himself, and he certainly didn't want to invite any conversation. He was trying to be invisible, but he was big, and big men on little planes drew attention. Later if asked, people might recall seeing a large man with a heavy beard sitting in the exit aisle, but if he didn't look at their eyes, they probably wouldn't remember much at all about his face.

He gazed out the window at the clusters of neat farmhouses and barns that dotted the quilted world shrinking below. Their tiny façades reflected the day's final light back towards the sun falling over Missouri. Long shadows stretched east across the Illinois landscape, the subtle landforms and colors of the emerging fields exaggerated in the low glancing light. Spring had arrived and the land was awakening.

Bryan leaned against the side of the plane and closed his eyes, focusing only on the drone of the engines. Within minutes, he had fallen asleep.

*****

When the plane touched down in Cleveland, the jolt from the wheels hitting the runway woke him. He sat up and looked out the window at the dark tarmac, then he checked his watch, remembering to add the hour for the change in time zones. 6:57 p.m.. The bus to Indianapolis was scheduled to leave a little after 10:00 tonight, and that gave him plenty of time to finish what he needed to do and get to the Greyhound station. If not, he would pay cash for a hotel room and catch the early bus in the morning. When he got to Indianapolis, he would rent a car and drive to the airport in St. Louis where he had left his truck parked in the long-term lot. He would pay cash for that too.

After he got off the plane, Bryan followed the signs to 'Ground Transportation' and walked out of the terminal into the damp air rolling off Lake Erie. Immediately he ducked into the open door of a waiting taxicab and slid across the seat.

"One-seven-six-four Curtis Street; it's in Huntington Park."

He was wide awake now, but closed his eyes again to calm himself. If the outcome of his visit tonight was to his liking, he would be returning to Ohio in just a few short weeks to finish the rest of his business.

*****

Karen Fischer kissed Peter on his forehead and lightly stroked his short hair with the gentle palm of her hand. "Good night little man—sweet dreams."

"Good night, Mommy; I love you." Peter turned to his side and pulled the comforter up over his shoulder. Karen knew he had to be tired; he had asked to go to bed almost two hours early. Life could be tough for an eight-year-old boy. She picked up the pile of dirty clothes at the foot of his bed and shut the door part way, leaving it open just enough to let some light spill into his room.

At the end of the hall she pushed his clothes through the hamper door in the wall and listened as they slid down the chute to the basement. She reminded herself to get the laundry done tomorrow; Peter was getting low on clean shirts for school.

She went back downstairs and entered the kitchen. After

considering the evening's dishes piled in the sink, she decided they could wait until morning; two people just didn't create enough mess to clean up after every single meal. She did a quick rinse and set them on the counter, then scooped out the sink strainer with her fingers and flicked the soggy clump into the trash. Karen thought about the unpleasant things that sometimes had to be done. She knew that one day Peter would be grown up and facing them without her; she wondered if he would be able to.

Feeling a little better about the mess around the sink, she rinsed her hands with warm water before drying them on her apron. "Good enough," she said out loud and hung her apron in its place behind the pantry door. She paused for a moment and listened. The house was quiet. The rest of the evening belonged to her, and although she was exhausted, she needed a little time to unwind.

Karen poured a half-glass of orange juice over ice and filled the rest with vodka, stirring it with her finger before giving it a taste. It was her nightly routine before retreating to her room where her bed was a big and lonely place. It was too easy to lie there and think, and without the vodka to help numb her thoughts, sleep would not come for hours, if it came at all.

She flipped off the kitchen light and walked to the living room. Sitting on the edge of the couch, she found the remote between the cushions and turned on the television. She adjusted the channel to catch the end of the local seven-o'clock news and turned down the volume. Karen frowned when she recognized the sportscaster bobbing his head behind the news desk. It annoyed her that she had to sit through the casualty lists from the various athletic contests around the country just to find out about tomorrow's weather. Professional athletics had little importance except to professional athletes, but the weather report was something altogether different. It told her if she needed to get up early to have more time to get to work. It told her how she should dress herself and Peter for the wait at the school bus stop. It told her which way she should drive downtown to avoid the usual weather related snarls or if she should put gas in her car for the longer commute. It was information she needed; *it* was important.

She decided to check the weather app on her cell phone later and turned off the T.V. She set the remote on the coffee table and glanced out the window to the front porch. Beyond the railing, a heavy fog hung between the trees like a gray veil. Soft rain, captured in the luminous cone of the street lamp, lightly washed the cobbled stones up and down Fowler Street.

Karen felt anxious but couldn't think why. *What have I forgotten?* Peter's clothes were ready for tomorrow, and his lunch money was on the counter where he would easily find it. The car had plenty of gas, the oven and stove were off; the back door was locked. *What am I missing?* She cursed to herself at the dark porch and hurried to the front hall to turn on the light. She parted the lace curtains and looked through the glass in the door. The red sparkle from the little pendant immediately caught her eye and settled her. It twisted back and forth slowly in the evening air, suspended from its invisible thread. She leaned against the door and thought about the note that had come in the package with the glass. It had arrived almost one week ago. *'You will know when it is done'*, the note had said. But the days had passed, and she didn't know anything at all. There had been nothing in the news or the paper about the murder of Boyd Duncan. *Maybe he lives in another city—his death wouldn't make the local news.* But she hadn't received another message either. She realized killing a man took time and wondered how long it would be before it happened. *How long will it be before I can begin again?*

She thought about the man who had sent her this small gift and thanked him silently for what he said he would do. Karen returned to the living room and lay down uneasily on the couch.

She thought about what he had written. He had said that he lost his daughter, that someone had taken her from him like Lindsey had been taken from her. She wondered if he had a family anymore, or had that been destroyed also? The note said that his daughter was hurt very badly. In Karen's mind she kept an image of the man holding his dead little girl in his arms. She remembered the relief and hope she had felt when Lindsey had come home alive. The mysterious man would never know that same joy or release, however temporary it may have been for her.

She knew how he felt, to lose his child. He would know the cutting sorrow and unbearable guilt; the burden of opening your eyes each morning and the fear of closing them again at the end of every day. And during the slow, painful hours that passed between crawling into bed and finding sleep, he would know the tortured replay of the wrong choices made. Few people in the world could know how they felt living with the gaping wound that would never close. No one else could even possibly imagine.

Karen stared at the cracks in the plaster ceiling and tried to think of the past she had but couldn't remember. It had all changed so suddenly, so abruptly. Her old life was a boat that had crossed the horizon, too far away for her to even see. She wanted to remember that morning, before this all began, when her life was simple and ordinary and predictable, just like the lives of the other people on Fowler Street. Some*thing* took her daughter, raped her and discarded her in a pile of rotting leaves. Some*thing* hurt her little girl so much that Lindsey chose dying over living. Some*thing* desecrated her life and family and destroyed her marriage. Some*thing* was a man locked away in prison, and some son-of-a-bitch therapist decided the man could now control his cravings and set him free. Free to make a new home and a new life wherever he pleased, free to wander the streets, the malls, the parks, the museums whenever he wanted to. Free to follow his thoughts and wants and desires—*free to* *crave another child.*

That *thing* was free and Lindsey was dead and Karen was the prisoner to all of it. Someone out there had offered her primal justice and she took it. Soon, He would come to punish the man who had hurt her family. Soon, He would come to send *him* to hell. She wished He would send *them all to hell.*

Karen closed her eyes; in minutes she was asleep.

*****

Bryan stood on the curb and watched the taxi drive to the end of the street and turn back toward Cleveland. He looked at the house at one-seven-six-four Curtis Street. It was a handsome dwelling, and he thought it might make a good home to raise a family. He glanced at his watch again: 8:02 Eastern Time. Turning up the lapel of his coat against a damp breeze, he crossed the street, then followed the sidewalk until he reached the wrought iron arbor that marked the entrance to Huntington Public Park. He ignored the sign warning the park closed at dusk and made his way along a weakly lit path toward what looked like the distant outline of a bandstand or picnic shelter. It was backlit in the lights of the parking area beyond and seemed buoyant in a heavy fog, the sole structure in the otherwise complete darkness at the center of the park. He had read about the pavilion in the police report; it said the girl had been taken from there.

He thought he heard something and stopped; his breathing was regular but audibly deep, and he made a conscious effort to sort out his own sounds from the sounds around him. He thought he heard a giggle far from where he stood, then a more masculine laugh. Next was the noise of an aluminum can striking something hard followed by more laughter, and it calmed him some. *Must be just a couple of kids—young kids who should not be in this park.* He continued along the path toward the sounds of the couple; his breathing became less relaxed the closer he got to where they were; he needed them to leave. It wouldn't happen if he wasn't alone.

When he reached the pavilion, he found it perched at the edge of a pond, the far side of the water obscured in absolute darkness. The weak smell of an abandoned cigarette lingered in the air. Fifty yards beyond was the parking area where he could see the two lovers embraced between their automobiles; they separated, and one shape chased the other around the cars. He heard doors slam and watched them drive off erratically. For no reason, he counted the twelve light fixtures that glowed at him through the fog before turning his attention back to the pavilion. *Good.*

Bryan climbed the steps and crossed the wooden floor to a railing that framed the pond below. A group of mallards quacked nervously as they shuffled into the black water and disappeared into the darkness. A single, dim light bulb hung from the rafters and cast shadows through the structure, like blue fingers reaching out to embrace his arrival. He leaned on the railing and moved his hand over its surface scarred by dozens of engravings professing one pair of initial's love for another. A few were scratched out altogether, probably, he thought, paired off with others in fresher carvings elsewhere along the rail or on the broad surfaces of the wood posts supporting the roof overhead.

A soft drizzle began to fall, gradually growing stronger until it sounded like hail striking the tin sheeting above where he stood, finally culminating in an angry chorus of violent white noise. Bryan ignored the loud intrusion on his thoughts; instead, he watched curiously as lost rain seeped from a crack in a part of the roof that projected out over the water. Like little magnets, the droplets attracted one another and merged to form larger ones, straining against their combined weight and the pull of the earth. Once freed, they struck the surface of the pond in a row of tiny water explosions. Their orderliness contrasted sharply with the chaos falling everywhere around him.

He was thinking of the little girl.

*****

In Karen's vodka sleep she is dreaming a hauntingly familiar scene. Each time she has had the same dream her mind has crafted the imagery in greater focus. Each time, the details have become more and more terrifying.

She saw the man who sent the letter again as she always did, in an unknown place, a dark, colorless cellar. His face is just a shadow as he stands over someone—or something. He is not alone.

His captive is kneeling, crying; its arms are behind it and its wrists are tightly bound to ankles hideously twisted together like rope. It is naked and bleeding but without human form. The face is raised and straining in the weak light to see.

The man in control is speaking in whispers; he claims that he is the Keeper of the Innocents as he pulls a shard of broken glass from his pocket; faint spots of red light wash across the alien face. He orders the mouth to open and his command is obeyed.

The Keeper pushes the glass into its throat, past two rows of broken teeth guarding a forked tongue, then places the razor edge of a knife below the shape of a nose. He pushes it up into the flesh that separates the flaring nostrils. Blood runs down the silver blade as the Keeper gives his command.

"Swallow!"

The ferociousness of the dream awakened Karen. She sat up and found her drink on the coffee table and finished it with a long pull; her hands were visibly trembling. In the few long minutes that followed, the vodka began to thaw the hollow chill she felt inside, but still she was alarmed. The images that filled her dream did not bring her comfort. Instead, she felt weakened by a horrible force pulling her deeply into a haunted world of nightmares and hate; a world far more terrifying than anything she had dreamed before, before the letter, before the... *pendant.*

Her thoughts reeled. *Please, God, not now! I'm not ready, not tonight; please! I'm not strong enough! What should I do?!* She had to stop it from happening; panic wrapped her tightly.

The light!

She hurried through the front hall, grabbing her long raincoat from the closet, and threw it over her shoulders. Cool, damp air spilled in as she opened the door. She pulled the coat more tightly around her and studied the light switch for a hesitated moment before turning it off, then stepped outside into the blackness of the porch.

*****

Bryan circled the pavilion floor with his hands deep in his pockets. She had been taken from here; he was sure of it—he could sense it now. The girl was abducted from the picnic shelter in Huntington Park early on a Sunday evening. She had gone alone to feed the ducks like she did every Sunday in good weather; the park was only two blocks from her home. She had followed a predictable pattern, and it had made her an easy target.

Bryan sat on a picnic table close to the railing. He blocked the sound of the rainfall from his mind and tried to imagine what the girl was like sitting where he sat now, tossing bits of stale bread to the mallards in the pond. He thought she must have looked very pretty there by the water and imagined the late afternoon sun streaming through the lacy fretwork and lattice that trimmed the posts and beams of the pavilion. In his mind he sees her deep in youthful thought. She is thinking of the important things in her life, a slumber party with her friends, a young boy at school, or the argument she had with her mother and now regretted and thought hard how to correct. Perhaps she was just here, at the pond with herself and the ducks and the warm sunshine.

Next, he imagined the demon, friendly-looking with a round face, its features plain and calm and not threatening at all, but it's a lie. On a sunny patch of lawn at the edge of the pond, it fakes a struggle with a pretend bad foot while it plays with its dog. The demon is very visible with animated movements and laughter that are just a charade, exaggerations to attract the girl's attention. It has probably worked before, and it is working again. She sets her bread on the table and stands at the rail to watch the script unfold. The demon appears to lose the leash from its grasp, and the dog runs off past the pavilion and past the girl just as the animal has been trained to do. She hurries to give chase and catches the pet easily; they are instantly friends. As the predator reaches them, she returns the lead, and it bends to calm the excited animal while looking up at her with soft kindness—thanking her. After they talk for a little while, the demon places its hand gently on her shoulder to test her comfort; she nods her head eagerly, then smiles and runs off with the dog clumsily nipping at her ankles. They turn on the path that leads to the parking area and disappear into a thick canopy of trees while the predator follows to catch up with them. It was all very easy.

Bryan sat on the table for a long while and focused on the pretty imagery of the girl. He fought back thoughts of the demon alone with her after it had taken her from the park—ugly thoughts. "Damn it!" He sputtered aloud through his clenched teeth. Wrapping his arms tightly around his knees, he pulled his chest to his thighs and rocked back and forth on the edge of the table. "Damn—damn—damn!"

The rain shifted suddenly on a gust of wind and washed across his feet; Bryan recognized the moment and looked up, feeling alarmed but strangely confident. He knew *it was time* and braced himself for the pain that would follow as it had before, but it would dissipate soon enough.

Just then his skin began to tighten, in isolated patches at first and then everywhere. The veins in the back of his hands vacillated under the growing pressure. It was as though his flesh was being stretched across his muscles to the point of ripping apart; he couldn't help but grip his legs tighter. There was a faint and distant ringing, first in one ear and then the other; objects fixed in his vision suddenly appeared as if they were far away, becoming lost in a blur. He shut his eyes and stared at the tiny white and red dots floating across the inside of his eyelids and sensed the pending arrival. The ringing in his head became unbearable; he closed his hands over his ears and pressed them hard against his skull. He clenched his jaw and shook his head violently; he wanted to scream but dared not release the pressure on his clamped teeth.

Then the ringing stopped. As quickly as it had tightened, his body now relaxed and he felt emptied of himself. Cautiously he released his hands from his ears, and his vision cleared. He now sensed her presence was here; he knew it would be. It was why he came. It was the little girl named Lindsey.

He stood cautiously and walked again, this time with careful, deliberate steps, slowly circling the pavilion, pausing to touch the painted surfaces, to feel the energy escaping; he breathed deeply and purposely. He removed his coat letting it fall to the floor and allowed the damp cold to penetrate into him. His awareness of the girl became very strong. Faint, ghostly cries began to seep from the wooden structure. They were weak and distant at first, but steadily grew stronger and louder until they collected in a haunting refrain that swirled all around him. Her cries, dark and whispery, fell from the sky and filled his heart with her sadness and fear.

Bryan paused at the steps and looked out into the veil of tears washing over the park. He raised his arms and stretched them wide with hands and fingers spread to the chilled air as if he could absorb all of the girl's pain. He screamed out in anguish at the life lost from this place and listened to the echoes of his own voice recede into the night. Motionless, he stood there for a long time. The rain slowed and moved off across the pond, seemingly carrying the girl's presence with it. The cries faded just as they had come to him, and he was alone again.

Feeling drained, Bryan shuffled back toward the table and found his coat where it had fallen. As he bent over to pick it up, he stopped, sensing something else, something very different. This time, it was something known. A fragile but familiar scent made him stand immediately, but cautiously; he was keenly alert now. As the smell filled the air and grew more intense, a comforting warmth crawled up the back of his neck and spread across the base of his scalp. He knew the scent and recognized the warmth that came with it; they had come to him not very long ago in just the same way. This time he knew what it was, and it didn't frighten him at all. It was his little girl.

Bryan closed his eyes and stood at the railing, forcing himself to be calm. He folded his hands and placed them against his bearded chin as if in prayer. At the right moment he let his arms hang, resting loose at his side and waited. The seconds passed slowly, but he didn't dare move; he was certain of what would happen next. Then one by one, he felt little fingers thread between his own. His body stiffened; his skin electrified. He wanted it to be real. He wanted *her* at his side again, but he couldn't look down, for he feared that she wouldn't really be there, and he refused to not believe. As he gently squeezed the air from his empty hand, he heard the young voice in his head speak to him.

Daddy?

"Yes sweetheart." His voice quivered.

Is she okay, Daddy?

He opened his eyes and gazed out across the pond where the girl's cries had drifted away just moments before.

"She will be."

Suddenly, he felt strong from the power of his promise rushing through his body. He needed to hear her sweet voice again just one more time; he hoped that she was still there. She was.

Pinky-swear Daddy?

He bit his lip and started to cry. "Yes; pinky-swear, Sweet Pea."

I love you Daddy...

Her words were fading away too quickly, receding into the lonely chamber of his mind where they could not be heard.

"Come back! Please don't leave me!" He hurt all over but defied the pain to speak once more to the nothingness, "I love you, Emma."

Bryan dropped to his knees. "I love you with every beat of my broken heart."

*****

Most of the time Karen's street was a deserted place, especially after dark and always when it was wet or cold outside. Even in good weather, the neighbors who were out for the night air or a walk around the park found their way home soon after darkness fell. Sometimes, on comfortable evenings, well-lit porches came alive with people gathered for a visit, but it wasn't often, and children, trying to capture the long days between spring and fall, were ushered indoors well before the daylight completely withdrew. Occasional birthday parties overflowed the small homes and front porches taking to the yards, sidewalks and street for their games, but the youngsters were always kept close and under watchful adult eyes.

It wasn't always this way, but had been since the girl who lived in the green house on Fowler Street was taken from Huntington Park, and, two months later, another girl was taken from the neighborhood grocery store just a few blocks away. One came home and committed suicide, the other had never been found. A few of the homes were now empty, the For Sale signs nearly lost in the weeds of the overgrown yards; those who hadn't left pulled their lives indoors. Karen's street had become a place to leave.

There was no one out to be seen or heard tonight; no parties or music or laughter; no games where flashlights lanced the dark. There were no nosey neighbors walking by to make pretend conversation with; there was no one out tonight but Karen, standing alone outside her front door.

The last leaves clinging to the oaks hung motionless in the still air; they would drop soon as the new spring growth pushed to replace them. Fog filled the street and shallow yards held by the facades of houses and short hedges that lined each side of the narrow road. It was the fog that sometimes rolled in from the Cleveland River; Karen could smell it.

Street lamps pushed their light down through the dense air and weakly rendered the cracked surfaces of the sidewalks. Karen counted the number of evenings she sat on her front steps, waiting for an unfamiliar car to approach and slow down just enough so that the driver inside would see the glass suspended from the ceiling of her porch. The waiting was horrible.

She sat down on the tired wicker swing her husband had hung for her a very long time ago. The rusted chains squeaked in their mounts as she gently pushed herself with the balls of her feet. It reminded her of the swing that was on her parents' porch when she was young. She had liked to lay with her head on her father's shoulder as he pushed them both in lazy gyrations; she always felt secure when she was with him. Sometimes they would sit together in the shelter of their back porch and watch great summer storms approach the small town in Kansas where she was raised. They would race inside just before the spears of rain forced water through the cracks around the windows and doors, leaving dark stains on the papered walls and puddles on the floors. The fierce winds bent and twisted the great trees in their yard, and lightning flashes bleached the sky; she could still hear the deafening claps of thunder that shook their house violently around them. Young Karen knew there was nothing her father could do to calm the frightening green skies, but when he was with her and held her, somehow she was never afraid. Her father had said that no storm would last forever.

She heard a noise and stopped the swing. First she listened for Peter upstairs, but the house was silent; then she listened for anything, but there was no sound. She lay down curled up on the swing and closed her eyes; she pulled her coat around her knees and listened only to the stillness. Lying there, the warm memory of her father's rough hand stroking her hair came easily to her; she missed him deeply. He had sung his favorite hymns to her many times on a swing just like this one when she was a little girl. Now, in a soft whisper, she sang for him the one he had often liked to sing for her.

Then the air began to stir. Leaves rustled in the oaks just as a gentle rain began to fall, soft and cleansing, not like the storms she remembered in Kansas. A gust of wind rolled up the street from the direction of Huntington Park, pressing the water before it. It crossed the curb and moved toward her, combing the lawn flat as it approached. The smell of the river fog was gone, and the night felt cleansed. The wind rocked her back and forth in the swing, but the chains remained quiet. The pendant roused on its thin line while Karen continued to sing.

*****

Bryan turned his back to the picnic shelter and walked along the path that followed the edge of the water. The fog had cleared but began to return as new air pulled the moisture from the wet ground. When he reached the end of the pond, Bryan crossed a narrow wooden bridge, each leg of its gentle arch firmly embedded in the ground with heavy stone walls. The dam between them held strong against the new burden of water brought on by the sudden, heavy rain. An opening in the top of the wall released a rush of turbulence across the rocky spillway. Farther below, the creek swelled against its grassy banks, impatiently waiting to push through the row of metal culverts that tunneled beneath the road winding out of the park.

He stopped on the bridge and watched the waters roil white at the mouth of the round openings. In his belly his stomach churned also, but his mind was quite clear; he knew how to find the monster that took the young girl from the pavilion, and now he was ready. He knew what her mother would do if only she could, but Bryan was strong, and he would do it for her; he was simply the mechanism for getting it done. Tonight, the mother's blessing was all he needed, but he wasn't worried about what her answer would be. A parent's love was the strongest force on earth.

He left the path and climbed down the embankment to the edge of the road, following it to the end before turning right on Woodson Street. Woodson soon joined Buckeye, and from Buckeye he turned left onto Fowler. Fowler Street was where Lindsey Fischer had lived and died.

*****

"*...was blind, but now I see.*" Karen listened to the final note softly resonate in the heavy air and then fade away. The sound of her voice was gone, but the night was no longer silent. She heard footsteps coming from down the street. Weak at first, the sound of hard soles scratching against the gritty sidewalk was getting louder and clearer. She froze.

Is it... him? Karen felt excitement—then panic as she realized she had turned off the light over her porch; still she could not move. The sound was loudest now, as if amplified by the front of her house. Then she heard a muffled cough; the closeness of it startled her.

It was a man.

Karen sat up as slowly as she could. She struggled with the swing twisting from her clumsy movements; the chains popped loudly as she regained her balance and her feet found the floor. She looked out over the railing and saw him.

The visitor was a mysterious profile painted black against a wash of yellow light from the street lamp across the road. The new fog hung all around him and softened his outline; she could see no particular features, only that he was an imposing man. He looked up and down the street and then directly at Karen. She wished she could see his eyes.

Karen spoke first, "Is it... *you?*"

"Hello Karen".

She felt suddenly nauseated; saliva poured from her cheeks and flooded her mouth. She fought against the sickening need to vomit. She swallowed and took several slow, deep breaths. His shifting movements only added to her anxiety. She struggled to speak.

"Please don't worry. I've been out here a long time tonight; I am sure we're alone." Karen took another deep breath; the urge to retch now passed. "I've wanted you to come; I've desperately wanted you to visit me, to see it, to see my... answer. It's right here; I hung it outside the day it arrived. It has, I mean—*I have* been waiting all this time for you." Karen stood and reached to push the pendant forward to prove to the visitor that it was there; then she turned it to look at it herself. She didn't know what to say next, "What does it mean?"

There was no answer.

Karen needed to talk, "I don't know what to say to you. I feel so much, but there are no words for any of it."

"Say nothing; I must go now; you have given me what I came for." He turned to walk away.

"Wait!" Karen almost shouted to him. "Do you believe in God?" She had to know.

The visitor looked back over his shoulder at her, then bowed his head as if looking to somewhere else; there was a long silence before he spoke again. "When they found her—," he began to choke on his words. Karen started to come down the steps, but he held up his hand and shook his head at the ground. He spoke through clenched teeth, "When they found her body, they asked me to come and identify her. She was so broken; she was so— I cursed God for what happened to her. She was just a child!" With soft, broken speech, he finished as if to remind God of His mistake, *"She was my little girl."*

Karen sat down on the bottom step and thought about Lindsey; she fought back the tears.

He continued, "But I had to keep believing. I couldn't accept the thought of her lying in the cold ground alone, forever. Do you see? I *had* to believe she had gone to a better place, where one day I could be with her again. I can think of no other outcome." His voice changed, becoming mechanical, "God took her from me, so I would do this work for Him. I know He will give her back to me when I am done."

Karen shuddered from the conviction she heard in the tone of his voice. Cautiously, she asked, "How many times have you

—?"

"Not enough."

"What was it like?" She wanted to know what he felt when he murdered them, but couldn't say the words.

"I am only half of the moment." He turned away, raising his hands, then looked up the street and spoke to it, like a pastor to an empty church. "I wanted to destroy each one of them *with these*. I thought it would help me." He placed his fingers lightly over his lips. "But I am just the hand that covers the mouth; do you see? I do not take their final breath away—God does. There is always one final breath I leave for Him to decide. Perhaps it is brief, but there is a moment of absolute fear between the release of my hand and the grip of God. I wonder what the monster thinks in that instant of reckoning. Did *it* repent? Did *it* beg for His forgiveness? God could not be capable of granting *it* forgiveness. How could He have compassion for *it* when He had none for my little girl?"

The visitor lowered his hands from his lips and reached in front of him as if he was trying to touch something. "Once I tried to kill one of *them* from a distance, but it wasn't the same. That final moment was lost. It happened too suddenly; it happened too far away. I could see the fear, but I couldn't smell it; I should have been closer to feel its fear. I wanted *it* to know *it* was about to die, but I was too merciful. I wanted *it* to hurt and...," he paused and leaned a little toward Karen, "I wanted to make *it* cry. I will never make that mistake again. Next time, for your Lindsey and for my—," he stopped himself. "I will be sure to make *it* cry."

Karen wiped her eyes; her hands shook uncontrollably. She spoke slowly and carefully; she didn't want the visitor to think she doubted him. "What if the police find you?"

"They won't," he answered abruptly. "The police do not care about *those* that prey on the innocents. I am a threat only to the demons. No one else is in danger; no one else needs to fear me."

"How long will you go on doing this? I mean, how many times will you—?" Karen stopped. From inside her house, she could hear Peter calling to her. "My son, he needs me upstairs. I have to go, but I'll hurry back. Please don't leave yet, I have to know something else." Karen moved toward her front door looking back to the visitor. She held up a finger as if to say '*wait one minute*' and then disappeared inside.

*****

Bryan stood at the edge of the walk and said a silent goodbye.

You want to know how I will kill Boyd Duncan, don't you, Karen? See to your son and watch over him; keep him safe. Don't fret about what I am going to do. If I told you, you would change your mind.

*****

−13−

GASKIN'S SWITCH

The girl in the blue jersey rounded second base on her way to third; her short legs pumped awkwardly but with determination. With a chirp from his whistle, the umpire signaled the play over and a stand-up triple. The parents and friends of the blue team were already on their feet and cheering wildly; there was only one out remaining in the first game of the new season, and it looked like the score was about to be tied. Bryan was standing and applauding quietly with the rest; his beard was now gone, and a ball cap was pulled down over his newly shaved head. He didn't look like the same man who had come to Ohio two weeks ago. From the top tier of the bleachers, he could have easily followed the action of the game but wasn't. He was sitting alone at the end of the row, so he could leave when it was time.

The teams playing on the adjacent field were older girls; Bryan guessed them to be twelve or thirteen. On the bench closest to him, the players were dressed in yellow jerseys and green shorts with a white stripe. 'First Baptist' was written in bold letters across the back of their shirts and the front of their ball caps. For the past hour-and-a-half Bryan had been watching them; even more keenly, he had been watching their coach and carefully watching how he touched the girls.

*****

Coach Boyd Duncan was new to the community and had become a zealous member of First Baptist Church. Every

Sunday since he began working there a few months ago, he could be found at the early service, seated in the same pew at the front of the congregation. He was employed as the church janitor and volunteered to cook for the fellowship suppers on Sunday and Wednesday evenings. For important church projects and special events, he was the first to volunteer to help, especially when it was for the children like the girls on the youth softball team. None of the other adults had come forward for the position; they were too busy living their own lives, but not Boyd Duncan.

The janitor didn't look or act threatening at all; he was very polite and particularly courteous to the older members of the church. He kept his shirt pocket full of lollypops for when the youngsters stopped him in the hallways to get him to play his little magic game. No matter which color the children asked him for, and without ever looking, he was always able to pluck just the right one from his pocket. Wearing a generous grin, he would wave the candy before their eyes, wide with amazement, and drop it in their little outstretched hands.

He had 'Boyd' monogrammed above the lollypop pocket on his uniforms and on the corner of the white handkerchief he kept folded in his hand to wipe the constant beads of perspiration that collected on his glossy forehead. He had 'Boyd' stenciled across the back of his yellow coaches' shirt. Even the brass letters on the door to his small office in the basement just said 'BOYD'. But the children of the church called him Mr. Dunk.

The congregation provided him with a small salary and three grey janitor uniforms that he kept clean and neatly pressed. He owned one suit, and wore it only for worship services and the occasional funeral he attended as part of the First Baptist family. It was cobalt blue with grey pin stripes, and he had it specially tailored to best flatter his unflattering body. He was quite short and walked with his chubby hands folded together over his round belly like a monk; his face, round and pink, always boasted a bright, toothy smile. At any Christmas party he would have made a perfect Santa. The church members were thankful that the man had chosen their community to move into; they probably wished that there were more good people around just like Boyd Duncan. They didn't yet know that he had come to their church so he could prey on their children.

*****

The sudden roar from the neighboring field distracted everyone on the bleachers, except for Bryan. He was already looking in that direction and had just watched the final play end the game to send the First Baptist team rushing to swarm excitedly around their coach. The shrieking girls bounced up and down hugging each other with Boyd Duncan caught in the middle of it all. Bryan didn't believe for a second that the grin on the man's face had much to do with his team winning the game. When the girls settled down, they moved to the bench to collect their gear as their parents and friends emptied the bleachers and gathered around them. Bryan became anxious that the janitor might disappear into the crowd without him seeing; he checked the sky and guessed it would be light for maybe another half hour. Even though he knew where Boyd Duncan lived and worked and could find him anytime he wanted to, he would keep his eyes fixed on this demon and not let it get away. Tonight was the special night he had chosen to kill it.

The prayer surprised Bryan. If it weren't for the sad reality of what the janitor was, the irony might have made him laugh. The parents had formed a circle around the girls and quieted them; Duncan was again at the center. With his hands placed on the shoulders of the two tallest players, he bowed his round head, and the others followed. The group stood that way for almost a minute before Duncan looked up while the others remained as they were. His lips were still moving, but his eyes were open and gazing over the girls huddled all around him. If Bryan could block out everything he knew about the predator faking the prayer, the scene might look very normal. There was nothing about Duncan's appearance and nothing about his behavior that would have signaled alarm in a trusting adult. He touched a lot, but not too much, and seemed very careful to do it only in ways that a father might touch his own child. Sometimes it was a light stroke of the hair or a quick hug or pat on the back, but his hand never stayed anywhere for long or strayed anywhere that would arouse concern. Outwardly, Bryan could see that this monster was a master at maintaining the deception; inwardly, he knew it would let its thoughts and desires roam freely as it pleased. When the prayer was over, Bryan watched with revulsion as the demon moved among the girls.

"Bastard!" The word escaped through his clenched teeth; he glanced at the people around him because he knew he must have been heard. Before anyone could respond, he jumped off the end of the bleachers and headed toward the concession stand. He would buy a cup of coffee and find somewhere to observe the janitor without drawing any more attention.

Bryan stepped to the counter just as a father and his young daughter were walking away with their food, and he tried hard not to think about Emma. He checked the field to make sure that Duncan was still there. The sun was getting low in the sky and shined almost directly in his eyes; it was hard to distinguish any features among the shapes of people moving about. *Where are you hiding, Boyd?* He turned back to the counter; behind it, a small distorted woman squinted at him in the harsh light. Her face was chiseled elegantly, but wrinkled with age. He checked over his shoulder once more toward the field and then looked down at the old vendor.

"Would you like something, Honey? We're closing soon; I'm all out of the chicken sticks and hamburgers, but I still have some hotdogs.

"Just coffee, ma'am. Black, large if you have it." He would

be up late, and the caffeine would help keep him alert.

"Sorry, Honey, we only have the one size; it's fifty cents." Her voice was coarse and loud, but her tone was friendly.

"Then make it two, please."

She retreated to the row of canisters along the back wall and filled a Styrofoam cup, then another. With her head bowed over the steaming beverages, she shuffled back to the counter, being cautious not to spill any on her shaking hands. "You be very careful, Honey, these are real hot." When she looked up, four quarters shined up at her from the counter, and the customer was gone.

*****

"Monica, give me a hand with all this equipment, would you?" Coach Duncan called up to the girl standing at the top of the bleachers. He was busy stuffing bases into a large canvas bag; perspiration dripped from the end of his chubby nose. The girl was on the last row with her back turned to the field, looking toward the steady stream of cars exiting from the parking lot; some already had their lights on ahead of the approaching night. Duncan dragged the duffle through the dirt to the edge of the grass; an orange-brown cloud rose in a dusty wake behind him. "Don't worry, Monica, I'm sure your mom will be here soon;" he paused to catch his breath, "I'll stay with you until she comes; now help me collect the rest of these bats while we can still see them."

Monica hopped down from tier to tier and paused on each one, dampening the annoying rattle of the aluminum stands. She walked up to her coach who was now kneeling on the ground, sliding the last of the wooden sticks into the open bag. "Mr. Dunk, what if my mom forgot to come get me? She dropped me off before the game, but she had to go back to work for a while. I can't call her; I left my phone in my room, and I can't remember her number; it's in my favorites."

Duncan looked up and wiped the sweat from his forehead with the back of his dirty hand and left a brown stripe across his brow. He smiled at Monica so she wouldn't worry. "I'll tell you what, young lady, help me get this stuff put away, and you can wait with me by the van under the lights. If your mom shows up now, she might not see us over here behind the bleachers. Let's hurry; it's getting dark pretty fast."

Monica collected the half-dozen batting helmets and pushed them into the canvas bag while her coach held it open. 'First Baptist' was stenciled in big black letters across the side; below it, Duncan had scribbled a not-so-naïvely mixed message in red permanent marker: *'We're Friendly at First'*.

*****

Bryan leaned against a tree just inside a wooded area that separated the parking lot from the main road leading back to town and watched as the few remaining cars drove away. He took off his cap and drew his hand across the smooth scalp; it felt like it belonged to someone else. It felt like he was a long way from home.

The sun hovered just above the horizon and cast long shadows in front of him, making him nearly invisible among the jumble of tree trunks eclipsed in the radiance of the dying daylight. His rental car was parked nearby and would be easy to get to when he needed to leave. From where he stood, he could see Duncan and the young girl struggle with the bag of equipment as they carried it toward a white van on the other side of the lot. It wasn't hard to follow them now; they were the only ones left in the ballpark.

He imagined the evening of Lindsey's abduction from the pavilion. He thought it might have felt something like this. The mechanics would have been almost as easy. But Bryan wasn't worried about that now; he knew this girl would not be another one of Duncan's victims—not this time. The fat little janitor wouldn't be that stupid. Bryan was worried that he wouldn't be able to get this demon alone with him tonight, and he was worried he wouldn't be able to do what he came back to Ohio to do.

*****

Monica stood in front of the van looking toward the road with her hands cupped at the sides of her cap to shade her eyes from the final sun. The janitor stood closely beside her with his short legs and arms crossed, awkwardly balancing his round body against the bumper. If he shifted his weight a little to one side, he could stumble to the ground or *maybe roll into the girl*.

The minutes passed, but there was no conversation between them. Duncan was happy to just stand there in the light breeze to receive the wash of air that bathed over her and carried the sweet young scent of her to him. Suddenly, his phone rang, and he fumbled to pull it from his pocket.

"Boyd Duncan." There was a short pause, "Yes, Mrs. Dwyer, she's right here with me. I'll let you talk to her." He handed Monica the phone.

"Mom? Where are you?" She listened for a moment. "I'm sorry; don't be mad, I must have left it on my bed. I couldn't borrow a phone because I can't remember your number; it's saved in my favorites." A few more seconds passed. "I'm sure it will be okay with him; he's been real nice. I love you, mom."

Monica ended the call and handed Duncan back his phone. "My mom had a flat tire and has to wait for someone to come and fix it for her. She said it shouldn't be very long and asked if you could take me to my grandma's house. She lives real close to the church, and I can wait for her there if it's alright. My mom's on the other side of town, and she said it would be quicker if she could pick me up at Grammy's. I still have a bunch of homework to finish when I get home. Is that okay, Mr. Dunk?"

"That's no problem at all, Monica; I'd be happy to. I drive right by the church on my way home, so it shouldn't be too far out of my way. But I have one condition: we have to stop and get an ice cream cone to celebrate our first win."

Monica smiled easily, "That's a deal, Mr. Dunk!"

Duncan's flesh began to stir beneath his clothes. *Don't you dare, Boyd.* He scurried to the passenger door and opened it but left only a narrow space for Monica to step through between him and the door. He inhaled her scent as she slipped by and watched her lean young body stretch and twist as she climbed up inside.

*****

Here we go. Bryan let the van exit from the lot before he stepped out of the trees and hurried to his car. In less than a minute, he was following behind them while keeping enough distance so as not to attract any attention. It was almost dark, and his headlights would soon disappear in the van's mirrors as they mixed in with the other traffic on the road. Even though he was careful to stay well back, he wasn't really worried that he'd be noticed; right now the demon wouldn't be paying too much attention to anything other than the young passenger sitting beside it in the front seat.

Bryan went through his mental checklist; everything he needed was organized in his rucksack in the trunk. The heavy plastic sheeting he had lined the sides and floor would contain any evidence his captive might leave as he drove to the remote place he had selected to exact his punishment. He had rented the car in Toledo and was now two hundred miles away at the opposite side of the state; there was no reason they would ever link the car to tonight's murder as long as he was careful. Everything was ready.

The girl was going to be a minor setback that he hadn't anticipated, but surely she was just getting a ride home. He sensed it wouldn't be long before he would have his prey cornered and all to himself. He had to stay flexible but alert; the opportunity to strike would present itself only if he remained patient, and he would adjust his plan for the girl if necessary. Bryan could take all the time he needed and right now felt quite calm and rested. As a matter of fact, he felt surprisingly strong.

They drove for a few miles before coming to a traffic signal that marked the beginning of town. The busy intersection was well lit from overhead street lamps and the white canopies of the gas stations glowing from two of the four corners. Bryan stopped his car several feet behind the van and a little over the yellow line so he could watch the demon in the large side-view mirror on the door. Its bald head was turned to the girl and bobbing up and down as if in nervous conversation. It glanced forward a few times to check the signal and then quickly returned its attention to the girl. Just as the light turned green, its round face filled the mirror and looked directly at Bryan looking directly at him.

Hello Boyd.

Bryan leaned slightly forward and sharpened his stare; he saw the demon's eyes flare just before the van pulled away. *Aw, did I scare the little creature? I can already smell your fear, but why so soon? You were thinking things you shouldn't, and you're afraid that I heard your thoughts—aren't you?* He accelerated slowly to let a car turning from the cross street merge between him and the van. It was hard not to, but he didn't want to provoke the demon into doing something that might jeopardize the night ahead. The seed of doom was already in the ground. Unknowingly, the demon had seen its fate reflected in the mirror. The haunting truth would now whisper to it at some level just below its consciousness. Bryan was in control now; he felt innately tuned to the rhythm of life and death. As he drove along toward the demon's destiny, he felt himself rising out of Bryan Rhodes and into the killer of the Short Roses, the imperishable servant of the meek.

*****

Duncan anxiously checked and re-checked the traffic behind him after losing sight of the car from the red light. He had seen something frightening in the eyes of the man in the mirror, but he knew he could sometimes be paranoid, particularly now with the girl beside him in the van. His paranoia always arrived as a mixture of fear and arousal; the fear that someone would come to punish him for his deviance, confused with the arousal that he might actually like it. Even thirty years later, he could still feel the shock of his mother finding him hiding in the closet with her silk stocking wrapped around his little fist wrapped around his newly discovered maleness. He could still hear the squeal of the door sliding open and the intense stimulation of her slender figure standing there above him in the sudden brightness. He remembered there had been no face or eyes, just the dark curves of her female body; it was the body he imagined in his closet fantasy. In her firm tone she had ordered him to finish and he had, easily. She had shaken her head in disgust and closed the door before walking away, leaving him alone again in the darkness with the addicting smell of her cheap perfume lingering around him.

Suddenly, Duncan felt the overpowering urge to take Monica to the empty church, to the special room he had selected in the basement, but now was not the time. Her mother knew he was with her. He had to kill this burning feeling and quick; his desires were consuming what little self-control he could sustain. Right now, the only thing Boyd Duncan could do to avert the craving was distract his thoughts, do something in public with lots of activity and people all around him.

He jerked the van into the parking lot in front of Twisties' Ice Cream stand and pulled into the first empty space. "I'm ready for that chocolate cone now," he swallowed a deep breath, "and what about you Monica?"

"Yay! A large chocolate one for me!" She threw her ball cap on the dashboard then jumped down from the seat and ran to the end of the line. The weather was mild and Twisties' was crowded with families out enjoying the pleasant spring evening. Duncan started to feel a little better; he could sense the urging subside almost immediately. In his desperation to smother his thoughts, he had forgotten all about the horrible man in the mirror.

They found an empty picnic table close to the road and sat on top watching the traffic crawl by. Duncan finished his cone before Monica had hardly started. "Do you need any help with that, young lady?" He smiled his toothy Santa smile. "You know I'm just kidding, right?" Monica nodded her head yes and kept licking her cone oblivious to the janitor's watching eyes. "We probably should get going though; we need to get you to your grandma's so she doesn't start to worry."

"Okay, Mr. Dunk. Thank you for the ice cream."

"No problem; you can finish it in the van. You look like you're enjoying it." Duncan turned away to temper another thought that had come to visit him. As he got up from the table, he extended his elbow and bumped Monica's hand; her ice cream fell out of the cone and rolled down her jersey and into her lap. She glanced at the trail of chocolate on her shirt and shorts and jumped up throwing the rest to the ground. "My mom's going to kill me!"

"Calm down, Monica; everything will be fine." Duncan tried to brush her shirt with his napkin, but she stepped back waving her hands defensively at him. He tried not to smile.

"Leave me alone! You made me do that! I wasn't supposed to have any ice cream; my mom grounded me and told me I couldn't have any treats for a week. Now she's going to ground me forever!"

"No, she won't. I'll tell you what," Duncan calmly calculated his next move, "I have some extra uniforms in my office at the church; I'm sure we can put something together that will fit you. We'll get you changed; rub a little dirt here and there like you just won your first softball game and *presto!* Everything's cool again. It shouldn't take us long at all. Then I'll drive you straight to your grandma's house; I'm sure we'll get you there before your mom. How's that for a plan?"

"Okay, Mr. Dunk;" Monica had settled down, "I'm sorry I got mad; I know it was an accident."

"I'm sorry about your ice cream; if you want, I can buy you another cone, but first we better get some more napkins and a cup of water to clean you up a little before I drive you to the church." His Santa grin was back. *It's a good plan, Boyd.*

*****

Bryan was parked at the fast food restaurant next to Twisties' and had been patiently watching the janitor and the girl from inside his car. There were plenty of people around, and the demon, busily doting on the girl, hadn't seemed interested in looking over its shoulder for the man at the traffic light.

When they got up from the picnic table where they were sitting by the road, he saw the girl spill her ice cream, and it looked like the janitor had caused it to happen. He saw Duncan try to brush her jersey with his napkin, but she stepped back frantically waving her hands. When she calmed down a little, they went back to the ice cream stand and walked away with a cup and a stack of napkins.

What are you up to now, Boyd? You're pushing your luck. Don't you know that your luck has already run out?

The van turned out of Twisties' and continued across town with Bryan following not too closely behind. When it turned into the First Baptist parking lot, he continued a few more blocks before turning around, to give the janitor and girl enough time to get inside, if that's what they were going to do. A few minutes later, he found the empty van parked behind the building near the entrance to the fellowship hall. He backed into a space at the edge of the lot not far away, where he could watch the door to see if anyone came or left. Someone would be coming to pick up the girl, he figured, and he hoped they would come soon. He would only be able to wait in the car for a short while; he wasn't about to leave the demon alone with the girl inside the church for very long.

Bryan took the keys from the ignition and made sure the dome light was switched off before he got out of the car. He retrieved his pack from the trunk along with his black leather jacket and gloves and put them on. Then he slid the pack across the front seat before climbing back inside and closing the door quietly behind him. He grabbed the roll of duct tape and a dozen cable ties from the side compartments and stuffed them in his jacket pockets. Next, he pulled out a large green bag and set it beside him on the seat. It was tied in a tight roll like a log and carried with a shoulder strap to keep his hands free. He smiled at the little dancing reindeers printed on the side. *Who would have thought a storage bag for a plastic Christmas tree would be a convenient way to move a body?*

He stared at the sleeping church through the windshield. The building and parking lot were dark except for the light that reached out through the glass entry doors, most of it absorbed by the asphalt pavement. The flat stone façade either side of the entrance connected the sanctuary at one end with a newer brick gymnasium at the other. Ten darkened windows were evenly

179

spaced and balanced by the doors in the middle; below them ten more were half-buried in the ground, tucked inside metal wells that held back the earth so the light of day might find the half-buried rooms. A hedge of boxwoods separated the wall from the sidewalk and was beginning to thicken with new spring growth. The last window on the lower level, next to the sanctuary, suddenly lit up.

Without thinking, Bryan placed the strap from the canvas roll across his shoulder and zipped up his coat. He hesitated a minute trying to think rationally about what things might be happening in that basement room before deciding he had to know. He jumped out of the car and rushed toward the window breaking through the hedge as if it wasn't there; he moved quickly along the face of the wall until he was close enough that he could hear the sound of the girl's voice through the glass. There was no fear or distress at all in what he heard—she was chatty and seemed relaxed.

He squatted down at the edge of the well, out of the light, and listened but couldn't make out what she was saying. Cautiously, Bryan leaned into the window, hoping the eyes inside were looking somewhere else. The janitor was standing in the doorway with his back turned to the room; the girl was leaning against a desk in just her socks and panties, pulling up a clean pair of shorts; her talking stopped while she slipped a new yellow jersey over her head. As she did, Duncan turned to steal a glance but looked away quickly. Bryan stayed focused on the demon; if the janitor moved toward her, he would be down the stairs and in the room before she could understand what was happening. He was ready to risk everything to prevent Duncan from putting his hands on the girl; how he would explain his sudden presence to her hadn't yet entered his mind. What he would do to the demon was an altogether different matter.

As soon as she had her shoes back on, Bryan heard Duncan say something that he couldn't understand, then saw the girl step past him into the hall and disappear in the direction of the sanctuary. *She'll be okay now,* Bryan assured himself.

Duncan stepped into the office and closed the door. There was a lamp on the desk, and he switched it on before turning off the harsh fluorescent lights burning above. He gathered the girl's soiled uniform from the floor and sat down, leaning back in the chair as he closed his eyes. He brought the front of the green shorts to his nose, then draped them across his face. As the janitor worked to undo his belt, Bryan retreated from the window and passed back through the hedge, moving in the direction of the entrance doors. He didn't need to watch what the demon did next.

*****

Inside the entry to the fellowship hall, Bryan found a stair landing halfway between the two floors. He held the glass door as it closed to make sure that it wouldn't make a sound, then locked the dead-bolt behind him. A steam pipe hissed overhead, inviting a momentary glance; he could hear the faint music of a piano begin to play on the floor above, coming from the direction of the sanctuary. *The girl.* He checked the top of the walls and ceiling around him but found no security cameras. Below was a darkened hallway; the polished floor glowed ominously red from an exit sign mounted above the bottom of the stairs. It was the hallway that would lead him to the office where his prey was now trapped, engrossed in some sick self-gratification, consumed by deviant lust for a child. It would be its final time; Bryan would make sure of it; his wait for this kill would soon be over. In his mind, the demon's presence alone with the girl had already violated her, and it had to be stopped; it had to be punished. He would overpower it quickly; then find a place to hide until she was gone.

Bryan moved swiftly but silently down the basement hall checking each of the four rooms he passed; the doors were all closed and locked. He could hear the hum of electrical equipment coming from behind the second door. In less than a minute he was standing in front of the last room that held the demon within. A bare light bulb glowed from the ceiling and cut deep shadows below the brass letters screwed to the face of the door: 'BOYD.' He glanced down each end of the hall at the exit signs peering back at him. The sign behind him was over the stair that led back to his car; in front of him two more were spaced at the middle and far end of the hall; the one closest to him marked a cross corridor and indicated an exit in both directions. Remembering the layout of the building outside, Bryan thought it probably led to the church foyer on the right and perhaps the pastor's office or choir area behind the rostrum to the left, but without checking he couldn't be sure. The sign farthest away would lead to a fire stair and likely an exit at the side of the building. If something happened, he would at least have four ways to escape.

Curiously, he reached across the narrow corridor to touch the damp stone wall and rubbed the moisture between his thumb and middle finger; he smelled the rank staleness mixed with the fresh leather of his glove. *I think it smells like you, Boyd.* Stacks of boxes lined the wall each side of the door and choked the hallway down so that there was barely enough room for Bryan to walk, let alone carry the demon out of the building. He could still hear the piano music above him; it was louder now but still far enough away that he felt safe. He would have to work fast. He hoped the girl would continue to play; it would tell him where she was and help mask the noise of the demon if it tried to resist its capture. He turned his ear to the door and listened; through it he could hear labored breathing. Almost instantly, it fell quiet.

"Monica? Is that you?" The demon's voice squeaked from behind the door; it sounded more like a rodent than a monster.

Like the vermin you are, Boyd Duncan. Bryan stood still in preparation, filling his lungs repeatedly, expanding them with each breath until the last one was all he could possibly hold. It was almost time.

"Monica?" the rodent squeaked again.

Bryan straightened up as the adrenaline raced through his bloodstream; the muscles in his arms and back swelled to attack, and he filled the doorway. The air in his chest screamed to be released, but he had to wait for the breathing behind the door to resume. *Then it did.* He crashed into the room and tossed the heavy wooden desk out of his way like it was made of cardboard, exposing the naked demon behind it. As the lamp hit the floor and went dark, the janitor screamed; his useless seed erupted all over the fat folds of his belly. He struggled to stand and pull up his pants but stumbled backward and fell against the wall and into a cast iron pipe standing in the corner of the room. His hands were flailing hopelessly at his attacker. "Wait mister; stop; it's not what you—!"

But it is. Bryan stood between his prey and the light from the hall, his big shadow blanketed over it. Calmly, he reached behind him and turned on the overhead lights; he pushed the broken door against the splintered frame and moved toward the cowering demon.

"Moni...!" Duncan tried to yell but Bryan slammed a fist into his face forcing him back against the pipe; his head bounced off the concrete wall just before his legs collapsed beneath him. He dropped to his knees, pleading through the blood pouring from his nose, "Please, stop! "Why... are... you—?"

"Shut up!" Bryan raised his big fist again, but before he could strike, the demon scrambled behind the overturned chair, holding it in front of its face like the bars of a cage.

"Wait!" the janitor spit the blood from his mouth, "You're the man in the car—the stoplight! Where's Monica; what have you done to her!?"

"*You?* You want to know what I did to *her?*" Bryan looked at the ceiling and then pointed upstairs. "Listen." Monica was still making music on the piano. "You have other things to worry about now, Boyd Duncan. Rest assured; I'll make certain the girl gets home tonight; you might have improved your situation if you had done the same."

"What do you want? I didn't touch her!" The janitor was shaking behind the chair, looking side to side for a way to escape; he could barely speak. Blood fell freely from his broken nose and stuck to the semen smeared across his swollen belly.

"But you were going to—" Bryan's angry voice abruptly dropped to a deeper pitch and slowed, drained of all expression, "—like you did with all the others." He delivered the rest of his message as if it was a matter-of-fact. "*They* have sent me to come get you; *they are waiting for you now.*"

Duncan began to weep, his voice begging, "Please; I'm not that way anymore; I've been good, but sometimes I am weak." Slowly, he crawled out from behind the chair and retreated to the pipe behind him; hand over hand he began to pull his heavy body up off the floor. "I wasn't going to hurt her; please, I'm not going to hurt anyone ever again. MONICA!!!"

The sudden scream surprised Bryan but he killed it immediately with the back of his hand. He stood motionless, waiting for a response from the girl upstairs, but none came. The building was old and solid, built of concrete and stone; the demon's cry would not travel very far or with any purpose. When the energy of it faded, the music from the piano was still playing above them. "She can't hear you, Boyd." He righted the chair and snapped off the arm that had loosened from the side and tossed it behind him. He set the chair on the floor and shoved it toward the demon. "Sit down." Duncan quickly stumbled into it, bending forward over his knees, shielding his face in his hands; the blood from his swollen nose dripped between his legs and collected on the floor. He didn't look up.

Bryan turned away and spoke to the room around him. "There's a pretty little hill not far from Cleveland; it rises gently above the Rocky River. You can still tell where the railroad used to run beside it, but it's long since gone. The place is called Gaskin's Switch; I went there last summer. It was warm and green and very pleasant. There were butterflies, thousands of them, Monarchs, returning south from Canada. I sat alone on a beautiful stone bench that was thoughtfully placed so it looked out over the shallow river valley; the rolling hills framed the blue expanse of Lake Erie in the distance."

The music above seemed louder now, haunting the air around him; Bryan casually gathered the demon's wrists behind its back and lashed them together with a cable tie from his jacket pocket. Its soft arms were limp and did not resist; it kept its face down, away from further harm. Its pitiful sobs were not lost to Bryan as he continued to speak. *I told you I would make it cry, Karen.* "The place has a visceral quality; it's as if it was created in a dream I might have once had. But I don't have dreams like that anymore."

Bryan pulled the roll of duct tape from his pocket and set it on the side of the overturned desk. "I met a woman who goes there almost every day;" he said, "she sits on the bench and talks to her daughter. It was Providence that I met her that day; she didn't know it, but we were both there for the same reason. She told me that all she really wanted was time to be with her little girl again, just the two of them together."

The janitor cried into his lap, "I don't know anything about that place, or that lady, or her girl!"

"Yes, you do." Bryan picked up Monica's soiled shorts from the floor and tossed them at the demon cowering in the chair. "You do know the girl, and I will make you remember her. Gaskins' Switch is a cemetery; the girl is buried there and the bench is her headstone. The time her mother spends sitting on her grave is the time you stole from them both."

185

"Wait!" Duncan raised his head and shook it as if a revelation had just occurred to him. "I've never killed anyone; you must have confused me with someone else; you have this all wrong!"

Bryan ignored the demon and delivered his findings like a magistrate's decree in court. "Her name is Lindsey Fischer. You took her from the pavilion at Huntington Park. You tricked her with your dog to follow you to your car and then you forced a rag soaked with ammonia and bleach into her face until she lost consciousness. Do you know that the chemicals could have killed her? Then you drugged her with GHB and drove her to the end of a dirt road in the woods not far from her home. When you were through, you left her there alone in the night, miles from nowhere. You took her clothes and threw her into the cold. For these insidious acts, Boyd Duncan, you will be destroyed." Bryan's face drew taught; his eyes blazed at the demon shaking his head in denial. "Why did you take her clothes? You shouldn't have left her like that."

"She woke up! She started screaming! I couldn't stop her! I can't take the screaming—the crying! She ran out of the car and disappeared into the woods and I," his voice trailed off, "... just drove away."

"Shut up!" Bryan stepped towards his prisoner with his two fists raised like hammers. The demon turned its head into its shoulder to shield its broken face. "Look at me, or I'll crush your thin skull right now!"

Duncan looked up slowly, still pleading; it was the only thing he could do, "I didn't kill her mister; please! I didn't kill her!"

"But you did." Bryan backed away, tempering his rage with the distance; he wanted to destroy the demon right now, but this was not how he planned it to happen. He stepped to the opposite corner of the room and thought about the girl's cries in the rain, the sound of her cries striking the tin roof of the pavilion in the park. "She was twelve years old, just like the girl upstairs; but you knew that, didn't you? Not long after you shattered her life, she surrendered the empty shell you had left her with. It made her mother very sad. Her mother's grief demands an answer, Boyd Duncan; I'm here to make sure she gets one."

"What are you going to do to me?" The janitor's voice was gurgling and weak; his desperation barely audible as if he realized that his end was now imminent.

"Are you afraid?" Bryan thought of his promise to Lindsey's mother. "You should be."

The demon responded with the stench of urine; a yellow stain spread across the front of its underwear; its pants and belt were still tangled below its knees.

"Can you imagine how Lindsey must have felt lying naked in the woods, curled up in a pile of wet leaves trying to stay warm. She must have hidden there for hours in absolute fear, a little child with no understanding of what had happened to her or where she was. I don't know how long she laid there; a farmer found her wandering in his field the next morning. She wouldn't let him touch her; she just cried for her mother over and over again." Bryan stepped toward the demon. "Lindsey's mother still hears her cries in the middle of the night—she told me so." Bryan grabbed the roll of tape and ripped off a long piece. He wrapped it around the demon's mouth and head staring closely into its eyes. "*I've heard her cries too.*"

Duncan tried to pull air through the caked blood in his broken nose; he could barely breathe. Weakly, he struggled against the tie binding his wrists, but it was hopeless. He tried to get up from the chair, but Bryan drove a fist into his ear, and he dropped to the floor, rolling to his side. He lay there barely conscious, twisting slowly like a dying snake, coiling into a fetal ball. Bryan pulled a plastic bag from his pocket and removed the rag he had soaked with ammonia and bleach. He pressed it against the demon's face until it surrendered.

*****

Monica rested her hands in her lap and sat still for a moment; she wondered why her coach was taking so long. He said he had some work to finish up and would only be a little while. She slid off the bench to go check on him but was distracted by the rack of choir robes lining the back of the music room; the shiny material felt soft to her touch. Her mother had told her she was more than good enough to play the piano with the choir, but Monica wasn't sure she could get up in front of a whole church full of people. She put on a child-sized robe and sat back down to play just one more song. She opened the music book to a hymn she liked that the choir sometimes sang. First, she played it in her head one time through to work out some of the more difficult ascending sequences of notes and chords. Then, when she was ready, she returned her fingers to the keyboard, and the music started to flow beautifully again.

*****

Bryan unrolled the green bag and laid it open next to the demon's body. When he finished binding its ankles and knees, he found a pen in the debris on the floor and poked two holes in the tape covering its mouth so it wouldn't suffocate prematurely. Next, he made sure that it was still breathing. It needed to be kept alive for a few more hours.

He rolled the body onto the bag and stretched the sides around it; in spite of the demon's girth, he was able to close the heavy zipper completely. Bryan stepped calmly to the chalk board next to the door and erased the work schedule charted across the green surface. In its place, he scribbled a message for the investigators who would surely follow him. "YOU SHOULDN'T FREE THE DEMONS. LINDSEY WOULD HAVE TOLD YOU." Bryan relaxed his hand and let the chalk drop to the floor.

You were right to bring me here, Emma. This one had to be stopped.

He sat in the broken chair looking down on his prize. *Just pick it up, Bryan, and get out of here. What are you waiting for?* But something gave him reason to pause; he checked around the room. A crimson brushstroke of blood marked the wall near the pipe where he had driven the demon's head against it. The desk laid on its side where he had tossed it out of his way; the floor was riddled with the broken lamp mixed with the rest of the clutter that had been on it. The arm of the chair landed in a scattering of hymnals that had fallen out of a bookcase, toppled over in the commotion. In the center of the floor, a drop of semen left a milky spot just a few inches from where the girl's discarded shorts lay. Squatting over them, Bryan peered at the reindeer sack stuffed with the monster. His head glanced back and forth between the two as he rubbed his eyes and face; the day's growth of a new beard dragged across the palm of his glove.

He had left nothing of himself, not even a lock of hair; he had seen to that. Even if he had lost so much as an eyelash at the scene, it wouldn't lead the police to him; his DNA had never been collected. His gloves and hat were still on; his clothes were freshly bought and would leave no history of him after they were burned. He had not been injured; traces of blood were everywhere from his defeat of the demon, but none of the blood was his. Everything looked acceptable, but still something felt very wrong.

The piano.

He couldn't hear it anymore; and just as he realized the absence of the girl's music, the janitor's phone started to ring from inside the bag. Bryan yanked down the zipper and found it quickly; he listened to the voice on the other end before deciding if he should respond.

"Yes, ma'am, it is." Bryan cleared his throat. "Uh, this is

John; I'm doing some work for Mr. Duncan at the church, but he can't come to his phone right now. I can give him a message."

The woman's voice was a mixture of anger and alarm. "Why is he at the church?! Dammit! He was supposed to bring Monica to my mother's house; mom just called and told me Monica's still not there. Where is my daughter?!"

"She's fine, ma'am. I heard her upstairs playing on the piano. I think it would be best if you picked her up here; we're in the middle of a little emergency right now."

"Well, you can tell *Mr. Duncan* that I'm not very happy, and tell him the deacons are going to hear about this! He should have called me. I'll be there in a half-hour. Tell Monica to meet me at the fellowship hall door; it's around the back; she knows where." The call ended. At least now Bryan didn't have to worry about anyone else coming to the building anytime soon. Dealing with the girl was going to be problematic enough.

Anxiously, he checked the hall. *Where is she?* Surely Monica was on her way to find the janitor and would show up at any moment. He had to do something quick; there was no way he could lock the office and hide in it—the top of the door was cracked in half between the 'O' and the 'Y' and the jamb was shattered from when he stormed into the room. With Monica wandering somewhere around the building, it was too risky to move the demon, let alone try to get it to his car. It would wake soon, and when it did, it wouldn't be quiet. He still had the rag with the ammonia and bleach, but it would only keep it down for short periods of time; he would have to stay close. He needed the syringe with the GHB to put it under for a few hours, but he had left it in the trunk of the car, and before he could get to it, he would have to hide the demon. But that wouldn't fix his other immediate problem... *But—but—but. She's coming here, Bryan, to this room, and there's nothing you can do to stop her. You can't confront her; she'll tell the police all about you. She is going to find you and the mess you've made and then what?*

Bryan studied his watch; thirty minutes was a long time; he needed a plan to keep Monica out of the basement. He glanced at the bare lightbulb above him and remembered the electric room he had passed down the hall. *She won't come downstairs if the downstairs is dark.*

*****

Monica closed the lid over the keyboard; she was tired of playing and was ready to leave. She didn't like being in the empty church. This was God's house, and since there was no one else around, He must be watching her every move. She felt very unsettled. It was time to go to Mr. Dunk's office and tell him she needed to leave; she didn't care about his stupid work; he could finish it after he dropped her off.

She returned the robe to the rack and entered the stairwell that led up to the choir loft and down to the classrooms in the basement. As she descended, she dragged her hand along the surface; the walls changed from painted concrete block to rough stone that felt cool and damp to her touch. At the bottom of the stairs, the door was propped open with the broken base of a plaster urn. She stepped over it and into the hall and stopped to listen for her coach, but there were no sounds except for the hum of the fluorescent lights overhead. A few feet away a pair of bulbs flickered as their ballast struggled to feed them enough power. The barren hallway looked very different from Sunday mornings when it was full of parents and other kids going to and from the classrooms. Now the empty basement gave her the creeps. It was a hollow but pressing feeling, something she would never be able to describe.

In front of her, the red exit sign marked the cross corridor where she would turn to the right to get back to his office. She didn't like going there at all; it was narrow and full of shadows and cluttered with whispering pipes hanging from the ceiling and old musty boxes stacked along the walls. She would never go that way when her Sunday school class was over. Even though it took much longer, she would always go back upstairs and cut through the fellowship hall to get to the doors where her mother would pick her up behind the church. She listened again for her coach, but it was still quiet. With uneasiness, she moved slowly toward where the hallways came together. She froze. She thought she heard a noise like wood splitting, then a moment later came a loud click, and the lights went out.

*****

Bryan jumped when he heard the scream. His hand was still on the breaker, and he jerked it away as if the scream was a jolt of electricity coming from out of the switch. Quickly, he felt his way into the hall as his eyes tried to adjust to the pitch darkness; he moved along the boxes toward the sound of the girl crying just around the corner. Her weeping was low and close to the floor. "Mr. Dunk?" Her voice shook with uncertainty. "Are you there, Mr. Dunk? Please tell me it's you. I'm afraid of the dark. I'm afraid to move."

Bryan stood still. *Now what?* He could hear the demon begin to stir behind him in the office where he had left it. He had to think fast.

"Mr. Duncan's not here, Monica; my name is John." He spoke loud to cover the sounds of the demon's rousing but was careful that his voice didn't sound threatening to the girl. He moved forward slowly, "I work for Mr. Duncan at night sometimes. There's a problem with the electricity, and he went to get a part from the hardware store before it closes; he should be back anytime now. Please don't be afraid; we'll get the lights back on soon; I promise."

Bryan thought he must be getting close to where the corridors crossed. He could tell from her sounds and the echoes of his own breathing that the walls had opened up, but he couldn't see the exit sign overhead. It had gone dark with everything else; its emergency batteries must have been too old or weak to keep it lit. He stopped short of turning the corner when he saw just hint of light on the opposite wall.

"Monica, your mother called just a few minutes ago; Mr. Duncan left his phone with me, and I answered it. She's on her way to pick you up. She said she would meet you at the back entrance." He peaked around the edge of the wall and saw the light spilling from the open door in the stairwell at the end of the corridor. *Good, not all of the power is off.* He could vaguely see Monica starting to get up off the floor and retreated into the dark. "You need to go wait for her; I have to stay down here until Mr. Duncan gets back with the part. I think you should probably go back the way you came. Don't try to come through here; we left some dangerous wires on the floor."

"Okay, but please don't follow me, mister. I can hear you, but I can't see you; it's so dark, and I'm scared. I'm not supposed to be with strangers, but I don't think I want to be alone. I just want to go home now." She was sniffling but wasn't crying openly anymore. Bryan heard the fear in her voice, and he didn't want her to be afraid.

"I won't, Monica. Of course you should keep away from strangers. I'll stay right here until you're upstairs." Bryan thought for a moment, "I'll tell you what; I have to take something out to my car; I'm parked right outside. I'll be out there in a few minutes. I'll stay in the car and keep an eye on you at the back door until your mom gets here. That way you won't really be alone, and you won't really be with a stranger. I promise I won't let anything happen to you, Monica." Bryan moved backward to block the office door; he hoped she wouldn't take the shortcut by the janitor's office to get to the fellowship hall entrance. He pulled the brim of his cap over his eyes and picked up a large box to hold in front of him in case she did; the less she saw of him, the better.

"What's that noise?" Monica's voice sounded close. Behind Bryan, the demon was coming around.

"I don't know Monica; stay back, I'll go check." His voice was loud and direct, "You better get going now; your mother will be here soon."

*****

Bryan listened while the girl's footsteps receded down the hall. When he was sure that she was gone, he spoke into the dark office, "Are we getting feisty, Boyd?" Moving quickly, he pulled the janitor's phone from his pocket and turned on the flashlight. The bag had migrated across the floor, and the prisoner inside was moaning louder now, twisting vainly to escape from the canvas cocoon. Bryan straddled the demon to keep it still while he pulled down the zipper; its retinas opened so wide in the bright light that he could see the blood pooled in the back of its eyes. He reached around its head and found the plastic bag where he had left it; the rag was still moist with the ammonia and bleach, and he pressed it across its nose and the two holes in the tape over its mouth.

Bryan was agitated again; things just weren't going very well. He wanted to kill the demon right now rather than have to carry it out of here, but within a few seconds it had settled back down and Bryan had too. He got up and checked the phone. *Twenty-two minutes; time to go.* He scanned the light around the office to find something to write with and then grabbed a church memo tacked to the face of the broken door. On the back of it, he wrote a short note and folded it in half, then sealed it with a piece of duct tape he tore from the roll in his pocket. On the front he wrote *"Monica's Mom"*; then quickly made his way along the hall and up the short flight of steps to tape it to the glass doors where the girl would find it. Her mother had to know that she needed to protect her daughter better. When Bryan was done, he went back down to the office to finish his business with the demon.

The body was heavy, but he hefted it to his shoulder with little difficulty. He wasn't going to stay in the building any longer; there was no way of knowing what the mother would do when she got to the church. As angry as she had sounded on the phone, there was a good chance she would come looking for the janitor or call the police when Monica told her the strange story of John and the dark basement. He decided that the stairwell at the far end of the hall was his best option. Once outside, he would carry the demon around the perimeter of the parking area, using the night to conceal his movements.

Bryan passed the cross-corridor and several closed doors before he entered the stairs; he lumbered up the steps and stood in front of a blank steel door. His breathing was rapid but regular; it felt good to be in control again. The landing glowed in a wash of green light from the exit sign above him; it looked new and was either connected to a live circuit or its backup batteries were still working. From the landing, the stairs continued upward, the green fading into the black. He lowered his load to the floor to catch his breath; he would need it for the long trek to the car. There were rips in the top of the bag, the frayed edges showed a hint of the demon's blood; it must have scraped against the metal brackets holding the low pipes in the hallway outside the office. The clock on the janitor's phone showed that he had eighteen minutes before the mother would come.

He ran the flashlight along the face of the doorframe to check for a security contact but didn't find one. He knew it could be hidden in the lock mechanism, but the door looked as old as the building, and the walls were solid stone with no place to conceal a wire. If security had been added, he would have found a contact and a wire leading away from it. The panic bar looked old too but worked smoothly and clicked when the lock released. He pushed the door open, and the night rushed in; a soft rain had begun to fall. He rinsed his lungs with the cool air several times, then hefted the demon back to his shoulder. It would be a short sprint across the lawn and driveway; then he would disappear into the shadowy fringe and make his way around to the car.

He smiled to himself. *It won't be long now, Emma.*

*****

Monica stood anxiously behind the glass doors with the man's note to her mother sealed in her hand. She knew she was in trouble but hoped her mom would take out her anger on her coach. It felt later than it was, and she was too tired to argue with her; she still had lots of homework to do when she got home. Hesitantly, she called down the stairs to the black hallway below. "John?" But there was no answer; the strange noise she had heard before was gone too. She rubbed a hole in the condensation on the glass with her shirt tail and peeked outside. The white van was parked nearby, and it made her wonder what her coach had driven to the hardware store.

She remembered she had left her ball cap on the dashboard but didn't want to get it now. She hoped her mom would come soon and take her away before he came back; she was still upset and didn't want to have to see Mr. Dunk again tonight. Other than the van, there was only one car, and it was backed in at the edge of the parking lot, but there was no one sitting in it. *Where is he? John said he would wait in his car; he said he wouldn't leave me alone.* As she thought about the voice in the basement, the trunk suddenly popped open; she couldn't see anyone behind it, and it seemed like it was open for a very long time. When it closed, someone quickly walked around the side of the car and got in. It happened so fast, that all she saw was a big man wearing a baseball cap.

*****

Bryan started the engine; the mild evening had turned cold with the rain. He was wet and felt chilled, not from the air but from the release of finally getting the demon in the trunk and injected with the drug that would keep it down for a couple of hours. He lowered the visor and turned on the dome light so that the girl would see him sitting in the car; the visor and the rain on the windshield would help obscure his face through the glass. The warm air was too slow in coming out of the heater; he turned the fan on high and revved the engine. A steady cloud of white exhaust blew over and around the car and drifted toward the building in a light breeze; it climbed the stone facade and swirled below the eaves before dissipating across the roof. A brown paper bag tumbled out from under the demon's van and skipped across the pavement, becoming caught in the hedge of boxwood trimming the entry to the fellowship hall.

Monica was standing behind the doors, waiting for her mother to come and take her home. The warm, moist air in the building had condensed on the glass and blurred her image unrecognizable except for the yellow and green colors of her uniform; it could have been any child behind the glass. Bryan gripped the wheel and leaned forward; his red eyes shot back at him from the rear view mirror. *It could have been any child in that basement room; it could have been Emma.* He reached into the pack next to him and grabbed his knife and a coil of heavy cotton rope and cut off four pieces, each about five feet long. Keeping an eye toward the girl, he began to lash the loose ends into loops about the size of his fist while the radio softly played a ghostly ballad from a long time ago.

Monica appeared anxious; her figure paced back and forth, sometimes disappearing, away from the doors, away from Bryan's view. Her movements made him feel uneasy; he wished she would stay still; he wished her mother would hurry and get there. *Why is it taking so long?*

He watched her clear a small hole in the condensation using the bottom of her yellow jersey. She cupped her hands between her face and the glass and looked out toward him; he flashed his headlights so she would know he was there watching her; he hoped that it made her feel less afraid. He considered the time. *Her mother will be here any minute. If I go now the girl will be just fine.* Bryan didn't want to be there when the woman arrived, but he couldn't allow himself to leave. He decided he would drive away with his lights off the moment he was sure that Monica was safely in the car with her mother. He was certain that she wouldn't try to follow him; a mother doesn't look for trouble when she's with her child; surely a strange man driving away from a dark parking lot in a dark car would look a lot like the kind of trouble she would want to avoid.

A flash, like lightning, startled Bryan. It was so sudden that he wasn't sure if the light had glanced across the whole of the church, or was it just something trivial greatly magnified in the wet windshield of the car? He fumbled for the switch to turn off the dome light, but instead the wipers jumped through their arcs, screeching across the glass. Quickly, he turned them off and found the switch for the light. The car went dark. He turned off the engine and the radio with it. Bryan crouched down in the seat and peered over the dashboard; a pair of headlamps swept through a turn, unexpectedly approaching from a street behind the church. The light moved erratically and ratcheted up the face of the building as the car drew near; its temperament seemed alarming. He held his breath thinking about the body in the trunk and prayed it wasn't the police.

The church door opened, just a little, and Monica's face appeared, her eyes squinting in the sudden harsh brightness. She started to step outside, but the car raced by and disappeared, its tires sliding on the wet asphalt as it turned the corner of the building. *Idiots.* Bryan sat up and re-started the car; he swallowed a deep gulp of air and turned the dome light back on. He tried to send a smile to the girl in the doorway even though he knew she wouldn't be able to see his face this far away. As if she sensed his gaze, she looked toward him for a moment and held up his note; then withdrew into the building with her head down; her hazy yellow-green image receded from the glass and then vanished.

Bryan checked the clock glowing in the dashboard, impatiently waiting for Monica to reappear; his vision traded between the empty glass doors and the blue dots pulsing between the numbers; soon the eighteen became nineteen and the nineteen became twenty. He turned off the radio. He didn't like that she had wandered away, even though the building was empty, and the demon was safely bound just a few feet behind him. He could hear it stir as the drug sent it someplace stored in its brain like a dog twitching its paws, as if running in its sleep. He knew the girl wouldn't go back down into the basement and find the mess in the janitor's office—but the mother might. *If her mother comes now, she'll wander around looking for her.* Instinctively, his hand went for the door lever but just as it did, the soft image reappeared behind the glass. Bryan sensed it before he saw it, but there was something very different about the girl.

He laid the ropes on the seat next to him and wiped the inside of the windshield with the sleeve of his jacket; the rain had stopped, and he cleared it one more time with the wipers. He studied the figure curiously, in a way that you might study a familiar room with something seemingly out of place. He tried to process what he knew to be so with what he sensed had changed. Then it hit him; it was her clothes; the colors of her uniform were no longer discernable; yellow was white, green was grey. *How could she have changed clothes?* And there was something else, at first less obvious but much more troubling; the girl appeared to be smaller than before. Bryan couldn't reason with what he saw; a river of thought swirled in his head as he climbed out of the car. He walked toward the door but slowed himself with uncertainty half-way across the parking lot;

his next few steps were tentative, and then he stopped. He remained still, afraid to advance and afraid to stand in the open, vulnerable to the mother if she should come at this moment. And he was afraid to turn his back to the girl, afraid she might vanish again. With his gaze fixed on the door, he measured slow careful steps backward until he felt the car brush along his left side and the idling engine vibrating through the fender. Across from him, the driver's door stood open where he had left it; he could hear the warning ding over and over from the key in the ignition. Then the figure raised a small hand and placed it to the glass. Bryan froze, and his heart stopped. His voice squeaked with hesitation, "Monica, is it you?"

The girl's little outstretched fingers pressed their warmth to the surface in a perfect array like the feathers of a wing; her small shape seemed to hover vaguely beyond. Her hand stayed where it was only briefly and then pulled away; then the likeness of the child pulled away too. It happened so suddenly that Bryan's mind tried to reconcile what his eyes couldn't believe with what his heart wanted to be real. His breathing went shallow until there was almost none. Pushing what little breath he had through his lips, he called to the girl again, "Emma?"

The sound of his dead daughter's name broke the night; a horrible anxiety overcame him. Pain enveloped him and burned through his flesh, rushing to the center of his chest, tightening around his broken heart, compressing it in what he thought would surely be its final pulse. His fingers pricked with numbness; the palms of his hands turned wet and cold, and with them he tried to steady his legs, but they began to fail. Falling against the car he groped for something to hold, but his knees buckled beneath him, and he dropped heavily to the asphalt. He lay doubled over on the ground with his arms folded around his waist, his lungs struggling for the air he refused to breathe. Her imagined cries resounded in his head, drowning the night echoes around him. The scar that never healed lay open, and through the gaping wound he could see the trace of Emma's little hand left imprinted upon the pane of glass.

An absolute hollowness, vast and empty as the infinite universe, engulfed him, siphoning off the last troubled remnants of his existence. He thought the end of his sad life to be with him now, and he desperately wished it to be so—it no longer mattered. Tears welled up in his eyes and spilled down his cheeks into his open lips, and he could taste the saline. He prayed not to God, but for the peace that surely comes just before death, but there was none. He turned his head toward the doors and lay still; in the corner of his eye he could see the pool of tears collecting on the pavement, and he thought it to be his blood. A final, sinking rumination pulled him closer to the ground. *You touched the glass, Emma, knowing I was somewhere on the other side. You were waiting in the church for me all that time. You were waiting for me to save you...* He surrendered the side of his face to the cold, wet asphalt. *And I didn't come.*

*****

Monica jumped into the front seat beside her mother; the heater felt good on her bare legs. She kissed her mom on the cheek and hugged her arm tightly.

"It's okay Monica," Annie said. She put her arm around her daughter and patted her back. "So where is Mr. Duncan? And where's that other man, the one who answered the phone?"

"Mr. Duncan never came back from the store, mom, but John's right over there." Monica pointed toward the parked car. The interior light was on, and the driver's door stood wide open, but there was no one there. She rolled down her window and could hear the engine running.

"Where *is* he?" Annie repeated.

"Mom, he's right there!" Monica pointed again but let her

hand drop when she saw that the man was gone. "He was there in the car a minute ago; I swear I saw him! He said he'd wait there until you came, so I wouldn't be alone."

"I don't like this, Monica; I don't like this at all." Annie rolled up her window and triggered the power locks; she idled cautiously toward the parked car, glancing all around, certain the man would appear suddenly out of the blackness. She stopped a few yards away from the vehicle. Against the backdrop of night, it glowed almost iridescent, washed in the high-beams of her headlamps. Monica slid over next to her, close, away from her door.

"Mom, he was—"

"Shhh!" Annie held her hand up to Monica's mouth. She lowered her window an inch and listened. From the abandoned car, the ignition dinged annoyingly through the open door. There was something else, but it was hard to distinguish from the drone of the two engines. Annie was frightened. *He must be somewhere close.* She waited. *There it was—the sound.* She heard it again, or thought she did. It seemed to come from the back of the car, a dull thump-thump. She strained to find the noise that she did not want to hear.

"Mom, can we *please* go now?" Monica squeezed her mother's hand. "I'm scared."

Annie hesitated, staring where she thought she had heard the sound, then swung the car around and sped away from the church, keeping an anxious eye on the rear-view mirror. She drove quickly and erratically, turning frequently through the maze of back streets to get her daughter safely back home. They continued in silence for several tense minutes until Annie felt sure they weren't being followed.

"Are you okay, baby?" She placed her hand on Monica's leg and spoke softly, "The man didn't touch you, did he?"

"No, mom; I never even saw him. I was in the basement

looking for the coach, and all the lights went out. John was there; he said he was helping Mr. Dunk work on the electricity, but it was so dark. I couldn't see him. He scared me at first because I didn't know who he was, but he was very nice; he didn't want me to be afraid." She looked down at her lap. "Mom, I have a confession."

Annie checked the mirror and made a quick turn down a narrow, one-way street; she pulled the car to the curb and turned off the headlights. "Good! Maybe you'll tell me why you were at the church instead of grandma's house? And where was Mr. Duncan?" Annie turned to look at her daughter; she could see the moisture gathering in her eyes.

"Mom, you see, I know I wasn't supposed to, but Mr. Dunk bought me ice cream because we won our first game, and I spilled it on my uniform, and I thought I'd be in trouble, so he brought me to the church to give me a new uniform, and after I changed I came upstairs because he said," Monica paused for a breath, "he had to do a little work. So I played the piano for a while, but I started to worry because he was in the basement for a long time. Then the lights went out, and John was there, and he said Mr. Dunk had to leave to get a part from the store to fix everything and—"

"Mr. Duncan just left without telling you?" It all felt very strange to Annie; she tried to put together the events at the church, but nothing made sense. She studied the empty street behind her in the mirror.

"I'm sorry, mom; I didn't mean to make you worry; I won't forget my phone ever again."

"You did make me worry, but it's my fault, Monica. I should have come to watch your game instead of going back to work. I'm so sorry, baby."

"That's okay, mom." Monica sounded relieved.

"John left you a note; it was taped to the door." She handed her mom the slip of folded paper.

Annie checked the mirror again and turned on the dome light, "He left me a note?" With a look of bewilderment on her face, she peeled back the tape with her fingernail and began to read silently.

'Boyd Duncan was a very bad man. He hurt little girls, and one day he may have hurt Monica. You need to protect her better. She's precious. But he can't hurt her now.'

"What does it say, mom?"

Annie didn't hear her daughter. She reread the first line subliminally alarmed by a single word. *'Boyd Duncan <u>was</u> a very bad man.'*

She folded the note and pushed it into her purse; she turned to her daughter and looked into her young eyes. Inside, her baby was still there.

"What is it, mom?"

Annie wrapped her arms around Monica and pulled her close. She thought to drive back to the church, but quickly dismissed the idea. There was an abruptness to the last sentence of the note which kept her from wanting to know. *He can't hurt her now.*

"Mom, will you tell me what it says?"

"He said you're precious, Monica." Annie kissed the side of her face and hugged her tighter. When she released her, Monica leaned away and looked at her mom curiously. She wiped a single tear from her mother's cheek and smiled.

Annie smiled back. "Let's go home."

*****

–14–

DUNCAN'S AWAKENING

H e spoke to each of the young girls drifting in a circle above him. *"I remember you, and you, too; I know who you all are."*

A dozen empty faces swirled all around, their dark eyes sealed closed under a veil of translucent skin. Absent life, they could offer no expression. He told his hands to reach out and touch them, but his arms were too heavy; as if sewn to his side, they wouldn't move. Other ghosts marched around him in a circle also; ugly, old women, pulled from the grave, hovered just above the ground and stayed nearly hidden at the limit of his vision. He could only glimpse them by shifting his eyes back and forth. Something gripped tightly against his forehead and held his face still. Floating over him, the young bodies were carried along by the darkness; their edges softly blurred where white flesh touched the black emptiness; form and void began and ended in a blended obscurity.

"Why won't you let me know your eyes?" But no answer was offered. His ears pulsed with a persistent hammering; metal to metal rang in a disjointed beat inside his skull. He watched curiously as the drifting girls raised their hands and grabbed handfuls of hair from their scalps. At first random strands floated down, then frightening clumps rained over him like plugs from a doll's head. Openings appeared where the hair was pulled, and he could see through to the darkness beyond. His morbid arousal turned to fear. He wanted what was happening to end; he cried up to them to make it stop, but the hair continued to fall. As it settled on his arms and legs, it wrapped around them and gripped tightly against his skin, as if he was prey caught in the spinning of a spider's web. He struggled to

break free but couldn't move. The hammering continued, and with every stroke he felt like he was being driven into the earth, bound and sinking to the bottom of a shallow hole— a cold, wet grave swallowing his naked body.

"Why is this happening?" He cried in desperation to the awful ghosts flowing faster in a current around him. Suddenly, the heads became grotesquely disfigured, the empty scalps stretched in impossible distortions, swaying to an invisible turbulence. Darkness encircled the sealed eyes and spread outward, erasing the human form of their faces; distant points of light shone through where the flesh had melted away. Traces of skin, like egg-white churning in boiling water, seemed to pull apart and then disappear. Soon the heads were gone and the old women too; everything had dissolved to nothing except for the mysterious eyes—like little moons swirling in the vacuum of space.

He felt incredible horror at the sight; the hair wrapping his arms and legs gripped him even tighter; he screamed at the hideously orphaned eyes, but no sound passed his lips. Slowly the veils split open to reveal haunting black orbs peering directly into his past. He had seen the eyes before, they were all the same, and now he wanted only to cry; he could never forget the look of constant anger and revulsion he had known in his own mother's eyes.

Terrified, he slammed his eyelids shut. "Mother, don't hurt me. I'll be good! I will be very good!" He repeated his whimpering pleas over and over. "Please don't hurt me, mother—I won't ever do it again!"

*****

Duncan thought he awoke but wasn't sure. Carefully, cautiously, he gazed around as he could, but his vision was cloudy, and his head was still locked looking up at the sky. The girl-ghosts were gone; the darkness had consumed them completely. His ears rang, but the hammering was gone now too.

Blurry points of light shined above him; he lay quietly watching them and blinked several times to see if he could will the setting of his dream, but the stars remained as they were. He fought to pull air into his lungs against the tightness binding his chest; a numbing paralysis, like a cloak of pins, gripped the whole of his body. He struggled to remember what had happened, but no memory was there. *Where am I?* If he could calibrate his other senses to whatever signals were around him, maybe he would recall. He could feel the coldness of wet leaves pressing to his back and sides; the smell of cut grass, strong like alfalfa and manure filled his clogged nostrils. The air felt crisp and chilled his skin. Night sounds began to drift to his ears as the ringing lessened; the shrill of distant cicadas peaked and lulled in audible cycles like waves erasing the shore. There was a hint of iron, like blood on his teeth, and a gummy taste lingered on his lips...

The tape.

It all rushed back to him: the man at the traffic light, the horrible attack in his office. He jerked against his immobility and then realized it was not of himself. He tried vainly to control his overwhelming panic. *What do I do?!* The snap of a twig jolted him—a shape swept through his vision and briefly blanked out the stars, then it was gone. He sensed someone at his side: a close, heavy presence. When he heard it clear its throat, he knew it was the man from the church.

"Do not struggle, Boyd; the ropes will only get tighter if you do; and don't bother to scream—no one will hear you. No one heard Lindsey; do you remember Lindsey?"

When the voice paused, Duncan wanted to vomit.

"Tell me now, how does it feel to not know where you are or

what will happen to you next? But I guess you might recognize this place; it hasn't changed much since you brought Lindsey here. The farmer's moved away, and his house is empty now. So go ahead and scream if you must; I will enjoy it. Your fear feeds me."

The janitor heard every word as he stared into the emptiness between him and the stars of the sky.

"It sickens me to say this, Mr. Duncan, but in the arcane judicial system of this country, money holds more value than the life of an innocent child. If I use a gun to rob a liquor store, I will be punished more severely than if I was to rob a little girl from her home and assault her body and kill her soul. And in the sad aftermath, her pain must also be endured by her family, and it destroys them all. They are all victims. An obscene, cowardly act by someone like you becomes a long trail of suffering from which no one recovers. The flesh may be restored in time, but the scars to the self are deep and will never heal. *This I do know.*"

The man squatted over him, nearly face to face, and looked into his terrified eyes.

"You are not him—I knew it at the church when you cowered on the floor. I would have known if you were. On that score you should consider yourself very lucky." The man got up and walked a slow circle at the edge of Duncan's vision. "Even so, I do not like you; you are a demon that preys on children. You did not ask to be who you are, and I am sorry for that, but you have destroyed many lives, not by who you are, Mr. Duncan, but by how you have allowed yourself to be. What you *are* does not hurt people; what you choose to *do* is an altogether different matter."

He watched his captor gaze out through the edge of the woods to the glowing sky just beyond the horizon. Out of the corner of his eye, Duncan could see a blood moon beginning to rise.

"You will be destroyed tonight and soon all the others who are like you." The man reached down and grabbed the coils of rope lying across Duncan's chest; the rough fibers dragged against the sides of his battered face as they were pulled away.

Duncan strained to see the man walking toward the bumper of a car. He closed his eyes and listened anxiously to the footsteps receding. It occurred to him just then that his rectum felt full and strangely cold. He started to weep. There was nothing he could do but wait.

*****

R. BYRON STOCKDALE

−15−

RESTORATION

The Ohio State Police cruiser slowed and pulled to the side of Old Wire Road behind a line of official state and county vehicles. Tom Russell thanked the highway patrolman for the ride and swallowed the last of his now cold coffee. He set the empty cup on the dashboard and exited the car. Kate slipped out from the back seat with her phone to her ear; she had been talking to Grainger for the past ten minutes.

Just ahead of them, a dirt farm road broke to the right and disappeared into a heavily wooded area about a quarter mile away. Several feet out from each side, yellow police tape traced the road from the county blacktop deep into the forest canopy. Uniformed officers and plain-clothed detectives were moving up and down the scene like an army of worker ants carrying black cases and paper evidence bags. The television crews were held back on the pavement, set up along the shoulder with their video cameras and telescopic lenses aimed into the activity. Gravely, reporters repeated the few known events into microphones and waited anxiously for more details about what was most certainly a horrible crime.

A four-wheel-drive Suburban bounced across the furrows of combed earth and stopped below where Tom and Kate stood, bridging the wet swale that separated the field from Old Wire Road. The sun was bright and high, but the air was cold, particularly for late April; a thin layer of clouds reached across the sky from the west. A few hours behind, a cold front was pushing across the Great Lakes, bringing falling temperatures and heavy, possibly freezing rain.

The agent climbed out of the truck and clamored up the embankment toward them; F.B.I. was stenciled in large yellow letters above the brim of his blue ball cap. He extended an open hand, first toward Kate and then Tom; he spoke almost in a whisper so as not to disrupt her call. "Welcome ma'am, you must be S.A. Morrow and that makes you S.A.C. Russell. Pleased to meet you both; we appreciate you getting here so quickly." He paused to take a breath as Kate stepped away to finish her conversation with Grainger. The agent looked at Tom, his voice now normal, "S.A. Chuck Akers, Cleveland field office, was mostly in charge, but that will be you now, sir. I'm the local NCAVC coordinator, and I'll take care of getting you any resources you might need." He took another breath. "We still have a little time, but I'd feel a lot better if we got the body downtown. They say we're due to get some bad weather later this afternoon. If you've ever seen one of our spring storms roll off the lake, you'd know what I'm talking about."

"Call me Tom, and Ms. Morrow should work just fine for the lady. You can relax, Chuck, it's still your case; we're just here to lend a hand and not get too much in your way." Tom surveyed the activity around him and scratched the back of his head. "If you put me in charge I'll have to talk to the press, and believe me, you don't want me talking to the press; they haven't been too kind to me in the past. Besides I don't photograph real well, just ask Ms. Morrow."

Kate nodded her head yes as she ended the call and clipped her phone back on her belt. "Fischer, that's her last name, Tom, Lindsey Fischer—the name that was written on the black board at the church. Grainger is sending us all the juvie history he can dig up between her and the janitor. He said he'd have it to us shortly, *before it's time for your afternoon nap*; those were his exact words." Kate winked at Tom and zipped up her jacket against the cutting breeze; she took a couple of steps down the embankment as she pointed across the field toward the woods. "What about all those men, Agent Akers?"

"Well ma'am, that fire road there splits Cuyahoga and Loraine County; of course our office is in on it because of the possible missing girl and the collection of kiddie porn found on the janitor's computer. We've got the Amherst PD and some Ohio State Troopers in on the deal too. Except for a couple of heated discussions earlier this morning, everybody seems to be getting along real fine, nothing even close to a fist-fight just yet. The county boys are pretty much staying out of our way; I think they're real happy now that we showed up. This isn't something most people want to deal with, and I bet if you were to ask them off record, they'd much rather be handing out traffic tickets, but I'm sure they'll be just fine with the overtime pay. We put them to work holding off the talking heads with the cameras and microphones.

We called you as soon as we got a positive I.D on the John Doe; as you saw in the report, the VIC is one Boyd James Duncan, janitor at the First Baptist Church down in Medina. You had a similar case last year in Iowa and another one recently in Colorado, right? We're not sure if this is the work of the same guy; won't know much about anything until we get the body downtown and the examiner gets a chance to look it over, but so far it would appear that the signature is similar. I saw the inter-agency release you sent out on your Short Rose Killer just a few weeks ago and of course the posting on VICAP."

He paused to sneeze into his jacket sleeve, "Sorry, it's my damn allergies; you'd think the cold air and rain last night would have helped. Anyway, the identification part wasn't hard; Medina PD got a 9-1-1 early this morning after the pastor at the church found the victim's office turned upside down, bits of him splattered here and there. The power to the basement where his office was located had been cut, and we're still trying to figure out why and what the connection might be. So far we've found blood and a spot of semen belonging to the janitor. We're running some prints, hair, cloth fibers and what we believe is a saliva sample through the lab. I'm sure some of it will belong to the girl and hopefully something will be from our unknown subject.

We were able to pull two partial sets of footprints from the blood on the floor. One set belongs to the janitor for sure, the other would have to be the UNSUB since the pastor said he didn't even go in the office. It looks like he was wearing hiking or work boots; I'm sure the tread pattern will match what we've found out here. The only items we believe belong to the child are possibly some hair samples, two small finger prints we lifted off the desk, and a softball uniform with what looks like dried ice cream stains on the front. We also found several pairs of child-size panties hidden in the bottom drawer, but we don't think they were hers. Other than the custodian, no one's reported anyone missing; that's the first thing we checked, so we're real hopeful we'll find her safe at home. The pastor said that the girls' team had a game last night, so we're canvassing all the restaurants and C-stores between the local ball fields and the church with a photo of the janitor. Maybe someone saw him with the girl, and if we're lucky someone might have gotten a look at our killer."

"Agent Akers," Tom interrupted, "you're looking for a white male, large build, probably six-four plus and physically fit; he'll be in his mid-to-late-thirties. Given his size, he probably stays in the shadows so as not to draw attention. I know it's not much to go on, but it might help a witness remember."

"Yes, sir." Agent Akers held up his finger and sneezed again. "We're also talking to the families with kids on the softball team as fast as we can but haven't identified the girl yet. There are fourteen names on the roster, so we should know who she is soon enough. If our killer is the same perp you've been looking for, I doubt he would have had any business with the girl. I'd say he might have done her a big favor by getting to the janitor first. Other than the stash of panties, we found some adult-size nylon stockings and a couple of large bras washed and folded behind the top drawer of his desk. Yeah, go figure. He did a crappy job hiding his porn on his computer, by the way; I guess he didn't figure anyone at the church would have a reason to be looking for it." Akers glanced down at the ground, then up at Tom, still standing at the edge of the pavement. "Agent Russell, you don't think our hero would have beaten the janitor up in front of the girl, do you?"

Tom didn't hear the question and was staring at his phone, scanning through the email he had just received from Grainger giving the history on the Duncan-Fischer abduction.

"I don't think so." Kate injected. "If anything happened, she'd either be missing or talking. If she's missing, we would have already heard about it, and if she's talking, we probably would have already heard about that too. She wasn't taken, and I don't think she saw anything either, or anything that would be worth reporting to the police. I doubt she even met the UNSUB. It's much more likely that the janitor gave her a ride home from the church and then went back, or someone picked her up at the church before the attack occurred. I'm sure we'll find her safe and sound."

*****

Tom was turned toward the business across the field from where they stood. He thought of his daughter Katie; she played softball too, and he began to question if he really knew her coach all that well. "I want to know the second you find the girl, Agent Akers. Of course we'll want to talk to her about her coach, but if she saw the killer, we'll need whatever she can give us toward a description of him as the first priority. We need every detail she can remember—all the usual stuff but, more importantly, how he *behaved* with her—his speech, tone, mannerisms. Did he seem threatening, or was he comforting to the girl?"

"Will do." Akers pulled a little notepad from his pocket and scribbled a few words. "Now, regarding our sorry fella lying out there on the road, as luck would have it we got the call early this morning; a pheasant hunter found him just before daybreak on his way out to kick up some birds in those grain fields just on the other side of that woods; well, actually the dog came up on the body first. The hunter lives a half-mile west of here but doesn't own the property where the body was found; says he's been hunting it for years since nobody lives on the place anymore. He said he didn't hear or see anything last night and fell asleep watching a movie on T.V.; I talked to him myself. He's pretty hard of hearing with some serious cataracts, so I'm sure he's telling the truth. Not sure how good of a hunter he could be with those bad eyes, though; I wouldn't want to be the poor dog flushing out the birds in front of his gun."

"Agent Akers, how about we stick with, um, the body?" Kate sounded impatient.

"Sorry ma'am, yes, of course—the body. Without un-wrapping it, it was hard to say if the description matched the janitor, but we were fairly certain it would. Anyway, we ran the thumb and a finger and got a hit. We only had two good digits to pull a print from; the rest didn't have much skin left on them from the dragging. Same guy alright, had a record, did time, pedophile, but I guess you already know that or you wouldn't be in Ohio standing out here in the cold with me. Kind of makes you wonder how a guy like that got the job coaching a young girls' softball team."

"Yeah, it does make you wonder." Tom had grown impatient also. "We read the report on the plane, Chuck. Now, if you could take us to the body, we sure would like to have a look."

"Right this way, sir, we haven't moved him—your orders." Akers side-stepped down the embankment. "Good thing it's been chilly; he's still in pretty good shape. Based on his body temp and rigor, the examiner put his time of death about 2:00 or 3:00

this morning."

"Wait, Tom." Kate held up her hand in front of Tom as he came down the slope. "Since we don't have a missing report on the girl, we can assume he had her in the church shortly after their softball game, which we know was over about 7:30, but probably not any later than when a parent would start to get concerned, otherwise there would have been a panicked call to the police. Or, the parents were aware that the girl was with the janitor and had made arrangements to pick her up or have her dropped off at her house. Either way, it seems likely that the girl got home at a reasonable time. Remember, last night was a school night. Since we don't have any reports of a witness to the beating, we can also assume that the girl was gone prior to when the perp started working over her coach; let's say she's home before nine-o'clock. But, according to the examiner, our buddy Boyd J. wasn't killed until a few hours after midnight. Of course the attack could have come anytime between 9:00 and just before he was hauled up here to these woods, but what would the janitor be doing at the church much past 9:00 or 10:00 at night?"

Kate paused for a second. "Maybe I should rephrase that question. What would the janitor be doing in his office after nine or ten at night that he couldn't be doing just as well at home? Then, interestingly, the report said the clock radio in his office was flashing 9:07 when they turned the power back on; that would mark the time when the main breaker for the basement level was tripped. I'll bet that time somehow coincided with the attack, and we can probably all agree that beating someone up in the dark doesn't make any sense. So, it appears that the perp killed the power just *after* he whooped up on the janitor to somehow cover up the scene, or maybe he was just telling us it was '*lights out*' for Mr. Boyd Duncan.

He may have kept him somewhere for a few hours before bringing him out here, but I doubt it. Why would he? Where would he hold him? No, he'd want some time alone with his prisoner where it would be safe for him. I think he brought him out here straight from the church in Medina; that's maybe an hour drive. That puts him in the woods with his prisoner for more than four hours, and that sounds like a very long time to me." Kate smiled and lowered her voice to Tom like she was about to tell him a secret. "It also sounds a lot like SRK."

Tom nodded his head and just smiled back.

"Sir, ma'am," Akers spoke from the running board of his truck, "if you care to jump in, I'll give you a lift through the field; it's a bit wet for walking, and we're staying off the road as much as possible until we've had a chance to go over this end of it thoroughly. It looks like we have a full day out here if the weather holds; we'll be bagging evidence for a while. Your SRK friend left us a pretty big mess."

Tom sighed. *Always does.* "How far is it?" He glanced across the field as he reached the bottom of the embankment.

"About three hundred yards give or take; see the group of agents over there on the other side of that scruff?" Captain Akers pointed at a thicket of hedge and under-story trees. "They're waiting for you to have a look." Fairly obscured beyond the trees and brush, a handful of blue FBI hats and jackets were grouped in a loose circle around the body which lay covered by a white plastic sheet. "The victim was dragged from a spot in the woods quite a ways farther down, we think pretty fast judging by the trail through the dirt and gravel."

"Let's go, Chuck." Tom opened the front door for Kate, then climbed into the back seat.

"One other thing, Sir," Akers pulled himself behind the steering wheel, "we believe he was still alive and probably conscious after the dragging. The wounds were severe, but they didn't affect any critical organs that might have killed him immediately. He was going to die for sure, just not right away. Given the amount of blood we found, he most likely bled to death. The examiner thought it would have taken maybe an hour or an hour-fifteen. Unless he was in total shock, he could have been somewhat coherent for a good thirty minutes or so. That kind of makes you wonder too, doesn't it?"

"What are we wondering about now, Chuck?" Tom asked.

"What the poor S.O.B. was thinking while he lay there dying. He would have been scared shit-less so to speak, and in a whole lot of pain."

Tom thought to himself. *That's exactly what SRK had in mind.*

*****

Tom and Kate stood ten feet from the covered body and observed an agent pouring dental plaster into a shallow shoe print in the dirt; another was recording the process with a digital video camera. Luckily, the pool of blood surrounding the victim had not drained into the depression.

"We made a careful sweep immediately around the body and then covered it per your orders," Akers said. "We've taken photos of the drag marks up and down the road, measured them and taped them off too. There were lots of places where it looks like the killer slowed down and then took off again. Based on the throw pattern of the dirt ejected from his tires, we figure he was moving at a pretty good clip; thirty, maybe forty miles-per-hour. It wasn't easy, but we found traces of brake dust all along the tire tracks like he was riding his brakes."

"Anything on the car?" Kate asked.

"Nothing yet, Agent Morrow, but we're talking to every land owner around here. If they saw anything we could at least nail down the time a little closer. I doubt they'll give us much in the way of details; there's nothing too suspicious about a lone car on these deserted roads late at night. Based on the trash we see everywhere, it looks like kids come out here to party now and then. It's a good thing the rain was light and let up around midnight; it helped soften things up without making a muddy mess. We were able to pull several good casts of the tire treads and got axle width and wheelbase measurements. We think it was a passenger vehicle by the tread pattern but there are also a few light duty SUV tires that could fit. We're sure it was rear or four-wheel drive and should know what type of brake shoes it has by tomorrow, but that won't narrow it down much. If we're lucky we'll find some fibers on the victim to tie the crime to the vehicle if and when we locate it. If it's your man from Iowa and Colorado, he's probably not local, so we're checking the rental returns around the airports in Cleveland and Akron for tire type, blood, soil residue, and any rope fibers that may be left on the frame or bumper. It will take a while, but if it was a rental, we'll find it."

Tom thought for a moment and shook his head. "No, I doubt you will. He's not going to return a car full of body bits and blood, and he could have rented it anywhere; all he needed was Ohio plates. You can get here in four hours from every corner of the state. It would be worth checking rentals that logged more than a hundred miles, but my guess is we'd be talking about a lot of cars. Focus your search on the bigger model sedans, nothing flashy; he'll have needed a big trunk. Forget about an SUV unless the windows are heavily tinted; our perp wouldn't take the chance of moving his victim openly. A panel van is a remote possibility, but it would have drawn attention out here. He may have specifically requested a car with Ohio plates, and that would be worth checking into. It's an unusual request that a rental agent might remember."

Tom rubbed his eyes and pinched the bridge of his nose. "Get with the locals to set up a check point a quarter-mile down that blacktop in each direction, closer if there's another way out. We've got quite an audience now; our boy may be up there mingling with the rest hoping for a little extra fix. We don't know yet if he collects souvenirs, but he will have left us one. Look for a small piece of colored glass, no more than an inch wide and a couple inches long."

"That's going to be a problem sir. This road's littered with broken beer and liquor bottles. Country kids, you know."

"And that would be a problem for who exactly, Agent Akers?" Tom didn't wait for a response. "They can ignore the curved glass, but collect everything else within ten yards of the body. If they're not sure—bag it. The piece we're looking for will be flat and probably cleanly polished; it will most likely be red but don't let that distract you. We think it may be part of the killer's signature. If he left us one, we have an expert who knows what to look for and will be able to cull it out from the rest."

"Yes, sir." Akers turned to his colleague overseeing the evidence collection to make sure he had heard the instructions. The agent nodded.

Tom continued, "Check all the local motels for a few days in case the killer sticks around for a while, but I doubt he will— too risky. The janitor's office and this dirt road don't look the way they do because he's careless; we're seeing just what he wants us to see or what he doesn't care that we see. He's smart, cautious and in control; this kill was too important to him. They all are."

"Yes, sir. We'll take care of it." Akers stepped to his truck to relay the orders back to Cleveland. When he returned, Tom had walked down the edge of the dirt road and was kneeling in the grass about a hundred feet away; Kate was kneeling opposite him on the other side. Their backs were turned to the victim, and they were both facing the woods.

Akers walked past Tom for a few yards and stopped. He took off his cap and scratched his thin scalp, "You see it too, don't you? It's the damnedest thing." He was looking at a deep

221

depression in the road forty feet away. "We figure the rope broke about there, and the victim skid and tumbled like a loose football before coming to rest here." Akers pointed at the dark residue of blood between where Tom and Kate were kneeling. "But we found him there." He motioned toward where the victim lay covered by the plastic sheet. "From the high concentration of blood and the more defined patterns in the dirt, it looks like our killer dragged the victim from here, over to there, by hand. Must be a good thirty yards; he had to work at it too. You're right; I'd say your man is pretty fit; the janitor is at least a couple hundred pounds plus, maybe two-fifty. Why break a sweat dragging him? He would have bled to death just the same right here."

"Hate." Tom responded instantly. "Hate is one hell-of-a motivator." He stood up and looked directly at Akers. "Before we get to see the main event, can you first direct us to where our killer set up his little sideshow?"

"Yes, sir. That's going to be a couple hundred yards farther down, well into that tree line. We figure he spent a little time getting things ready and used the woods for cover. You'll see what I mean when we get there."

"If you don't mind, S.A. Morrow and I would like to go over the scene with a fresh set of eyes," Tom said. "I'm sure you won't mind."

"Not at all, S.A.C. Russell; we haven't done much of anything out there. It's a little bizarre if you ask me, and we wanted to make sure you had a chance to look it over first. We can compare notes later. I'll wait for you and Miss Morrow back at the body."

*****

Kate had already started moving toward the woods on the other side of the road; Tom followed opposite her, trailing a few yards behind just outside the police tape. He moved slowly, kneeling occasionally, keeping his eyes focused on the drag marks and the random deposits of blood left in the dirt and gravel. The dragging had made distinct patterns indicating that the body had slid and tumbled back and forth from his side of the road to Kate's side repeatedly. "See anything?"

"Just what you're seeing, Tom; I'd say Boyd had a rough ride."

"Yeah, it looks like he did. What a way to go."

They walked for a while in silence until they were deep into the trees; the canopy above was filled with new growth that weakened the daylight and slowed their progress. They stopped where the police tape turned out to form a box, capturing an area fifty feet square. The center was defined by a mound of wet leaves with a depression in the middle about the size of a man; it looked like a giant nest. One end was scattered, blown away, leaving a trail of leaves that pointed back down the road in the direction of the body. Toward the other end, two steel rods were driven into the ground roughly eighteen inches apart. Kate stepped over the yellow barrier and moved slowly inward, deliberately placing every step until she reached the edge of the leaves. She reached into the nest and put her gloved hand on the tip of one of the rods; she tried to move it, but it wouldn't budge. "Now what do you think these were for?"

"Probably to keep Duncan immobile while SRK did God-knows-what to him. It reminds me of the stake he used to restrain Bart and Alice Lowen while they starved to death; this time it doesn't look like he required any chains. I'm sure we'll learn something more when we have a look at the janitor." Tom walked a slow circle around the scene. It was obvious that SRK had raked the ground to form the pile of leaves, but everything looked extremely neat and orderly as if the killer wasn't in any hurry at all, as if it mattered to him how his kill-site appeared. There was nothing left in a thirty-foot circle except combed dirt and gravel, not even a sapling or twig; it was clearly a presentation meant for someone to see. From above, it would look like an artist had painted the rays of the sun, using a rake as his brush and the ground as his canvas. "I can see how he spent four hours out here." Tom spread his arms wide to embrace the scene. "This is significant, Kate; every bit of this will tie back to the Fischer girl in some way—all of it will."

"Tom, there's something over here." Kate was standing at the end of the mound of leaves where it was scattered down the road, marking the initial moments of the dragging. She bent down and moved some sticks and leaves to the side. After taking several photos with her phone; she carefully pulled a pair of nylon stockings out of the debris.

Instantly, Tom re-opened the email from Grainger and was quickly scrolling through it, "Nylons—they must have been involved in the assault on Lindsey Fischer, but Grainger doesn't even mention them." He looked up at Kate, "Did he say anything to you when you talked to him?"

"Not a word, Tom. Where in hell is this guy getting his information?"

"The sooner we can answer that question, the sooner we'll find SRK."

*****

When they were finished at the nest, Tom and Kate made their way back toward the corpse, this time walking together on the same side of the road. Kate followed several steps behind, allowing Tom to concentrate on what he called the 'trail of anger' leading to the victim. As they reached the agents waiting around the body, Akers began immediately where he had left off.

"From what we saw at the church, the janitor would have been in bad shape when the killer brought him out here. You're about to see that the dragging busted up what was left of him pretty bad; I need to warn you it's a bit graphic." He was looking directly at Kate. "A few of his fingernails were torn off, and there's plenty of gravel stuck in his hands, too. That's why we think he was conscious. Even though he was wrapped up tight, it looks like he was desperately trying to grab what he could as he was pulled along. You ever see a motorcycle wreck?"

Kate shook her head yes.

"Well, it's sort of the same. If it weren't for the ropes protecting much of his torso, he would have come out a lot worse. I guess the end result would have been the same either way." Akers continued, "We've got five sets of foot prints, not counting the dog, of course, one by the farmer, two by the officers who first responded and one set is ours. That leaves this one." Captain Akers pointed to the large print they had seen being cast for analysis earlier; it was near the head of the victim and had dried plaster residue all around the edges. "The one good print was all we could pull. Other than prints by the hunter and his dog, there weren't any more in the woods. Did you see how he combed the site around that pile of leaves? How'd he manage to do that without leaving any footprints?"

"Good question. Is there just the one?" Tom asked.

Akers nodded. "There's another one on the opposite side of the victim's head, but it's hardly a depression in the gravel. The rest of them are shallow with no definition and go off that way about a hundred feet to where the killer got back in his vehicle. They're mixed in with impressions coming this way, probably left from when he got out of the car to finish the dragging by hand. Go ahead, we completed our camera work an hour ago and swept the area very carefully. By the way, we didn't find any glass meeting your description, but we collected all of it anyway."

"It's here; we'll find it." Tom approached the body and

stood just behind where the prints were made, behind where the killer had stood. He looked down at the frayed ropes that emerged from below the plastic sheet and then towards the woods over two hundred yards away.

"We already have a jump on running the rope fibers and tape through the lab," Akers said. We should know something about the type in a day or two—maybe less, and we'll use it to help tie the killer to the crime; that is if we can get a match with any exemplars we gather from his car, if we're able to find it. It's a long shot to check all the stores that carry rope and tape locally; it could be in the hundreds, and who's to say he didn't bring it with him from wherever he came?" Akers continued, "It's cold enough that we're not worrying about decomposition, but the examiner would like to get him downtown before the weather turns."

"Thank you, Chuck." Tom motioned for him to be silent. He looked up at the weakening sun and took a long breath. "Let's have us a look."

Akers lifted the plastic sheet and stood back out of view; the other agents stepped back as well or walked away toward fresher air; it wasn't something they needed to see or breathe again. Tom squatted down and surveyed the body. It was positioned face down in the dirt, naked and bound in windings that had pulled it almost into a ball, precariously balanced on the face, shoulders and one folded knee. *He placed it this way.* The victim's left leg had worked loose during the dragging and was bent to the side, nearly perpendicular to the corpse in a mess of twisted rope and tape; his splintered fibula jutted through the flesh of his thigh. His pelvis was torn apart, and a gaping hole spilled his lower abdomen on the ground. An iron pipe, the thickness and length of a man's forearm, projected loosely from the wound and rested in the stew of the janitor's insides. Its end was tightly wound in rope, and the exposed length was covered in what looked like burnt baked beans. The scene reeked of feces and the unmistakable smell of sour blood.

"Okay, let's turn him."

Akers nudged the body over carefully with the ball of his foot; it rolled to its side exposing half of the janitor's disfigured face. A pair of ropes lead from the pipe across his groin and ran the length of his body to each side of his neck; the broken ends draped on the road. Deep grooves crossed his cheeks, nose, and brow and marked where the ropes had sawn on his face during the dragging. A broken tooth was deeply embedded in his lower lip.

Tom looked away and closed his eyes. His mind focused on the frayed ends of the ropes that had dragged the body for such a great distance; he saw the strain of the weight they pulled; their fibers stretched and deformed until they had to fail. He imagined the energy they must have held—*the energy of hate*. His thoughts went to last night and the dark, sleeping countryside, the victim tumbling through a cloud of dirt illuminated red in the brake lights of the speeding car. He opened his eyes and grinned at Agent Morrow.

"Is there something you want to tell me, Tom?"

Tom shook his head in frustration at how obvious it was. "SRK wasn't riding the brakes to slow the car, Kate; he was riding the brakes so he could see Duncan in his rear-view mirror."

Before Kate could respond, Akers stole the moment, "Sir, I do have to ask. Do you think there's a chance we could be dealing with someone unrelated to the other crimes; maybe a local sicko, someone who has a real problem with pedophiles or, more likely, someone connected to the Fischer girl or another one of the janitor's past victims?"

"No, I don't." Tom nodded toward the body without looking at Akers. "This was SRK, and you're partially right; he did pick this victim and this site for a reason. The woods back there is the exact place where Lindsey Fischer was taken and assaulted eleven years ago. It happened under a lunar eclipse—a blood moon, just like last night. Dragging Boyd Duncan by a thick metal pipe shoved in his ass was how SRK wanted this particular predator to go out, and if you read the case file, you'd know he had a good reason to do it exactly this way. But the killer has no personal connection to the girl. It's obvious that this was revenge for the horrible things that happened to little Lindsey under those trees, but it was also something more. It was about claiming redemption for all the other children *just like her.*

SRK isn't seeking gratification for himself; he's trying to restore something greater that we don't yet know about, and there is a difference." Tom tugged on the end of one of the ropes. "The Iowa scene had a similar feel, and when you look at the photos of some of his early victims, you would have to agree that we're looking for the same man. The murders are carefully planned, ritualistic, and particularly grim. We're dealing with an assassin personality of the highest order. This kill's *exactly* like all the others; it was a trial, followed immediately by an execution."

Tom walked around the corpse and stopped just opposite of where Agent Akers stood; he squatted down next to what had been the janitor's buttocks and gestured toward the protruding metal tip of the mechanism that had caused his horrible death. "Call it a hunch, Chuck, but I think you'll find that piece of glass we're looking for hidden inside this pipe."

*****

–16–

MIDNIGHT SLOOP

B ryan couldn't get back to sleep and didn't want to. The violent storm that woke him an hour ago had moved off quickly, but he could still hear the faint farewells of thunder grumbling off to the east. The dream had not yet come to him tonight.

He slid out of bed and descended the stairs with Molly trailing sleepily behind. In the small dining room next to the kitchen, he sat down at the table and turned on the computer; the monitor glowed solitary blue waiting for the login prompt to appear. He looked around the room in the dim light. It had been Mary's home office for a long time and looked very much as it did the day she died. The old hutch and breakfront were covered with dusty corrections journals and volumes of operational manuals from each of the prisons her company managed. Bryan never liked her career much or understood why she got into the field in the first place. The money was obscenely good, but the industry was populated with abrasive people who were frustrated with working in the bowels of law enforcement.

Mostly, he hated the system that released evil men to walk the streets. *They should just keep the monsters inside where they belong.* Mary wouldn't defend how it worked; she hated it too, but the bureaucracy was too big, and she had learned that there was nothing she or her business could do to change it.

She had aimed boldly by naming her company *American Corrections*, and it was her creation, something she had built from nothing except a college degree in Criminal Administration and a little seed money her parents had loaned her. She had started small, in this little room, just a consulting business to a vast industry, but she carried good instincts and had done well. In time, she moved her growing company to a prestigious office building in the city and added staff and a few trusted partners over the years. Bryan and Mary talked about moving their home, getting a bigger house and all the fancy things that came with success, but she liked how they lived and wanted to keep her private life simple, just like it was when they were first married. Instead, the plan was to retire very well, and they would retire very well while they were still very young.

When Emma was a little girl, Mary didn't want to move; she thought the rural life would be good for their daughter and maybe a little brother someday too. After they lost Emma, Mary didn't want to stay there any longer, but she soon became sick and surrendered the will to do much of anything. As her health rapidly declined, her partners had offered her a generous buy-out, and Mary decided to accept it. All she wanted was time with Bryan for as long as possible, and when the illness inevitably won, he would be able to live comfortably without her. Bryan would never have to work again.

He leaned forward and entered the password. The screen went dark, then filled with the photo of Mary posed in the companionway of their sailboat. He paused for a while to think about her and everything that had changed on that day. He could never forget their last time together on the water; he could never forget because of what Mary was going to ask him to do.

*****

Breathless heeled obediently in the brisk twenty knot wind. Mary turned the helm just slightly as Bryan tightened the mainsheet, purging the remaining twist from the sail and coaxing the cruiser even tighter to the air. The boat responded without delay, heeling harder. The conditions were ideal; if other sailors had tried the lake that afternoon, they would have thought that

God had graced them with the perfect day.

With the boat this hard over, the water raced by less than a foot below the cockpit rail. Spray washed over the forward deck in spasms as *Breathless* cut through the legions of whitecaps marching toward her. When she was this stirred up, Table Rock Lake roiled gray-green and came alive for the few boats that might try to ride her. Bryan reached over the side, surrendering his hand to the water. His arm danced across the chop, pulled backwards in the clear sluice rushing through his fingers. Compared to the crisp autumn air, the water felt comforting and warm. The boat was moving close to her hull speed and maybe a little bit more.

For most of the lake, the steep Missouri hills and bluffs held the shorelines less than a thousand yards apart to form the twisting narrows of the flooded White River valley. But here the lake was broad and straight, giving *Breathless* miles of open water to run. Even better, the hills to the north and west lifted more gently leaving this stretch of water naked to the insistent autumn winds. Beating at the long side of eight knots, they could have sailed this course for the better part of an hour before having to come about.

Mary surrendered the helm to Bryan and climbed down through the passageway in the bulkhead, grabbing a rail to overcome her uneven footing; she stayed low to avoid the spray breaking across the cabin top. When she turned around to look back at him, her face was drawn but happy. He glanced aloft at the wind vane, its angle was perfect for their point of sail. The telltales told that the rigging was tuned and trimmed, while the steel shrouds whispered their peculiar cry under the tremendous load. He turned to Mary peering back at him through the open companionway, and then at the beautiful curve in his mast. The stretch of water beyond the bow was open and waiting for them, but it was cold, and he sensed that Mary was ready for a break.

Reluctantly, he loosened the mainsheet and eased his grip on the wheel. The boat rolled off its chines coming broader to the current of air, the mast pointing more directly into the overcast sky. Immediately, he felt a little warmer and knew that she would too. They weren't going to make the marker at Lost Bridge on this tack, and it wasn't important. The calmer point of sail would slow their progress down lake, but they weren't really trying to get to any particular place in a hurry. It wasn't the distance they would cover in front of them that mattered; it was the distance they would leave behind.

As they came out of the wind, Mary smiled at him but in a forced way, her mouth moving to configure a silent word of thanks. He studied her lips; they were still soft and subtly curved. Across the years their fullness had lessened and fine lines drew away, but beautifully, like wisteria vine clinging to a winter garden wall. He missed how they used to blush red when she smiled; even more, he missed the warmth of them touching his own. They still kissed, but not often, or for long, because his mind was never completely free to take pleasure in her.

Bryan watched her eyes gaze out across the water to the golden bluffs receding slowly in their wake, and he followed her there. "Do you see the eagles?" he asked, but Mary looked lost in a thought. He answered himself, "I don't think we will. It's a bit overcast, and the lake is churning—there won't be very good fishing today."

Mary released a wistful sigh. "I haven't seen any, just a few buzzards and a pair of cranes. I think it's still a little early." She pulled away the hair that had blown across her face; it had already lost most of its color. "We've never seen them before late November, but I think it would be a good omen if we did. A good omen would be very good today."

She went below and returned with binoculars hanging from her neck. She aimed them high, just above the bluffs, scanning the tops of the naked trees where the gray limbs threaded the gray forest with the gray sky. Bryan held his eyes on Mary while he eased the lines and wheel a little more, and the boat slowed. "See anything?"

"Nope." She adjusted the focus. "Do you remember the pair we saw that one year when we took Em..." Mary stopped abruptly.

Bryan knew where she almost wandered, but she wasn't ready, and neither was he. They would have to go there sometime today—but not yet. He spoke quickly to avoid it, "The young ones? They should have their white head-feathers by now." He looked around at the shoreline and the pattern of the hills, trying to find something else to say to mask the pain he felt beginning to stir. "Do you remember the shape of those rocks?" He pointed at an unusual formation at the top of a bluff. "I told you I thought they looked like a stampede of horses;" Bryan almost smiled, "you said they looked more like a stampede of rocks. I remember what you said because you laughed." He turned to look at her. "I don't think you have since."

Mary acknowledged his words with a long silence, and Bryan instantly regretted saying them. She lowered the binoculars and drew her coat zipper tighter to her chin before going below.

Bryan gazed across the rail at the vast expanse of water windward of their tack and was grateful that they were alone on the lake. Right now, he didn't want to see or be with another human being except for his Mary, and for no reason at all he had just carelessly picked at her wounds.

Left alone in the cockpit and alone on the lake, he sailed for a long while, watching the hills crawl by, wondering how she must feel knowing that she was going to die before summer came again, and he wondered how he was going to go on without her. It was killing him inside.

*****

Mary emerged from the cabin and pushed her hands deep in her coat pockets. She sat across from Bryan with her feet propped up on his legs; her face was turned in profile against the gray hills beyond. He could tell that she was hurting; he knew because of the way she was quiet.

"Potter's cove is just ahead, Mary; I'll reach over to it, so we can get out of this wind and warm up a bit. Maybe we should eat something; I can make us some tea."

She kissed him without saying a word and went forward to get ready to drop the sails. He turned the helm slightly, easing the boom across the cockpit and pointed *Breathless* toward Potter's Cove.

*****

The anchor dropped from its cradle at the bow and splashed through the calm surface; the windlass clicked loudly as Bryan released thirty feet of anchor chain and rode. He let the forward momentum of the boat embed the flukes into the lake bottom, then gave a hard tug on the line to see that it held firmly. He secured it to the forward cleat and waited for the light breeze that filled the cove to ease the stern around toward the shore. Mary had released the sails and let them drape across the foredeck and cabin top. He helped her gather them in loose folds, securing them to the boom and bow rail with short lengths of elastic cord.

Above the cove's shelter, the wind pushed freely through the barren limbs of the walnut and black oak that populated the Ozark hillsides. The native cedars were alone among the trees in their resistance to the turbulence. As if to try and calm the blustery afternoon, they voiced a whispered *hush* in yielding to the moving air. High aloft, a red-tailed hawk soared with outstretched wings in patterns of figure eights, watchful for movement on the forest floor that might signal a late afternoon meal. The waves that reached the end of the cove lapped lightly against the side of the boat, then dissipated their energy in recursive rhythms on the rocky shoreline. Thin fissures in a limestone outcropping freed a spring that spilled down across its face and helped freshen the lake.

Mary leaned against the mast and surveyed the unspoiled landscape. "I don't remember it quite like this; it's been a long time. Beautiful."

Bryan sat on the curved roof of the cabin and let his legs hang over the side; he crossed his arms over the rail. "Yes—very pretty."

Mary sat down with him and let her legs hang next to his. "Do you remember the night on that bluff just before you left for college?" Mary pointed to the ledge at the top of the rock wall towering in front of them, high above the end of the cove. "We had an amazing view across the lake. I remember we stole a bottle of wine and a blanket from my parents' RV and snuck away from their camp, but I think they knew we disappeared, and I'm sure they had a good idea why." She nudged his hip with hers. "The moon was big that night and rose so quickly that it made me dizzy; I could almost feel the earth spinning toward it like we were on a giant rollercoaster. I suppose it could have been the wine."

She kissed his cheek with a girlish smile. "You made love to me then, Bryan, under the moon; it was our first time." She kissed him again and let her lips linger. "I'm glad I can still remember that night; I don't ever want to forget it. Please tell me the story again when I get too..."

He put his fingers gently on her mouth and wrapped his arm around her; "I know; it was wonderful, Mary; I promise I won't ever let you forget."

*****

They sat quietly for a while before Bryan remembered something that he thought would make her happy.

"When we were up there on the bluff, you know, *afterward*—the sailboat; do you remember? You saw it first; it appeared out of nowhere and crossed the lake right in front of us like it was gliding above the water in absolute silence. The sails were shimmering in the moonlight as if they were made of silk. I remember we talked about getting a boat just like it someday so we could sail together under that same moon. Then we talked for hours about what we would do after college, something about white picket fences and swing sets, as I recall."

Mary rested her head on Bryan's shoulder. "I love you, Mr. Rhodes."

"I love you even more."

"Do you remember the name of the sailboat we saw that night, Bryan, the name on the side of the midnight sloop?"

"Of course, lover, how could I ever forget?" He rested his head gently against hers. "*Emma* was her name."

*****

A long time passed as they sat holding each other, listening to the lake gently wash against the shore. Bryan's thoughts were wandering to places he didn't want to go—uncomfortable, frightening places. He wanted to raise the sails and head back out on the lake to cleanse his mind in the wind, but he knew they weren't finished talking. Death was coming to their home again, and there was so much more that needed to be said. He lifted his head and dried his eyes.

"I've always liked this cove, Mary; it's like coming home." *I hope Heaven will be just the same for you.*

She took a deep breath and surveyed the carvings of time in

the stone walls wrapping the cove; she began to gently stroke his hand, threading her fingers neatly in his. "How long do you think it's been, since we last anchored here?"

Bryan hesitated a moment while he thought, then lowered his head when he found the memory. There was always a memory.

"Bryan? Are you okay?" Mary asked.

"I'm fine." He glanced at her bravely but his voice grew shallow. He formed the words with short breaths as if the memory was churning his stomach and bile might suddenly spill from his mouth into the water. "We moored here for the night, in Potter's Cove." He released a sigh. "It was the Fourth of July; it was the last time we watched the fireworks by the dam." '*Last*' was almost inaudible; his voice trailed off even more. "Emma was four or five, I think. It seems like a very long time ago."

Mary kissed him and whispered into his ear. "It *was* a long time ago, lover."

Bryan forced a smile. "They were spectacular that night, the fireworks, I mean. Emma could barely stay awake, even with all the bright explosions and noise. Do you remember?" He drew a breath. "And I promised Emma before we went out on the lake that afternoon, if she was good—" he stopped and let a tear run down his cheek, "—if she was good, we could sleep on the boat in Potter's Cove."

He started to wipe his tear, but Mary did it for him. She looked in silence at the pain on his face, and, like a mirror, Bryan saw it reflect on her too. He pulled her coat tighter around her and let her head fall to his shoulder.

"*If-she-was-good.*" He repeated the four words slowly through his teeth. He placed his head on hers and kissed her hair. "You know, sweetheart," he could feel his voice quivering, "she was always good." He squeezed his eyes tightly and let the tears fall. Mary nodded her head yes.

Bryan said nothing for a while, but as much as it was going to hurt, he knew she wanted him to talk—that's why they had come out on the water. His mind raced with random memories of his little girl that he needed to share but was afraid to release, as if he would lose them when he did. Like moving pictures they flashed through his head: *Emma knee deep in autumn leaves she helped rake in the back yard... the plaster handprint she made him for Father's Day... the scent of her skin and the smell of her breath... the popcorn he pulled from her hair as she slept on the boat on the Fourth of July... her shrouded dead body in his arms...*

Bryan started to get up. Not all of the memories were memories he wanted to keep—but Mary stopped him. It was her turn. He gripped his eyes shut and sat back on the deck, waiting for what she would say. He wasn't sure if he could do this any longer.

"Do you remember that time you called me at the office from the pet store?" She began carefully. "I could hear Emma crying in the background. I think I could pick out her crying in a stadium full of children crying. She was pleading with you to let her talk to me. She had fallen in love with a little orphaned dog in the store. You told me she carried the pitiful thing around with her for an hour and wouldn't put it down. She begged me to let her bring it home. She told me she would care for it; she promised me she would be responsible."

Mary stared over the side at her reflection in the dark water. "I told her no; I was real firm. You know me, the tough prison lady. I told her we already had Molly, and we didn't need another dog. I told her we would get her a new puppy when she was older—a puppy just for her. I can still hear her heart breaking."

Bryan squeezed Mary's hand gently. "Emma was only six years old; she couldn't even pronounce 'responsible'. She wasn't ready for a dog and neither were we. You thought you were pregnant again, and you were hardly at home with your company growing like it was. I was still in the reserves; I had no idea when my next deployment might be. We had our arms full." He moved his hand under her chin and tried to raise her face to look at him. He spoke softer and kinder, "Mary, the timing was all wrong; we couldn't possibly have another dog. Please don't punish yourself, you couldn't have known."

Mary looked directly in his eyes, "I promised her we'd get her a puppy…"

He wanted to look away but couldn't.

"…when she turned seven."

Bryan started to cover his ears; he didn't need to hear what Mary was about to say.

"She never turned seven."

He let her words dissipate across the surface of the cove. There was nothing he could say, or wanted to say, to lessen their damage. The truth sometimes just was.

They sat together silent and broken; Mary with her arms crossed around her folded legs and Bryan with his forehead resting on the railing. She pulled her knees to her chest and placed her face between them; the tears fell freely. Her back shook in spasms as she released the pain. Bryan gently stroked her hair. He wanted her to say something, anything that would help her purge the aching inside, anything except for what she was about to say.

"You weren't home then. You were deployed to some God-awful place, and it was just Emma and me. I dropped her off at the bus stop that morning and went to work, Bryan. I should have waited with her," Mary's voice could hardly be heard, "and for that terrible mistake, I will be eternally punished."

She left him at the rail and went below again. This was the

part he hated most; it was how it always ended whenever they tried to talk about Emma. It ended with Mary's guilt—*and his.*

Bryan stared across the cove with empty eyes. He had been a soldier in a terrible war half-a-world away, but he had never felt more alone or more afraid, until now.

*****

The weak sun had moved behind the bluffs, and the cove was slowly losing daylight; the cold afternoon was drawing to a close. Bryan got up to ready the boat so he could motor back to the marina; he no longer felt like sailing. There were too many memories for them drifting out here on the water, and he wanted to get off the lake before nightfall. They still had the long, silent drive back to St. Louis ahead of them.

Mary surprised him when she suddenly emerged from the companionway with dried eyes; it seemed like they had aged a dozen years. She was holding a large envelope and handed it to Bryan as he climbed down into the cockpit with her.

"What's this, Mary?"

"Open it."

Bryan pulled out a stack of paper; about thirty pages were stapled together. He scanned his eyes over the first page, then the next and the next. At first he didn't understand; the pages appeared to be computer generated reports of some kind. They were full of legal-looking information: plaintiff names, detailed prosecution evidence, trial verdicts, sentencing, incarceration status, release dates, terms of parole, addresses... Every ten to twelve pages held the record of a different man, but the crimes listed all seemed the same: *aggravated assault of a minor, serial child abuse, child molestation...*

"These are convicts, Mary—they're child predators. Where did you get this information?"

"Bryan," Mary sat down and leaned against the bulkhead; she patted the seat so he would sit with her, but he didn't move. "My company manages prisons in seventeen states—*we have resources.* I only printed the first few to show you. It's sickening, but there are tens of thousands just like these, so when I began my search I filtered all the filth that went into the state and federal system during the year after Emma was..." she took a deep breath, "They couldn't find him, Bryan, because he went inside—that has to be why. It makes too much sense. If he was in prison, the attacks would stop, right? The police and FBI said that all their leads were weak and had gone nowhere; they thought surely he would strike again, and that would give them more to go on, but he didn't, and thank God another child didn't have to endure what happened to our baby. I've been watching the reports ever since and there hasn't been anything even close to it. Emma was his first and last; don't you remember?"

"Of course I remember! Dammit, why would you suggest that I didn't? How could I ever forget, Mary?"

"I'm sorry, Bryan. I've been working on this for a long while, and suddenly I'm running out of time. I don't want your pity, but I'll be real sick soon and won't be able to keep sifting through all the files to shorten the list like I had planned." She rubbed her eyes, "Look, I limited my search to inmates who had lived within three hours of our home at the time when Emma was taken. From that search, I generated a list of names, including a file for each with all the information you have in your hand. Almost all of them are still inside; some have been in and out of the system several times, but all of them went in during that period, *during the time of Emma's investigation—* that's how I was able to narrow down the number of names on my list.

I have a protected link to pending release dates; it's updated every few days. Every federal and state lock-up is required to file a notification of release with the D.O.C., and they compile it in their secure database with all this other information. They issue alerts to law enforcement as part of the predator laws, but I can get to it through my security clearance under my corporate login. After I generated each of the files, I copied them to my computer at home and erased them from the company servers. Seventy-eight demons made the cut; Emma's murderer *has* to be one of them. You can start with these three; they're all out on parole now; the others will be getting released later as their sentences run out. The alerts will tell us when. It's just a simple process of elimination."

Mary pressed her finger to the first page. "One day you will find the son-of-a-bitch that murdered our baby. He picked the wrong daughter, Bryan; make sure he knows it when you look into his eyes—*just before you kill him.*"

Bryan leafed through the pages to read the names: Chapman, Randall, Levy. "What do you want me to say?"

"Say that you want him dead." Mary stood up and put her arms around Bryan; she laid her head to his chest for a moment, then pulled away. "Look at me, sweetheart. I'm going back to the cancer center for the last time; I'm not going to be here very much longer…" Tears welled up in her eyes; she was trying hard to smile. She spoke softly, "I'm going to be with her soon, and I'm finding my peace in that—I have to. One day we'll all be together again, but right now this is something you must do for Emma and me. I gave birth to her. I'm her mother. I give you my *permission.*"

Bryan looked up at the top of the bluff where he had first made love to Mary and then out to the main channel across the expanse of empty water; the lake had settled and was patiently waiting for night to arrive. Mary crossed the cockpit and sat at the helm. She gripped the wheel, resting her chin on her hands and just stared at the water; she looked so tired. He thought of all the loss and sadness they had endured together, and now all of that was going to end sadly as well. Something evil took

Emma away from them, and now that evil had returned to claim his wife, *and it made him very angry.*

"I want him dead, Mary—I want them all dead." It was easy. It wasn't a decision. It was like taking one breath before the next.

He leaned into Mary and put his lips to the lips he so loved; then he stepped away and went forward to raise the anchor, because that was the only thing that could happen next. He paused to look up one last time. The clouds had begun to clear and freed the late sun to kiss the tops of the highest trees. He listened to the wind softly whistle through the sleeping Ozark forest; winter was coming soon. High overhead, the red-tailed hawk circled in lazy patterns of figure eights. From a small crack in an ancient limestone ledge, the lake graciously took in all that the spring would give her.

He watched Mary turn the key and felt the engine rumble to life before he heard it. It was time to say goodbye to the cove.

Bryan knew he would never be back.

*****

The computer monitor had timed out and went dark; the photo of Mary on the boat was gone. Bryan entered the sequence of keys that opened the directory he wanted. He found what he was looking for and double-clicked on the file. At the password prompt he typed *1midnightsloop.*

Seventy-eight names filled the screen; nine had a line struck through them. The woman from Moline was not on the list, but her husband was. *The bitch got what she deserved.* It was the same thought he had every time he scrolled across Bart Lowen's name. He found Boyd Duncan, right clicked, and put a strike through it too.

Bryan opened the Internet in another window and keyed in

the Department of Justice website, then selected the inmate locator page. It still irritated him that he wasn't able to access the secure link through Mary's company servers anymore; her partners had shut down her user account just a few days after she died.

I could have been so much further along.

*****

By the time Bryan lowered Mary's body into the ground, he had killed Michael Chapman and Allen Randall; Greg Levy's fate was already set in motion. As Bryan walked away from the cemetery that morning, he decided that his next victim would be the first to receive the brunt of his newly-acquired rage.

One week later he was stuffing Levy's lacerated corpse in a plywood crate and felt quite pleased with the creativity of what he had just done—*the demon's screams had been intoxicating.* But in the wake of that third kill, in the days, weeks and months that followed, Bryan grew unbearably alone and restless. Mary was gone, and he no longer had access to American Corrections—he didn't know when the next demon would be released, and he didn't know what to do with the list. *Mary must be angry...* It took all of his energy to keep from going completely insane.

Then one day, not long after the third anniversary of her death, a miracle appeared to Bryan on the Internet that set him free. Websites began to offer inmate locator services. All that was required was a name or identification number to find one of their demons in prison along with its release information, and Bryan had both. Now he could begin hunting again.

*****

Randomly, he selected one of the remaining sixty-eight

names and entered the I.D. number at the top of the page. A moment later, a window appeared that showed the inmate was still locked away. Bryan tried two more numbers before a date appeared; this one had gotten out five months ago and was living in Fort Wayne, Indiana. *Good.*

He returned to the list and double-clicked on the name; the first page of the predator's file opened; at the top of the screen it said *Hill, Jared Dwayne.* He read through its criminal history and the descriptions of the several victims Hill had claimed; the first was a little girl named Caroline Evans, and she caught Bryan's attention. He sent Jared Dwayne Hill's file to the printer and then closed the website and the Internet. The picture of Mary standing in the companionway of *Breathless* reappeared on the monitor. He leaned in and kissed the screen as the printer released each of the dozen pages that told him everything he needed to know about the next demon he was going to kill.

He reached for the rucksack hanging over the back of his chair and pulled out the wooden box. He put on the pair of cotton gloves he kept inside the lid before carefully removing the pane of red glass with the amber swirl. He held it along the edges and looked through it at the light above the table, through the center where the smudges of Emma's burned fingerprints had been found. He set it on the table and grabbed the glass cutter from the side pocket of the pack and scribed a small piece before snapping it off with his thumb. *That should be enough.*

He put everything back in the box and the box back in the pack. Then he checked to make sure his hand gun was in the bottom compartment and the magazines were fully loaded.

Then he walked outside, passing Mary's dead garden without looking, and entered his workshop.

*****

245

R. BYRON STOCKDALE

−17−

CAROLINE EVANS

C aroline Evans woke just before dawn, like she had every morning since before she could remember. She pulled the same worn robe from the hook behind the closet door and slipped on the same tired house slippers that she kept under the bed. She started to grab the end of the quilt to pull over her pillow but stopped when she felt the soreness in her left thumb. *That's so odd. Now what did you do to yourself this time, Caroline?*

She flipped on the light in the hallway and shuffled from her bedroom toward the kitchen, gazing down at her swollen finger. She paused in the hall bathroom to brush her matted hair. Bits of wood and little clumps of white powder fell into the sink as she did. Even looking in the mirror, she didn't seem to notice. Her eyes were fixed on the mysterious damage to her thumb as it moved up and down with the brush. She thought hard about how she came to hurt herself but quickly lost interest and decided to think about it again later. Besides, her head hurt and her bladder felt full, but that would also have to wait until after breakfast. *You know the order, Caroline; the doctor said you must stay with your routine if you ever want to get well again.*

She stopped at the grandfather clock that crowded the narrow hall and carefully moved the little hand from the four to the five. It lost an hour every day and, almost without knowing, she corrected it each morning on her way to the kitchen. She didn't remember where the clock had come from but couldn't remember a time when it wasn't there in her hall. Side-to-side, tick-then-tock, the pendulum swept through its lonely arc slowly failing in its measurement of time like a pulse that can't quite keep up with the life it was supposed to sustain.

Next she straightened the sampler of the Lord's Prayer hanging beside the clock. Her grandmother had stitched it when she was little and left it to her when she died. It hung next to a single photograph, the only picture she kept in the house, and she adjusted that too, just as she did yesterday and would do again tomorrow. It was a black and white photo taken of a woman next to a taller man, a handsome man with a thick beard, and two older boys. They looked to be standing in the busy midway of a summer carnival. On the right side of the image was a pretty young girl, perhaps eight or nine years old, off by herself. Some days Caroline knew these people as her family and the girl as her. Most days she didn't and struggled to understand why their picture was even in her house, but she never dared to consider taking it down. *Sudden change is bad, Caroline. Don't you remember what the doctor told you?*

In the photo, the handsome man's arm was draped over the woman's shoulder; his big forearm folded across her chest; the other extended toward the little girl as if to pull her closer to him in the picture. Oddly, she felt his eyes in her past looking directly at her eyes in his future. She reached out to touch him through the glass; a tender smile surprised Caroline's face and then disappeared. She glanced up the stairs climbing above the picture and clock and yelled to the empty bedrooms. "Mom, can I make breakfast now?" *Oh wait; silly Caroline! This is Saturday; let her sleep for heaven's sake. Daddy has to mow the lawn before we can eat. You know that we never eat breakfast on Saturday until daddy is finished cutting the grass.*

She listened for the mower through the walls of the house, but it was quiet outside. She turned back to the girl in the picture standing in the carnival midway and tried to form a thought out loud, but the only word she could speak was her name.

"Caroline?"

One of her five cats threaded through and around her ankles, purring loudly. "Oh, Sammie, are you hungry again? *Him's a little sweet kitty, the best little kitty in the whole world—yes him is!*

Okay, momma's going to get you some food; you're an impatient little guy, aren't you? Yes you are." *Yes you are, you fuckin' little cat.*

She reached down and scratched the animal roughly between his ears then gripped her hand firmly around its neck, pulling its face toward hers. "If he asks for a fish, will momma give Sammie a serpent?" The instant she released the cat, it scurried away down the hall and up the stairs. The agitation that just visited upon her left as fast as it had appeared and was already forgotten, but it would come again.

She stood up and adjusted the picture one more time. In the photograph, the girl held a little toy horse and an ice cream cone that had melted over her hand and down her arm. She wasn't smiling into the camera like everyone else, but seemed to be looking past it at someone or something beyond the photographer. Behind the girl, a crowd of people stood in a long line that grew blurry as it stretched into the distance. Through the steel lattice of carnival rides that rose above them, dark clouds filled the sky. For a moment, Caroline thought that the girl looked afraid, like something bad was going to happen to her, and she felt afraid too. *The storm is going to get you, Caroline!*

Then she remembered her nightmare, the nightmare she had again last night:

She was running with the bearded man and the two boys to escape a terrible thunderstorm, but it had come upon them too suddenly. A fierce, confused wind screamed at them from every direction. Tables with colorful umbrellas tumbled across their path. They were running toward a massive wall that filled their vision, an endless light-blue surface with a single purple-red door, and it seemed like they were being beckoned toward a clear sky on the other side of the storm; if only she could get through the door! In front of it, a carousel of disfigured horses turned in disconnected images, as if from a camera that had only captured their dance every few seconds; her only escape appearing and disappearing behind each horrible animal as it flashed by. The young girl from the picture was running with Caroline, but her short legs were moving too slowly, slowing them down. She could feel the warm stickiness of the ice cream filling her hand as she pulled her along. The handsome man and the boys were running ahead and getting farther and farther away. The distance separating them was growing so fast that Caroline became frightened she might never see them again.

A violent burst of wind and rain suddenly broke their grip. She spun around to grab the young girl's hand again, but she had disappeared somewhere into the storm. And Caroline could now see that the stickiness on her hand wasn't ice cream at all— it was blood. As she turned, terrified, back toward the others, they had disappeared too, beyond the carousel and the purple-red door and the cloudless mirage of the light blue wall.

*****

As quick as it had appeared, the memory just stopped. Caroline leaned her forehead against the wall and tried to think, but couldn't recall what happened next. A chill crawled across the back of her neck. *The tempest comes out from its chamber— the cold from the driving winds...*

She pulled her robe tighter to her shoulders and shook off the feeling. "So sayeth the Lord; right, little Sammy?"

*****

Caroline entered the kitchen and switched on the light above the electric stove. After moving a dirty skillet to the sink, she turned on the empty burner, holding her hand above the metal spiral until it began to glow red. She crossed the floor to fill the dish by the trash can with kibble and added some fresh water to the bowl beside it. At the end of the counter, an effusion of light from a muted television flickered across the walls and animated the ceiling with a pulsing, bluish glow. It was always on, tuned soundlessly to the twenty-four hour weather channel; filling the corner of the room with silent images of a turbulent world not so removed from her own abandoned and confused existence.

She pulled a carton of eggs and the last of a loaf of bread from the refrigerator and proceeded to prepare the same breakfast she made every day: a fried egg on one slice of thin, dry toast that she served herself on the same yellow plate with the same yellowed silk napkin that her grandmother had embroidered for her when she was a little girl. It was the same meal she knew from then, from the lost times, and the doctor had told her that the certainty of its appearance on her table, and the smell and color and taste of it every day, would help her regain some of her memories. The doctor had also told Caroline that even if her mind still failed her, at least the sameness of her routine would make the anxiety of facing each unfolding hour perhaps a little more tolerable.

She sat at the table and bowed her head. "I am the bread of life. Whoever comes to me will never go hungry. Lord, if we eat we are better, if we eat not, Lord we are the worst." Finishing her prayer, she opened her eyes and studied her meal in the weak glow that reached across the table from the light above the stove. When she saw that the bread was burned along one edge of the crust, she jumped to her feet knocking over her chair. "Unacceptable!" She grabbed the loaf off the counter and counted out the remaining slices. *Three? Three fucking slices? Really?*

"What the hell is wrong with you, Caroline!? This is unacceptable!" She took several short breaths, shaking her head violently side to side as fragmented thoughts clicked by in her mind. *Okay, the nice young lady from across town comes on*

Tuesday and drives me to the market. You only get in the brown car with the white top, Caroline. Yes, Tuesday is shopping day with Alyssa—no, that's not right; it's Allison with the 'n'. That's it, you must remember it's the 'n', Caroline, not the 'a'. Oh, Allison is such a good driver, but she does drive too fast!

She paced the floor from the table to the stove and back, again and again. *Tuesday is... uh, today is Saturday; I need to get mom up. Wait, that's wrong, I still have to wait for daddy to cut the grass first before it gets too hot outside, but one slice is for Sunday and one is for Monday, and the last one is for Tuesday. Okay, I'm okay. If I can just eat this fuckin' burnt bread now, I'll be okay.*

She closed her eyes and swallowed a bite of the fried egg on the ruined toast. *You cannot partake of the table of the Lord and the table of demons Caroline...*

She fought the urge to vomit and forced down another bite. *You better finish your food, Caroline, or the doctor will be very disappointed!*

Maybe, she thought, her mistake wouldn't matter this time if no one told the doctor, but maybe it would... *It bringeth forth sin; and sin, when it is finished, bringeth forth death...*

As the first hint of early sun threatened to wake her house to the idle sameness of yet another day, Caroline Evans stood calmly in the middle of her kitchen, between the table and the stove, licking the yellow plate.

*****

When her tongue grew tired, she wiped her mouth on the sleeve of her robe and stepped to the sink. She dipped the plate in the cold dish water left standing from the night before and placed it in the rack to dry. Next she grabbed the skillet from the stove and tossed it in the sink. *It—burned my damn bread!*

She grabbed a rusted pad of steel wool and scrubbed on it violently, turning the water oily brown. "Wash you, make you clean and then, and then I will... I will sprinkle clean water upon you; put away the evil of your doings, and ye shall be clean from your filthiness from before... from before mine eyes!" It annoyed her that the stuttered, jumbled verses spewed out of her mind and across her lips without effort or invitation. She swatted at the air around her as if the words were invisible gnats encircling her head and then, when she thought they were gone, she cupped her hands over her mouth. *Shushhh!!! Quiet now, Miss Evans, not so loud please; you might distract my driving. It's okay—be still. There is no one else in the car. See? We're almost to the store, and you have to be calm. I'll slow down a bit for you; there, that should help. Why don't you tell me all about your week? Do you need any bread?*

Caroline grabbed the plate from the rack and started to lick it again. The words of the nice young lady from across town played back from somewhere inside her troubled brain as she tasted the soapy porcelain. *Healing is a slow process, Miss Evans. These things do take some time.*

She shuffled past the television toward the hall, holding the plate to her mouth and lingered for just a moment, studying with some interest, the grainy images of a violent storm unfolding on the other side of the world. She made her way to the living room and dropped the plate in the basket filled with junk mail and old magazines that she kept below the big window that looked out over the porch and front yard. Next to it was a small table and the soft chair where she would idly pass much of this day. She opened the curtains just enough to let in a hint of the early morning and checked the empty street to make sure no one saw her. *For He maketh his sun to rise on the good... and the evil.*

She measured the light that fell across the chair and closed the gap between the drapes by half, leaving just a slice of early daylight, enough for her to sit and look through the small pile of mail that she had collected from the box at the street two nights before. She was especially tired yesterday and had left the mail for the morning, when she thought she might feel a little better. The fireplace smelled of burnt paper and melted plastic and she vaguely recalled burning her trash yesterday morning... or maybe it was the morning before. *For God is a consuming fire.*

Caroline looked at the half-smoked cigarette left in the ash tray and the empty glass on the table next to it. She remembered filling it last night with bourbon but couldn't remember how many times she did. She gathered the mail and set it on her lap. There was an opened letter on the floor that she reached down to collect also, and without looking at it, she folded it and placed it on the top of the stack. She wrapped her hand around her sore thumb and felt the pulse push against her grip. Releasing it, she raised it in front of her face, curiously studying the obvious clue to an unobvious riddle. Her brain searched the clouded time between when she ate dinner and when she somehow made her way to bed, but found nothing at all. She cursed herself for her drunken sloth. *Who hath woe? Who hath sorrow, Caroline? Who hath redness of eyes? Who hath wounds without cause?*

"I do!" She shouted out loud. *Drunkards shall not inherit the Kingdom! You are weak, Caroline; you are a very weak woman.*

She closed the curtains and settled herself on the edge of the chair, rocking gently back and forth, then closed her eyes also. Yesterday had been a bad day, but she decided it didn't really matter, and she didn't really care. It was Saturday now, and that day was Friday. She would take her time going through the mail, but decided it could wait until later. Breakfast had upset her. She glanced down at the letter on the top of the pile and thought there was something she needed to do but couldn't think of it. *You keep yourself busy, Caroline, if you want to feel better. The medications can only help you so much.*

The doctor said she would need things to do to help pass her days, but right now she wanted to do nothing. She wanted to feel nothing too and closed her eyes again, waiting for the quiet to calm her mind. The pressure in her bladder helped clear her thoughts. Calmly, she disciplined her urge to pee. *Not yet Caroline—soon. Through faith and patience you will inherit what is promised.*

*****

The minutes crawled by, and the house grew still. Everything was silent except for the lonely pulse of the clock down the hall. For a strangely lucid moment, Caroline became keenly aware that the tick-tock-tick of the pendulum was not quite keeping pace with each second that passed.

Then, beyond the window, something felt suddenly familiar; a long-ago memory that had attached to a sound—a sound that she could now hear. She opened her eyes and jumped to her feet; the mail spilled to the floor as she did. She stood in front of the closed curtains, listening, wishing with dread for what couldn't possibly be. Outside, the idle hum of a lawnmower pushed through the glass and brought the sketch of a morning she knew from years ago. That morning belonged to her, and that sound belonged to her too. Caroline found the memory.

The man with the beard was walking behind the mower, pushing it from the driveway to the fence at the side of the house and back again. In and out of the long shadows, he crossed the yard, over and over. From the steps of the porch, young Caroline had watched him on that beautiful spring day. Daddy?

Tears began to fall from her eyes. She had found him again.

The man in the picture is my daddy.

In her mind he turned to smile at her, standing now at the window, but the curtains were still closed. She reached to open them but stopped, her wrinkled hands quivering at the edge of

255

the lace. Somehow she knew he wouldn't be there on the other side, and the sight of the empty yard frightened her. The cadence of the mower pulled her from the window to the door, but she didn't want to open it either. He couldn't be there, she was sure. That was impossible. *They're dead Caroline. They're all dead.*

Gathering her robe around her, she tightened the sash and wiped her eyes before stepping out onto the porch.

The yard was empty, the grass still overgrown. Newspapers wrapped in their plastic sleeves lay scattered along the walk where they had fallen; trash overflowed from the cart that sat at the end of the driveway. She could hear the mower but not see it; the sound came from across the street and several houses away. Tears filled her eyes again, but as she wiped them dry, she noticed a glimmer of light at the edge of her vision. A small piece of red glass hung on a plastic thread from a nail driven into the side of her house. A hammer lay below it on the porch, leaned against the wall. She looked down at her sore thumb. *He drove the peg through her temple and she died?!*

Agitation quickly found her again. She kicked the hammer into the bushes losing a slipper as she did. With a snap of her foot, she flicked the other shoe high into the air and watched it bounce against a tree before disappearing into the tall grass. *Fuckin' neighbor boy, dammit!*

Her mind rattled. *Can't he leave me be? Evil miscreant, always up to his wicked shit! I'll kill the little prick when I find him!*

She yanked the pendant from the wall and wrapped it tightly around her hand. "I'll show you what-for, you rat-bastard!" She screamed at the vacant cars parked along the empty street.

Caroline rushed back into the house, shouting to her imagined father. "Daddy!" *Where the hell is your gun?!*

She threw open the door to the closet below the stair and

reached into a thicket of moth-eaten coats, her hand blindly grabbing back and forth until she felt the cold steel. *There will be righteousness when you burn my bread!*

Confused anger overwhelmed her. She swung the rifle around, knocking over the lamp on the table next to the closet. Her momentum carried her through the open door, across the porch, the yard, and to the edge of the street. Her heart pounded heavy in her chest. *I know where you live, you little horse fucker! You WILL appear before the Judgment!*

She took three more measured steps on to the pavement and stopped.

And there she stood, barefoot and defiant in the middle of the street. Her robe had fallen open, exposing two white, sagging breasts that pointed toward the ground. Warm pee flowed down between her legs and spilled around her feet.

An approaching car slowed and steered to the curb to avoid hitting her, but she didn't move. The driver's eyes flashed wide at the insanity of the scene. She chambered a round and aimed the rifle toward the car. The pendant sparkled red as it dangled from her hand, gripping the stock of the gun. *His mischief will return upon him, and his violence will descend upon his soul!*

Then Caroline slowly lowered the gun, searching for the driver through the windshield, but the car was backing away into the low morning sun, her sight blinded by the intense light.

Allison? Is that you?

*****

−18−

OPPORTUNITY

Tom's desk was cluttered more than usual. He had spent the morning looking through a box of cold case files he had brought home from the Bureau. It was a long shot, but one of the unsolved murders in the box might have been the work of SRK. The loose piles of folders stacked at each end of his desk left only a small area in between, barely wide enough for his laptop, cell phone, and a now-empty cup of coffee. He listened intently to the voice on the other end of the call coming through the speaker while he scanned through a budget memo from Grainger.

Kate was in the room behind him, somewhat pacing back and forth. She hoped the call might bear a little good news in the case. They had spent another late night working, just allowing themselves a few hours of rest around 4:00 a.m. Tom slept intermittently, leaned back in his desk chair. Kate, on the couch, had stayed awake trying to fill in the gaps between some random and related thoughts behind closed eyes. It wasn't yet mid-morning.

"S.A.C. Russell, S.A. Morrow, um, this is Lieutenant Wade Jennings with the Gibson Police Department in Gibson, Indiana. We had an FBI alert come across on our N-DEx recently, said you folks were interested in any information about reports of an anonymous letter requesting the recipient's permission to six, um, I mean kill a specific sexual predator that had previously victimized the recipient. Let's see, there's a reference to glass and, um, a locket of some kind…"

"Pendant." Kate interrupted officer Jennings before he could finish the sentence. She knew what the alert said and was too tired to hear it read back to her. They had posted it a month earlier on the N-DEx national information and situational awareness system. Any law enforcement agency with access to the FBI's law enforcement portal would have seen the alert. The Gibson police department had an intern that monitored activity on the portal and provided an email briefing for the officers each day.

"Please tell us what you're working with, lieutenant," Kate said.

Lt. Jennings got to the point as best he could. "We recovered a letter from a private residence where we answered a couple of 911 calls early this morning. One call was from a motorist who said the homeowner pointed a rifle at him as he drove in front of her house. He saw her run back inside afterward. The other call came from a neighbor across the street who said a lady was disrobed and peeing in the middle of the pavement. Funny thing; he didn't even mention the gun or the car. Anyway, let's see, there was also the piece of colored glass, um, red, attached to some kind of fishing line; looked like eight-pound test to me. The post office believes it was delivered two days ago, but it could have been earlier. We can only speculate because the carrier that has that route remembered the owner yelling at him for trying to pet one of her cats in the front yard— God forbid. He's not had to deliver any mail to her address since.

We couldn't find an envelope with a postmark, so we don't know the origin or when it might have been mailed. The homeowner apparently nailed the pendant to the front of her house per the instructions in the letter, but she took it down for some reason. She's quite agitated, I might add. Anyway, we're running prints on all of it now but don't expect we'll find anything that doesn't belong to her. The recipient is a one Caroline Evans, um, white, fifty-eight, lives alone with four or maybe five cats. We know her pretty well here at the PD—nothing serious, mostly complaints from the neighbors calling when she acts up from time to time. She's certifiably crazy, by the way. Keeps some old rusty hunting rifles like the one she waved around half-naked in the street. They probably don't shoot, but we took them in anyway. Apparently she's been there in the same house for all of her life... hold on." They could hear some chatter on a police radio in the background. A few seconds later Lt. Jennings continued, "Sorry, I'm manning the console this morning until our dispatcher gets in. She had a doctor appointment—you know how it—"

"Wade?" Kate interrupted.

"Um, yes, sorry. Caroline's mom and dad were killed in a car crash about thirty-five years ago and had left everything to her. She had two older brothers. The younger of the two died in the wreck with the parents. The other brother was by her mom's first marriage and was quite a few years older than her. Wendy, that's our dispatcher, dated him for a short stretch in the mid-sixties when Ms. Evans was about ten or eleven. She said he moved out west soon after, San Diego she thinks, and got caught up in drugs. Looks like he deceased a while back, but we don't know the C.O.D. Caroline has a nephew by him in Arizona and that's about it. The rest of our information is a little sketchy, but she might have some second or third cousins around here somewhere but no local relatives that we know of for sure. Her grandparents on her dad's side did have a farm over in Highland, but the property sold shortly after they passed on."

Kate responded first talking over Tom's shoulder. "Does Ms. Evans have anything in her jacket about any victim history such as rape or sexual assault?"

"Negative Agent Morrow; that threw us a little bit with your N-DEx alert. There's nothing. If she does, um, have any history, it would have to be as a juvenile. We can't pull anything up like that without a court order."

"Get one." Kate said. "Have it for us when we get there this afternoon."

"What do you want me to tell Judge Martin?" Lieutenant Jennings asked.

Kate continued impatiently, "Tell him or *her* that this event appears to be directly related to an ongoing FBI investigation dealing with the apprehension of a known serial killer that's been targeting sexual predators of children. We believe Ms. Evan's juvenile history will likely confirm this. The body count currently stands at six, with one additional target that survived his wounds. We suspect there are other bodies that we haven't found, since his early kill sites appear to have been deliberately obscure and scattered across a wide swath of Midwestern states. There will be at least one more if Ms. Evans has succeeded in signaling our UNSUB her permission for him to kill again. That's a real possibility, given when you said the letter was delivered to her house. She may have had the pendant on display for the better part of a couple of days now, depending on when she opened the package and how quickly she acted on it.

If he's received her blessing, he'll have a significant head start in carrying out his next kill. Keep in mind that he already knows who his target is and where to find him. That would put him at least one day ahead of us, which is all the time he'll need. Tell the judge that the identification of the target will likely be in Caroline's juvenile history, and we are out of time."

"Roger that." Wade Jennings started to ask a question, but his voice trailed off as if he was distracted by more chatter on his police radio.

"For the time being, Lieutenant, let's assume we got lucky, and the UNSUB hasn't yet shown up. Have a couple of officers keep an eye on the house until we can get there."

"Yes ma'am."

"If he does come looking for the signal, a uniformed officer will spook him off, and we'll lose this chance—so no uniforms. We're looking for a white male in his mid-to-late-thirties; strong build, well over six feet. He'll most likely be in a vehicle, but he could be on foot just walking by the house if he thinks he needs to take a closer look. Either way, he'll pause just long enough to find his answer. Do you have a white female officer on staff?"

"Yes ma'am; that would be Maggie; I mean Officer Pace," Jennings responded.

"Good. That's even better. Have Officer Pace sit on Ms. Evans porch for a few hours, just until we get there. She'll need to be in casual, just-another-lazy-morning-reading-a-book type clothes. It's unlikely that our UNSUB will show up during daylight, but it's a remote possibility. Did Ms. Evans hang the pendant where it could be easily seen from the street?"

"Well, I'm not real sure." Jennings' answer sounded hesitant and a little apologetic, like he should have done something obvious but hadn't thought of it. "She had it wrapped around her hand when we questioned her in the house. We wouldn't have paid any real attention to it except she made sure to point it out to us. We just thought it was her jewelry or something. That was before we saw the letter. She showed us where it was hanging, but I didn't check to see how visible it would have been from the street. She doesn't remember nailing it to her house; thinks it was some neighbor's kid pulling a prank on her. We found the opened letter inside on her living room floor, but when we showed it to her, she acted like she was seeing it for the first time. Like I said, she's about a half-bubble off. After she read a few lines, she got real upset, threw it back on the floor and locked herself in the bathroom."

"Give us a minute, lieutenant." Tom pressed the mute button. "What do you think Kate?"

"I think we should have them hang the pendant, but not in plain view. As we now know, he needs the victim's permission to act for some reason and will probably have a lot of head space already invested in this kill. SRK *needs* to find it, but let's not make it easy for him. I don't think he's been by the house yet, or that's what I want to believe at this point. If the letter was delivered only a couple of days ago, that's probably too soon for him to show up. He would have allowed a conservative amount of time for the letter to arrive in the little town of Gibson and then make it to her mailbox. He'd also want to make sure Ms. Evans had enough time to make her decision—but not enough time to change it. His offer takes a little cerebral processing time, and he knows it. He needs the kill but understands not everyone he contacts will feel the same, at least not right away. Based on the delivery date, it's unlikely that Ms. Evans had known the contents of the letter for much more than twenty-four to forty-eight hours."

"That's not enough time for most ordinary people to make that kind of decision," Tom said, "although I'd probably have the pendant swinging in the breeze in just under five minutes."

"You're not ordinary Tom—but you are right about how most people would process his offer. So let's assume SRK allows three or four days for Caroline to contemplate the letter before he comes looking for her decision, and I definitely think he'll be careful to make sure he's clear on what that decision is before moving on. If we hang the pendant where it's plain to see, SRK might spot it easily from a moving car and be on his way without attracting anyone's attention. If he doesn't see it, he'll spend more time lingering to find it, and time is what we need. He'll hang around long enough to confirm it's absolutely there or it's absolutely not. If he's in a car, we want to force him to get out on foot—maybe approach the house. My guess is it might irritate him enough that he could make an error, and that error will make catching him a bit more likely. You and I should be inside. We'd catch SRK totally off guard if we came at him from in the house. We'll want things to appear normal, and normal means there should be a woman shuffling around inside. Besides, he won't be expecting the front door to open, but when

it does, he'll expect to see a female. If I'm there it could buy us a few crucial seconds. If we don't catch him in Gibson, we should get another shot when he goes after this target; that is if the judge comes through, and if SRK doesn't make us at the house. I know—*if, if, if.* Once we have the history on Ms. Evans, it should be easy to put eyes on her perp and be waiting there when the SRK comes to claim his prize." Kate paused a few seconds to process another thought that couldn't be avoided. "It's crazy when you think about it."

"What's crazy?" Tom asked.

"Well, some sorry-ass assaults young Ms. Evans—real bad I suspect. It happened what, maybe forty, forty-five years ago? He probably doesn't even remember her or even what he did to her. Who knows how many more victims he took over all those years? I doubt she was his only one or else he wouldn't have shown up on SRK's radar. So he'd be at least in his early sixties by now but could be much older. Picture this: he's long outlived his proclivities, sitting on his front porch all relaxed, sipping his nightly Milk of Magnesia in some idyllic little southern retirement community, sun's setting, old dog at his feet; Social Security check's waiting in the mailbox. Life is good, right? SRK strolls up, says all howdy-pleasant-like, 'lovely evening mister, nice dog, how about those Braves?' So Mr. Sorry-ass invites him to have a seat and stay for a little visit, maybe even offers him a glass of sweet tea. An hour later, Sorry-ass is gripping the side of his bathtub with his insides now on his outsides, hopelessly trying to recall who the hell Caroline Evans even was. *That,* Tom, is crazy."

"Yep, that's crazy alright." Tom un-muted the phone. "Lieutenant, we're going to assume that the UNSUB has not been by Ms. Evan's house and proceed accordingly. Re-hang the pendant where it's not easily seen from the street. We want the killer to have to look for it. If he doesn't see it, he'll likely approach the house on foot to confirm. We want to make him work for it, to pull him out in the open. Officer Pace needs to act domesticated on the porch, like she's just enjoying the beautiful spring morning, but she needs to scrutinize every person or car that goes by for anything that looks suspicious. Have a couple of cruisers close in the area, but keep them off her street and the surrounding streets. We prefer that they're not mobile. The more they move, the more likely they'll be seen. Stage them in restaurant parking lots or more populated venues where they likely won't stand out. We're confident our UNSUB will sweep the area for any scent of the law before he goes in for a closer look. Our people will arrive to set up discreet video surveillance ASAP. If the UNSUB hasn't shown up, we have zero to no time to get in place before he comes looking; he won't waste a lot of time coming for his instructions. S.A. Morrow and I have a few more minutes before we need to leave for the airport. We should be there by noon. It would help if you could give us a description of the house and surrounding properties."

The lieutenant answered in surprisingly thorough detail. "Sir, ma'am, it's a solid working-class neighborhood a bit on the decline since they closed the fertilizer plant a few years back. The house is an old brick bungalow, with a half-level upstairs tucked under the roof. It sits sixty feet back from the sidewalk, large oaks each side of the street about thirty feet apart. One-way traffic east to west, a few cars parked each side most of the time, especially at night when folks that still have a job get off from work. Ms. Evans' house is on the south side facing north, so the front's in shade and makes it hard to see much detail in bright daylight. Um, there are two more large oaks each side of a large front porch, and the grass and landscaping are seriously overgrown. Neighbor houses are close on either side, maybe twenty-five feet apart on the east with a shared drive and maybe twenty feet on the west where there is no drive. She has a one-car garage in back but no car. Small rear yard—overgrown also. Has a five-foot privacy fence in bad repair between her and the house to her south and no gate. The neighbors behind and each side of her have a pretty similar set-up, except their places are in decent shape. The house just east of her is vacant, up for sale."

"Excellent," Tom responded with a note of optimism. He spoke to Kate while Jennings listened on the line. "We'll set up our surveillance team next door in the vacant house. Lieutenant Jennings needs to talk to the real estate agent to keep her or him away. No appointments until we get through this. He can tell the agent it will only be two to three days, and we'll tidy up Ms. Evans' yard as part of the deal. Once we're set up in the house, no one will come or go for the next seventy-two hours, so we'll make sure we're well provisioned. We'll load in from the back yard and do it quickly. Hopefully the neighbors are mostly at work and don't get in our way. If they do, we'll make sure they understand it's some benign police matter, to mind their own business, there's nothing to worry about, etcetera. Our UNSUB could monitor local police channels, so limit your communication to walk-around mode or cell phones only. We'll get Gibson set up with some encrypted devices when we arrive."

Lt. Jennings spoke hesitantly. "Sir, ma'am, all this manpower you're talking about is going to be a problem for us. You haven't seen Gibson, but it's a small town with a small-town police budget. Our normal workload doesn't require much in the way of staff. Gibson is a pretty peaceful place mostly; nothing serious happens much around here. This will be the first big deal we've seen since forever. Usually we rely on the Washington County Sheriff for the heavy lifting, and they cover the night shift for us. Not counting me and the chief, we have six officers, a couple of reserves, one intern and just three cruisers. They're a little tired, um, the cars I mean, and one's still in the shop with a broke transmission.

"That won't be a problem, lieutenant," Tom answered. "Your people will concentrate on the perimeter net; we'll take care of the surveillance and close-in work. I'll mobilize a team out of our New Albany Resident Agency as soon as we're off this call." Tom was looking at a map of the FBI's Indiana Division on his laptop. "They should be there before we are. We'll put a second team on stand-by in Bloomington in case we need more help. We can evaluate our resources once we get there. Don't worry about it, we should be just fine. Also, we think our UNSUB will most likely *not* be armed, but we can't be sure. We don't believe he's dangerous to anyone except his prey, but if he's cornered and does have a weapon, he will most likely use it to avoid capture. He's an excellent shot, by the way."

"Yes sir—understood."

Kate continued, "In the meantime, lieutenant, contact a landscaping company to trim up any low hanging limbs or tall shrubs that block a clear view to the street from the for-sale house next door. Bribe them to show up this morning, and send us the bill. From what you describe, a crew sprucing up the yard might normally look a little out of place in that neighborhood, but since the house is for sale, it shouldn't generate too much gossip."

"Roger that," Jennings responded immediately. "Anything else you need me to set up before, um, your people get here?"

Kate answered in a friendly but firm tone. "We can't over-emphasize the importance of being invisible with this guy. We think seventy-two to ninety-six hours after the letter arrives is likely when he comes for a look. He doesn't want to give anyone a chance to change their mind, but he won't be sloppy either. If it smells bad he won't like it, but he'll move on to his next opportunity."

They ended the call. Kate moved a stack of folders to the floor and sat on the edge of Tom's desk. Her eyes brightened when she leaned into him for a kiss. "Let's go get him, Tom."

*****

–19–

BROKEN LIVES

Gibson, Indiana, was a typical rural small Midwestern town with streets mapped out from the main square in a grid aligned more or less with the compass points. When the federal highway came through in the early 1950's, about six miles east of Gibson, they may as well have plowed the town under as avoid it. The highway turned out to be just close enough not to kill it quickly and mercifully, but far enough away to slowly bleed off almost every measure of progress achieved by the town since the first cornerstone was laid just after the Civil war. It didn't take long for the steady stream of travelers on the interstate to convince most of the local businesses to abandon their handsome brick and limestone edifices downtown to cluster in cheap metal buildings next to the single highway interchange that connected anyone left in Gibson to anywhere they wanted to go. The old state road still came through town but saw little use, except for the local farmers that came in every couple of weeks to pick up provisions at the IFA feed store and maybe take in the daily lunch special at Hannah's restaurant.

Kate was navigating a Google map on her smart tablet, snacking on a bag of corn chips she bought from a vending machine at the Clark Regional Airport where they had landed just a half hour earlier. She looked up as Tom slowed the rental car at the top of the exit ramp and stopped. The sign in front of them indicated that Scottsburg was just a mile to the right and Gibson was six miles down State Highway 56 to the left.

"Tom, there are five primary ways in and five out, so there will be a lot of checkpoints to set up in a hurry if our boy takes flight. He could take 56 here back to the interstate or west through Salem; State Road 39 heads north out of the center of town, and there's a short connection to Old Highway 56 heading southwest and southeast. That's about it for improved roads." Kate tapped on the screen. "I've traced a number of these smaller streets that lead out of town, and most head a few miles into the country and turn to gravel. Most of them dead-end at someone's property, but some eventually find their way back to blacktop. A number of them cross into Scott County and link up with two-lanes that cross into Jackson County up north and Clark County to the south. I'd say they're all in play if SRK gets spooked."

Tom was scrolling through the recent email subject headings on his cell phone, looking for anything recent from Lt. Jennings. When Kate stopped talking, he tossed it back in the console between them. He glanced at the mirror for any cars coming up behind them, but there weren't any. "All bets are off if he runs. He's smart and will have assumed by now that the Bureau is involved or will be eventually. I don't think you can approach people and offer to kill another human on their behalf without considering one or two might object to the principle of the thing and let the authorities know about it. Remember the Hoffmans? If he senses we're this close, he might change his game or go quiet for years. We'd have to start over, Kate. I've been there before, so let's avoid that cluster if possible." Tom re-checked his mirror. "My guess is he plans to come in and leave by the interstate, nice and quiet. Once he makes it back to this interchange, it doesn't matter which way he turns. He'll be just another car on the highway. I suppose we might think him clever to work his way cross-country, but why would he? If it all goes like he expects, he's come and gone without raising so much as an owl's eyebrow. No sense risking a breakdown or mishap on some one-lane gravel road out there with all the nosey farmers around. That horse would be hard to get back in the barn."

"So it's Mr. Country Boy now, is it? All owls, barns and horses all of a sudden? Should we find us a honky-tonk to get some cold beer, vittles and a little Loretta Lynn on the jukebox?" Kate walked her fingers across his thigh. "Giddy-up partner?"

Tom could only manage half a grin. He turned left from the exit ramp and drove a hundred yards to the three-way stop sign and made another left to stay on the state road. It ran parallel to the interstate for a quarter of a mile, then curved west into open country. On both sides of the road soft green fields, dotted with round bales of freshly cut spring hay, rolled gently toward the horizon. Cattle grazed blithely under a low overcast sky. Three miles farther, they passed a small brick motel with a single car parked in front of the office. Next to it was Hannah's restaurant with a half-dozen pickups scattered around the gravel lot.

"Kate, get Lieutenant Jennings to have a plain-clothe check out the guest registry at that motel. Our guy's not likely to get a room, but we need to be sure. Maybe he settles in for few days to scope out some final details or as part of his pre-kill ritual. I doubt it, but shoot, I don't know. Forget it. It doesn't fit the profile. Our guy's a vigilant hunter, not a sociopath, at least not yet. I don't want to over-think this, Kate." Tom paused. "On second thought, we better check it anyway. Grainger would chew my ass if he could hear me right now. Jesus, I really could use some sleep."

Kate nodded in agreement, then relayed the message to Lieutenant Jennings on her cell phone. When she finished, she rode along in silence as the green fields gave way to shaded yards and small, but tidy white homes on the outskirts of Gibson. A mile later, a few brick commercial buildings began to fill in at the side of the road; half of them looked empty.

"So what's your take on all this?" Tom asked. "I mean what's your read on Caroline Evans? I need a woman's perspective."

Kate didn't smile. "Well, she had to be a victim as a young

girl years ago. It just fits. Maybe it was at the hands of someone she knows or knew back then. The little prick might still live somewhere in this half-a-town, but he probably moved on a while ago to better hunting grounds, or at least someplace where no one knew him. This *is* a small town, after all. Obviously he'll have done some time and be in the system. It's scary to think that Ms. Evans would stay in Gibson all these years and in the same house to dwell among her ghosts. Even if it didn't happen in that house, she would have re-lived the nightmare every night alone in her bed. It sounds like the damage festered all these years and caused her to go bananas. She's likely too far gone for any closure that an SRK kill might bring to help. But if it was up to me, I'd sure give him the opportunity to *try*." Kate paused to shake off the feeling. "Tom, do you think I should be hoping instead that Jennings made some hay with the judge?"

"Hay? Now who's gone all country?" Tom pulled into an empty space between the two Gibson Police cruisers that were parked in back of the old courthouse on the square. The sign in front of them read "Police Vehicles Only - $200 Fine". He turned off the engine and looked directly at Kate. "If Jennings was able to convince the judge, I suspect we'll know what we need to know about Caroline Evans soon enough."

*****

Midday traffic in Gibson was light. A few townspeople strolled along the storefronts that lined the square, sometimes pausing briefly at the window displays of the businesses that had managed to remain open. The coffee shop on the corner seemed busy enough, with a steady trickle of lunch customers that came and went through the open front door. From the end of a bench on the courthouse lawn, along the walk that led from the street to the entrance, an old man was feeding a flock of pigeons with bits of bread he broke off from his sandwich. Twenty feet behind him, the life-size statue of Union Colonel Benjamin Harrison, forever captured in bronze and elevated on a noble limestone podium, stoically presided over the center of town. At the opposite end of the bench, a man maybe half the old man's age was reading the Indianapolis Star from below the broad brim of a denim cowboy hat. The cowboy's attention switched to the two strangers as they got out of the car and hurried toward him on the sidewalk. As they approached, he tipped his hat to the young lady and then went back to reading his paper. After they had passed, he resumed watching with interest until they had disappeared through the back door of the old courthouse building.

*****

Tom and Kate followed the signs to the police department and lockup on the lower level. Jennings was waiting for them just inside the door. His smile was barely concealed behind a thin beard and mustache. He looked older than he had sounded on the phone. "Welcome to Gibson, folks. Chief Crawford is on his way back from a fishing trip up in north Michigan; otherwise he'd be here to greet you himself. I hear the Walleye's been hitting pretty good. He should be back by early evening. Your New Albany people got here about an hour ago, and they're setting up in the house next door now. They brought some pretty impressive gear with them, I must say. Your crew chief from Indy is down the hall in our briefing room. You'll meet him in a minute. Um, this is for you." He handed a folder to Tom, who passed it off to Kate after glancing at the cover. It read: Case #WC-71-021, Evans, Caroline, Juvenile vs. Jared Hill, June 1973. "Judge Martin was all too happy to oblige, by the way."

Kate smiled back. "Nice work lieutenant. Based on Ms. Evan's current age that would make her what, about thirteen years old at the time of the incident?"

"Yes ma'am; you are correct. Young Caroline was attacked in her home just prior to her fourteenth birthday. Her parents were over in Scottsburg shopping for a few hours and came home to find her that evening. Some neighbor kids did it. The young perp was sixteen; the older perp, Jared Hill, had just turned nineteen and stood trial as an adult. He got sentenced to fifteen years not far from here at Chain-of-Lakes, the medium security lockup in Albion. I got a hunting buddy who works nights over there. Anyway, looks like the younger one tagged along that afternoon to watch or just couldn't get his pecker to cooperate..." He stopped himself. "Oh, I'm very sorry, Ms. Morrow; that was rude of me."

"Forget it, lieutenant." Kate answered. "We should be glad it didn't. You were saying?"

"Yes, well the younger boy apparently got scared and ran off before things got real serious with Ms. Evans. He flipped on Hill and pleaded out in exchange for a slap on the wrist and a six-month juvee tour in Madison. His family moved him far away from Gibson as soon as they could. You know how it can be in a small town; no way to live a normal life after that. I couldn't find anything on the Internet but was able to dig up some old news clippings off of microfiche down at the library and stuck them in the file there. Yeah, I know, we still have microfiche. It's hard to use 'progress' and 'Gibson' in the same sentence, but that's not always a bad thing." Lt. Jennings chuckled. "The case was a big deal around here, evidently. The older Hill boy got paroled after nine years, was out for about eighteen months, then sent back in for another rape conviction up north at Ball State in Muncie. Somehow he had gotten a job in the kitchen at one of the girls' dormitories. Go figure. Anyway, because of his prior with Miss Evans, they sent him back in for a solid twenty that time. Got out for a while and then back in for another seven-and-change on a drug possession charge. He got released on parole about two months ago. We're checking the Sex Offender Registry to run down his whereabouts now. I also sent an N-DEx back to your folks in D.C. as a backup. Unless he jumped parole, we should know where to find him right quick."

"Good work, lieutenant," Tom said. "I suspect you have Ms. Evans somewhere where she won't be in our way while we wait on a visit from our UNSUB? We'd like to keep her there for a while if at all possible."

"Yes, sir. She's over in the psych ward at the county hospital in Scottsburg for observation. With the gun violation we have on her, not to mention the indecent exposure, we can keep her for a couple of days before we have to charge her or cut her loose. She's sedated, so she's not complaining much. I think we can manage to stretch her time at the hospital to three or four days with the help of the meds, but we sure ain't going to press any charges. I can take you to see her if you think it might be helpful."

"That won't be necessary at this point, lieutenant. Do what you can to hold on to her for a while, but please keep her comfortable. It sounds like she's been through enough already."

"Yes, sir; agreed. Also, if you want, Maggie, um, Officer Pace, can remain in the house if you think we need the place to seem normal, whatever that is."

"S.A. Morrow will take care of that for us," Tom said. "I think we can make the house appear lived-in without committing any more of your resources. If she needs something to do, I'd prefer she works with your perimeter team in case the UNSUB takes flight. If that happens, we will definitely need all the help we can get."

*****

Lieutenant Jennings led them down the hall to the briefing room, where the five Gibson officers were standing in a loose circle drinking coffee. They stopped talking when Kate and Tom entered the room. A bald, plain looking man in jeans and a loose, flannel shirt was sitting on the edge of a table at the back of the room. He was twirling a red Indians baseball cap on his index finger while listening intently on his cell phone. There was nothing interesting about his appearance. He ended the call and approached with his hand extended. "S.A.C. Russell, S.A. Morrow; pleased to meet you. I'm ASAC Caleb Voight, Indianapolis. We spoke earlier on the phone. I came down to lead the New Albany field crew and liaison back to our office if we need any more resources. I personally trained this team, and I know they'll do good work. They're setting up at the subject location as we speak, loading in from the back yard as you instructed. No issues with any nosey neighbors yet. I think officer Jennings took care of that for us. Everything's good so far."

Kate shook his hand firmly. "We're glad you're wasting no time, Agent Voight, because at this point we have none."

Tom greeted him next. "Good to meet you. It sounds like we'll be all set before it gets dark. Nice work. Kate's right, this had to come together quickly." He turned to the other officers who had been joined by Lieutenant Jennings. Kate moved to the window to review Caroline's case file in more detail, while Tom addressed the assembled officers.

"I'm Special-Agent-in-Charge Tom Russell with the FBI. The young lady with me is Special Agent Kate Morrow, and this is ASAC Caleb Voight down from our Indy Field Office. S.A. Morrow has been working closely with me on this case for a couple of months now. Agent Voight will be running the surveillance team from the house next door. I assume Lieutenant Jennings has already briefed you on the matter of Ms. Evans' history and the particulars of our current situation. We don't have much time, so I'll keep this brief." Tom paused to clear his throat. "We have good reason to believe that we're dealing with a serial perp we've labeled the 'Short Rose Killer' and will refer to as 'SRK'. SRK's been around for about five years, but went quiet for three of them before he showed up on the FBI's radar recently. So far we have him down for six confirmed kills and one failed attempt, but there could be others we're not yet aware of.

Lately he's not been too shy about dropping his victims where he's sure they'll be found. He targets pedophile predators but first requires permission from someone, or the family of someone, previously victimized by his target. He's made contact with Ms. Evans through a letter he sent requesting her blessing to avenge what Jared Hill had done to her when she was a young girl. This is the second incident of victim contact through a letter that we are aware of. With his letters, SRK includes a small pendant that he makes with a piece of colored glass and monofilament. Ms. Evans was to hang the pendant by her front door, to signal her consent to SRK for him to proceed with the kill. Our job is to apprehend SRK when he comes looking for his answer."

Tom reached for a bottle of water from the table behind him and paused for a drink. Kate was propped against the wall near of the window reading through the file. She looked up at Tom and shook her head with a pained expression on her face.

He continued, "That brings us to the current operation. As I said, Caleb's team will handle eyes and ears from the empty house next door. S.A. Morrow and I will position ourselves in Ms. Evans' place for a frontal response should our SRK decide to approach the house on foot. We'll have a resource at each end of the street to monitor anyone entering and leaving. Your team will need to position cruisers as close as possible without drawing attention. I know Gibson P.D. has limited assets, but you'll need to be prepared to respond should SRK take flight in a vehicle or as a second perimeter to back up Agent Voight's team if our man decides to flee on foot. Just slow him down, but don't engage. We'll take care of the rest—no heroics are necessary.

ASAC Voight will distribute tactical radio kits here in a few minutes. They have very reliable encryption technology, so we won't get picked up on any scanners that might compromise us.

Use them exclusively for this operation. They're very similar to your Motorolas, so you won't have any trouble using them—but take some time to get familiar with the wireless finger PTT if you've not used one before. Agent Voight will walk you through the other features. We've established frequency 151.400 with the state for communications. If SRK skates, switch to four-four-zero. I've already briefed the Sheriff's office. They know the situation and will be monitoring four-forty to assist, but only if our boy gets outside of Gibson town limits. An excessive law enforcement presence in town could run him off before he even gets close. We don't expect SRK to be armed, but use extreme caution; he's known to improvise. Before we head out, are there any questions?"

Kate closed the file and stepped to Tom's side. She turned away from the room briefly and whispered to him as quietly as she could. "It's worse than I imagined, Tom."

*****

A tall, older officer stepped forward and glanced back at the other officers standing behind him. "Sir, I do have a comment." An expression of sincerity was revealed on his face. His voice held a hint of nervousness. "My colleagues and I've been talking about this little matter, and I can say that I speak for all of us here and Maggie over at the house." He paused to gesture over his shoulder. "All of us know Ms. Evans, and we know she's prone to these crazy spells, but we also know why. I've spent my whole life in this town, and I've known Caroline personally since she was maybe nine or ten. We lived a few doors down the street from her house, and she'd come over to babysit me and my younger brother from time-to-time. She even taught me how to ride a bicycle and did a good job doing it. Caroline was fun to be around and always seemed happy to me. She took good care of us. She was just a real good kid, a lovely young girl.

I didn't see her much after it happened." His voice broke off, and his eyes started to tear up. He drew a breath and continued, "I knew that Hill kid too. He was a bona fide S.O.B. creep show. Most of us young kids back then knew he was bad, and we knew to stay away from him. I can't say I was surprised when they said it was him that did it; except at the time I was too young to really understand what had happened, just heard a bunch of rumors around the neighborhood and at school. They all turned out to be nothing compared to what Hill really did to Caroline that day; God bless her. Since they sent Hill away, this little town's been a much better place for it. But what he did to that young girl was nothing short of pure evil, and me and my colleagues here just want it to be clear that we're prepared to do our job, and, make no mistake, we *will do it,* but to tell you the truth, we would be just fine if you'd catch your Mr. SRK some other time, after he's had a chance to execute, so to speak, his particular form of justice on Hill. That's all I gotta say."

A long pause held the room; no one moved. Kate looked at Tom, but his eyes were still with the officer. She set the folder on the table and quietly cleared her throat, responding in a soft but sincere voice. "We appreciate your compassion, Officer Lockman, is it?" She read the name tag pinned to his uniform over his silver badge. "I read the file on Ms. Evans just a moment ago. It was horrible what Hill did to her. I can't imagine what went through her mind that afternoon or how she's had to cope with the playback of that day for all these years. Tom and I have read too many files not very different from hers while working this case. Over and over, each one tells a story of unimaginable human suffering. Each paints the same picture of family tragedy and heart-breaking loss.

We're not immune to the contradictions of this case, and we don't necessarily believe we stand on the moral high ground. Statistically speaking, SRK's targets would have likely preyed on other victims, and in that sense he has prevented immeasurable pain. You're right, Officer Lockman, why should we stop him? Why would we even want to?" Kate paused for a long moment to think carefully through the answers to her own questions. "I know it's backwards. This all seems upside-down because at some basic human level SRK's response to these child predators feels like the natural one. If we're really honest with ourselves, he's doing what each of us would be compelled to do if given the same circumstances. What SRK does, Officer Lockman, isn't what keeps me up late at night. That we are tasked with stopping him sure does. But we don't get to make a choice about which laws we uphold and which ones we don't. The fact of the matter is, if we don't keep it between the rails, we'll all go over the side."

*****

−20−

A LITTLE BLUE ROOM

Tom surveyed the front of Caroline's house from an upstairs bay window of the empty house next door. Downstairs, the field agents could be heard stepping through the testing protocols on the surveillance equipment. "It looks like her overgrown shrubs may help obscure the view to the pendant." Tom tapped the glass. "You'll need to check it, Kate. We'll change the porch light to a low wattage bulb also. We'll have the light on, but it won't help him see much. I'm sure we can find something that we can make work. If not, we can have Jennings pick one up. I want to force SRK to approach the house; it's our best chance. In his mind it has to be there for him, and he'll take some risk to find it. He's probably rehearsed this kill a hundred times. Now he just needs the nod to go through with it."

"How do you know he'll come at night?" Kate asked.

"I really don't for certain, but I think it's likely since it would be much less exposure for him. It's supposed to be overcast for the next several evenings with no moon. That works in his favor. He won't come too late, though. The risk goes up after people start going to bed. An unfamiliar car driving slowly on the street or a strange man lingering outside late in the evening would get noticed around here." Tom stepped away from the window. "Let's get over there. We need to be in her house before it gets dark." Aside in a whisper, Tom added, "Besides, I understand Ms. Evans walked around half-naked most of the time. You'll need to get into her character. I say we go for authenticity."

"Yeah, sure Tom.   SRK shows up and I'm modeling

underwear for you."

"Is that a problem?"

*****

They slipped through the backyards and entered Caroline's house through the kitchen door. Before closing it, Kate surveyed the overgrown yard and checked the visibility between the neighbors' homes to the street behind. She wondered if SRK would do the same, only in reverse. She pulled the small curtain across the glass in the door and closed the shade in the window next to it. In the dimly lit room, the air felt thick and stale. A foul odor emanated from the sink piled full with dirty dishes. The water had drained away from when Caroline had left it that morning, leaving the dishes covered in an oily orange-brown residue.

"See if you can find the thermostat, Tom; let's hope the air conditioner works. I'll fill the sink to help mask that nasty smell. I think we're in for a couple of long days; we may as well be a little comfortable."

Kate turned on the light over the stove and found the switch for the ceiling fixture on the wall by the door, but only one of the bulbs came on. She turned on the hot water and waited for the sink to fill. Half-empty bowls of cat food littered the floor in a pattern that looked strangely deliberate. She gathered them up and set them on the counter next to the darkened T.V. *Less things to trip over if we have to move quickly.*

Tom called back to her from the hall. "The cats must be hiding somewhere."

"Jennings had them moved to the local shelter. He thought they'd get in our way," Kate answered. "He said he'll bring them back so they're here when Ms. Evans gets to come home." When the sink was full, she turned off the faucet and went to the front of the house to make sure the curtains were closed. She picked up the broken lamp and pile of unopened mail and set them on the hall table before stepping to the window. The street in front of the house was quiet. There were a few cars parked along the opposite side, but Caroline's curb was empty except for the trash cart at the end of her driveway. A pickup truck passed slowly, and Kate immediately saw that it was a female driver. She thought it fortunate that the street was one way, right to left, and they would be able to more easily identify the drivers. She pinched the curtains together and went to the front door to check the feed from the miniature camera installed earlier by ASAC Voight. From the outside, it looked like a normal peephole viewer in the door. On the inside, a small monitor was connected through the hole to the back of the camera and mounted to the face of the door. A wire ran from the monitor to a digital recorder and flat video screen on Caroline's dining room table. The recorder sent a wireless signal to the equipment monitored by the field agents positioned in the house next door.

Tom came up behind her and placed one hand low on her waist. With the other, he handed her a small light bulb he had taken from the vanity light in the bathroom and an old but clean bathrobe that he had collected from Caroline's bedroom closet. It looked as though it had never been worn. She let herself lean into him. "I like it when you bring me special gifts." She kissed him on the cheek and put the robe on over her clothes.

Tom walked to the dining room and looked over the equipment. He pressed the talk button on his lapel microphone. "DC's in place. Gear appears to be working fine. Clear to step out?" He released the button and went back to Kate standing in the front hall while he waited for the response. The agents next door kept track of seven different camera feeds to their computer screens. The monitor on Caroline's dining room table cycled through the same series of images. Six high resolution cameras had full pan, tilt, and zoom capability; one each looking east and west down the street and sidewalk, two showed cross views of

Caroline's backyard and two showed cross views of her front yard taken from cameras carefully hidden in nests of oak pollen at each end of the gutter. The peep-hole camera in her front door was stationary and was limited to zoom control only. The screen immediately jumped to any camera that picked up movement with its motion sensor, and the screen split to multiple views when more than one was engaged. Currently, all cameras reported zero activity.

"Roger, DC, all clear to step out." It sounded like Agent Voight. "We'll advise immediately if the weather report changes."

Tom looked up into the hall at the top of the stairs. "Kate, while you're outside, I think I'll do a quick check of the second floor. Jennings didn't mention anything about it. Make sure you cover your ear piece. Here, let me help you." As he tossed her hair to cover the device, a playful grin appeared on his face. "There you go, Caroline; that's *much* better." He left her in front of the door and bounded up the stairs two steps at a time. Kate was only slightly impressed. She slipped out of her shoes and started to open the front door but first checked to make sure Tom wouldn't be seen from outside when she did. Around the corner, the grandfather clock chimed six times but it was almost quarter-to-seven. It would be getting dark soon.

*****

Kate stepped outside onto the porch. The coach light next to the door was low enough that she could easily reach up into it and change the bulb. The pendant hung from a small nail hammered into the wall below the light just a foot away. Hanging there, she knew it sealed the fate of someone's life that was probably not worth saving. *Nonetheless, here I am.*

She removed the pendant and held it in her hand. It was crystal red and flat; a quarter of an inch thick, about two inches long and perhaps an inch wide. The edges appeared broken, not cut, but polished so they were smooth to her touch. It was shaped roughly in the form of a tear drop with small air bubbles that were suspended in the glass like stars in a tiny frozen sky. It reminded her of the bits of colored glass she collected on the beach when she was little. She wondered about the significance of the pendant. *It had to be linked to some horrible event that triggered SRK's urge to kill. Was the color or shape of it important?* Eventually, she knew, they would solve the mystery. Kate replaced the pendant on the nail and checked the visibility to the sidewalk and street. Jennings had done a good job concealing it behind the lacy upper sprigs of an overgrown Juniper. It would not be easily seen when SRK came looking for it.

Kate moved back inside, but before closing the door, she flipped on the switch and made sure that the light was working. She went to the dining room and watched the monitor cycle through the seven images several times through. Once, the camera sequence jumped ahead to show a car approaching from down the street, then immediately switched over to the next camera showing the car driving away. It was moving too quickly to be of interest. When the car was out of view, the normal pattern of the seven images resumed. Above her, Tom's footsteps could be heard shuffling at the back of the house over the kitchen. She sensed him moving slowly closer toward the room above her. Through her earpiece, she listened to the agents next door settling into the typical chatter that came with the boredom of the long wait.

A loud bang suddenly shook the ceiling, startling her. Small bits of plaster dust drifted down on the table. "Is everything okay up there, Tom?"

Tom's voice echoed down the stairwell with a hint of urgency. "You might want to see this, Kate."

*****

It happened in the little space next to Caroline's bedroom. Her dad had finished part of the unused attic where the roof was too low for big people to stand, and he had connected it to her room with a child-sized door so that she could crawl in there any time she wanted to. It was her play closet, *'an imagination space'* her mom had said, where she could read and play and make believe. The walls and sloping ceiling were well insulated and finished with drywall trimmed with some fancy boards that her dad had been saving in the rafters above the garage. There were no windows, so he mounted a pair of adjustable lights in the ceiling so that Caroline could aim them for whatever activity she might be doing. To finish, he installed a small remnant of carpet that almost fit the size and shape of the floor exactly. When her dad was done, Caroline helped her mom paint the walls and ceiling a light blue because she said it looked like the sky over her grandpa's farm. They painted the door deep-red, almost purple, just like the big sliding door on the barn where he kept his horses.

For her eighth birthday, her grandpa had given her a little red yearling that she named Strawberry. She loved to stay there on the weekends during the warmer months so she could ride Strawberry alongside of him while he rode his mare around the farm and surrounding countryside. Often they would take a lunch basket with them and follow the fence line to the trail that led through the woods, down to the shady meadow and the stream that meandered through it. After they ate, Caroline would wade in the cool water while her grandpa watched, resting on their picnic blanket under the willow that grew at the edge of the glade. The horses would wander close by, drinking leisurely from the stream or grazing on the thick Indian grass. At the end of their first summer of riding, he gave her a little toy horse that he had carved from wood and painted to look just like Strawberry.

After it happened, her mom took Caroline to live with her at the farm for almost a year, so she might have the time to heal. The morning after they left Gibson for the country, her dad walled in the opening to what was once the little blue playroom. He removed the purple-red door and the frame with the fancy trim and tossed them into the hole before it was covered. Then he painted her bedroom walls a pretty soft yellow and bought her a big, new dresser that he set in front of where the opening had been. He screwed the legs to the floor and the back to the wall, so it couldn't be moved. Lastly, he cut a door in the hallway outside her room and made a linen closet from the taller side of the play space, because he wanted more than just a thin wall between him and where his daughter had been brutally attacked by that neighbor boy. He made certain that what was sealed behind the closet would never see light again. You couldn't tell that Caroline's imagination space had ever existed. If he could erase the room, he could erase the memory of what happened inside.

*****

Kate found Tom kneeling, leaning into a large hole in the back of the hall closet. A weathered, long-handled axe with a rusty head was buried deep in the frame of the door to her right. The shelves and back wall had been violently destroyed; linens and towels were mixed with debris that covered the floor and spilled into the hall. "What is it, Tom?"

"It looks like a little playroom that someone closed up." He handed Kate his flashlight. "Well, it used to be a playroom anyway. Take a look inside."

The air was stale and acrid with the smell of rot. A heavy layer of dust and the shells of dead insects covered the carpet. Kate took off Caroline's robe and laid it inside on the floor before she crawled through the hole. Tom leaned in behind her. She swept the flashlight slowly over the light blue surfaces. A corner of the sloped ceiling sagged noticeably, ringed in an orange stain and speckled with black mold where the roof had leaked for years. About a foot away, the straw and feathered nest of a pack rat sat empty; the dried carcass of the animal lay just beside it. Broken pieces of trim and the purple-red door lay in a jumbled pile at one end of the little space. At the other end, the rectangular opening where the door had been was now closed with wood framing and the back face of the gray wallboard of Caroline's childhood bedroom on the other side.

"This is where Hill assaulted her," Kate said. "They must have closed it off afterwards as a way to make it all go away." She carefully reached into the pile of trim to avoid the rusty nails and handed Tom a plastic toy horse about eight inches long. "There's another one over there, but I can't get to it. I guess she liked horses. Her file said Hill used a wooden one just like it in his assault. The med-exam said she would most likely never be able to have children."

Tom looked at the toy horse and shook his head. "Sick bastard," he seethed as he set it down. "The outside walls of the house are solid brick, Kate, a foot thick, and the roof in here is probably well insulated." He hit the ceiling above him with the side of his fist. "Most likely her screams weren't heard, or no one was home next door to hear them. Her old room is just behind that wall. On the other side of that hole is a dresser that's been screwed in place. I couldn't budge it. It looks like Caroline hacked away at it for a while before she gave up. When she couldn't get through the dresser, she apparently started on this closet. I guess she knew the room was still in here somewhere and was determined to find it. The axe marks are fresh, so she must have done this recently. I'd say as recently as last night."

"I'll bet SRK's letter was the trigger," Kate said. "It's obvious that Caroline wasn't supposed to see this room ever again." She scanned the flashlight one last time over the light blue walls and followed Tom back through the opening into the hall.

*****

Caroline's childhood bedroom was at the front of the house and fit below a large shed dormer that ran the width of the room. A bay window projected toward the street, just like the house next door where they had looked over her yard an hour earlier. "It doesn't appear like anyone's been in here for a very long time," Tom said, as he brushed some dust off the top of the sash and gazed out at the darkening street. His reflection was clouded in the milky-green residue of dirt and pollen that had collected on the outside surface of the glass. Below one end of the window, the curtains lay in a pile where the rod had pulled away from the wall. "I checked the two bedrooms at the back of the house, and they look about the same. Both rooms had some nice clothes that were laid out neatly on the beds. I guess after her family was killed in the car wreck, Caroline, or someone, had gone through the closets and dressers looking for something to bury them in. The doors and drawers were left open like they were in a hurry. Apparently no one bothered to come back to put things away." Tom watched the street light flicker off, then back on, several houses away; he turned toward Kate who was still standing in the doorway next to the dresser. "Other than neglect, I'd say her room is probably exactly as it was when she buried her family. That was thirty-five years ago."

A hand-painted sunrise on the face of the door seemed to have distracted Kate's attention. She was tracing the outline of the golden rays one by one with her finger but stopped when Tom approached. "It's easy not to think about it until you see all of all of this," she said.

"What's easy not to think about?"

"That she had a life once." Kate pointed around the room at

the toy horses displayed on the shelf that ran along all four walls just above the height of the door. A veil of cobwebs draped between them and occasionally to the ceiling. "There must be a least a hundred up there, Tom, maybe two. Look, they're perfectly spaced and organized by the pose they were cast in. It's like each is a small piece of the life that she lost."

On the length of shelf above her, the toys had fallen over from the impact of the axe hammering through the wall. Several were on the floor, scattered around her feet. She picked one up and reached above her to set it back on the shelf. "It doesn't look like Caroline ever came up here again," Kate drew her hand lightly across the splintered axe marks in the top of the dresser, "except to do this."

*****

Their ear pieces lit up. "D.C., we have a walker, white male, early-to-mid thirties. Subject has stopped in front of the prize, but has not approached. Repeat—the subject is stationary. He's holding a long, narrow box. Copy D.C.?"

"Copy that." Tom bolted down the stairs to the dining room with Kate trailing two steps behind. Within seconds they were leaning into the monitor, their faces just a foot from the screen. It showed a man standing on the sidewalk looking both ways, up—then down the street. There wasn't enough light in the image to read his clothing clearly, but he had on a light jacket, long pants, and what looked like running shoes that he was nervously shifting his weight back and forth in, as if he was getting ready to leave in a hurry. He looked directly at Caroline's house, then turned around and looked at the house across the street. The long box was tucked under his arm, his hands buried in his jacket pockets.

"I can't gauge his height, but he looks about the right age, maybe a bit young; his frame is lighter than I imagined. But it's possible." Tom clicked off his observations out loud as the recording equipment captured the man's movements on the screen. "Hold on, he's heading east."

As the subject walked out of the frame, the monitor immediately switched to the camera that was aimed down the east end of the street. Tom triggered his mic. "Wade, he's moving in your direction; drift to the east ready point and hold for an update." The subject stopped abruptly in front of the for-sale house and stood looking toward the front door. "Hold on, Wade, our friend may have changed his mind. Let's see what he does next. Caleb, you tracking this?"

"Yes, sir—we have very good eyes." The response through his ear piece was immediate.

A few seconds later the subject turned back toward Caroline's house, but instead of heading up her walk, he continued moving right on by. For a moment the screen split into two frames; one showed him coming, the other going, but as he passed the midpoint between the two cameras, it filled with the view of him walking away. He stopped in front of the house on the other side of Caroline's. "Now what?" Tom pushed back from the table but kept his eyes on the screen. The next minute passed too slowly. "Shit—something's wrong, Kate."

"Patience, Tom; let's give him some time." Sliding the mouse forward, she zoomed in the camera as tight as it would allow, but the image was too grainy. She pulled back out to return to the full view.

"False alarm." Tom's excitement deflated like a balloon burst with a needle. He backed away from the monitor and started to pace the floor. As he did, he stretched his hands in the air, locking his fingers behind his neck as though the game was over, and it was time to add up the score. He turned back toward Kate, and stabbed his finger toward the screen. "That's not SRK."

"What?" Kate shook her head like she wasn't convinced. "How can you be sure?"

"Look at the guy; he's nervous—uncommitted." Tom sounded certain; the overriding aggravation was evident in his voice. "SRK would be cautious but collected. He would focus on locating the pendant on the house, just a glance to the side as he's walking by, or maybe he'd dwell for a moment longer, but he'd do it casually. If he didn't see it, he would move on but then circle back after a while for a closer look. SRK wouldn't go here then there, then wherever, and he wouldn't just stand still long enough for someone to paint his portrait. Skippy here can't make up his mind. The man is confused."

Kate zoomed in the camera until the clarity just started to grain. She tapped the image. "Tom, he's reading something on the box." The subject had pulled the box from under his arm and held it lengthwise in front of him. He was tilting it toward the light from the house and looking down at it, so he could read whatever was written on the lid. "Look at this side of the screen, Tom; it's brighter." Kate pointed at the green glow on the left side of the image. "It's out of the frame, but that's the light from the front porch. He's not confused, he's checking house numbers. He couldn't see the number on this house; the bulb's too dim, so he's checking the one on each side of us."

Tom grabbed the mouse and panned the camera left. The image brightened dramatically. "I'll be a son-of-a-bitch." Just then, the subject appeared to make up his mind. He moved deliberately now. Tom's excitement returned instantly. "Get ready, here he comes!" The screen split to two images, then three as the man turned up Caroline's walk and headed straight for the door in an aggressive stride. The view from the peephole camera filled the screen as he bounded up the steps.

Kate was already there. She threw open the door just as he reached it. Her gun was drawn, pointing squarely between the man's eyes. "F—B—I! DO NOT MOVE!"

The man stumbled away reflexively, falling backwards down the steps. Kate heard the air rush out of his lungs when his back hit the concrete. The box landed several feet away, spilling dozens of flowers across the walk. His hands were shaking wildly in front of his face as if they could block the bullets when the gun was fired. Gasping for oxygen, he struggled to speak but could only manage labored gasps. "Please—la—dy—don't—shoot!"

Tom charged past Kate in the doorway and was the first one off the porch. He holstered his gun and rolled the subject to his side, locking handcuffs tightly around his wrists. "I'll give you a minute to get your wind back, sir. Then you and I are going to have a little chat. When you're ready, we can start with your name, okay?" The man shook his head yes as Tom got back on his feet.

"Tom, look at this." Kate waved her flashlight over the flowers scattered on the walk. "They're roses; at least several dozen." Tom's attention was still distracted by the subject's shallow breathing. Out of the corner of his eye, he tried to follow the light as Kate moved it side to side, but she was standing in the way. Her voice was soft, like she was talking to herself. He could barely hear what she was saying. "Most of them are white, and they look fresh. I see just a few red ones, but they're all dried and dead." She bent over and picked each one up, then turned around to look directly at Tom. "The stems, all of them, they're cut off just below the bud." She reached out and put seven dead roses in his hand. "He doesn't know Goethe is alive. It's SRK."

Instantly, Tom opened his mic to reach Agent Voight, but he was already coming across the yard, followed by two other agents. Lieutenant Jennings had just pulled his car to the curb a half-minute before and was trailing a few yards behind. Tom yelled to the group as they approached. "Have we located Hill yet? His world is about to go to hell—if it hasn't already."

Caleb looked down at flowers and the handcuffed man curled up on the walk. Confused, he handed Tom his phone. "Good timing. It's Agent Lockman on the line sir; Fort Wayne." Kate came up next to Tom just as he hit the speaker button. He held the phone out between the three of them.

"This is S.A.C. Russell; do you have eyes on Hill?" Tom's voice was anxious, as if somehow he knew it was already too late.

"Negative, sir, we're in position at his residence but have not made Hill," Lockman responded. "We've had surveillance on all openings for almost an hour now. No movement's been observed. There's just one car in the driveway, and the lights are on inside and out, but the drapes are closed. It looks normal enough. Our crew has stayed dark and not approached per your instructions. We have some loud music coming from in the house. It's loud enough that some neighbors have called it in. We've requested that the local PD not respond until we wrap this up."

"Shit!" Tom barked into the phone. "Get in there now! Call an ambulance, and you better call the medical examiner too. It's probably too late for the EMT's. I want to know what you find immediately!" Tom checked his watch. "We'll be there in two hours. Don't touch a damn thing!" He ended the call and dropped Voight's phone in his pocket. He turned to the man lying on the walk, then at the two agents standing nearby. "Get him up."

*****

They sat the handcuffed man on the steps of the porch. His breathing was still labored but improving. "Are you ready to talk now, Mr. FTD?" Tom's tone suggested that he didn't care if the man was ready, or not. "Let's start with your name, and you can keep talking until you've told us everything you know about these roses here and Caroline Evans."

"Uh, Levi Quint sir. I work for Goldberg's Florist, just delivering flowers; sometimes I work late to make some extra money." His speech was nervous and weak. He stopped every few words to take a breath. "Honestly, that's all I was doing."

Tom waited impatiently for Quint to continue, but he appeared to be done talking. "Okay, Levi." He sat down on the step above him and laid his hand firmly on his shoulder. Quint tried to scoot away, but Kate sat on his other side, blocking him in between. "We really don't have much time, so we're going to try this once more, but it will be *only* once more. Understand? Let me give you a little background here, so you will get an idea of the mood I'm in." Tom glanced down at the dead red roses in his hand and tossed them into a half-empty water bowl on the step next to Quint so he would see them. Printed around the top of the rim it said: *'Drink from me and you will never thirst.'*

"Mr. Quint, you have just delivered flowers for a serial killer, who, thanks to you, has now confirmed that he has killed six people." Tom picked one rose out of the bowl and tossed it aside. *There you go, Thurman.* "The last one he killed was with a two-foot pipe, two inches thick, rammed most of the way up his victim's anus. Right now, he's probably in the middle of killing his seventh target with just as much creativity, while you and I sit here and have our little chat. And that makes you an accessory before the fact. Now I, and the lovely Agent Morrow over there, would like to go try and stop him, or at least be there soon afterwards to clean up the big mess he's going to make, but, right now, you're keeping us from actually doing any of that. So, Levi, shall we start again?"

"No shit? A serial killer?" Incredibly, Quint found his voice and was suddenly cooperative. "Okay, when I got back from lunch today, there was a note folded on the seat of my van; it had fifteen twenty-dollar bills inside. I don't ever lock the door; you know, why bother around here? The money fell all over the floor, and when I picked it up I thought, shoot, this is going to be my lucky day, right? So the note said to put, you know, those dead roses in a box; they had to be red, and I was to fill the rest of the box with fresh white ones, as many as I could get in it. Well, I figured Goldberg wouldn't miss a few flowers; shoot, the old man has greenhouses full of them and sells them wholesale upstate. So I took a few dozen, okay? Then the note said to cut the stems of the red ones real short, you know, like below the bud and deliver them to this address. Oh yeah, and it had to be today, just after dark. I was supposed to park my van a couple of blocks away and walk here, set the box against the door, ring the bell, then leave. That's it. I kept the note; it's right here in my jacket if you all want to look at it. You'll see; I ain't lying to you people. How was I supposed to know it was a freakin' serial killer? I figured it was just some pissed-off boyfriend or something. I didn't see no harm in earning a few extra bucks on the side. Shoot, three hundred dollars is a week's pay. My wife lost her job last month; we sure could use the money."

Tom slipped on cotton gloves and pulled the note from Quint's pocket. He unfolded it carefully as he stepped back up on the porch to the open doorway where the light was better. Kate followed, pulling her gloves on as well. The note was written on the back of a letter-size flyer for the Annual 4H Junior Rodeo to be held in Scottsburg the following weekend. The corners were torn like it had been pulled off a surface that it was taped to. Tom read through it quickly before handing it to Kate. He knew the analysts at the forensic lab in Quantico would thoroughly process the note for fingerprints, handwriting, ink chemistry, and any trace evidence to be found. For now, the content was important, and it was just as Levi Quint had described. "It does look like this is your lucky day, Mr. Quint; these men will see to it that you get home to your wife shortly," Tom said. "They just have a few more questions for you to answer, and you should be on your way. Lieutenant Jennings here will give you a ride to your vehicle. And, by the way, you'll need to hand over the money to him. If we don't find any useful prints on it, the Lieutenant will make sure that it's returned to you. Then it's all yours."

"He must have pulled it off a shop window," Kate said. "These flyers are all over the place. I saw one back at the airport this morning. SRK's smart. If he bought some paper around here, we might be able to track it down to the store where he got it and get a description. This was spontaneous, Tom; he hadn't planned on any of it. Why wait around to set this up? I don't get it. If he saw the pendant, he'd be gone. If he didn't see it, he'd be gone. SRK must have seen something that compelled him to change his plan. But what? It had to have been something he saw today."

"He saw me," Tom concluded. "He had to—*the short roses.* That's something between us. He remembers me from investigating the kills in St. Louis. The case was in the news for months. I started to call him the Short Rose Killer, and they all ran with it. But where could he possibly see me here, today?" Tom thought hard. "We've been in Gibson, what, six or seven hours and haven't been any place other than the PD where someone got even close enough to recognize me."

Kate looked overwhelmed, as if by a sudden realization. "Tom, when we got to town, on the bench outside the courthouse." She pounded her forehead against his shoulder. "The cowboy. That was him, Tom. The son-of-a-bitch tipped his hat at me!" She stepped away and leaned on the railing overlooking Caroline's front yard like she wanted to vomit. "That was SRK."

Tom hung his head and was quiet for a long moment. Rubbing the new stubble on his face, he realized he hadn't shaved since early yesterday, maybe the day before. He thought it peculiar that he would even think about something so insignificant. He smiled wryly to himself as he looked around the porch. *What did I miss?* He reached for the pendant and took it off the nail. "Kate, do you still have the bulb you changed out for this one?" He tapped on the light next to the door.

"It's in the robe. I left it upstairs in the closet. I'll be right back." She disappeared into the house. Tom rubbed the edges of the glass in his hand while he waited. *You made this; you shaped it to make it smooth. You held it in your hand and felt it, just like I am now. You ran your fingers along the edges just like this. What do you think about when you polish the glass? It connects you to something bad or someone good, doesn't it? Or is it both? But then you had to wipe away every trace of yourself before you sent it. That had to be hard for you to do.* It occurred to Tom just then that he had never felt closer to the presence of SRK. Then he thought about the cowboy on the park bench. *You saw this piece of glass again this morning, didn't you? Why did you wait to go after Hill? He was all yours. Were you waiting for me?*

Kate came through the doorway and handed Tom the light bulb. "I'm glad I didn't kneel on it in the closet; the filament's broken. It's burned out."

"SRK was here," Tom started, "probably last night. He came by and couldn't see the pendant. It would have been too dark. So he took a risk and came by again early this morning. He had to have seen the pendant *and* the police at the house and connected the two. If he just saw the pendant, he would have left quietly to go after Hill. If he had just seen the police and no pendant, he would have likely been scared off. He had to have seen them both in order to come up with the idea for the flowers—but how?"

"Okay, try this," Kate said. "SRK gets to the house just after the incident with the motorist, but before the police show up responding to the 911 call. He's driving or walking by and sees the pendant nailed to the house, but the police are coming down the street, so he leaves. Then what?"

"Nope—doesn't work," Tom responded. "Jennings said Caroline had it wrapped around her hand when they got to the house. He said they were inside asking her questions when she made sure to show it to them, remember? SRK would have had to be extremely close to her to see it. That puts him with her just before the police came as you suggest, either in the house, which is extremely unlikely, or close enough to her when she was outside with the gun..."

Kate interrupted Tom, "Okay, SRK came just as Caroline is running back into her house after the motorist. He sees the pendant wrapped around her hand...," now Kate interrupted herself, "but it would have been several minutes; at least ten, before the police would respond to the call. He wouldn't wait around that long, so how could SRK know the police were even going to arrive unless— *holy shit!* He's the one who made the call!"

Agent Voight's phone came to life in Tom's pocket. He grabbed it immediately; it was still on speaker mode. "It's Agent Lockman sir. Hill's dead. Probably this side of a couple of hours, I'd say. We found him downstairs in the basement. It's a real mess."

"Don't touch the body," Tom ordered. "Photograph the hell out of the place but don't move a thing. The med examiner's just going to have to wait. We're leaving for the airport now." He ended the call and tossed Voight's phone back to him. "Kate, get a hold of the pilot and tell him we need to get to Fort Wayne. Tell him we're on our way. Where is Jennings?"

"I gave him the keys," Kate said. "He went to get our car."

"Good. I'll wait right here." Tom groaned as he sat back down on the steps. "I may have moved a little fast back there, Kate, coming off the porch. It sucks to get old. Call Jennings and tell him we need the audio of the motorist's 911 call. He can have dispatch email it to me, and we'll listen on the way to the airport."

Tom watched Kate step off the porch and walk to the edge of Caroline's driveway to make the call. He looked down at the dead roses left floating in the water. *Six red, six dead.* One of Voight's team was photographing the box and the lid that had landed in the tall grass. As the camera flashed, Tom thought he saw another dark bud mixed in with the long stems of the white roses and got up to see. He stepped around the scene, careful not to disturb it more than it already was. He considered reprimanding Kate for removing the short red buds but decided there really wasn't any value to them as evidence anyway. He believed Levi Quint. There was no physical tie linking them to SRK. There would be no fingerprints and no trace evidence to find. Still, Kate didn't know that when she picked them up and handed them to him. *She should have known better.*

Tom bent down and pulled another red rose from the nest of long stems. Below it he found another. *Eight and nine, that makes two we haven't found.* In front of him, the white buds lit up with every flash of the camera. There were more than he cared to count. *You're not even close to being done. How many will you kill before I find you?*

Just then, Lieutenant Jennings came up the driveway and handed Kate the keys. He called over to Tom, "Wendy has the transcript, but she has to get the recording from county. She'll have it to you shortly."

"Okay, good." Tom walked across the grass toward Kate and the lieutenant. "Wade, let's back this bus up."

"Sir?"

"The 911 calls; you said you received two calls this morning. Tell me more about them."

"Well, we didn't actually take the calls. The Sheriff handles our 911. We just get a dispatch request if the call is inside Gibson. The county notifies Wendy and she dispatches our guys…"

Tom stopped him. "Wade—the calls please?"

"Sorry sir, anyway, there wasn't much to them really; as I said before, one was from the neighbor across the street who didn't even mention the gun. The other caller was the motorist, but he didn't I.D. himself. I figure he must have soiled his britches and left. We get dispatch requests all the time where the caller didn't give their name. We have to answer them just the same. You know, most people don't want to get involved."

"You did track his number, didn't you?" Tom asked.

"We tried, sir, but it was a burner phone." Jennings smiled weakly like he just realized he had neglected something that might have been important.

Tom just started to laugh.

*****

−21−

TRANSFERENCE

Tom turned the car off State Road 56 back onto the interstate heading south. Jennings was in front of them in his cruiser, setting a pretty good pace with the emergency lights on. They would be at the Clark Regional Airport in less than twenty minutes. Tom had just gotten off the phone with Agent Lockman in Fort Wayne, who had provided an update and a few more details. "Kate, do you remember your *idyllic southern retirement community* scenario? It turns out you were wrong about the bathtub, but not by much; it was a washing machine. I conditionally surrender on the C.O.D. though; you nailed *the insides on the outsides bit*." He glanced over at Kate to see if he drew a smile, but she was busy checking the in-box on her tablet. "Lockman says Hill lost a shit-load of blood. He couldn't say how since I told him not to touch the body, but the wounds would have to be severe."

The device pinged, and Kate looked up. "We just got the email of the motorist 911 from the Gibson P.D. She sent the transcript also. Oh, that's helpful—the subject line says the call came in at 6:43:47 a.m. and ended at 6:44:22. Shall I?"

"Please."

Kate double clicked on the audio file attachment and adjusted the volume.

911: "What's the emergency?"

Caller: "She's on the street with a gun. She doesn't mean it."

303

911: "Who has a gun, sir?"

Caller: "Please send someone. She needs help. None of this is her fault."

911: "Sir, do you know the woman?"

Caller: "I just don't want her to hurt anyone. She wouldn't want to."

911: "What is she doing now?"

Caller: "I don't know. She just ran back in her house."

911: "What's your location?"

Caller: "Twenty-one Poplar Street."

911: "Sir, please move to a safe location. Officers will be there shortly. I'll stay on the line with you until they arrive. Okay?"

Caller (barely audible): "*a...gas...uz...ery...gud...to...see.*"

A click is heard on the call

911: "Sir? Sir, are you there?"

"Shit. Play it again;" Tom said bluntly, "just the last part."

When the recording ended, Tom slammed his open hands against the top of the steering wheel. "His last words on the call—he said: '*the glass was very good to see.*' That's him! Dammit! I'm going to kill that lieutenant." He pressed the accelerator until they were fifty feet from Jennings' cruiser and approaching fast.

Kate put her hands on the dash. The flashing lights filled the windshield. "Take it easy, Tom!"

Tom let up on the gas to let Jennings pull away. "Sorry, Kate; I'm just pissed all over. SRK had his answer—the son-of-a-bitch! Why did he wait around?" Tom checked his watch. "He had six, maybe seven hours on us. That's still plenty of time, but he would have had more if he had just left after he saw the pendant early this morning. We'd have been here for days waiting for him to show up. He could have taken his sweet time with Hill. SRK could have had the flowers delivered two days from now, and we'd still be sitting back at the house in Gibson like idiots."

"Sure, we'd have waited a few more days in the house," Kate answered, "but he knew he wouldn't have much time with Hill regardless. Look, after seeing you, he knows the FBI is involved, and he'd also know that we'd dig into Caroline's background and find out about Hill, and, with our resources, we wouldn't have to work too hard to locate him. He knows we'd lock onto Hill as soon as we found him. SRK had a very narrow window of opportunity and took a huge risk going after him. His six-hour head start didn't matter if we had Hill's house under tight surveillance. Since SRK beat us to him, he probably dispensed with any ritual he had planned to be real quick about it. That would be messy and messy means he may have left us some solid evidence we can use to track him down. It's puzzling why he would waste what little time he had to set up the little delivery stunt, unless he just wanted to jack with you. But that doesn't fit the profile, Tom."

"No, it doesn't". Tom drove for a while in silence while he pondered the significance of SRK's ruse. "After the 911 call, he must have stuck around to see what happened next. He wanted to see if they'd bring us in after they talked to Ms. Evans and learned about the pendant, so he waits on the bench outside the police station. It would be a huge tactical advantage for him to find out the scope of the investigations into his killings, if they were just isolated local efforts or a nation-wide man hunt. So he waits.

Then there's a big surge in activity when Voight's team shows up, and he begins to wonder where it's all heading. His overwhelming urge is to get to Hill, but his instincts keep him on the bench a little while longer, trading risk for information. If the FBI hadn't shown up, he'd have all the time in the world with Hill. But when they did, the clock started ticking. He would have to get to Hill quickly or lose his chance. And then something unexpected happened; we, or rather I, appeared, and his world shifted completely. After seeing me, he must have come up with the idea for the roses. For some reason, he wanted me to know just how close he was; close enough to recognize me, and I didn't have a clue. I looked right at him and don't remember a single detail except the stupid hat. And that, Kate, is going to twist my little brain into a giant pretzel. SRK will learn from this and adjust. He'll change his pattern, and that's going to make it that much harder to catch him next time—*if there is one*. The roses were his little way of letting me know it's him. Killing Hill as I'm picking them up off Caroline's sidewalk is his way of telling me he can't be stopped."

*****

Jared Hill had rented a small ranch house in a modest neighborhood on the south edge of Fort Wayne. It was just a few blocks from the junior high school, but that was more a coincidence than a convenience to Hill, now sixty-four years old. Kate was kneeling at the bottom of the basement stairs talking to ASAC Voight on her cell phone as she was placing an evidence marker next to part of a tooth that was embedded in the bottom step. Two other agents from the Fort Wayne resident field office and the local police remained upstairs, as Tom had instructed them to do. Other detectives were already canvassing the neighborhood for witnesses who may have seen SRK.

Tom stood alone near Hill's body. He needed some time with the corpse to absorb every nuance and detail that would help him refine the killer's profile. The other agents and techs would formally process the scene and gather the physical evidence that could lead them to SRK; it would tie him to the crime when the case went to trial. But unlike most murder scenes, this killer and his motive were already known. Tom knew why Hill died; he needed to know how. Everything about the position and condition of the body would tell him something more about SRK.

Jared Hill was folded over, his body wedged tight in the corner between the basement wall and the washing machine. His back was toward the room with his arms tucked between his legs that were straight and vertical against the concrete foundation. The tail of his shirt was soaked red with blood and hung loose at his waist. In slowing motion, a few droplets still gathered along the hem and reached for the floor. His head was twisted impossibly to the side, so much so that his chin was locked over his shoulder in an extremely tortured-looking pose. Even though his body faced the corner, Hill was looking directly at Tom.

"He was pushed down the stairs, Tom, and dragged to there." Kate moved toward the pool of blood in the middle of the floor. "I found his broken glasses under the stairs and some blood residue on about every third stair tread. There's a tooth embedded in the railing near the top and part of another one at the bottom. It's all consistent with a hard fall. From the looks of things, I say he bled out and either died right here or between here and there." Kate motioned to where Tom was standing next to Hill's body and pulling nitrile gloves over his hands. "The blood trail is minimal going toward the washer, which tells me his heart had most likely stopped pumping by the time he was moved. If he was already dead, why would SRK bother to stuff him in the corner?"

"Good question." Tom grabbed Hill's shirt collar and pulled. Hill was a small man and Tom was able to easily unfold his lifeless body from the corner. He carefully laid him out chest up on the concrete; the head remained grotesquely turned backwards, the face now to the floor. "His neck is badly broken, Kate. It could have happened on the stairs and is probably the

C.O.D., but I've never seen one broken this bad. That suggests SRK made it much worse after the fact, but I'm not sure why he would. My guess is Hill expired before SRK was ready for him to, and that really pissed him off. That would also explain *this* mess." Tom waved his flashlight back and forth over the multiple stab wounds in the abdomen. "His gut's been punctured at least thirty times from hip to hip. Look at this pattern. The spacing between the holes is consistent; these four seem to repeat over and over."

Something in the light caught his attention. "That's odd. Fetch me the small pliers from the evidence kit, Kate, and hold the light right here." When she returned, he handed her the flashlight. "I think there's something in there." Tom rolled Hill to his side. From the back of his hip, in the meaty area just above the pelvic bone, a round, pointed object, twice as thick as a pencil, protruded about an inch. "It looks like a sharpened bone." Tom gripped the end with the pliers. As he slowly removed it they could see that the point was carved at the end of a five-inch long leg from a plastic toy horse. "Whaddya know—that's interesting. Let's have a look around. I'll bet the rest of Mr. Ed is around here somewhere."

"Mr. who?" Kate asked.

"Never mind—I hate when you do that."

Kate scanned the side of the room opposite from Tom with her flashlight. The single light beyond the base of the stairs left most of the room in shadows. Other than the water heater, furnace and some boxes stacked against the wall, there was nothing much to see.

"What exactly am I looking for?" Kate asked.

"A three-legged toy horse like the ones we saw in Caroline's room. The legs will be sharpened to a point like the one I just pulled from Hill. If you find it, don't move it. There could be a message in where he left it."

"He might have taken it with him," Kate said.

"I suppose, but he had no more use for it. It was intended specifically for Hill, and he'd leave it here with the body so we'd find it."

Kate checked the narrow space between the furnace and water heater and then looked between the furnace and the wall where a sump pit was cast into the floor. At the edge of the hole, she saw the toy horse balanced precariously on its back. The bloodied tips of the sharpened legs pointed toward the ceiling and reflected her light like three small flares. "I got it; over here!" She took a few pictures while Tom crossed the room. "Well, it looks like it could be a message, Tom. Or, maybe he just threw it across the room, and this is where it landed. I'll agree it's pretty interesting how it just happened to end up teetering on the edge. You couldn't do that again if you tried a million times." Kate squeezed herself behind the furnace; her outstretched hand barely reached the toy. "SRK's a big guy; there's no way he could fit back here. We might want to file this one in the freak coincidence file right behind Caroline trying to kill SRK in front of her house."

"Yeah, you're probably right." Tom sighed. "I'm over-thinking again."

Tom set the bloody toy on Hill's belly just above his wounds and sat on the floor with his back against the washing machine. The cool metal felt good through his shirt. He pulled off his gloves and rubbed his eyes with the palms of his hands. "I'm exhausted, Kate. We missed him by only a couple of hours. We were *that* close. And *that* also means SRK didn't have a lot of time to waste, and he knew it. Hill was dead on the stairs or not long after, yet he took the time to do all of this anyway."

Tom gestured to the body. He paused a few seconds to reconstruct the scene in his mind. "Okay, let's work through this. Hill takes the dive. He's either pushed or falls, but either way, when SRK gets to him at the bottom of the stairs, he's not moving. SRK needs him to be awake for the main event, so his anger flairs, and he drags him to the middle of the room where the light is better and starts stabbing him with the toy horse over and over. That was his plan all along, but Hill's not responding like the other victims because he's already dead. SRK's frustration works into a rage, so he throws the weapon across the room, drags Hill to the washer and jams him in the corner like a broken lawn chair. To top it all off, he torques his head and does the one-eighty on his neck just so that Hill's face is the first thing we see when we get to him. That's a lot of pissed-off."

Tom got to his feet and walked to the pool of blood, shaking his head. "But here's the real interesting part: SRK would have to sit here for a long while waiting for gravity to drain the blood from Hill's body. You said it yourself, Kate; his heart had stopped pumping before he was moved to the corner. Even considering the number of punctures to his abdomen, it would have taken twenty minutes or more to drain this amount of blood on the floor. That's an eternity of time for SRK to sit still, knowing that we're coming for him. What the hell did he do for twenty minutes?"

"He waited," Kate said. "He waited for the rush that comes with each kill, but it didn't come this time. Think about it. Not too long ago he was just a regular guy doing regular guy stuff, but something very bad happened in his life, and that set him off—so here we are. And here he was, sitting alone in this dark basement next to a corpse of his own creation. A moment earlier was pure violence; suddenly it's pure silence. Maybe sitting in that silence he began to realize that all the killing he's done won't begin to bring back what he's lost."

Tom took a long, deep breath. Something important began to fit together in his mind. "You're right, Kate; the killing won't bring back whatever SRK lost, but it will help him heal, or *at least he believes it will*. Waiting for Hill to bleed out wasn't about discovering some path to redemption. Just look what he did next." Tom glanced at the back of Hill's head where his face should have been. "No, this one got botched, and I don't think it would have done anything for him except make him hungry for another target. Shit, he may have one lined up already.

He needs his prey alive and conscious when he goes through his kill rituals. Hill was supposed to be breathing while SRK made a pin cushion out of him, but he wasn't. Sure, he wanted Hill to remember young Caroline Evans and what he did to her. And for that, he would hear him beg for mercy just before he died. But all that was secondary effect. What SRK *needed* was Hill to be in absolute, terminal agony, and that, Kate, is the whole point of what he does: inflict horrific, unrelenting pain—as much as possible for as long as possible. That's how this works for him.

SRK wasn't waiting for the rush; he was waiting for the release—a *transference* from him to his prey. But dead pedophiles don't feel any pain, so now he has to go out and find one alive that will."

*****

R. BYRON STOCKDALE

–22–

ELLIS GROVE

Thurman Goethe was released from the hospital in Colorado Springs seven weeks after he entered the ICU with less than a ten percent chance of surviving his wounds. No one could explain how he did it without crediting Goethe with a remarkable desire to stay alive. On the morning he shuffled out of the hospital, he checked into a cheap motel to take his time searching for a suitable place to stay. He needed a few more months to finish healing, and he wanted a place that was quiet, something comfortable where he could think and write his poetry without interruption. The hospital had been almost as bad as the prison.

A few days later he found a room and bath for rent in the basement of an old house on Nevada Street a mile north of the center city; it was located next to a bus stop where he could catch a ride to the grocery store and his physical therapy sessions at the clinic downtown. The last thing he wanted to do was walk any distance in the rain, and a late spring snow was still a possibility. A fall would be a huge setback to his recovery. Nothing was going to get in the way of finding the man who did this to him.

The room he rented was spacious but with a low ceiling and had little windows high on the walls that reminded him of the window at the back of his prison cell. At least now he could walk outside and look at the sky as often as he pleased. It had a small wood-burning stove in the corner that the owners allowed him to use because the stone walls of the basement stayed cool, even through the summer, and Goethe needed to keep his legs warm to help with their poor circulation. And for an extra fifty-dollars, they gave him access to the bin behind the garage that they had already stocked with firewood for the next heating season.

The room had an outside entrance at the top of a short flight of stairs and led to a brick path along the side of the house. The path ended at an iron gate that opened to the street where he waited each morning for the bus to take him to the clinic. The owners of the house hadn't asked any hard questions when Goethe answered the ad for the room and especially after he offered to pay six-months' rent in advance and in cash. They hadn't asked about his background or his injuries, and they hadn't caught the news coverage of the shooting outside the Rockville Prison nearly two months ago.

The landlords' only concern seemed to be whether or not the applicant would be able to negotiate the five steps in and out of the apartment. Goethe assured them that stairs were a minor challenge that he could manage without much trouble, and the extra effort would be a small price to pay for his privacy and to be this convenient to public transportation. He also assured them that he lived quietly, and as soon as he completed his rehabilitation in a few more months, he would be moving on to live with his sister somewhere back in the Midwest.

*****

The buzzer rang a third time as Goethe reached the landing and unlocked the door. Behind it stood a short young man, perhaps nineteen or twenty years old, pointing a pistol at Goethe; the weapon was shaking noticeably, even though it was gripped tightly between the visitor's hands. Goethe retreated slowly down the first couple of steps then calmly turned around and finished descending the stairs. For some reason he started to smile.

If you come to me

Oh sly dementia,

Then be aware:

You may steal away,

Only what

I will not remember.

He shuffled across the floor, dragging his left foot to help with the pain, and opened the stove to expose the glowing embers; a chill had followed his visitor into the room, and the heat felt good on his stiff legs. "I'd say that gun is just a bit big for you, son. But please come in; be my guest."

The young man pushed the door closed behind him with his heel and followed Goethe down the stairs, keeping the pistol and his eyes aimed awkwardly at the center of Goethe's chest. He brushed the perspiration from his upper lip and brow with the sleeve of his jacket and glanced at the walker folded against the wall.

"As you can see," Goethe continued, "I'm doing much better getting around, thank you, and I don't need that contraption anymore." He shifted his weight to his right side over the stronger leg. His colostomy bag was full and was starting to smell, but he kept it in the heat so the stench might distract his visitor. He raised his palm in the air to show the scar, then formed a fist and opened it again, stretching his fingers wide.

"The hand's doing fine also, if you want to know. By the way, that was a damn good shot, or did you just miss?"

As soon as he said it, Goethe knew he was wrong. He hadn't felt afraid since he answered the door, and if this was the shooter who crippled him outside the prison, he would have felt fear by now. Instinct would have told him that he was about to die, but his guest didn't frighten him at all. No, the brutal attack on him would have required something that this person was clearly lacking. *The boy-man looks more like he's about to wet his pants, Thurman.*

Goethe felt around behind him until he found the handle to the heavy iron poker he used to tend the fire. "So, you must be little Blake Jefferies; it's been a while hasn't it? I do remember you, but not too fondly, you must know. As you can imagine, I spent a lot of time in a concrete box since we last met; it had something to do with your big mouth, and since you're standing there in front of me with that big gun, you obviously remember me also. So, Blake, however did you find me?"

"The *s-s-s-s...*, the *s-s-s-s...*, the offender *r-r-registry; it, it, it* was easy." *I, I, I ch-checked* it every *d-d-day* when I *f-f-found* out you *d-d-didn't* die. It *s-s-said* you lived here."

Goethe often wondered how the shooter could have found him—before he had been released—before he had to register. *And how would he know Thurman was getting out of Rockville that morning?*

"Come closer, and let me have a better look at you."

Blake took a step forward but stopped well short of being close enough for Goethe to strike. He knew he'd have only one chance to smash the little man's head, and if he missed, he was sure the nervous young Blake would panic and squeeze the trigger repeatedly until the gun was empty.

"It looks like you're all grown up now and became a man, well *s-s-sort* of, and how'd that happen *B-B-Blake?* You were such a lovely, *s-s-sweet* boy." Goethe couldn't move very fast, so he needed Jefferies angry and off guard,

"Don't *m-m-mock* me!" Jefferies leaned toward him, but not enough; his eyes briefly looked into Goethe's, then quickly retreated back to his chest. The gun was shaking almost uncontrollably. "*I, I, I* have this!"

"Yes, you do, Blake, but you seem a little upset; are you going to use it?"

"He *m-m-messed* up, so I have to *f-f-finish* you."

"Who messed up, Blake?" Goethe eased his grip on the poker; the afternoon just got much more interesting.

"My *m-m-mother* said a *m-m-man* was going to kill you; he *p-p-promised* her *in, in, in* his *l-l-letter."* Blake reached into his jacket pocket and held up a folded envelope; he tossed it on the floor a few feet in front of Goethe and put his hand back on the gun. "It *c-c-came* in the *m-m-mail.* He said he *woo-woo-would* kill you for us, but he *m-m-messed* up."

"I suppose he did." Goethe held up his one injured hand as if in surrender, with the other he tightened his grip behind him. "Before you kill me, Blake, will you let me read it? I'd like to know who did this horrible thing to me before I die." He moved his bad leg slightly forward and swept his hand across the front of it, presenting the crippled limb as evidence to the crime.

Blake stepped forward and pushed the envelope toward Goethe with the toe of his boot.

"Would you mind? I can't bend over with my bad hip." Goethe moved away from the stove; the envelope was too close. It looked like he was giving Blake a safe distance to pick it up and hand it to him, but he was positioning himself so that the barb on the end of the poker would land squarely in the side of his skull—*and it did.*

The sound of Blake's head collapsing was substantial; he didn't even scream. Blood and bits of his brain sizzled on the side of the hot stove and smelled like burning bacon.

"That, young Mr. Jefferies, is for the last eight years."

Goethe bent over slowly and picked up the envelope. It was postmarked back in January from Ellis Grove, Illinois, two months before his release. Not surprisingly, there was no return address. Thurman thought for a moment; the town sounded vaguely familiar to him, but every memory he had from before his time in Rockville was vague. He removed the letter before tossing the envelope in the stove and hobbled to the end of his bed. He glanced over at the boy-man bleeding out on the floor, "You really were a *s-s-sweet* boy, Blake." Then he sat down and began to read.

When Goethe was finished, he threw the letter in the fire as well and watched it burn. It had helped him to remember everything he needed to remember about Ellis Grove, Illinois.

*****

−23−

THE EMAIL

Tom stared at his computer screen, scrolling through the dozen or so emails that had collected in his inbox while he and Kate were flying back from Indiana earlier that afternoon. None looked particularly interesting except for Charlie's invitation to go out fishing on *Lady Luck* first thing Sunday morning. The rest of the emails would have to wait until tomorrow—or maybe Monday. It was late Friday evening, and he was tired of using his brain.

"You up for some fishing Sunday? Charlie's asking."

"Hell yes!" Kate walked into the room carrying two cups of hot tea. She handed one to Tom and set the other cup on the floor before plopping down on the couch where she had been working for the past two hours. "Anything to distract my mind from *you-know-who*."

Tom typed 'hell yes' in his reply to Charlie and hit send. He stretched his arms over his head and grabbed two fists full of air. "Please Kate—make this all go away."

"I'm trying, T. So, uh, shut up please." She glared at Tom nicely until he managed to fake a smile.

"How about a little music then?" Tom asked.

"Nope." Kate picked up a folder and got comfortable on the couch. Why don't you go for a walk and clear your head?"

"My knee hurts from gazelling off Caroline's porch."

"Whose fault is that?"

"Mine."

"Well if you're quiet and let me get back to work, I'll rub it for you later."

Tom shut his mouth but left the grin across it and went back to his emails. He had a separate secure line to his study for confidential Bureau communications; it was the same line used for voice and fax whenever he had to be consulted about sensitive case material at home. His secure private email address was well guarded, known only at the Bureau by select agents of the Criminal Investigative Unit and, of course, Charlie Grainger. Only two persons outside the Bureau knew his address and neither had ever used it unless it was absolutely necessary. For emergency reasons, his ex-wife had it in case something happened to one of their kids and Tom couldn't be reached by the usual methods. The other person was John Fleming, Tom's old friend and college mate from his days at Dartmouth. He switched the router over to the secured line and keyed in his special Bureau account address. Next he entered the twenty-seven-stroke password. Within a few seconds he was connected and waiting for any new messages to appear.

He took a sip of his tea and looked over at Kate; she was already back to reading the lab reports on the evidence collected at the church where Boyd Duncan was abducted and the scene in the countryside where he was killed. Things were moving quickly in the case, but it had only been a few days since they were standing in Jared Hill's basement looking over *his* mutilated body, and it was too early to have any results in from the lab dealing with Indiana.

The contents of the red folder were sorted into a dozen piles on the floor next to her where she could easily reach them. Her head was propped up on a throw pillow and her bare legs stretched out lazily across the cushions; she had her reading glasses balanced at the tip of her nose and a red pen clutched lightly between her lips. She was wearing one of Tom's thin

FBI t-shirts with no bra and a pair of his white boxers; her hair was pinned up loosely above her slender neck, and she was toying with some stray strands that had fallen behind her ear. Tom smiled openly; he was happy that Charlie had gotten them together; he was also glad to have found a better reason to keep his study warm.

"You were right, Tom;" Kate uncrossed her legs and sat up, "they found the piece of glass exactly where you said it would be, although you did miss the part about it protruding from the business end of the pipe— the one that SRK shoved up Duncan's backside."

Tom shook his body like a chill had just come over him. "That had to hurt."

"Yep, and that's not all. This particular piece of glass wasn't exactly red; it was closer to amber with some red along one edge." Kate handed Tom the document as he came over and sat down next to her.

"Well, I'd say that could be good or bad;" Tom leaned back looking disappointed, "either the amber is significant or the red never was."

"Maybe they both are. Maybe the red is *sooo* significant that he didn't want to desecrate it by putting it up Duncan's hoo-ha."

"Or maybe they both aren't, and, by the way, the word you're looking for is 'heinie'. A 'hoo-ha' is the, uh, front crack on a—" Tom pointed between Kate's thighs and got up. He scratched the back of his head and shuffled around the room, passing in front of Kate twice before sitting back down in front of his computer. "You know, Kate; this one's getting my knickers in a wad."

"I think this is fun!" She swung her legs back on the couch and lay back down. "Do you know you have a big hoo-ha in your ceiling?"

Tom laughed, "Yeah, it's on my to-do list, bottom of page forty-seven right after 'finding a new career'. Don't worry, the crack's been there forever, so I don't think it's going to come down on us, and if it does, I'll throw my body on top of yours to protect you."

"Just give me a little warning first so I can get my heinie in a comfortable position." Kate blew him a kiss before turning her attention back to the report.

*****

Tom looked at the screen; he expected to find several emails waiting for him but only one appeared. The subject line read:

"Dartmouth professor needs student intern for special assignment. $5/hour. No experience necessary."

"Fleming, you're a sorry-son-of-a-sheep-herder." Tom double-clicked the heading and went to pour himself a glass of Scotch from the bottle of Glenfiddich that sat on the shelf above his desk between his college textbooks on *Preliminary Statistical Analysis* and *Criminal Psychology*, classes he and John Fleming had taken together as sophomores. He kept the bottle handy for just such occasions. He held it up so Kate could see. "You in?"

"Like a glass eye."

"Should I be worried, Kate? You're starting to talk like me." Tom handed her a tumbler half-filled with scotch and sat back at his desk.

"You should be flattered." Kate took a sip.

"I am, actually." Tom paused what he was doing to study the incredible woman reclining on his couch. "I am *very* pleased."

"Good; I hope you stay that way."

"I just got an email from my old college buddy, John Fleming."

"Really? The James Bond writer?"

"No, that's Ian Fleming; but John is as Scottish as the single malt you have in your hand. He and I were frat-rats together at Dartmouth; we roomed together for three great years; of course we could never afford the good stuff back then. After school, I went straight south to start my drills at Quantico, and John stayed behind in Hanover for graduate work and went on to earn his doctorate in Forensic Psychology; he's quite the brain guy. Those who can—can; those who can't—teach, right?" Tom paused to savor the smell of his scotch before taking a healthy drink.

"Anyway, he's been there so long they had to promote him to faculty chair or have him stuffed. He's been a real help to me on some past cases and should prove useful to us in capturing SRK—*once we know what the hell is going on.* I'm indebted to this guy. If I'm fortunate enough to outlive John, I'll probably have to return to campus and bury him below the 'green' in front of Old Dartmouth Hall. I have a very special bottle saved for that particular occasion."

"I have a sorority sister from OU that means a lot to me too; I'm not real sure where she is anymore, but I do have a six-pack of Corona in the back of my fridge that I plan to knock back at her funeral, unless I drink it before then." Kate shot an exaggerated grin at Tom, then went back to reading. She made it politely clear that she wasn't very interested in hearing about Tom's old roommate at the moment.

Before Tom returned to the email, he took a moment to reflect on his friend; they hadn't seen each other since their tenth reunion too many years ago.

*****

John Fleming had been a vital resource to Tom throughout his FBI career; his brilliant and objective psychological analysis had steered the profiles for several particularly troublesome killers. Those profiles had led to five criminal convictions and ultimately two federal executions; most recently a killer by the name of Silas Filer, known prior to his capture only as the 'Trenton Butcher'. Fleming's mind was quite adept at analyzing deviant human behavior from the hills of southern New Hampshire. It seemed that his distance from the crimes, removed from any distractive personal feelings for the victims, helped him to evaluate the case information from a purely intellectual perspective. Sometimes Tom needed a little help seeing the forest through the trees.

This time around though, Tom hadn't yet contacted Fleming about the Short Rose Killer. They had collaborated on the early case when it was unfolding back in St. Louis, but Fleming had been just as stumped as he was. Now, the current events were coming too fast, and Tom hadn't had a chance to pull anything tangible together. Each time he thought he had, some important detail changed—*like the color of the glass.* There was also something about the case that kept him from wanting to move too quickly. Perhaps his private thoughts were right; why should he care so much about catching this one? The half-dozen murders he was trying to solve and the ones he was trying to prevent didn't involve college coeds or helpless children. In fact, it was quite the opposite; the longer SRK was free to hunt, the more sexual assaults against children were prevented. This killer went after the monsters that preyed on kids like Haden and Katie; even Grainger didn't seem like he was pushing too hard about making a quick arrest.

For this new dance with SRK, Tom would take his time to compose a few theories and maybe have the chance to test them before approaching John for his help in the analysis. Besides, he really liked working with Kate, who looked a lot better on his couch than John ever would, and he wasn't sure if he wanted to rush on to the next assignment knowing she might not be part of it. Tom raised his glass to his old friend and took a drink; the

Scotch felt warm going down his throat and brought him back to younger days at Dartmouth. He thought it funny how the Scotch and ancient memories could be so tightly woven together.

*****

Tom spoke silently to the flat screen; *so what do you have to say for yourself, Nippy?* It was the name he endeared to his friend, well-earned for a propensity to take winter swims in the Hanover River—even without the persuasive influence of copious amounts of alcohol. First, Tom clicked the .jpeg file attachment; the screen prompted for another password before it would open the document. As an additional precaution, all documents shared between Tom and John were automatically password protected. After he confirmed his entry, the screen filled with a photo of his friend sitting on a giant ice sculpture of two tangled lions. A banner promoting the 123rd winter carnival at the college hung across the front of Baker Library in the background. After he checked the format of the image, he sent it to the color printer; he thought that Kate might want to have a look. Besides, his other Katie would want to see a picture of Uncle John the next time he had his kids for the weekend.

Tom clicked on the attached .txt file and reentered his password at the prompt. The text read:

"Dear Russ,"

"How are the little Indians? It's been a while since we've swapped notes. I understand Silas got the chair. Bravo! I suppose you couldn't have done it without me! What a team; good work, huh?"

Tom smiled and took another sip before he continued reading.

"Follow along with me, Tom, and be patient, it's important—I'll get to the point soon enough, but I want to take

325

you through all the steps—you know, all things in order. I may drift into the dung a wee bit but we haven't chatted in a while, so humor me. I trust by now you've indulged yourself to a little splash before reading this?"

Tom refreshed his glass before returning to the text.

"Do you remember Two-Drop Dudley? Well, someone's been through our alumni directory, and the attached message arrived to me through him. I just heard from the Dud a few months ago, so this came a little bit out of the blue. We had a few laughs at our 15th reunion, and we've stayed in touch maybe once a year around the holidays ever since. You should have been there just to see him; I guess he's gained a good hundred pounds and, besides needing a stair master, he could use a little sod upstairs, and he still can't hold his booze. He's done well for himself though, and his new wife was a stunner, mostly store-bought; had bloody fine pappies that defied gravity, if you know what I mean. Anyway, to my knowledge he's the only one from our class that has my email, and I'm definitely the only one that has yours. That makes the fact that you're getting this a long shot.

The email chain I got went back only three levels past Dudley; the names in the copy list were mostly fellow grads, but a dozen or so were from different years. If we discount the names in the first three levels, we can't say who it might have come from at all; someone along the line stripped out the early CC's as well as the original sender. I'm making calls to the rest of the guys from our frat-pack, but it will take a little time, and I doubt it will turn up much. I'm sure your Q-boys will be able to trace it better than me. We're in the middle of mid-terms, so I'm a little strapped for time. I couldn't see much more than some familiar names among the copy lists, but you might find one or two that might mean something. I did sacrifice my alum directory and clipped out the photos of the guys I could identify in the chain in case their pics would help you in some way. I sent them to you in the overnight mail yesterday, and don't worry, I billed your account number. Remember, I'm still just an impoverished college professor! You might want to fetch it."

Tom got up from his desk and went to the front door; he had to step over Jake who was curled up in the middle of the hall, sound asleep. Outside, a FedEx priority envelope rested against the stoop next to a rolled up copy of the Washington Post. He grabbed the envelope but left the paper and returned to the study. Before sitting back down, he kissed Kate on the forehead and was rewarded with a sexy, but phony, little moan.

"The last directory came out about a year ago, Tom, so whoever used it had fairly current address information— except for yours, of course. I checked it myself and only one hundred thirty-six of two hundred and seventy-four classmates had provided their email address for publication. My guess is that the attachment has been widely circulated among the grads. I figure it was sent to one or all of the emails listed, and most of them probably forwarded it on to the rest of the alumni in their address folders. With the way a message can proliferate across the web, it only took two days before it ended up in Dudley's inbox, then in mine, and now in yours. It's clear that whoever sent it was fishing for you through one of us. He obviously knows you're a son of Dartmouth and also the year you graduated. Who knows how he got the information, but he did, and he wanted you to get this. Wouldn't it have been much easier to just send you a note at the Bureau via U.S. Mail? For what it's worth, I think he's just trying to impress you with how clever he is."

Tom looked over at Kate lounging on the couch; she was still intensely occupied by the Duncan lab reports. John was probably right; he usually was.

"The missing child is legitimate, I checked the origin of the file attachment, and the mother and kid are for real. The County Sheriff's report was filed shortly after the New Year. Her boy

327

was taken about ten weeks ago from some little town in West Virginia just outside of Wheeling, but you can read that for yourself. You'll see that the email came from her brother who supposedly attended Dartmouth, but I checked, and there is no brother. The fact that he doesn't exist makes this little conundrum begin to stink. The mystery man that sent this must have made it up to help ensure it was widely circulated among the Hanover community—so it would ultimately get to you; otherwise the email would have just died at the first or second level."

Tom stretched back in his chair; he was pleased that his friend had already made an effort to sift through some of the front-end work.

"There's an embedded .txt file attached but it's password protected. There must be a clue somewhere in his short message, but it's probably a piece of information only you both share. If you can't solve it, I'm sure one of your lab geeks will be able to pick it apart in no time. I can't do much else from here until I know more, but I'll help as much as you let me. Is there something you're working on that you want to share? If I knew, this might start to make a little sense, and I might actually be able to H-E-L-P you."

Tom took off his reading glasses and rubbed his eyes. He finished his Scotch and poured another splash; he figured at this point it couldn't hurt and was actually beginning to help. He glanced at Kate's glass but she had hardly made a dent in it.

The two attachments in the heading had been forwarded along with the original email. One was the password protected .txt document; the other was an unprotected graphic .gif file. He clicked on the .gif first. It was a picture of a boy, perhaps fourteen or fifteen, and looked like a school photo, taken against a phony backdrop of the Appalachian Mountains in autumn. 'Blue Ridge Studio' was embossed in gold letters across the lower right-hand corner. He was a good-looking kid, thin but with a strong athletic frame. A big 'R' was sewn to the left breast of his sweater. Tom checked the size of the file format and sent it to the printer. Next he scrolled down to the original email message, from the bogus brother, at the bottom of the chain and began to read.

*****

"I'm a fellow Dartmouth Indian, class of '82. Please read the following plea from my little sister. She needs your help. Please forward this to <u>everyone</u> *you know. I remember reading that one of Dartmouth's later esteemed graduates ended up in a high-ranking position at the FBI. Russell is his name; he's supposed to be the best. I'm hoping that each of you will take a moment to forward my sister's plea to your Dartmouth friends in the hope that it will reach Mr. Russell and that he will be able to use his resources to help find my young nephew. There's a great wooded spot in Iowa where I'd like to take him hunting again."*

Tom thought for a moment. He dropped to his knees next to the couch and rifled through the stacks of files Kate had spread out on the floor until he found the tab labeled 'Iowa'.

"Lose something, Tom?"

"Nope, I got it." Tom quickly thumbed through his notes but couldn't find what he was looking for. "What's the name of the place where the Lowens were found—the woods where the hunter tripped over Bart's remains?"

"Turner's Wood," Kate answered without any hesitation. "Are you alright?"

"Yep. That's it! Thanks!" *TurnersWood: that has to be the password.* He was certain of it.

"What's going on, Tom? You seem a little excited. Should I get, uh, ready?"

"Not yet—*but don't lose that thought.* John sent me something that could be almost as interesting; give me a few minutes, and I'll know more." Tom *was* excited, but he knew he should read the mother's plea next. *All things in order...*

"My name is Emily Cooper, and this is a picture of my son Jamie. It was taken this past October. We live near Wheeling, West Virginia." Tom let the picture exit the laser jet and laid it on the desk where he could see it. Jamie Cooper looked back at him, frozen in time and place at the Blue Ridge Studio. *"On January 12, Jamie didn't come home from orchestra practice. It's dark then, but we live close to school, and it's just a short walk. I love my son, and we're very close. He would never run away from home. I know he must have been taken against his will. Please, please if you've seen him since that day, call Sergeant Mark Griffin at 1-304-555-2000. It will save precious time. Please send this message to everyone you know. I hope that someone, somewhere may have seen him. Please pray for his safety. Pray with me that someday soon my Jamie will come home."*

Tom clicked on the .txt document and entered 'TurnersWood' at the password prompt. The file opened immediately.

"Hello Thomas."

Tom thought he heard a sudden loud noise like thunder; he looked to see if Kate had heard it too, but she was still focused on the Boyd Duncan report. He glanced at the picture of the boy on his desk as he emptied his glass; his hand was trembling. He got up from his chair and walked around the room to shake it off. Kate followed him with curious eyes but quickly went back to her reading. When he felt settled, Tom sat back down at his computer and started to read.

"It was good to see you; it's been a long time. I was almost surprised when I saw you and your young lady friend at the courthouse in Gibson. But I knew you'd come to find me

eventually. We do what we do.

The newspapers said you found Hill before his body got cold—very impressive work!

I've liked you ever since you told that troll of a reporter in St. Louis that I wasn't a threat to decent people. We share a distain for the press; they have no interest in the truth. They just exploit the victims and their families so that they can sell their damn newspapers."

"Um; young lady," Tom motioned for Kate to join him at his computer, "you need to see this—*like right now.*"

Kate sprung off the couch and quickly settled in behind Tom. She leaned over him and rested her crossed arms on his shoulders; her face was close, next to his. "So what does Mr. Fleming have to say?"

"It's not John; it's SRK. Let me know when you get to here." Tom pointed at the bottom of the fourth paragraph and got up out of the chair so Kate could sit down. He leaned against the desk, watching her read.

When Kate finished, she didn't move or react; instead, she began to read the rest of the note out loud and slowly to Tom.

"You once said that my work is the work of a grieving father. You are quite correct. You're a father just like me and know in your heart that killing these demons is our primal right—it is virtuous and just. You and I, we're on the same side; we dispose of the bad people. My solution is more effective. It's also permanent.

This poor boy from West Virginia needs us, and there are tens of thousands more who need us too. Let me finish my work, and I promise I will go away peacefully. Wouldn't that be easier for both of us?"

Tom collapsed back on his desk like he was pushed by a strong headwind, leaving him sprawled across his case files and the empty red folder. Looking up, he noticed a crack in his ceiling that wasn't there before.

"It turns out I don't need John's help to find SRK after all, Kate. It appears that SRK has already found me."

*****

–24–

EBB TIDE

C harlie eased *Lady Luck* out of the marina just as the sun was trying to break over Turkey Point. The sky was overcast and heavy with cool morning air resting on a flat rising tide, great conditions for catching Striped Bass on the Chesapeake Bay. He called down to Tom, who was working below on the aft deck preparing the rods and tackle before securing them along the transom rail; he spoke loudly over the noise of the engine.

"As soon as we clear the markers, I'll bury the throttle and head north to the Route 50 Bridge; we'll drift along the concrete pilings and let the current push the fish to us. We should be able to fill the well in no time—should be a piece of cake. It's a ten-mile ride out, so we ought to be getting our hooks wet in about an hour." Charlie did a one-eighty scan of the water opening up in front of them and then turned back to Tom. "The forecast expects these conditions to burn off by mid-morning, and that'll push the fish into darker water. Even if the sun doesn't come out by then, the tide's supposed to crest about the same time, and then the good fishing, if the *Lady* is kind enough to give us any, is going to turn off like a switch."

Tom only half-listened to what Charlie had said; he didn't much care where or how they caught the fish or if they caught any at all; after the five-alarm cluster that happened out in Indiana that week, followed by SRK's little email note, he just wanted to get out on the open water and cleanse his body in the fresh salt air. He tossed a stick of gum in his mouth and set the last rod in a holder before looking up at Grainger piloting the boat from the fly bridge. He shook his head at the sight of his boss wearing the same silly fishing cap he always wore, trying his best to look something like Ernest Hemingway standing at the helm. The Deputy Director just had a hard time looking casual. Tom felt the boat surge forward as they slipped out from the shelter of the cove; he sat on the edge of the transom and watched the shoreline receding in their wake. Ahead, the great bay was wide and smooth, beckoning him to enter.

*****

The last time he checked, Kate was still asleep under a scramble of sheets and blankets in the forward berth below. Charlie had invited them to spend the night on his boat so they wouldn't have to make the long drive in from Virginia at some ridiculous hour in the morning. He told Tom that he planned to stay home and get some work done before he took the day off to go fishing; he didn't live far from the marina and would catch up with them at the dock a little before sunrise. Tom didn't swallow the excuse; he knew Charlie really wanted to stay on shore so he wouldn't embarrass himself in front of Kate by getting up every hour during the night to pee, especially if they spent the evening drinking a few beers. Tom was happy just the same; the boat wasn't that big, and the sleeping accommodations were far from private. He didn't want to wake up to the sound of Grainger's bladder draining every hour either. Besides, *Lady* was tied up at the end of the pier away from the other boats, and, without their host on board, he and Kate had had all the privacy they needed.

He climbed the ladder to the fly bridge and took the seat across from the helm. "How's it going, Captain?"

Charlie glanced at the two fish-finders mounted above the console. "It's quiet down there right now; we're in the no-Bass zone—too far from shore where they like to feed in the morning and too far from structure where the bait fish tend to hide. I expect we'll see a bunch of hungry Stripers at the bridge.

There're some binoculars in that compartment in front of you. Keep your eyes open for gulls or terns feeding on the way out; they eat where the Bass eat, if the bait is shallow enough."

He tapped on the fuel gauge, and the needle jumped from empty to full. "I need to get that fixed before I'm stranded out here with no diesel." He tapped it one more time, and the needle stayed put. "So how's our favorite case coming along?"

"You mean other than chasing our butts in a circle across the Corn Belt? I'm afraid it's mostly come down to the lab grunt work right now until we get another break. On top of Quantico's insane caseload, they've been cranking on what our evidence teams have been collecting in the aftermath of SRK's handiwork; there's quite a lot to process. And now this past week, we've added the mess from Jared Hill's basement into the mix. I don't know how they do it." Tom stopped short of mentioning the email; it was still processing in his brain.

"Fast, cheap or right; pick two." Charlie eased back on the throttle slightly and settled some odd vibration coming up from the engine bay.

"What?"

"The Lab crew is fast, and they're typically right, but they sure ain't cheap. *That's* how they do it."

"I don't suppose they are; I've seen their budget." Tom spit his gum over the side. "You won't believe it, but they found some glass residue in the ballistic blobs they dug out of the tower at Rockville. They're still testing the glass against the exemplars we have already, but I suspect they'll find a match; SRK wouldn't have gone through the trouble otherwise. It would appear that he prefers to hand-load his ammo, or at least in this case he did. Smithson over in Chemistry discovered the glass; he also found two different types of lead mixed in with the jacket debris; he figures after the heel of the bullet was drilled for the glass, a different lead was used to fill in the hole behind it. The second lead type is a little heavier, so maybe it was used to get the bullet weight back up to spec. That's some pretty impressive tooling and machine work, if you ask me; it would require some expensive equipment."

"I heard a lot of snipers like to roll their own, or they used to until the military started offering the new match-grade boat tail rounds out of Lake City Ammo," Charlie offered. "I understand the really good hand-loaders can tune a charge, length and load for specific field conditions. They are *that* good."

"Apparently they are. We've already suspected a military background or specialty law enforcement, but they're just one piece of the big Rubik's Cube we've come to know and love as SRK. I imagine we'll find something similar with the toy horse he used to make Hill into a pin cushion; he probably drilled out the legs along the same lines."

Just then Kate stepped off the ladder with a Styrofoam cup gripped between her teeth and a donut wrapped around her thumb. She took the coffee in the donut hand and gave Charlie a good-morning pat on the back with the other; she shuffled over to Tom and leaned into him. "Thanks for the use of your boat last night, Skipper 'G'." She looked out across the grey Chesapeake at the orange-cotton clouds filling the eastern sky and then up at Tom's approving smile. "This is the *most awesome* way to wake up *ever!*"

"I thought you two would like it," Charlie said. "I'm sorry I couldn't join you."

Yeah, too bad you had to work, Charles. Tom mused to himself as he wrapped his arm lightly around Kate's shoulders.

"So, what's the plan, boys?" Kate asked before half the donut disappeared into her mouth; she raised the other half to Tom, and he gladly took it. She let her thumb linger for a moment between his lips.

"Catch the fish before they go deep," Charlie answered

matter-of-factly. "That's the plan."

"We used to night fish for Striped Bass on Lake Texoma, but I don't remember my dad sharing that little factoid. Why do they go deep?"

"Stripers don't like the bright light of day. Their eyes are designed for low light or night conditions; that's probably why your dad took you out at night. Once they go deep, they tend to get lockjaw; you won't catch them."

"Interesting." Kate bounced on the balls of her feet for a few seconds like she was warming up a thought, then hurried to the ladder and disappeared below without any explanation.

"Is she okay?" Charlie eased the throttle down to an idle, and the boat slowed immediately. "Did I say something wrong again?" He sounded genuinely concerned.

"She may be a bit hung-over. I'll go check on her." Tom descended the ladder almost as quickly as Kate. He crossed the salon and went below to find her in front of her laptop on the settee opposite the galley. Tom hadn't known Kate for very long, but he knew when her sharp young brain had locked onto something juicy. "What are you thinking?"

"Ted Bundy."

"The serial killer?"

"No, the family guy on TV. Of course I mean the serial killer, silly. Teddy decapitated a dozen or so women before the freak got arrested for some other non-head-removing type offense. They had no idea that the handsome fellow sitting in their lockup had already committed close to thirty homicides in seven states. All those murder investigations kept right on chugging along because no one knew that the guy they were looking for was already sitting in a municipal jail cell somewhere in Utah. It was only later that they started making the connections."

"Yeah, I studied that case too; he was actually pulled over for running a stop sign. So, how does it fit?"

"Well, it doesn't exactly, but it helps to make my point." Kate brushed a frustrating strand of hair away from her face.

"Which is?"

"Captain Charlie said you won't catch the Stripers when they've gone deep."

"That's right."

"Well, you can't catch a killer if he's gone deep either; that is, if he's gone inside like Bundy did—well, sort of like him. *Oh never mind.*" Kate opened her SRK case directory and started scrolling rapidly while selecting several files. She stopped for a moment when Tom sat down next to her. "If you're looking for the unknown bad guy in a particular case, and he happened to get picked up for some other crime during the investigation, you're not going to make him, right? You can't arrest someone who isn't around to be arrested."

"Yeah, and I suppose the case would go cold pretty quick. So you think that explains why SRK went quiet for a few years?"

"I'm not talking about SRK; I'm talking about SRK's *victims*. Look at this." Kate turned her laptop toward Tom and pointed at the initial arrest date listed at the top of the page. "This shows Bart Lowen was apprehended eight years ago in April and ended up at Joliet after his trial." She selected the next file queued up on the task bar. "This one is Hill; he's been in and out several times, but he also happened to get nabbed on a rape charge in August—*the same year as Bart.*" She clicked on the next file. "Here's Goethe—*March, same year.*" Another file opened. "Duncan—*March also.*" Click. "Levy—*June.*" Click. "Chapman—*November.*" Click. "Randall—*June.*" Kate slumped back against the bench. "Every single one was pulled off the street during the same nine-month period during the exact same year. Tom, they all went *deep* at the same time."

Tom didn't move; he could feel Kate's excitement boil up next to him, but he blocked it out so he could think. "Okay, you're on to something, so let's try this: your child is taken and brutally murdered or, far worse, the child is never found, but the police have no suspects, no leads, nothing. The investigation drags on for months but goes nowhere. Everything they've tried turned out to be a dead-end. With no other options available, their case strategy digresses into a wait-and-see approach; I've seen it happen fairly often. Anyway, all they can do is sit tight and wait for the child's body to turn up or another murder to occur with the same M.O., but it doesn't. Maybe someone in the investigation suggests to you that the UNSUB must have been killed by some coincidence or maybe arrested for some other crime. You're told that there is nothing else they can do until the perp strikes again, if he ever does. Then all at once the task force is dismantled to work other cases, and you're left alone—kicked to the curb. You're a bitter, grieving father, and now you're angry beyond the known limits of human anger. What do you do next?"

Kate didn't even hesitate before answering, "You find every predator in your area that went inside during your child's investigation. You hunt them down, and you kill every single one of them. You believe your pursuit is righteous, and, because you do, you also believe that eventually you are going to come across the actual monster you're searching for; it's a simple process of elimination, Tom. When you find him, you will show no mercy."

"Bingo."

"And how do you do that? I mean, how do you know who you're looking for in the first place?" Kate leaned against the side of the cabin and put her legs on Tom's lap.

"I've been asking that question for five years." Let me see that. Tom slid the laptop in front of him and scanned through each of the files Kate had loaded. "Of course, his victims would have likely been jailed on child assault charges or maybe something benign along the lines of your Ted Bundy example, but they would definitely have a predatory record of one kind or another—that's how SRK would identify them. Unfortunately, it looks like they all went to different correctional facilities scattered roughly around the Midwest, except for Goethe, of course, and... do you have a folder for Bobby Mayfield?"

He slid the computer back to Kate. She found the file and opened it.

"Sorry, *Georgia*," Kate sighed, "another one of those pesky dead-ends you like so much. I was hoping for a tighter geographical spread. Now that we know the general timeframe of the investigation, it would have been real convenient if SRK's victims had been arrested in the same area; then we could have easily found a case or two that matched. But based on the range of these locations, I'd say we can't get any more focused than a five hundred mile radius around, I don't know, Missouri or Illinois maybe? At least that will reduce the number of possible unsolved crimes we have to sift through. There has to be something else threading them together, Tom; the common dates alone don't answer how SRK would have compiled his list and hunted them down."

"Let me see that again." Tom scrolled to the top of Mayfield's file and then reached across to the galley and grabbed a napkin and pen that were lying on the counter. He jotted down a seven-digit acronym and then did the same for each of the other victim files; three of the eight acronyms shared the number that appeared at the end.

"What are those Tom?"

"D.O.C. correctional codes; they're assigned to every slammer in the country from the county level on up to the federal facilities. The first two letters identify the state; the other three letters identify the facility, sort of like airport codes; the last two numbers after the dash identify if it's a privately owned or managed prison. Each company is assigned a different I.D. number. If you see zeroes, it means the facility is public. Look, these three are the same: Mayfield, Goethe and Levy; company number one-two; the rest just show zeroes."

"That's interesting, but there are only a handful of private companies, and I'm sure they have multiple facilities in their portfolios. I was hoping we'd find something a bit more significant. Couldn't these three just be a coincidence? I mean, this case seems to have had its share."

"Maybe—but I intend to find out." Tom pulled out his phone and opened his contacts. When he found who he was looking for, he placed the call. "Kevin? This is Tom Russell at the Bureau. I'm sorry to call you so early on a Sunday morning, but it's important." Tom listened for a moment, "Yes, Charlie's fine; I'm actually out with him on his boat right now." Another pause, "I'll tell him you said hello, but I don't want to keep you. Kevin, I'm looking at a prison code for a private operator, number twelve; that's one-two. Can you tell me what company it is?" Tom jotted down the name on the napkin. "Thank you so much, Kevin. Yes, all the best." He set his phone down. "Kevin's been at the D.O.C. for decades; he knew it off the top of his head. *American Corrections*—would you care to guess where they're located?"

"Can I buy a vowel?"

"No."

"Then I'll have to go with St. Louis."

"Correct."

Kate sat up as Tom slid off the settee. "Well, Thomas; so much for spending another wonderful night rocking Charlie's boat."

"And whose fault is that Miss *they've-gone-deep* Morrow?" He bent over and kissed her on the forehead. "I'll see if the

Skipper can make a call and get us one of his planes to St. Louis this afternoon, otherwise we'll go commercial. Before you shut down your machine, try to book us a room somewhere in the city—maybe with a view of the Arch. Kevin said American Corrections is located downtown by the river. As long as we're making the trip, we may as well take in some of the sights."

All of a sudden Tom felt a little more like catching a fish.

*****

−25−

DETOUR

Josh Bolen had gotten a late start out of the refinery in Chalmette and was running heavy on the Route 11 causeway over Lake Pontchartrain with twenty-five tons of gasoline filling the tanker behind him to capacity. The load was a rush order from a good customer in Knoxville, and he had volunteered for the Sunday haul so he could get home to his little place not far away in the Smoky Mountains in time to surprise his wife for their fifth wedding anniversary.

Normally he would have taken the I-10 Bridge, but the northbound lanes were backed up from an accident at the St. Tammany Parish line. Bolen could pick up a little time on the old causeway as long as the drawbridge halfway across wasn't raised for boating traffic on the lake. The sun had set a few hours before, and he was willing to gamble that navigation would be fairly sparse, especially at this time of night. Overhead the stars hovered alone in a moonless sky, but in the glare from the approaching cars Josh couldn't see them; he couldn't even discern where the water met the shore. Somewhere off to his left, the concrete spans of the Norfolk-Southern Railroad were converging toward the roadway and would run parallel with it from the drawbridge all the way to Eden Isle, but he couldn't see them either. Right now, he didn't care what he saw, and it didn't matter anyway; he was too irritated with the idiot driving in front of him, crawling along at thirty miles an hour, slow-hauling a bed on the top of his car like it was held down with Scotch Tape or kite string and might blow away. This was not a good start to his trip, and it sure wasn't putting him in a very good mood.

Josh took a deep breath and spit some chew in the plastic

bottle he kept next to his seat; he didn't need to get his blood pressure all worked up over this minor setback. There was nothing he could do about it anyway; his load was much too heavy to attempt a pass, and even if he was pulling a dry trailer, there weren't any breaks in the oncoming traffic long enough to even consider trying. At least he was making better progress than he would have made otherwise if he had stayed on the interstate. He decided to queue up a little bluegrass on his I-Phone and settle in for the short detour over the lake. It was going to be a late run through Dixie, and he would be back on I-10 soon enough, crossing into Mississippi on four lanes where he could pass any idiot he wanted and make up the lost time. He'd push his rig between eighty and eighty-five all the way to Tennessee.

Without looking, Josh knew he was passing over the drawbridge; for a few seconds the sound of his tires rolling under him changed from a dull drone to a low-pitched whine, then back again. *Half-way there.*

As he finished his thought, the car in front of him began to gradually increase its speed, and, as it pulled away, Josh started to sing along with the music; maybe his luck was beginning to change. He pressed the accelerator to stay close; there was nothing like ninety thousand pounds of truck filling a rearview mirror to hasten a driver along, and this asshole deserved a little tailgating. At first Josh was more than happy to pick up the pace; even his old diesel seemed to like it better; but when they broke seventy-five miles an hour, he became a little concerned and started to back off; two-way traffic on a narrow bridge with no shoulder was a dangerous combination.

Just as he began to slow, the mattress went airborne coming broadly at him, suddenly filling his vision as if he was driving into a square, white tunnel.

Time slowed to a crawl; there was not enough of it to react and nowhere to steer; to the right he would crash over the concrete rail and drown in the lake, to the left he would perish in a fiery collision with the line of approaching cars.

Reflexively, he slammed on the brakes triggering a deadly fight to maintain control of his truck as it began to jack-knife between the yellow lines and the edge of the bridge. In his right mirror he could see sparks trying to ignite the tanker where it dragged against the rail; in his left he saw the taillights of cars swerving to miss the wheels of his cab as they skidded into the oncoming lane.

He thought of his wife and young boy at home and wanted to cry out loud for them to hear, but all he could to do was release a loud moan through his clenched teeth. Gripping the wheel like a vise, he braced for the impact, certain his life was about to end. Strangely, the only thing he felt was the pulse of his heart throbbing against the wedding ring on his finger; and between the beat just before he closed his eyes and the one after he did, time stood still; and in that frozen instant Josh Bolen heard a horrifying scream and glimpsed the terrified face of a man trapped inside the white tunnel, hurling toward him with shiny red eyes at a hundred feet per second.

Then as abruptly as it had stopped, time skipped forward with a click, and the last of the scream died just as the mattress smashed into his grill and disappeared beneath his wheels.

*****

–26–

AMERICAN CORRECTIONS

"**G**ood morning, miss." Kate showed her credentials to the receptionist, who had watched her and Tom step off the elevator and cross the granite and steel entry hall to the penthouse floor of American Corrections. The space felt more like they had just walked onto a Hollywood sound stage for some futuristic prison movie than a corporate office. "I'm Special-Agent Kate Morrow with the FBI; this is my colleague SAC Russell. Tom stood next to her casually thumbing through the company brochure he had pulled from the display in the lobby downstairs. For this visit, they had decided that Kate should run point; it might soften any perceived threat associated with a couple of federal agents showing up at their offices first thing on a Monday morning. "We need to speak with someone in senior management please," she handed her business card along with one of Tom's to the young woman, "and as soon as possible, if you don't mind."

"Just one moment, ma'am; I think everyone is in a meeting; let me see who is available." She politely rolled her chair away from the desk and left the lobby with their identification. When she returned a minute later she was accompanied by a tall athletic looking man, perhaps in his late thirties, casually dressed in khaki's and a red polo shirt with the 'AC' logo embroidered to the left of his open collar. He had a photo ID clipped to his belt and a noticeably long scar down the side of his face that only added to his imposing appearance.

"Hello, I'm Frank Buchanan, managing partner with the firm." He shook Kate's hand and then Tom's. "How can I assist the two of you this morning?"

"Is there somewhere private where we can talk?" Kate began.

"Of course." Buchanan led them to a vendor meeting room around the back of the elevators and closed the door after they had stepped inside.

"Mr. Buchanan, we'd like access to your employment records from the years and facilities highlighted on this list." Kate handed him a copy of the spreadsheet she had pieced together after they had gotten back from their fishing trip with Charlie yesterday. The list included the corporate offices of American Corrections in St. Louis, the prisons where Levy, Goethe and Mayfield had been incarcerated, plus the six other Midwest facilities that the company operated during the period between four and eight years ago. Eight years because that's when all the victims were taken off the street, and, based on Kate's *gone deep* theory, would have coincided with the dead-end investigation into whatever happened to SRK's child; four years because that's when the killing had stopped with the murder of Greg Levy, his body found less than eleven miles from where they now stood.

"I can't impress upon you enough the importance of keeping this request confidential," Kate continued. "We're only interested in those employees with high enough security clearance to access non-public court records and offender databases at the county, state and federal levels. We believe one of those employees may have some information regarding a series of interstate abductions and murders that we are currently investigating. Three of the victims were inmates in facilities your company owned or managed during that time, and those facilities are also included on that list. We have reason to believe that secure government data accessible to one of your employees may have been compromised."

"That's a serious accusation, Agent Morrow; we have very stringent policies in place regarding the confidentiality of private records. Is this a causal connection, or something a little less worrisome?"

Kate was watching for Buchanan's reaction. She was hoping for body language contrary to his verbal response. She wasn't disappointed. *You glared at Tom as you were talking to me. That's not a good sign, Frank.*

"There is no need to worry, Mr. Buchanan;" Kate said, "I thought I chose my words carefully so as not to make an accusation; but I'm afraid we're not at liberty to discuss the details of the investigation. To keep this simple, we're just interested in the names of the employees and their current status with the company. We do not require any additional information at this time, but that could change."

"Well, that shouldn't be too difficult, then." Buchanan raised his eyes to the ceiling and then settled on Kate. "I think we can help—I don't see any reason not to cooperate with the FBI, but if you don't mind, I'd like to run this by my partners first. They're a little tied up at the moment; we're reviewing our architect's proposal for a new high-security facility we're trying to land with the Illinois DOC, but we should be wrapped up shortly. Would you like to step into the meeting? I wouldn't mind a little input from the federal perspective. I think you'll find the architect's design approach to special management housing quite clever, and we've been grilling him pretty hard about it. It might be fun to see how he defends his ideas with a couple of feds in the room."

Kate addressed Buchanan but looked at Tom. *See, I can do that too, Frank.* "I think it would be very interesting; it's always good to know how corrections intend to take care of the bad boys we send their way. Besides, it sure would be more entertaining than sitting in here." She sensed something defensive about Frank Buchanan and thought they should spend a little time with him and his partners before someone thinks it might be a good idea to call the attorneys. *If he's uncomfortable with us, why would he ask us into his meeting? Maybe he has the same idea.* "If I may impose, Frank; would you have any coffee? We had a long day yesterday."

"I'll have some fresh brought to the conference room. Follow me this way, please." He led them down a short corridor to a secure door where he swiped his I.D. through a card reader mounted on the wall. The red light on the ceiling above turned green just before the panel slid out of their way.

"That's a bit theatrical; is it necessary?" Kate asked.

"Well, if you must know, the lights were added just for effect, but, yes, the secure door is a good idea. We don't normally make a lot of friends in our business." Buchanan winked at Kate from the eye on the damaged side of his face.

*****

They entered a large atrium lined with glass offices and conference rooms on two sides. A skylight centered overhead bathed the room in a pleasant morning light. Over-sized portraits of the four partners hung in a row along the wall at one end. The photo of Buchanan showed him in a slightly turned pose with his injury prominently visible, as if he thought promoting his scar would help the company earn favor with prospective clients from a violent industry. The wound was obviously there on his face, but most people would never be so blunt as to ask why, *but Kate just might.*

On the wall opposite the partners, a series of aerial photographs were displayed depicting the twenty-eight correctional facilities currently under AC's operational control. Several detailed architectural models occupied the middle of the room and showcased the more well-known facilities in their portfolio. Kate immediately recognized the Florida State Prison. "Look at this one, Tom." She pointed at the model, "That's Raiford, where Ted Bundy got the chair." Kate scratched her head as if stunned by the coincidence. "I recognize this part from the photos; it looks like a big zipper. What are the chances that we'd see this here after our little Bundy discussion yesterday?"

Tom just shrugged, but Kate decided it was an omen.

"Very good, Agent Morrow. I'm impressed." Buchanan had walked ahead and was standing patiently inside the door to a large conference room. Through the wall of glass behind him the stainless steel sweep of the Gateway Arch rose dramatically above the banks of the Mississippi River. The sun had slipped behind the southern leg, and as it emerged a sudden flare of bright light seemed to momentarily make a section of the monument disappear. As they stepped inside, Buchanan picked up the phone on the back credenza and spoke briefly before hanging up. "Your coffee will be on the way shortly, Agent Morrow." He turned to the small group seated around the table; in the middle was a large-scale model of an inmate housing wing. "I'd like to introduce agents Kate Morrow and Tom Russell with the FBI. They've come all the way from Washington D.C. to grant us this little visit." Heads nodded along with a few smiles. The architect standing at the front of the room looked pleased. In back of him the wall was covered top to bottom and end to end with detailed drawings of his prison design.

"This is John Bishop and James Haas, partners in the firm, and that's Kelly, our construction estimator. John oversees business development and James handles our technology division." The three men stood up and politely shook hands with Tom and Kate. "The smart-looking guy over there is our architect, Ben Baunach. His firm does all of our work, but they haven't figured out how to make any money doing it yet." Ben bowed his head to say hello.

As everyone began to sit back down, Kate kept her eyes glued on Buchanan, who was still standing by the door; he was typing a message on his phone. The moment he finished, she

351

heard two simultaneous pings; Bishop and Haas both looked down at their phones. *What did you just tell them, Frank?*

Bishop set his device on the table face down and abruptly plopped into his chair; his expression had changed noticeably. "We've had about every other department in Washington pay us a visit at one point or another ," he said, "but this is the first time we've had agents from the FBI. Did Buchanan try to pass some counterfeit twenties again?"

"Very funny, John; it's nothing major; we can talk about why they're here after the meeting."

But you already have. Kate looked at Tom, whose eyes were fixed on her; she could tell he had observed what she had.

Buchanan pointed at two empty chairs, "Please have a seat, agents, and we'll finish this discussion; I'm sure you'd like to be on your way, and I've got to get ready for a meeting tomorrow in Atlanta. I'll let John brief you on our opinions of the design so far. I'm going to go check on that coffee."

Sure you are. Kate watched him hurry across the atrium and disappear through the sliding door.

Bishop leaned back and folded his hands behind his head. "Our architect friend here is suggesting we take the correctional system back one hundred years. Frank rather likes the proposal and thinks it's innovative; I'm more of the opinion that its total B.S., and James is on the fence, so your perspective would be rather helpful. Ben, if you don't mind, please give our guests an overview of your design." Bishop picked up his phone and started typing.

"Certainly," Baunach cleared his throat, "what I am proposing is a paradigm shift."

"A pair of what?" Haas seemed to be laboring over the message from Buchanan and only partly paying attention.

"A paradigm shift." Baunach repeated. "Remember when the

Japanese came out with quartz movement for watches?"

"No." Haas set down his phone.

"Well, the Swiss had actually come up with it first, but dismissed it as too radical; it would have meant restructuring their whole industry. When they bailed on the idea, the Japanese grabbed onto it and developed the hell out of it. It was a whole new way to keep time and catapulted them to the lead spot in the industry. The Swiss are still trying to figure out what hit them. It, James, was a paradigm shift."

"I know what a paradigm is, John; I just didn't hear you correctly; try speaking into my good ear next time." He picked up his phone and looked like he was reading another message.

"It's total sensory deprivation." Buchanan walked back into the room with a mug of coffee in one hand and two in the other. "That's why I like it." He set them on the table and slid two in front of Kate and Tom.

"I started out as a prison guard in this business seventeen years ago and carry the scars to prove it." He looked directly at Kate in a rather intimidating way. "Now I'm an owner in a company that manages prisons. I know how the DOC thinks; they're paranoid S.O.B.'s and will embrace anything that helps them control inmates or costs. They can do both with Ben's concept." He waved at the drawings on the wall. "Remember, this isn't a run-of-the-mill slammer like our other facilities; it's a *Super-Max,* and it's meant to hold the nastiest pricks in the Illinois system. These boys can't be mixed in with the general population, and to prove my point, they routinely assault the other inmates and sometimes the guards. I don't mean they rough somebody up from time to time; I mean they're into some serious shit. Their volatile behavior warrants extreme management precautions. This will be a first of its kind for Illinois, but their budget is strapped, as always, so they'll be looking for efficiency in costs and operations."

Buchanan swallowed a drink of his coffee and continued. "I know the head of the selection committee; he toured the Connecticut facility last week with the rest of his group. The warden out there is a friend of mine and called afterward to say they were impressed with how he managed their inmates. They do a pretty good job keeping everybody separated from each other, and that's what keeps the peace, but from what I've seen, the problem at Connecticut is that they're labor intensive. They have too many escorted prisoner movements, and that loses points on the operations side. Anytime you move one of these animals, you need two guards minimum, sometimes three or four. That adds up fast if you have to escort a lot of them to and from wherever, and it's a big hit to your bottom line. From what Ben has presented, it looks like he's worked all that out in this design. To make my point, let me show you a draft of the new training video we're coming out with next month."

Buchanan grabbed the remote off the table and pressed a button that lowered black shades over the windows and dimmed the lights at the same time. He pressed another button, and a flat-screen monitor descended from the ceiling over the architect's head while the video began playing. Baunach ducked out of the way and moved to the side of the room to watch.

"This first scene will show a forced-cell-move." Buchanan said, "Basically we want the prisoner out of his cell, but he doesn't want to leave, and, as you will see, he's not real inclined to cooperate."

'TECHNIC ONE' appeared over the image, followed by an audible blip. Two guards were shown in riot gear behind a third who held a large plastic shield in front of him. The image froze while the voice-over explained the positioning tactics of each of the officers; emphasizing the correct positions of arms, legs and heads. The motion continued as the camera zoomed out to show the door to the cell sliding out of view. It stopped again while an arrow pointed at the guards' bent knees to illustrate the proper readiness position. When it resumed, the inmate could be seen at the far end of the cell pacing back and forth like an animal; his face blurred to conceal his identity. With the suddenness of a rattlesnake strike, the prisoner charged, vaulting off his bunk at the approaching guards. In one swift choreographed move, the lead officer raised the acrylic shield and the flanking officers braced their shoulders against it. The instant the inmate landed on the guards, they rushed forward and slammed him against the back wall of the cell. A fourth officer approached from the bottom of the screen and shackled his ankles with two rings of steel separated by a short rod. The officers backed off and let the prisoner fall forward to the cell floor. An instant later, two of the guards were on top of him, pinning his forearms against his back before securing a set of handcuffs. The video stopped, and the audio went dead.

"We'll have to edit out the screams that come next; they're a little graphic." Buchanan set the remote on the table as the shades raised, and the lights came back up. "We broke the guy's jaw when he hit the floor. It happens sometimes."

"Better them than you. I'm sure it keeps your legal team busy." Tom pulled the model in front of him and looked it over carefully and then glanced over the drawings on the wall. "So these are small individual day spaces adjacent to each cell?" Tom pointed at the rooms depicted in the model.

"That's correct," the architect answered. "Rather than cycling the inmates through a large dayroom one at a time, all day long, we attach a small individual space to each maximum security cell. There's a shower and window for daylight; they can even turn a lever to let in outside air if they choose. With this concept we can arrange the cells in these long wings and control everything remotely; one officer can manage a hundred inmates. There's no need to build large dayrooms with cells around the perimeter; it's very expensive construction and requires 24/7 observation from multiple control rooms. With this approach, we cut operational and construction costs significantly, while meeting every A.C.A. requirement to the letter."

Tom sat back and folded his arms. "I'd say you have that sensory deprivation thing nailed down, but you won't hear me complain. I assume this would work well for special management inmates such as, oh, I don't know, child predators?"

"Yes, sir. It would be quite effective in keeping them sequestered."

Kate's jaw dropped. *Nicely played, Tom.* She checked Buchanan for a reaction, but it came from James Haas. He had been silent since they entered the conference room but finally had something to say. "Mary would have loved it."

Out of the corner of her eye, Kate saw Bishop shake his hand at Haas as if to shut him up, but he kept talking anyway.

"Mary was always concerned for the safety of our officers," Haas said. "She told us we could never pay them enough to risk getting injured, or worse. I'm in, guys, Frank convinced me; I'm off the fence."

Kate thought of the portraits in the atrium, the one on the left, the first one of the nice looking woman in the dark blue suit. *But why did Bishop want Haas to keep quiet, and why did Haas just speak about her in the past tense?* A fuse had been lit—now she just needed to make sure the bomb went off. "I was meaning to ask about your other partner, the picture of the attractive woman we saw out there." Kate pointed her thumb over her shoulder. "Um, where is she?"

Buchanan looked at Bishop, and Bishop looked at Haas.

Boom.

*****

Kate stood in the doorway to the vendor meeting room, making sure the hallway was clear. She turned to Tom, who was leaning against the table. "Well, that was fun. I don't know why they acted that way," she said. "Their lady partner is dead; I get it; people get sick and die all the time; so how come all the weirdness?" She checked the hall again.

"You nailed this one Kate. They're hiding something, and I don't know what it is; but I'd have to say you got the hornets stirred up nicely."

"So what's next?"

"Buchanan gives us our list of names and we're on our way."

"I know, but after that?" Kate asked.

"Based on what we just saw in there, Mary Richards' name will show up on our victim-suspect list. Then we figure out who's been doing all the killing and how it links back to Buchanan and the others. SRK will undoubtedly be her surviving husband or maybe a close brother. I do think we'll pay James Haas a personal visit as soon as possible. He wants to talk; something's eating at him."

Kate motioned to Tom that Buchanan was coming down the hall. "That was quick." She backed into the room as Frank handed her a single page of names and a thumb drive.

"That's it. Everybody on that list meets your criteria, including the partners. Mary's name is on it too, but I don't see how she could possibly be connected to your investigation."

Buchanan extended his hand to Kate and then to Tom. "Now, if you'll excuse me, I really need to get back to my desk. The elevators are right behind that wall."

"Mr. Buchanan," Kate just couldn't help herself, "I've wanted to ask you about your injury." She glanced at his scar.

"A stupid car wreck in college, but don't tell anyone; the mystery makes it much more interesting."

*****

As soon as the elevator doors closed, Kate turned to Tom and straightened his neck tie and brushed some lint off his jacket lapel. "She wasn't wearing a ring in her portrait."

"Yeah, I noticed. *The mystery makes it much more interesting*—don't you think?"

"I do." Kate kissed him lightly. "It is possible that she wasn't married, Tom; maybe a widow or divorcee. SRK could be one of her partners," she speculated, a "lover-boyfriend perhaps, or maybe it's all the partners; kind of like the most intense support group on the planet."

Tom didn't laugh. "No. I would have seen it in someone's eyes." He pushed the button for the ground floor. "They are definitely involved somehow, but I don't know..." Tom held up a finger; he pulled out his buzzing phone and put it to his ear. "Good morning Charlie." He found a pen in his pocket and made a note on the back of the American Corrections brochure. "Yeah, it looks like they're going to cooperate but..." Tom went quiet and listened; thirty seconds later he ended the call. The expression on his face looked like shock.

"What's the matter, Tom?" The elevator had stopped, and the doors were standing open at the ground floor. Kate had her finger on the button and wouldn't let them close.

"Well, two things. First, I had asked Grainger to leverage a priority rush out of our I&O Support people to chase down the addresses on all of SRK's victims during the twelve-month period just prior to them *going deep*, as he now likes to say. As you'd expect, they're a pretty transient group, but at some point during that year, I&O found that every single one of them, with the exception of Alice Lowen, lived within two hours of this building." Tom tapped the brochure in his hand.

"And the second thing?" Kate wasn't surprised at all by the first.

"Charlie thinks they found Bobby Mayfield," he glanced at his scribble "in a pile-up on the Route 11 Bridge outside of New Orleans. He wants us there *right now*." Tom stepped off the elevator into the lobby but Kate didn't move.

"What do you mean Charlie *thinks* they found Mayfield?"

*****

−27−

BOBBY MAYFIELD

Tom gazed down at the brackish water of Lake Pontchartrain lapping against the causeway pilings. He was bothered by what Kate had told him on the plane; they both were. Mary Richards' name was not on their list of victim-suspects; neither were her partners or anyone else who worked at American Corrections—then or now. Still, Tom wanted to talk to James Haas, and they would be flying back to St. Louis tonight to do just that, right after they finished piecing together what happened to Bobby Mayfield on the Route 11 Bridge.

He traced his finger through a freshly cut groove in the top surface of the concrete barrier; the white marks continued for thirty yards to where the tanker was jammed sideways across the bridge; the back end was cantilevered out over the lake, and its eight wheels were hanging precariously in the air. The tractor had separated from the trailer and was lying on its side another hundred feet up the road. In the lane opposite Tom, a huge boom crane was staged and ready to go to work setting the tanker back on the pavement. The operator was passing the idle time fishing from the side of the bridge and appeared to be having pretty good results.

Behind the crane, a handful of Louisiana State Police cruisers and over-sized recovery vehicles were lit up and waiting for the FBI to finish their business so they could clean up the mess and reopen the highway. Even in the bright of day, the flashing lights were giving Tom a terrible headache.

Between where he stood and the wreckage, were the

scattered remnants of the mattress as well as a dozen or so plastic sheets covering the parts and pieces of Bobby Mayfield that looked very much like he had been puréed through a giant blender. A couple of patrolmen were swinging their batons at the circling gulls, trying to dissuade them from stealing an afternoon snack. Tom looked up when the black Suburban pulled alongside him and rolled to a stop. The passenger in the front seat was shouting at someone on his phone while he waved his hand at the wreckage in front of him as if the person on the other end of the call could see it. The driver climbed out of the SUV and walked over to Tom. "S.A.C. Russell?"

"That's me."

"I'm Resident Agent Carlisle, New Orleans Office." He shook Tom's hand. "Per your request, the young fellow riding along with me is Josh Bolen, the unfortunate and somewhat agitated driver of that tanker truck over there." He pointed toward the trailer in front of them. "Sorry sir; that was dumb. I don't think there should be any confusion as to which tanker we're talking about."

"Don't worry about it; we appreciate you bringing Mr. Bolen back out here, Agent Carlisle. I understand he wasn't banged up too badly; I'm sure at this point he's ready to get home."

"Yes, sir, just a couple of cracked ribs; it's amazing that he walked away from the crash, but they checked him out pretty good anyway. As you might imagine, he's still a bit shaken up from what happened last night; who knows for how long he'll be seeing that mattress coming at him every time he closes his eyes. I'm not sure what to say about the poor bastard who took the ride in the bed, but it sure was nice that someone carved his name across his forehead to save us the trouble of figuring out who he was. That's when the Highway Patrol called us in, and, of course, we called your boss in D.C."

Carlisle paused for a moment to check the phone buzzing on his hip. "The Medical Examiner said the body temperature and rigor suggested that Mayfield could have been alive when the mattress flew into the truck, which is consistent with the scream that Mr. Bolen heard just before the impact. I'm sure he'll be excited to tell you all about it when he gets done yelling into his phone. Except for the tractor, they've cleared all the damaged vehicles on the east side of the tanker, and there's nothing much left to clean up on this side other than the stuff our people are collecting. I will say that L.H.P. is getting a little antsy to haul away Mr. Bolen's rig; it's not leaking fuel, but it's going to be a delicate operation nonetheless, and they'd like to get it done while they still have some daylight and all this expensive salvage equipment assembled. There's a lot of fire apparatus waiting for us to release the scene, and they'd like not to lose any of it responding to another call. On top of all that, it won't be long before the tree-huggers show up to begin their nonsense. I'm sure Louisiana wants their bridge back before the sideshow has a chance to get started."

"Tell them to take a Xanax and lie down. They can have their highway just as soon as we can get everything photographed and bagged." Tom turned toward the scene. "Based on what I'm seeing, I don't think we'll have to keep them too much longer, and if they still have a problem, I'd be happy to talk to whomever is in charge."

"Yes, sir; I'll let them know."

"Anything yet on the car?"

"No sir; the truck driver really hadn't paid any attention to the make or model of the vehicle. It was a black sedan or maybe dark blue, and he can't remember anything about the plates it had on it."

"It would have been a rental, probably rented two hundred miles from here," Tom said. "No one pulls a stunt like this using their own car."

Kate walked up next to Agent Carlisle and handed Tom a

piece of blood-stained fabric roughly the size of a paper towel.
"It appears that Mayfield was sewn up inside the bed like a
cocoon, Agent Russell. These tears along the edge are from
lacing that must have been ripped from it when the mattress
came apart in the wheels under the truck. The cord is pretty
strong stuff; it's still intact and threaded through a large section
right over there that matches these tear marks; it's just under the
back end of the trailer. I'd say it's the bottom half of the bed,
based on what little I know about gravity from the fifth grade
and the amount of liquefied feces I saw in it. I mean there's a
whole lot of it, Tom, like Mayfield drank a couple gallons of
bowel prep before he went on his little roof-top road trip."

Tom gave Kate a funny glance, then put on his latex gloves
before he took the fabric in his hand; he could smell the residue
of the watery stool. When he turned it over the pattern put an
involuntary smile across his face. "Red roses; *nice... how
thoughtful of him.*"

"Yeah, real considerate," Kate said. "SRK must have
shopped for that mattress a while back when he thought he'd get
the green light to go after Mayfield. Let me show you
something." Kate walked away and Tom was glad to follow; he
didn't feel like talking to Mr. Bolen just yet; the guy looked
hostile, and Tom was in no mood to talk to an alpha-male
wannabe. The way he felt just now, he wasn't about to take any
grief from anyone.

*****

They ducked under the belly of the trailer and kept moving
until they were standing at the front of the tractor. An agent had
just finished photographing the blood and debris stuck to the
windshield, crushed radiator grill and engine cowling; he was
gathering his equipment and stepped away as Tom and Kate
approached.

"So whaddya got, Kate?"

"I'm not sure, but it looks interesting; I've already taken pictures." She reached through the hole in the center of the grill and pulled carefully on a plastic grocery bag. As she removed it, they could see that the entire back side was covered in a cross-layering of gray duct tape extending well beyond the edges of the bag; there was plenty of short, black hair stuck to the glue. "It's pretty obvious that Mayfield had this taped to his chest." She turned it over and read the writing across the face of the tape, then handed it to Tom. "Um, it's addressed to you, Agent Russell."

Tom squatted down on his knees and set the bag on the asphalt. He took photos of the tape and the bag, then emptied the contents in front of him and photographed them too. There was just a note and a small, stuffed toy monkey. Sewn to its shoulders was a little cape that said 'Atlanta Zoo', and wrapped tightly around its neck was a pendant made of monofilament threaded through a piece of sharp red glass with Mayfield's blood all over it. The note was brief but direct:

"Christopher Hoffman wanted Mayfield dead. He told me so."

Tom stood up with the toy and handed the note to Kate. He walked to the barrier and looked out over the vast expanse of Lake Pontchartrain; a light breeze was beginning to build off the water, and it felt good against his face. A moment later, Kate was standing next to him. He wanted to tell her something that made sense, but he couldn't think of anything she didn't already know. He looked at the red pendant and thought of the jagged red glass planted under Bobby Mayfield's eyelids. *I guess that's what he got for forcing the Hoffman boy to watch him jack-off, that, and the ride in the mattress air show.* His headache was gone, and he wondered why; he thought by now his skull would be exploding all over the bridge.

"SRK has taken control of who he intends to kill, Kate, and

this mess is just his way of letting us know. We must have pissed him off royally in Indiana last week, and it now appears that he's eliminated the weak spot in his method."

He surveyed the wreckage everywhere around them and then peered deep into Kate's eyes with as much humility as he could muster; she looked almost as tired as he felt.

"I messed up, Kate; I should have put a team on Mayfield until this was finished; at least he would still be alive. Although I can't say I'm too disappointed."

Tom held the stuffed monkey over the side of the bridge being careful not to touch the glass pendant; he watched the cape flutter lightly in the wind.

"SRK is acting on his own now," Tom said. "There won't be any more letters."

*****

—28—

EMMA'S SONG

Bryan backed his pickup into an empty space at the edge of the Food Mart parking lot. He could have parked much closer, but chose a spot away from the overhead lights and the other cars. He had gotten back from New Orleans an hour earlier but had first stopped by his neighbor's house to get Molly and take her home before running back out for a few groceries. Even though there were two markets closer to his house, this one stayed open until 10:00 p.m., and it was on the far side of town where he would be less likely to run into someone he might know. It wouldn't take much time; he would buy just the items he needed and maybe a special treat for Molly, then leave. As the wipers intermittently cleared the film of light rain from the windshield, he thought of the truck driver on the bridge and was glad that the news report said he was okay. He was also glad he could now strike Bobby Mayfield's name from Mary's list.

He moved his rucksack from the seat to the floorboard and checked his watch before opening the door—*eleven minutes until closing.* He hurried through the rain to the sidewalk under the canopy and paused for the automatic doors to open. In spite of the several cars parked outside, the store seemed empty. *Good.* He found a dry shopping cart and pushed it in the direction of the dairy corner while meandering down the aisles filled tall with cereal boxes, snacks and canned items. He stopped when he got to the display of dog food but couldn't find the kind that Molly liked.

"Bryan Rhodes?" From behind him came a quiet, hesitant voice, but it felt like someone had stuck him with a pin. "Is that you?"

Bryan turned around and stared blankly down at the woman. She was short and round with narrow eyes painted wide with too much lavender makeup. He figured she must have known Mary from years ago, but he couldn't remember her and didn't care to; all of those people died for him when Mary did. He flashed a weakly-formed grin before looking away.

In return, the woman managed a compassionate smile and touched his arm lightly as he tried to leave. "Bryan, I'm Judy Sawyer; John and I are from the subdivision that backs up to your road. We're Jimmy's parents; we live next to the Friedman's, you know, Doctor Friedman? I didn't know you shopped here."

Bryan didn't remember Judy, John or Jimmy Sawyer, and he didn't remember any Doctor Friedman either, but she pressed on. "How have you been? We don't see you much anymore since, well, we just see you drive by from time to time. If there is anything you need, I hope you know you can feel free to call us for help." She fumbled around in her purse and pulled out a pen and a scrap of paper, then wrote down her number and handed it to Bryan.

"I will. Thank you, uh, Judy." He tried to be polite but didn't want to encourage any more conversation. "We're okay, Molly and me; but if you'll excuse my rudeness, I have to get a few things before the store closes. Really, we're just fine." He pushed the paper with her phone number in his pocket but crushed it in his hand as he did. Bryan knew the woman didn't ask her stupid question to hear the truth, and he didn't want to speak it. *How am I? Do you really want to know? What I can't possibly describe— you can't possibly imagine.*

*****

During the long days and weeks after Emma disappeared,

Bryan had become convinced that his neighbors were less concerned about him and Mary and more concerned about hearing something that would make them feel better about *themselves.* Then, after Emma was put in the ground, all of them went out of their way to avoid him and his wife. They were a neighborhood in denial; mothers and fathers too caught up in their own petty lives to have taken a few minutes to wait with their own children at the bus stop that morning.

Except for the rare occasion when Bryan's reserve unit was training or deployed overseas, he was there to walk Emma to the end of their road and wait with her for the bus, and he was there every day after school when it dropped her off. And while he watched over her, he watched over *their* children too. Then, in the most tragic distortion of fate, Bryan was half-a-world away fighting evil when the evil came to claim his daughter half-a-mile from his home. His bitterness was cold and real.

Any one of you, no, every one of you should have been there because your precious child could have been the one who was taken. Was there no one who could have prevented that monster from taking my little girl? Where were all the other parents that morning? Where were you, Judy Sawyer? And what about your doctor friend? Why didn't the bus driver see what was happening? Why didn't someone do something?!

*****

Bryan's gut tightened. He looked down and through the empty cart at the brown and green specks in the terrazzo floor. He didn't want the woman to see the anger gathering in his eyes—*but maybe she should.* His big hands tightened around the handle attached to the cart so she wouldn't see them shake. And if he kept his grip on the handle, maybe he wouldn't strangle her throat.

"Give my best to your family, Judy. I have to go." Bryan

forced the words bluntly through his teeth, and, without raising his head or waiting for a reply, he pushed his cart down the aisle and turned into the next. If she had said something else, he didn't hear it.

Bryan stopped the cart. Now he couldn't remember what he needed to buy—the stupid bitch had angered him. The store would close soon, and he tried to think, but the list of items had vanished from his mind. He gazed up at the stark-white ceiling; the rows of fluorescent lighting seemed to stretch to infinity and only emptied his mind even more. When he looked back down, he was startled by the shape of a little girl who had appeared beside him out of nowhere. There had not been a sound or movement, yet there she was, both sudden and strange. A naked cloth doll dangled from her hand, almost touching the floor; her matted hair and worn black coat told that she was less fortunate than most. Everything about her appearance defied her age, but her size said that she was perhaps six years old. She was too young to be walking around the store alone. *Where is her mother or father?*

The child stood still and quiet—the tips of her shoes almost touching Bryan's. She glanced up through clouded green eyes; her face was dirty and obscured by the matted hair gathered in tangles around it. Bryan wanted to speak. He wanted to ask the child if she needed help; he wanted to reach out and take her hand and lead her somewhere, but he couldn't move his limbs; he couldn't move his lips. *Emma had green eyes too.*

Then the row of lights overhead flickered and went dark. Without saying a word, the girl drifted away silently down the blackened aisle, dwarfed by the enormity of the canyon of food.

Bryan turned his cart in the direction she had gone; he was compelled to follow her, but she had disappeared. A moment later he heard what he thought was the sound of the girl's voice from the opposite end of the next aisle over—she was singing. The words of the melody were upon him but receded so abruptly that Bryan wasn't sure if he had heard anything at all. Even so, his heart leapt. He froze and gripped the cart tightly so the wheels would be silent. Without realizing it, his mouth was forming the familiar song. His lips moved effortlessly; the same words had passed over them a thousand times. He strained to hear what he knew was impossible to have heard. It was a song that Mary had taught him years ago; they were her words, and the simple melody was hers as well. It was a song known only to them in their home, but it had not been heard there for a very long time. It was a private song. It was a bedtime song. It was Emma's song.

Bryan panicked. He spun around quickly without releasing the cart, and it crashed on its side; he stumbled and ran past where the sound had escaped his ears. He stopped to listen for it—but there was nothing. He raced to the end of the aisle but halted himself, afraid to turn the corner and afraid to go any farther. It wasn't possible.

"Emma?!"

Bryan murmured the paternal cry through his trembling lips. It was barely audible, but its echo screamed loudly through his mind. He slumped to the floor shaking because he knew the song wasn't real—it couldn't possibly be. It was happening again, and he knew what he had to do. First he would sit for a while to arrest the violent thoughts racing around in his head, then he would get up and leave. He clamped his eyes closed to center himself. *Just get through this, Bryan; it will pass soon—it always passes. Then you will walk out of this building, and you will go home. You have to get home, Bryan—while you still can.*

He tried to calm himself and think through the sequence of steps he would have to follow to escape this place and this feeling. He had to push the guilt aside before it consumed him sitting there on the aisle floor, but he knew it would only remain dormant for a while. The guilt would be there waiting for him when he got home tonight—just like it always was.

I will stand and leave this building. I will get in my truck and find my way to the other side of this town. I will pass her bus stop and will look the other way. I will turn at the rusted mailbox and drive slowly down the long gravel road where she last walked, but I will see only the wipers sweep back and forth across my vision. Then the old oak tree will appear in the headlights, and on it will hang the swing that I can never take down. I will enter the house that I want to burn and will fill my glass more than once, and sometime late tonight I will go upstairs and walk past her room to the end of the hall. I will not pause outside her closed door. I will shut myself inside my bedroom and listen to the sound of my empty dwelling. I will study the file on the next demon I will soon kill—but the planning and the alcohol will not be enough to keep the guilt from finding me.

So I will take Mary's pillow from the drawer and place it beside me on our lonely bed, and I will cry until I can't. Then I will touch her lock of hair and tell her that I have always loved her. I will turn off the light and stare into my dark world, waiting for the sleep that will not come kindly. I will hear the truth beating in the hollow chambers of my heart; it will tell me again and again that the blame for all of this is mine. If only I had been there, they both would still be alive.

*****

—29—

REST IN PEACE

James Haas lived in a fine old house built at the west edge of St. Louis City just before the beginning of the last century. It had always been an affluent neighborhood, having been platted from virgin land across the avenue from the new campus of Washington University and not far from Forest Park where the grandest of World Fairs would be held soon after the house was completed. The rooms on the main level had thick plaster walls with marble floors and held onto the cold and damp that leaked in through the leaded windows whenever the weather turned foul. James sat in the parlor in his favorite chair beside the fireplace, sipping a glass of cognac brandy; the bottle was warming on the hearth next to him and within easy reach.

It had been a long day, beginning with the FBI showing up at his office in the morning and finishing in a heated argument with his partners after everyone else had gone home. A light rain was falling outside, and he felt chilled; it wasn't too late in the spring to enjoy one last fire, or too far into the evening to enjoy a few more glasses of brandy.

The book he had been reading lay closed on the arm of the chair with a pink ribbon marking the chapter he had finished before going to bed the night before. He set the book aside and removed the ribbon from the binding and placed it lovingly on the ottoman in front of him, next to the items he had been pulling from the scrap book he kept of the firm. It was the commemorative ribbon that Mary had given him on the day of Emma's Christening.

*****

James had first met Mary when he moved from New York City to escape the demise of his eighteen-year marriage to a woman who had no intention of letting him off the hook without first taking him through a financial meat grinder. He wanted a new start, somewhere far from Manhattan where he could re-establish his I.T. consulting business, and St. Louis seemed to be a good central location. Mary was just setting up American Corrections in a new office space downtown and had hired James to build and manage the computer networks for the company. A couple of years later, she invited him in as a junior partner to oversee the complex systems he had put in place to keep up with the firm's growth. With their day-to-day operations, there was a lot of sensitive interface with government agencies, keeping track of inmate records and court orders, and all of it had to be securely implemented and maintained. James Haas had written the protocols for the Federal Bureau of Prisons as well as the Justice Department and could worm his way anywhere inside the system to find any information he needed. If it existed, he could find it because he was the best in the industry.

He had fallen in love with Mary easily, but he knew he had no business imposing on her youth; he was twenty-five years old on the day she was born, and no matter how much he yearned to be with her, he couldn't get past the difference in their age. She would still be a young woman when he could no longer function as a man, and the inevitability of that biological failure terrified him. He knew that Mary loved him also, but it was the special kind of love reserved for the closest of friends, and it wasn't the kind that would have ever made her desire to be his wife. So, by necessity, James' feelings for Mary evolved into a paternal form of love, where he would be free to express it honestly without things getting awkward. He wanted to stay at American Corrections to be near her, and it was the only way that his love for her could exist.

Mary had lost her father before she was old enough to remember him, and James began to feel comfortable thinking of himself as the dad she never had. If he couldn't love her as a husband, he could love her as a man who dearly loves his daughter, and when that shift in his heart occurred, it suddenly made sense for James to introduce Mary to the other favorite person in his life, his stepson and only child: Bryan Rhodes.

It was difficult for James at first, watching the two people he most loved fall in love with each other, but with time he realized he was growing closer to them both; and when they made him a grandpa, he knew his life had been blessed by nothing short of a miracle.

*****

James picked up a photo of the partners huddled around Mary at her wedding reception and moved it next to the one of Bryan sitting in a chair dressed as Santa for the Christmas party; Mary was sprawled across his lap in a silly pose. He smiled to himself when he remembered that the costume they rented was too tight for Bryan, and he had ripped out the seams when he put it on. Below that was the picture of Emma pulling her little red wagon through the office, delivering four-leaf clover plants to the staff for St. Patrick's Day. Molly was trailing behind on her leash; she couldn't have been more than a few months old. Next to it were the invitations to each of Emma's six birthday parties laid neatly in a row. James adjusted each more perfectly, then took the sixth one, her last birthday, and held it against his heart. It was impossible not to cry—so he did. The pain was just too much.

Alone at the corner of the ottoman was the most precious and saddest of the pictures he had ever taken of Mary. He and Bryan were with her at the cancer center, and he had snapped it right before they brought her home. The photo was face down and waiting for him to drink enough brandy before he could look at it again. He wiped his eyes and finished off his glass before pouring another; he really didn't need to see it; the memory of that day was just as vivid as the image in the plastic sleeve—maybe more, but he turned it over anyway and sat back with it in his chair. He tipped it toward the glowing firelight so he could better see.

Mary was so small by then, and her skin had become pale, like milk thinly brushed across her bones. Bryan had filled the room with flowers the night before and told her he had picked them from her garden, but it was a lie; her garden was dying—just like her. In the photo, Bryan was sitting next to her on the bed, propping her up because she was too weak to sit on her own; his strong fingers were threaded loosely with hers as if he was afraid he might crush them in his closed hand. He had been so sweet to her all that morning, but hadn't yet been able to give her a smile and he couldn't manage one for the camera either—but Mary did.

Everything in the photo was crystal clear except for the features of Bryan's face, like he had moved his head just as the shutter clicked. Strangely, the only thing in focus was the anger that could be seen welling up in his eyes. The doctor had just told him that there was no way to stop the disease; he would be taking Mary home for the final time.

*****

Eight months before James took his last photo of Mary, he had helped her compile her list of predators. It took a while, but it wasn't really hard, and he did it mostly to be spending time with her. When it was finished, she was going to take it to the FBI and give them the names and locations of all the suspects they needed to investigate to solve Emma's murder. At first he thought it was a fool's errand; there were so many possible reasons why they couldn't find her killer; him sitting in a prison cell seemed like an impossible reach. But then he saw the hope and life it was giving Mary; it was as though she had regained the will to live just so she might have the chance to one day watch them execute the monster that had murdered her little girl. Grandpa Haas was more than happy to oblige.

But then, only weeks apart, the murders of two child sex-offenders were reported in the local news, and James knew immediately that it was no coincidence. The victims were on Mary's list, and Bryan had killed them both—he was sure of it. James tried to reach through to Bryan, but his stepson had already shattered. Emma's loss had been too great, and then watching helplessly as the cancer ate Mary alive had dragged Bryan to the bottom of a pit he could not or would not escape. His anger had coalesced—collapsing unto itself, like light trapped in the gravity of a black hole. Evil had taken his daughter and had now come to claim his wife. Bryan was hell-bent on making sure he would be the one to destroy it.

James didn't know if Mary knew about the murders; he would never speak of them to her. It was a secret that required no one to share, and he intended to protect Mary at any cost. Too much pain and sadness had already visited on the woman he so loved—he was going to make damn sure there wasn't any more. Then after she was laid to rest in the ground, James thought the killing would stop; he hoped that Bryan would somehow be able to move on or maybe just give up and turn himself over to the police. But it was only a few days before the news reported on the murder of Greg Levy, and James knew that he had been deadly wrong. Levy's name was on Mary's list too; in fact, Levy had been an inmate at their prison in Sedalia, Missouri. Bryan's killing wasn't over, and it had arrived on the doorstep of American Corrections.

Immediately after he learned of Levy's murder, James shut down Mary's private server account—he wished he had done it sooner. If his stepson couldn't access the information on the release dates of the inmates, Haas figured he wouldn't be able to hunt them down. Surely that would stop the killing, and for a long time it did.

Then four months ago came the news of Thurman Goethe, gunned down outside Rockville Federal Penitentiary, the high-security prison in Colorado managed by the firm. James knew it had to be Bryan, but he didn't know how he could have possibly found out the details of Goethe's release. It didn't occur to him at first that Bryan didn't need access to the secure servers at American Corrections to locate his prey anymore; the world-wide web had already taken their place. Sometime during the past year or two, victim advocacy groups had won the fight to make inmate location and release information easily accessible on the Internet. Thanks to James, Bryan already had the list of names and identification numbers—now, the rest was just a few clicks away.

*****

James kissed the picture of Mary, then set it lovingly back down on the ottoman. When he heard the buzzer to the gate at the end of the driveway, he was emptying the last of the brandy into his glass. He looked up through his fog at the security panel on the wall and saw the face of Tom Russell leaning into the camera; his pretty lady friend was sitting next to him in the car. "Good evening, Agent Russell, Miss Morrow; I was expecting you both. The front door is unlocked. Please come in. You'll find me in the living room."

He staggered up and pushed the button to release the gate, then fell back in his chair, careful not to disturb the memories of Mary, Bryan and Emma spread out in front of him. One by one, he painfully placed each into the fire, and when they were gone, he laid the scrapbook on the flames and watched it burn as well. Then he put the cold barrel of his revolver to the side of his head and pulled the trigger.

*****

–30–

RELEASE

B ryan couldn't see his house at the end of the long gravel drive; the rain was coming down heavier now but not enough to overwhelm the wipers and blind his vision. He was sure he had left some lights on when he went to the market, but all he saw ahead was darkness as if nothing was there; he thought maybe the power had gone out again.

His house was in the middle of eighty acres connected to the world by a single wire, and he was used to outages from time to time, but the weather could not have been the reason to have one tonight. He parked his truck behind the garage and ran up under the roof of the back porch and stopped to listen; Molly should have been barking by now; she always barked when anyone came to the house, even if it was Bryan. Something wasn't right.

He looked across the yard through the window in his shop and saw the blinking red light from the battery charger sitting on the workbench next to his tractor. *That's a good sign; the electricity isn't out. The main breaker for the house is probably tripped at the pole in the front yard. The damn rodents must have eaten through another wire.* He was too exhausted to deal with it tonight; he would track down the problem and fix it in the morning.

Bryan turned his key in the lock and stepped into the dark kitchen. "Molly?" Out of habit, he found the light switch on the wall and flipped it on, but nothing happened. "Molly, are you there?" He called into the house, but there was no sound except for his voice vibrating off the walls. "Where are you hiding? Come here, girl, do you want a treat?!"

His next thought came to him like a premonition: she wasn't a young dog anymore, and he should stop expecting her to live forever. He traced his hand along the wall as he moved toward the front of the house, keeping his eyes glued to the floor as best he could. When he recognized the black shape lying still in the middle of the living room rug, he knew she was dead. "Molly!" He dropped to his knees and brushed his hand gently across her long face, but she didn't move. "My poor, beautiful lady; you've been such a good dog to me. I am so sorry, Molly; it's not fair." Tears filled his eyes, but he quickly wiped them away; he drew his hand through the fur along the nape of her neck but stopped when he felt the warm blood and his fingers fall into the open wound. Bryan froze to process what he had just found; someone had been here or was still somewhere in the house.

His senses sharpened; anger flushed his bloodstream with fresh adrenaline; his muscles grew taut preparing for a fight that he wasn't afraid to have—but wasn't fully prepared to win. As a Green Beret, his team had cleared dozens of hostile houses in Kabul and Ghazni under the veil of darkness, but this was different. In battle, he had night vision goggles and a gun in his hands; right now his shotgun was leaning next to the back door, and he had left his sidearm in his rucksack that he had forgotten in the truck. *Neither one are any good to me now.* He decided it didn't matter; he would use his hands. Some coward had killed his dog, and there was hell to pay.

*****

The Taser hit Bryan high on the shoulder, and he collapsed, twitching to the floor. Instinctively, he tried to get up but was hit again and rolled over on his back; this time he couldn't control the spasms raging over him. A needle punctured the side of his neck, but he didn't feel it; instead he heard a shrill voice ring out from the dark, "Oh my! You are a big one; I think you will probably need another." The second injection came below the jaw and pierced his tongue; he tasted the bitter drug as he tried to spit out what he could. "You'll be asleep shortly, Mr. Rhodes; or would you be more comfortable if I called you by your first name, Bryan, is it? Now, you're going to have a sleepy-time nap while we take a little trip down memory lane, okay? I think you're going to like this stuff by the way, *your daughter did*."

Bryan was busy fighting the muscle contractions and wasn't sure of what he heard. He struggled to find his assailant but couldn't hold his head still long enough to lock on the man attached to the voice. Out of the corner of his eye he saw a shape recede slowly toward the kitchen; it took each step with one leg only, pulling the other behind it like a hobbled lizard dragging its tail from the room. It was several seconds before he heard the clap-clap of the screen door and the voice babbling nonsense as it descended from the porch into the yard.

"A farmer boy danced on a razor blade..."

Slowly the seizures began to recede, first coming farther apart, then gripping him with less intensity—but his eyes felt heavy as stones, and his vision was starting to blur. His training told him to fight the drug for as long as he could; the longer he stayed awake, the more information he would have to improve his chances of surviving the night. Next he recognized the squeal of the rollers over the big door to his workshop and a short while later the sound of his tractor rumbling to life. He could barely move his right arm, and all he could think to do with it was reach out to touch Molly.

"Don't you worry, girl; *I got this*."

The minutes passed slowly as Bryan lay paralyzed on the floor; for most of them he tried to remember what the voice had said; *something about my little Emma;* but he couldn't remember what he heard or if he had heard anything at all.

Light flashed through the windows and swept in anger across the room, but the drug polluting his thoughts kept him from understanding why. He knew the sound of the tractor that followed, but the noise seemed to cycle in and out of his ears in contrast to the movement of the light, and he couldn't decide where it was or where it might be going.

Time slipped backwards, then forward again; one second he was holding Emma's little hand at her bus stop and in the next he was kneeling over Molly reaching into her wound; and in his confusion of time and space, everything was collapsing into a surreal otherworld. He told himself the distortions of his mind were from the narcotic, yet they felt hauntingly familiar—the lights warping across the ceiling; the ceiling shrinking away as if he was being pulled toward the roof; the floor folding around him like a vise and twisting the walls into impossible shapes; the pulse of the diesel engine murmuring in the background... *This—is—my—dream.*

Then, in the narrow moment that arrived just before he blacked out, in the sliver of reality that marked the very edge of his consciousness, Bryan's fracturing brain coalesced around one final, illuminating thought: *the voice belongs to Emma's killer.*

*****

Kate ended the call and entered the address in the GPS on her tablet as Tom ducked out of the rain and climbed behind the wheel next to her. He started the car and took one last look at the stone walls of Haas' old house lit up in the flashing lights of the emergency vehicles; the day certainly seemed to have been full of them.

"Sorry for the wait," Tom said. "I got a follow-up call from Smithson in Chemistry; I guess he's been putting in the overtime for us. It turns out the lead alloy used to fill the bullet we dug out of the Rockville tower had a slightly lower tin and antimony content, making it similar but heavier than your basic ballistic alloy. Get this, Smithson called it 'restoration quality' lead; he said they use it in replacement caning to repair old stained-glass windows."

"Interesting, Tom; hold onto that thought until you hear what Scarface had to say."

"What did Buchanan tell you?"

"He sang like a canary in a coal mine." Kate shifted to the front of her seat and turned toward Tom; she was obviously quite excited—almost giddy. "Actually, his coal mine is filling up with carbon monoxide, and the canary won't be singing very much longer."

"Kate; *the call?*"

"Oh yeah, right; Buchanan said Mary Richards kept her maiden name for the company, like it was some sort of brand or persona; everyone in the corrections industry knew her by Richards, so she didn't change it, but according to Buchanan, she also liked to keep her private life very private. Get this: James Haas was her father-in-law. Can you believe it? That explains his sentiments toward her in the meeting today. Now I feel real sorry for the guy. He must have been carrying a heavy load." Kate motioned to the paramedics bringing the gurney through the front door with the body bag strapped to the top of it.

Tom glanced over but was distracted by the dot pulsing in the middle of the GPS glowing on Kate's lap; the dot connected to a blue line zigzagging away from where they were to someplace they needed to go. Suddenly, he was impatient and wanted to leave but had no idea of where they were going; he bumped his horn at the police cruiser blocking the driveway behind them and, without waiting, jumped back out in the rain. The officer was talking on his radio and looked up just as Tom tapped on his window and pointed toward the street. A moment later Tom climbed back in the car shaking the water out of his hair; he jammed the transmission in reverse but held his foot on the brake, "Haas' name didn't show up on our list of victims, K."

"I know; that's because Mary Richards was wedded to his *stepson* who never took Haas' last name. I've already checked; the stepson's name is definitely on our list." Kate pointed to the red dot in the lower right corner of the screen; it was at the other end of the blue line and somewhere south of St. Louis City. "Tom, meet Bryan Rhodes, or if you prefer, the *Short Rose Killer.*"

Tom's eyes lit up like a sunrise, and a big grin spread across his face. He leaned over and gave Kate a long, wet kiss. "I think I love you."

"You'd better; 'cause you're not getting rid of me after we catch this rascal." Kate then slid back in her seat and calmly put on her seatbelt as they backed out of the driveway. "They had a daughter together, Tom." Her tone immediately turned somber. "She was six years old when she was abducted and taken to some abandoned church in southern Illinois. She was badly abused by her captor for eleven days before she was killed."

"What was her name?"

"Emma." Kate paused a moment to clear the moisture from her eyes, "It's a nice name, Tom."

"Yes, it is."

"Buchanan couldn't give me any more details; he was pretty broken up about what went down tonight; I think he really liked James Haas."

"Yeah, it's a shame; I kind of liked the guy myself, but what's done is done. Get a hold of Charlie; ask him to send everything we have on the Rhodes case ASAP." Tom pointed the car toward Forest Park and buried the gas pedal. "How far to his house?"

"GPS says forty-five minutes," Kate shouted over the noise of the tires trying to grip the wet pavement, "but at this rate we'll be there in thirty if you don't kill us first." She braced her hands against the dashboard and talked fast. "Make a right at the stop sign, and in about a mile turn on 44 East back toward downtown, then head south on I-55. I'm pretty sure that sign up there says *STOP!*" She nodded at the red octagon rapidly approaching in the headlights.

Tom braked hard before they reached the end of the street. "Sorry, Kate; I've been waiting for this moment for a long time—but I'm good now." He turned right on Hampton Boulevard but kept pace with the flow of traffic. "After you talk to Charlie, call the Resident Office and brief them for some S.W.A.T. back-up; they'll have to mobilize fast; tell them to position their fire power at a choke point in case he runs, but keep it out of view until we know what's going on. I don't want them to get to Rhodes' house before we do, so tell them to give us one hour, no more, no less; that should give us enough time to go in quietly. Rhodes has some skills, and I don't want to spook him into using them; if we get in any kind of trouble, it will be good to know the cavalry is on the way."

*****

Bryan snapped awake when his head dropped off the door threshold; he could feel rope tightly wrapped around his ankles and tension in his legs as he was dragged across the front porch; his mind was gripped by a deep stupor, and he still couldn't move. Even if he could, his wrists were bound together behind him with thick plastic ties. When his feet crossed the edge of the top step, the pulling stopped and the rope went slack. He felt the vibration and heat of the engine as the tractor moved closer, and out of the corner of his eye he saw the arms of the front loader raise just before he heard the violent cracking of wood from the steel bucket cutting into the porch beneath him. Then, as abruptly as it had begun, the destruction stopped, and the engine slowed to an idle. From out of the rain, a shape appeared, but Bryan couldn't focus his eyes in the blinding work lights of the machine. When the figure leaned over him, he thought he recognized the stench of fecal rot mixed in with the diesel's exhaust.

"Let's see, Bryan; I've almost got you loaded. You should consider yourself lucky that I didn't crush you with that thing. I'm very impressed by you farm boys; it's not at all easy to operate." The voice moved lower in the light but stayed close; Bryan felt his legs being tugged just before his body fell into the tractor's bucket; nails and broken wood pierced his skin but he could hardly feel it. As he was lifted into the air, the rain washed over him, and he sensed a lightness wash across his being—as though his release was finally near.

Bryan rode along high above the tractor blinking at the raindrops falling into his eyes, and still he wasn't afraid. The droplets appeared from out of the black like they had fallen through the sky, just to find him lying there, and in return, he was smiling back at each one of them. He passed under the tree in the front yard with the broken swing and along the picket fence still waiting to be painted; he followed the eave at the side of his workshop and knew that Mary's dead garden lay below. And as he was dropped into the bed of his pickup truck, he was looking directly at the window of Emma's room.

The tractor backed away, and the engine fell quiet; he could hear the voice curse as it climbed down from the seat. "You know, Bryan, I was planning on just killing you here," the words were getting louder as the voice approached, "but when I looked in your workshop and saw your little glass chamber of horrors, I got a better idea; and with this bum leg of mine, thank you very much, your truck and that tractor made it a no-brainer. I hope you don't mind, but I borrowed the gun I found in your backpack—it's much better than the one I brought with me. Now that I see how big you are, I doubt the bullets in mine would have even slowed you down. I also took a few of your more interesting tools. Who knows? They might come in handy. Oh, and by the way, you owe me a hundred dollars; it's a long way out here from the train station. I thought the cab was never going to find it." The voice was now at the side of the pickup; he heard the handle click and the familiar groan of the rusted door as it was pulled open. "Let me just give you a couple more of these sleepy shots, and we'll be on our way. I'll wake you up when we get to where we're going; *that* I do promise." A syringe stabbed Bryan's thigh, then another, but he didn't look toward the voice; he just continued to stare at Emma's empty window while the drug worked its way through his flesh. Then it all went black as the bed cover was latched down over him, and the tailgate slammed closed.

"His severed balls are gonna bounce to the floor..."

*****

Tom and Kate crossed over the Meramec River Bridge heading south on Interstate 55. Ahead of them, a billboard advertised the exit for Mastodon State Park a few miles down the road. Kate glanced up from reading the information Grainger emailed her on the Rhodes case and caught a glimpse of the sign just before they passed it by. "Wow, I had no idea." She did a quick search on the Internet and scanned through the webpage when it opened. "It says that one of the hairy critters is actually buried near the park, right under this highway. Wouldn't you think they would have dug it up and stuck it in a museum?"

"I don't know." Tom didn't want to talk about prehistoric elephants, although digging up bones had a certain resonance with how he felt just now. His enthusiasm for where they were going had dissipated almost as fast as it had arrived. He had kept mostly quiet since they got on the interstate in St. Louis, letting Kate read through the information that Charlie sent. It had given him time to reflect on what it would be like to lose one of his own children, and it wasn't pleasant. He gripped the wheel as if he couldn't let it go. SRK had been a thorn in his life for a long time, and now he finally had a name to attach to the drawing he kept in his red folder, the drawing of the shadow-man standing in the hallway outside Greg Levy's apartment door. Tom knew he would soon be in the home of the Short Rose Killer, but up until tonight, he hadn't thought of SRK as a human being.

His name was Bryan Rhodes, and he was the broken father of little Emma and the husband to Mary Richards; both of whose lives were brutally taken from him. Tom was about to dig up some bones, but he was beginning to think that maybe they should just stay buried in the ground. He tried to shake off the thought—maybe talking would help.

"So, what did we get from Grainger?"

Kate set the tablet on the armrest between the seats and folded her hands lightly across her lap; she just stared into the windshield. "It was a sad deal, Tom, from the very beginning. It looks like Emma's investigation spun its wheels for a year to come up with basically nothing. Toward the end, they were just waiting around for another body to turn up so they could hopefully harvest additional forensics to give them some new leads to go on. Can you imagine waiting for a little kid to be killed just so you can do your job? My dad would have been sickened by it; he never would have given up like that."

"Sometimes we just don't have a choice." Tom rubbed the stiffness in the back of his neck, then reached his arm over the seat behind Kate and put his hand on her headrest. He wanted to pull her close but hesitated; the thought of another dead girl sickened him too. "The early SRK case went pretty much the same way, Kate, all smoke and no fire, but you already know that. At least we weren't waiting for a child to die."

Kate looked through her window into the wooded darkness racing by. The rain was finally starting to let up. "Buchanan said Haas had told him about a list of inmates he put together for Mary Richards years ago, but according to him, he never saw it, and he never really thought much about it. Apparently Haas used his I.T. skills to hack the information on the pretense that Mary was going to take the list to the FBI; it was supposed to be some sort of Top 40 Countdown of child predators to help our colleagues at the Bureau ferret out Emma's killer. Initially, none of the partners had a problem with her little project since they all loved Mary and would have done anything to help with her daughter's case, especially when she became sick. After she died, everything eventually got back to normal, and Haas' inmate list was forgotten.

But when Thurman Goethe was dropped to the dirt outside one of their slammers a short while ago, Haas had to confess to his partners that Goethe was on his list and, as you already know, so was a wannabe-barber creep named Greg Levy, another esteemed graduate of American Corrections who was killed several years before. Once was a coincidence, twice was a big problem, and all of a sudden things got real interesting at their firm. They've been in a five-alarm cluster mode ever since." Kate paused to listen to the voice on the GPS; the volume was turned down so she had to lift it to her ear. "Siri said to take the exit in two miles, just on the other side of this town coming up; then make a left at the top of the ramp."

Tom glanced at the clock on the dashboard. "We're on schedule, maybe a few minutes ahead. Check your gear."

Kate pulled the Glock from her shoulder holster and made sure the magazine was full before she chambered a round; she took the gun off safety and then tucked it back under her jacket. Next, she turned on the short-range radio clipped to her belt and slipped on the wrist transmitter before planting the wireless speaker bud in her ear.

"Anyway," Kate said, "after Goethe, Haas must have come to the conclusion that his stepson had taken the matter of his daughter's death into his own hands, and that's when Haas came clean with his partners. What I find amazing is that no one went forward to the police—*talk about a major corporate secret.* I guess when we showed up this morning, Haas had just about hit his breaking point. He didn't even know about Bobby Mayfield yet, but we must have pushed him over the edge. It was this morning, right? I'm exhausted just thinking about it."

Tom nodded his head and kept driving; Kate wasn't alone in how she felt. A lot *had* happened today.

*****

They left the interstate and crossed the overpass through a little commercial area with a gas station and a half-empty strip center. Vacancy signs were peppered across the windows, and a handful of For-Sale by Owner cars were lined up in the parking lot along the edge of the road. A minute later they were back in the countryside, following a winding valley toward the rich bottom land along the Mississippi River. Tom squinted at the bright headlights approaching from around the curve ahead; he flashed his high beams as the pickup passed but the driver didn't dim his lights. He watched the truck disappear in his rearview mirror as he entered the curve but quickly forgot about it. "We should be getting close to the river."

Kate looked down at the GPS. "Stay on this road for another mile; then turn left on White Oak Lane; it looks like it cuts through a subdivision, but stay on it. It will take us right to Rhodes' front door. And you're correct; it shows the Mississippi about a half-mile east of his house."

Tom sat up in his seat; he could feel his pulse quicken and didn't know if it was excitement or trepidation. During the past five years he had made dozens of other arrests, important arrests, but this one felt very different. This was the one he had really wanted, the one that was supposed to matter the most, but all of a sudden he wasn't sure why. He liked the hunt because he liked to win; he liked to solve unsolvable crimes, and he liked to out-smart the bad guys. His side was the side of the Law; Justice and Humanity were right there riding along beside him in the car. SRK had killed some horrible people, that part was for sure, but Tom wasn't thinking about them. He was thinking about Bryan Rhodes the father, about what he had lost and the pain he must have endured, and about the kind of rage that would fuel a sane man to murder again and again. Tonight was the end of something that never should have begun, and it was going to be the hardest thing that Tom ever had to do.

*****

"There it is;" Kate pointed to a sign coming up on the left, "White Oak Lane—turn here."

Tom lifted his foot off the gas and let the car drift through the corner before letting it slow to a crawl; he could hear the texture of the pavement change beneath the tires. Ahead of them, the neighborhood had already gone to sleep. Except for the intrusion of their headlamps and the glow of a few porch lights standing guard, everything was tucked in for the night.

They crept forward in silence with the motor barely spinning above idle, passing simple ranch boxes wrapped in pastels of plastic siding. Lollypop-shaped trees lined the sides of the road and were sprinkled randomly throughout the yards. Everything looked fairly neat and clean; nothing looked much older than a dozen years, and nothing spoke of what had happened on this street one morning to a six-year-old girl. If there had been a memorial for her, it would have been taken down or fallen into neglect and blown away a long time ago.

"Stop!" Kate blurted out, "Just for a second, Tom; please." They had come to an intersection where they could go left or right or keep driving straight ahead to arrive at the house of SRK. On one corner a single rusted mailbox clung to an old wooden post, and above it a newer yellow sign showed the silhouette of a small boy and a girl in a ponytail walking together with book bags hanging from their shoulders; "SCHOOL BUS" was printed boldly in block letters below, and below that a bundle of deflated Mylar balloons draped over a home-made sign pointing to where a birthday party must have happened the weekend before. "This is where Emma was taken."

Tom took a deep breath and closed his eyes; he tried to imagine this simple place on that tragic morning: *Children waiting their turn to climb the steps of the bus; one little girl distracted by something nearby, walking away to see the unseen; the unknowing bus pulling forward without her, leaving nothing but this empty street corner behind.* He took his foot off the brake and let the car roll forward a few yards before opening his eyes again. "What makes this so hard, Kate," Tom bit his lower lip, slowly shaking his head, "it could have just as easily been my baby girl."

Kate leaned into Tom and wrapped her arm around his. "You know, we could just go back to the hotel and let someone else do this."

"And our resignations would have to be in Charlie's inbox by morning."

"That's true. Fight or flight, Tom. We can't do both."

"I know, but I'm not sure what we're actually fighting for anymore. This really sucks, Kate."

They passed another dozen homes before dropping off the end of the pavement; the street had narrowed abruptly and turned into a dirt and gravel drive lined by large, crooked trees and over-grown brush entangled with barbed-wire fencing. The car dipped in and out of shallow ruts, splashing water to the side. Tom killed the headlights and let the car roll to a stop. "I'm going to let you out here, Kate, so I can beach it against the fence. It'll be tight, but I think I can leave enough room for our backup team to get through."

"Okay, but make sure the dome light is switched off first."

Tom turned a knob on the dash, "You're good to go."

Kate got out of the car and transferred her Glock to between her belt and waist; she unsnapped the straps of the holster and threw in on the seat before closing the door carefully until it clicked. She adjusted her jacket and pulled the zipper to her neck to cover the bright white of her blouse.

Tom eased the car against the fence and stopped when he heard the barbed wire cutting into the paint. He got out and shut the door quietly, then ran through his routine with his gun and radio before sizing up the space between the side of the car and the opposite fence line. "It should work unless someone shows up in a Hummer."

Kate spoke in a whisper, "The house sits about a third of a mile straight ahead. Google showed three structures and maybe a small well house. It looks like there are two out-buildings; one's a garage, and the other looks like a machine shed or shop, but I'm not sure. I can't see any of it from here; we could use a little moon right now, but I guess that works in our favor too. I'm glad it stopped raining."

"Me, too. The wet ground will help dampen our steps, but keep off the gravel as much as possible to stay quiet. I'm sure he has a dog or two; let's hope they're deaf or heavy sleepers."

"Tom, can I ask if you're scared?

"Sure I'm scared," Tom whispered. "Rhodes doesn't want to be taken, but he's not likely to run. Where would he go? This whole thing only worked for him because no one knew who he was. He has to know that eventually we'd track him down, and I'm sure he keeps an eye out for unwanted visitors. I really have no idea how he's going to react, but I don't think he'll go down quietly."

"I'm scared, too. My offer still stands, Tom; let's go back to our hotel room—we can just cuddle like an old married couple."

"That sounds wonderful, Kate, but I'll have to take a rain check." Tom stopped to give her a soft kiss. "That's just in case this deal goes bad."

She kissed him back. "It won't; *Super Girl* has your six."

They walked the rest of the way in silence. When they were close enough to see the house and out-buildings, Tom stopped. "It's too dark, Kate; there should be a yard light on or something; this doesn't feel right. It's awful quiet."

"Maybe he's not home; I don't see any vehicles—just the tractor over there. The garage door is open, but it looks like it's just full of junk."

"Check the shop for a car; then set up at the back door in case he runs. I'm going around front."

Tom moved slowly between the overgrown shrubbery and the walls of the house, ducking under the windows to keep out of view. The dead growth snapped audibly in the still night air as his legs pushed through it; if there was a dog, it would have been barking by now. *Kate's right; Rhodes isn't home.*

Tom started to breathe a little easier; maybe he wouldn't have to do this tonight after all. Kate's hotel offer was starting to feel like a good plan; all he really wanted to do was fall asleep beside her. When he reached the corner of the porch he paused to confirm his thoughts: *No dogs, no lights, no vehicles. No one is here.*

He had just convinced himself that the house was empty, but he stayed alert anyway before glancing through the porch railing. What he saw made him stand up and press his radio microphone, "Agent Morrow, you have to see this!"

A few seconds later Kate was standing next to him looking over the raw hole ripped into the porch floor; it looked like a small bomb had gone off, but there was no smell of explosives or fire, just the lingering odor of hydraulic fluid and diesel fuel.

"You don't suppose he could be remodeling, do you?" Kate asked, not really requiring an answer.

"No, I don't." Tom had just finished calling in for their backup. "But we do need to get some lights on. I'll go check the panel on that pole where the overhead power comes in; maybe the main breaker is tripped. Stay out of the house until I get back; everything in this place feels wrong."

"Then you won't mind if I tag along with you."

"Not at all, K, but point that thing away from me." Kate still had her Glock gripped in her hand; she put it on safety and slipped it back under her belt.

"Sorry, Tom; this is a little different than the incident drills at Quantico."

"Yeah, I know; reality has a funny way of training us. For some reason, the test always comes first—*then the lesson.*" Tom walked to the pole and threw open the panel below the electric meter. He found the main switch and flipped it over; the overhead yard light came on instantly and most of the ground floor of the house lit up as well. "Now isn't that interesting? Let's go have a look inside."

*****

Tom pushed on the front door with the barrel of his gun; it was already standing halfway open but didn't show any evidence of a break-in. The first thing he saw was the dog lying motionless on the floor; there was a trail of smeared blood coming from the hall, and it looked like it had crawled to the living room where it died. The carpet was bunched up and pulled toward the front door like something heavy had been dragged over it or on it. Kate kneeled over the animal and took a photo of the wound. "It's deep and wide with a slight curve to it. I'd say it's too irregular for a knife—a shovel maybe?"

"Could be; I'm going to check around upstairs." Tom pointed through a window at the flashing lights racing down the gravel drive. *"Here we go again."*

"Meet them outside, Kate; I don't want anyone in here traipsing around until we've had a good look. They can start by getting a little exercise and walking the property. Have them spread out all the way to the river." Tom nodded toward the dog. "I wouldn't be surprised if they found another body, human or otherwise. In the meantime, give Charlie a call to brief him on the status of the take-down, which apparently didn't happen, and then have a closer look at that shop or shed, whatever it is. I'll meet you out there as soon as I can, or I'll give you a shout if I find anything else inside. This is going to be a very long night."

*****

Kate couldn't find the light switch; she knew the building had electricity because she could see a red light blinking from a dark box on top of the workbench next to her. She had dropped her phone outside in the tall grass after talking to Grainger and couldn't find it either; she didn't have anything to help her see except for the yard light shining through the big opening in the side of the workshop. The second half of her little assignment was just not going very well. *Tom is going to think I'm an idiot.*

There was an empty area in the middle of the dirt floor marked by a large stain and deep tread impressions. Kate thought it must be from the tractor she saw parked outside. The remainder of the space was cluttered with what had to be farming implements, but she had no idea what they were used for; she grew up in Oklahoma as the daughter of a city cop— there wasn't a drop of farmer DNA in her. She thought she saw what might be a door on the far wall and wandered into the gauntlet of steel shapes without too much hesitation. *Surely there has to be a switch over there.*

"Are you okay, Kate?"

She jumped at Tom's voice, almost falling backward over a mower deck; he was standing in the light of the big doorway. "Might you be looking for this?" He reached up to pull something hanging from the ceiling, and a moment later the lights flickered on. "They call it a pull string—uh, for obvious reasons."

Kate wanted to scream at Tom, and then she wanted to cry. She wanted so badly to impress him, but her anxiety kept getting in the way. "It's just not going very well for me tonight, Thomas; I'm just about ready to start walking back to Oklahoma."

"We've had a couple of very long days, Kate. You're tired, I'm tired, the whole world is tired; it can mess with your ability to think." Tom stepped around the stain on the ground and walked toward her. "No pressure, Super-girl; we'll do this together."

"There you go making me feel all good again. You need to stop that."

"Make me."

Kate glanced outside to see if there were any agents standing around, then gave Tom a peck on his lips. "That's just a deposit."

"And I aim to collect, someday; now let's get back to work, Kate." Tom made sure he had left her with a smile before surveying the equipment spread around the floor; most of it looked like it hadn't been used in a quite a while. "Other than what we've already seen, Kate, I didn't find anything unusual upstairs or anywhere else inside, for that matter," he said. "The house sits on a stone foundation, but the only access is from outside—probably just a bug-infested crawl space or storm shelter. I'm saving that lovely task for last. I cut the guys loose to look for trace, and the techs are in the dining room doing a number on Rhodes' computer; hopefully they can crack into it while we're here. We've got some blood mixed in with the debris on the porch and here and there in the house; I'm sure it doesn't all belong to the dog. The tractor's still warm, so my guess is Rhodes' little demo project happened earlier tonight. I'd sure like to know what the hell went on out here."

"Me, too." Kate looked back at the door she had been trying to reach before Tom showed up and turned on the lights. "That wall looks like it cuts the building roughly in half. What do you say we have a look at what's on the other side?"

"I'm right behind you. Oh, and here's your phone, Sherlock." Tom held it out for her. "Charlie called you back after your little talk, and I found it ringing on the ground. He said to make sure *I* don't screw anything up."

"Yeah, right." Kate grabbed it out of his hand and gave him a friendly shove on the shoulder before heading toward the door. She brushed against a steel shank protruding from an implement and ripped her skirt. "Dang it! You know, Tom; this is turning out to be a very bad day."

"The good news is this particular one will be history in about an hour," Tom offered. He looked up from his watch and glanced at her exposed thigh. "Buy yourself a new skirt, and put it on your expense report, but don't get rid of that one; I think it's kind of sexy. Surprise me with it sometime."

Kate flashed him a come-hither grin before she pushed on the door; it wasn't locked or latched and didn't make a sound when it opened. She took one step up to the raised concrete floor and another to enter the dark room; Tom was right behind her with his hand resting lightly on her waist. This time she had no trouble finding a switch and flipped it on. As soon as she did, she fell back against Tom like she had been hit by a strong gust of wind. "Whoa! *Jackpot.*"

The room was a radiance of colored light, a confusion of

every pigment and pattern of glass imaginable piled high on luminous shelving and stacked in boxes and plastic buckets littered across the floor. Kate found her balance and rushed into the room like a little girl; she spun around on the ball of her foot to absorb the entire scene. Her shoe ground on a layer of sparkling sand and made a gritty, abrasive sound. Beside her, several barrels overflowed with long, dangerous looking shards; above, jagged pieces hung like colored lightning, suspended by invisible threads and moving ever so slightly in the disturbed air. A large work surface glowed in the middle of the room as if it held the sun, and it was covered with layers of glass cuttings and loose sticks of lead caning. The light pushed up from an array of bright lamps in the cabinet below and created a shattered rainbow of randomness across the ceiling. Kate's eyes were wide with amazement like she had just walked inside of a giant kaleidoscope.

"Tom, would this, um, suggest to you that Rhodes may have had a psychotic break?"

Tom circled the room, snapping pictures with his phone. "Affirmative—this is unbelievable." He ended his walk in front of a long workbench on the wall they had just passed through; it was where Rhodes kept his tools. "Glass cutting *and* ammo loading equipment, interesting. This reloading press right here would have set him back at least two thousand bucks." He pointed at the manufacturer's logo cast into the base. "He's got some high-end stuff here." Tom took a step along the bench and tapped his finger on a row of empty 20-volt battery chargers. "Hmm, this is for a cordless glass saw, and this one's for a hammer drill, but I don't see either one of them. Maybe he took them with him—wherever he is."

"Maybe." Kate was standing at the glowing work surface. "Tom, there's something under here; help me move this stuff. I can see part of a wooden frame; it looks like it could be a window. The Rhodes file mentioned the girl's finger prints, partials actually—her fingers were badly burned; but they were found on a stained-glass window at the church where she was taken."

Tom stood across from Kate as they carefully removed the layers of glass and caning spread across the table. As they did, a beautiful image began to emerge of a bearded man in a golden robe holding a small child. They continued to work until the full window was exposed for them to see. About four feet wide and ten feet tall, the frame had a deeply arched top and was ringed by a heavy bead of dried, brittle caulk and thickly covered in layers of white, blistered paint. It was obviously quite old, but the colored glass it held looked refurbished; all of the caning and cement had been cleaned or repaired. The image in the window was complete except for one pane of glass, about four times the size of Kate's outstretched hand. It was missing from the bottom corner of the window.

"I know this." Kate moved to the end of the table to look at the window from the orientation it would have been installed in a wall. "It depicts the Holy Innocents, the babies that King Herod ordered to be killed. Herod was one effed-up S.O.B., if you were to ask my opinion. That's God on His throne cradling one of the little kids; all the other children gathered around Him have died and are waiting to be received in Heaven by God—do you see the halos?"

"I do. And you know this how?"

"I grew up Lutheran, and, for the record, it was at gunpoint and against my will. December 28th was *Childermas*; we called it *Innocent's Day,* and it was a big deal in our church. FYI, it's one of the twelve days of Christmas and traditionally commemorates the first Christian Martyrs—the little kids Herod had murdered. I'll bet you a back-rub that this is the window from the church where Emma was killed. The place was abandoned somewhere out in the sticks; no one would have missed it. He must have taken it years ago, probably when this whole killing thing got started; it makes sense if he was in total meltdown. It looks like Rhodes spent a lot of time restoring it," Kate held her hand over the empty space, "except for this missing glass right here. I bet he cut it up to use for his calling cards."

"So what's with the big mess on top, covering it up? You'd think he'd have a deep reverence for it."

"I don't know; I'll probably have to get back to you on that. But I will say that this one corner was the only part of the window that wasn't covered; maybe he's waiting until he's finished, or can't bring himself to look at the rest of it."

"Or, maybe he's psychotic." Tom crossed his arms. "This is the kind of stuff that drives me crazy—the stuff we may never know."

Kate drew her finger around the empty spot left in the depiction of the martyred children captured in glass. "Take SRK alive, and we might find out."

"I'm afraid I'm going to have to let Rhodes make that choice."

*****

Goethe was lost; he vaguely remembered the dirt road to the old church had wound through the woods, but he felt like he had gone too far; nothing looked familiar in the headlights at all. He drove slowly between the trash littering the sides of the road, while low branches scraped against the roof of the truck and made an irritating sound that put him on edge. *This doesn't feel right, Thurman.*

When the road split off in two directions he stopped, and he tried to think of which way he was supposed to turn. Then he saw it in the headlights, the granite post with the marking that pointed to the cemetery; it had fallen over and was lying against a rock on the ground. He remembered that he needed to go to the right and then he would be there soon.

The road followed a dry creek bed for a short while, then took a sharp turn back into the woods. As he crested a low rise, he caught a glimpse of the weathered bell tower lifting into the moonlight; vines had grown almost to the top, and it was much shorter than he remembered, or maybe the trees around it had just grown taller. As he got closer, the sides of the road began to choke around him until the road was gone, and he was forced to plow the truck blindly through the thick undergrowth. He remembered a clearing around the church, but it was gone now; the woods had spent the years reclaiming its ground, and all that remained was a narrow crescent of driveway in front of the building where the stone cobbles had kept nature from taking hold. He parked the truck just past the steps in front of the entry doors and got out.

Goethe's legs were stiff, particularly the bad one, and it hurt to put any of his weight on it; he had driven out of the rain an hour ago but could still feel it lingering in his joints. He had left the keys in the ignition, and the warning ding quickly irritated him; he slammed the door and a startled owl took flight from a hole in the broken roof of the tower. In the distance, a hundred bullfrogs groaned for the favor of a female, but Goethe wasn't listening; he had come to the church to settle a score.

The first part of his retribution would be to make Bryan Rhodes listen to the details of what Thurman had done to his daughter inside these walls; the second part was to inflict as much physical pain as possible before allowing him to die. He was glad the farmer was a big, tough man; that meant he would be able to endure all the suffering that Thurman could deliver— and for a very long time. Getting that big man out of the truck and into the church was going to be a challenge but with the rope he brought from the workshop and the winch mounted to the front bumper, he was sure he would be able to figure something out. He centered himself behind the bed of the truck. *Shall we get started, Thurman, my feisty little friend?*

The heavy tailgate slipped from his hands the moment he released the latch. It made a loud bang as it bottomed out at the end of the chains. *Dammit, Thurman! Why did you allow that to happen?*

Goethe shook off the sudden irritation and threw back the bed cover.

Bryan Rhodes was gone.

*****

Tom pulled himself out of the crawlspace and stood up while dusting off his pant knees and the soiled elbows of his shirt, "What time is it?"

"Two-ish." Kate didn't know what time it was; she just guessed and figured it was close enough, considering she had been awake for twenty hours or more, and it was middle of the night. An hour one way or the other right now didn't make much difference to her. "Find anything, Tom?"

"Nope, mostly dirt, a couple of dead rats and lots of cobwebs. Just like I thought."

"S.A.C. Russell?" An agent came up from behind Kate and politely stepped around her. He looked at Tom's wide shoulders then grimaced at the small opening in the stone foundation he had just witnessed Tom crawling through. "Tight, huh?"

"Yeah, it was. Whaddya have for us?"

"Sir, we definitely have blood from three different sources— one belongs to the dog; that would be the pooling and splatter you saw in the kitchen, as well as the trail from the kitchen to the living room where it died. The second source we pulled off the debris on the porch which was a match for the blood we found inside the front loader of the tractor. We also found multiple blood droplets on the floor from a third source that indicate it was first in the kitchen, then in the living room near the dog, and then moved back through the kitchen, across the porch and climbed up on the tractor. Source number three also went up the stairs to the second floor, but we didn't find anything in the upper hall or in any of the rooms; just a couple drops of blood on the top step."

"Good work, uh…"

"It's Agent Billings, sir, and don't worry about it." Billings took off his hat and scratched the back of his head. "There's something else, sir. We found fecal residue pretty much lockstep with blood source number three. We first found it on the tractor seat, then traced it back into the house."

"Any of it in the workshop where we found the glass?" Tom asked.

"No, sir. No blood either. A lot of dog hair but it's clean otherwise." Billings' phone rang; he raised his finger and abruptly stepped away.

Tom motioned for Kate to follow him to the front porch, but there was something she needed to do first. "Can you give me a minute, Tom? I want to check something upstairs."

"Sure. I'll meet you out front."

*****

Kate entered the house through the kitchen and climbed the stairs, being careful not to disturb the evidence markers that Billings' team had placed on two of the steps and along the landing at the top. They had left all of the lights on, and it was easy to see. The first room she came to was directly in front of the stairs and at the back of the house; the door was closed and the hinges moaned when she pushed it open. As soon as she entered, she knew it had belonged to Emma.

She turned around before she went any farther and proceeded to the room at the other end of the hall, passing the open doors to a bathroom and a vacant closet. Once inside, she quickly inventoried the king bed with rumpled linens on the left side only, a dresser, a single chair draped in men's clothes, a dog's bed near the door and a wood stove tucked back in the corner. Nothing interesting caught Kate's attention. She started toward Emma's room but paused at the top of the stairs before going back in. She thought of Emma's father having to pass that door every night just before he climbed into his side of an empty bed and each morning when he climbed out of it. There was no way it didn't cause him terrible pain every time he did.

*****

Kate stepped through Emma's doorway into a time that had long ago passed; everything that was her life lay gripped under a mantel of dust, arrested in a moment that would never move forward. Years ago someone must have lovingly put things in their place, and it was there that they still remained. It didn't look like anything had been boxed away or discarded, but it didn't look like a room that a six-year-old girl would have left behind before leaving for school on that final morning. The bed was tightly made, and the children's books were closed and neatly placed on a shelf above the desk; there were no toys on the floor or clothes on the bed, just a row of stuffed animals on top of the colorful quilt leaning against each other and against the wall. The tracks from the last sweeps of a vacuum cleaner could still be faintly seen in the carpeting. Except for the dust, it looked like a child's room that Kate might see in a department store display.

She went to the window and looked out over the back roof and down at the orange tractor parked in the light spilling from the workshop. A half-mile straight ahead through the darkness would be the Mississippi River, and she imagined the sun rising soon over the bluffs on the other side that she couldn't yet see.

She glanced down at the pillow on Emma's bed beside her; it wasn't quite perfectly in its place and straightened like everything else. For no reason, except maybe a tender thought for the little girl, she slid it toward the wall so it would be centered on the mattress, and then she saw it—a single drop of fresh blood. *Well, hello source number three.*

*****

Tom was standing beside what was left of the front porch when Kate found him. "There you are, Kate. Okay, try this." He talked into the gaping hole as if he had practiced talking to himself. "An intruder enters the kitchen and mortally wounds the dog. Rhodes walks in and gets cut by the bad guy before he's able to overpower him; there's no evidence of a fight, so he must have done it quickly. That would make Rhodes blood source number three. He carries the intruder, blood source number two, out to the front porch before he goes to his shop to get his..."

"Or—" Kate put her hand gently under Tom's chin, and he stopped talking; she coaxed him to turn his face toward her. "Are you suggesting, Tom, that SRK had a case of the drizzly shits while he climbed up on his tractor and then deliberately did *this* to the front of *his* house? Are we talking about the same guy who almost split Duncan Boyd in half with an iron pipe and made a pin cushion out of Jared Hill with a plastic horse? You do remember what happened to Greg Levy and the Lowens, right? Let's not forget Bobby Mayfield, *the Flying Mattress Boy.*" Kate spoke with confidence and no hesitation whatsoever in her voice, "Rhodes wasn't the guy driving the tractor, Tom, Thurman Goethe was."

"Goethe? Are you kidding me? How?!"

"First, keep in mind that Goethe certainly had motive to come after SRK, although I have no idea how he could have found him; but please hear me out." Kate paused to take a deep breath. "Remember Locard's Principle?"

Tom nodded yes. "Of course."

"Well, Goethe left a trace, so to speak. First, he enters the kitchen and wounds the dog, as you say, but not before the dog scores with a couple of defensive chomps. One bite causes Goethe to leave a trail of blood drops through the house, making him blood source number three; the other punctures his *colostomy* bag—remember that nasty little detail? Now he's also leaking do-do everywhere he goes, and that puts Goethe right up there in the tractor seat. That also makes Rhodes blood source number two and puts him in the middle of *this* hole and in the front loader of *that* tractor." Kate pointed her finger through the house and at the orange machine parked behind it.

"You *are* Super Girl!" Tom placed his hands at the sides of Kate's arms. "You can lose your cell phone, fumble around for the lights and rip your skirt *anytime* you want."

"Good to know; I'll be right back." Kate disappeared but returned in less than a minute with her tablet. She was working the GPS screen as she walked up to Tom. "We can cross the river at the Chester Bridge; it's not far."

"Cross to where?"

"Illinois, silly, we need to get to Ellis Grove; it's only an hour from here."

"Why do I know that name?"

"It's the post mark on the envelope turned in by the Hoffman's, you know, the couple in Roswell, Georgia, with the autistic boy. It's also real close to where the abandoned church is located, where they found Emma's body eight years ago."

"How the hell did we miss that?!"

"The Rhodes file listed the crime scene in Randolph County. We missed it because there's no mention of the town name."

"Well, shit. Okay, Kate, you have my attention; but why do you want to go there right now?"

"Tom, I think Mary Richards was correct; call it mother's intuition or whatever; but she knew Emma's killer had *gone deep,* and she knew where to go fishing to find him; that's how she came up with her list. That said, there was a good chance that as long as Bryan Rhodes kept killing he would eventually clip the right guy, and I think Goethe is that guy."

"Keep going."

"When I went upstairs, I looked in the daughter's room and found a drop of fresh blood covered by her pillow; the guys must have missed it. Tom, Goethe *is* blood source number three, and he was in her room but nowhere else upstairs; he was *leaning* over her bed, and that suggests intimacy. For some reason, he wanted to see where she slept, and that means he has a connection to the girl. Call it a wild hunch, Agent Russell—but Goethe is going back to the church where he killed Emma Rhodes, and he's taken SRK with him."

*****

–31–

RECKONING

Goethe felt suddenly tired; his one good leg could barely support his weight. He leaned against the tailgate to get some air, and think. The gun was lying on the front seat; he would get that first and then wait for dawn; there was no way he was going to hobble around and hunt for Rhodes in the dark. He thought about getting back in the truck and driving away, but Rhodes had found him once before, and after what Thurman had done tonight, he would certainly find him again. *This has to end now.* Goethe decided it would be best to hide somewhere inside the church and wait for the big farmer to come to him.

*****

Bryan was standing in the woods shifting his weight from side to side; he was forcing himself to keep his heart rate up and hasten the drug along. Through the trees he could see the front of the church, maybe fifty yards away, lit up in the weakening moonlight; it would be daylight soon, and he needed to move quickly, but he was only able to stay awake for brief periods of time. The drug was still plying its way through his system, and he needed to hold it together for longer than just a few connected minutes. It had been enough time to cut the ties binding his wrists on a broken board in the back of the truck and long enough to break the plastic latch on the bed cover, but each time he had blacked out from the exertion and didn't know for how long. When he woke to the sound of brush scraping against the sides of his pickup, he had used the noise to mask his escape but soon fell asleep again not far from where he was now able to stand. The short bursts of consciousness had been long enough to enable his escape, but they weren't yet long enough to kill the demon leaning against his truck.

*****

Goethe thought the church felt damp and reeked of molded plaster and rotten wood; the floor was soft under the weight of his good foot. A bed of dead leaves covered the rostrum where the roof had collapsed and below where the big colored window used to be. He remembered there was a bathroom and a pastor's office in the basement where he might hide, but the narrow stair was gone, and he was lucky he hadn't stepped into the dark, empty hole it left behind. He shuffled to the only place he could go where he wouldn't be easily seen: the little room next to the entrance to the church where a bride would wait before walking down the aisle. Goethe slumped against the wall and closed the door with the gun pointing toward it. Perspiration burned his eyes, and he wiped it away with his sleeve; then he counted the bullets in the magazine of the gun with his finger because it was too dark to see.

Nine rounds; that should be plenty, Thurman. But the farmer was a big man, and Goethe knew he had to make every one of them count.

*****

Bryan moved in a tightening circle converging on the church; he shook his head often and violently to fight off the drug and kept pressure on a sliver of wood buried deep in his arm so that the histamine released in the pain would help keep him alert. He had watched the demon go inside with a gun and knew it was in there waiting for him. He had no intention of making the demon wait for very long.

He paused to rest for a moment. Through a clearing in the trees, he saw the opening in the back wall from where he had taken the window so long ago, and he abruptly remembered that this was the last place his daughter had been alive. Before he could process the thought, a sudden chill passed through him, an essence briefly sharing his body. He felt it first enter his back, then pass through his heart in the direction of the church, drawing the breath from his lungs as it pulled away. The undergrowth parted to receive the invisible presence, the leaves on the ground lifting, lowering, ever so slightly, like a barely perceptible wave rolling into the night. *Emma had arrived.* He closed his eyes, believing she would return to take his hand, but it didn't happen.

His anger ignited as soon as he understood: Emma was waiting for him to follow her to the church, to finish what he had obviously been brought there to do. He had had no plan other than to stay awake long enough to tear apart the demon inside, and the only thing stopping him from doing that had just vanished in the wake of his incumbent rage. He released his grip on the shard in his arm because the pain didn't matter anymore. The drug was now gone. The time had finally come to slaughter the monster that killed his little girl.

The time of reckoning had arrived.

*****

Goethe heard footsteps on the cobbled stones in front of the church. His arms were tired but he kept the gun raised and pointed at the heart of an imaginary man standing outside the door to the small room where he waited. He knew Rhodes was coming inside and would have to walk by the door; and when he did, he would pull the trigger again and again until the gun stopped firing because he knew he wouldn't have another chance.

413

But Rhodes didn't come. Instead, the ignition of the truck turned over, and the engine roared to life. The sudden noise startled Goethe, but he tried to stay calm and listen for what might come next. Sitting in the dark room he had begun to change his mind—he had lost control of the night, and now he had lost the chance to leave. He just wanted Rhodes to drive away and disappear; they could settle this score some other time. But the sound didn't move, and he knew that meant there wasn't going to be another time. Next he heard the whine of an electric motor but couldn't imagine what it was. *Don't worry, Thurman; it's going to be just fine...*

More confusing sounds filled his ears; the truck door squeaked open, then slammed closed; the footsteps came near then moved away, several times. It sounded like Rhodes was unloading the broken boards from the back of the pickup; he thought he heard nails dragging across the metal tailgate. Then the sound of Rhodes finally went away, and the only things his senses could find in the dark were the rough idle of the engine and a hint of gasoline drifting in the air. It stayed that way for a long time, and then everything went quiet, and all that was left was the lingering scent of unspent fuel and the chanting of the bullfrogs in the distance.

Goethe couldn't take it anymore.

Oh, not to be seen,

Or heard,

Or known,

Oh—not to be.

He didn't understand how things had gotten so turned around tonight. His bad leg was folded under him and hurting badly; the waiting was getting to be too much. Rhodes was just walking around outside and would make an easy target. If the farmer didn't want to come to him, it seemed to Goethe that he might just have to move the night along. *You should have killed him in his house when I gave you the chance, Thurman! Just how stupid are you? You're still the weak person father always said you were.*

He struggled to get up from the floor, reaching for the doorknob to pull himself up, but just as he did the door was ripped from its hinges, and all he could see was a big white hand coming at him; he fired the gun once before the farmer grabbed it and tossed it across the room.

Shit—Thurman.

*****

"How long?" Tom had just turned north on Route 3 after crossing over the bridge at Chester.

"Ten miles to Ellis Grove; then we're on our own, honey— there's no address for the church, so the GPS is about useless right now. It's somewhere between the town and the Mississippi River, and it's a good thing we borrowed Agent Billing's SUV; I think we're going to need it. The map that Grainger sent is a bit sketchy, but we should be able to find it. It shows that it's near the river in the flood plain; I guess that's why it was abandoned years ago; you just can't beat Mother Nature." Kate looked out her window at the slightest hint of light emerging on the horizon. "We should be there just before sun up."

"Works for me."

Tom was speeding but not like he was convinced by Kate's wild hunch. Her hunch felt more like a stretch of the imagination, but it was hard to argue with her batting average lately. He had been driving like he didn't want it to be true, but it suddenly occurred to him that on the off-chance that Kate was right, Bryan Rhodes would be in a lot of danger right now. He pushed the accelerator toward the floor, "Radio Ellis Grove PD or the county Sheriff or whatever they have out here. Tell them we're coming in hot, and brief them on what we think the situation is at the church; they're welcome to tag along, but no one gets there before us. If we're wrong about this, Kate, then we're wrong; I'll worry about my new career later." He switched on the light bar concealed at the top of the windshield and shook his head at the lights dancing across the hood. *Here we go again.*

*****

Bryan grabbed its leg by the ankle and yanked it out of the room; he heard the other leg break when it got caught sideways in the door. The demon screamed but Bryan didn't care; *pain* was the whole point. He took it by the nape of the neck and the back of its belt and threw it out of the church and halfway down the stone steps.

"Wait! Thurman did it; *it was him!*"

But Bryan didn't care about the demon's pathetic cries either; they only made him stronger and more determined. He hefted the thing to his shoulder and carried it to the front of his truck where he dropped it on the cobbled drive; then he reached into his cab and turned on the headlights. But before he could get back to the demon, a pain ripped through his gut like a bear had just buried its teeth into him. He bent over in agony, inching toward the light, sliding along the side of the fender to brace his weight; he needed to see why he hurt so badly, and then he remembered the gunshot in the church. He could see that the front of his shirt was soaked with blood but couldn't tell how bad the damage was without taking it off. He had been shot once before in the fleshy muscle above his hip, but it had gone clean through; this wound felt entirely different, as if his insides didn't fit together anymore. He clenched his teeth before straightening up to see if he even could, but the pain almost sent him to his knees. He took a deep breath and focused on the man-snake curled up in front of him.

"It's time, Bryan." He heard Mary speak.

"Yes it is."

What he had to do couldn't wait; he would push through his pain just like Mary and Emma had done with their suffering; he would deal with the hole in his belly only when he was finished destroying the demon.

Bryan pressed his hand tight against his wound and struggled to lower a knee to the ground; in the light he saw his assailant clearly for the first time and realized he had dealt with this one before; it was the demon called Goethe. Slowly, he lowered his face onto its face and peered into the hollow eyes to confirm what he already believed to be true. When he did, he knew he was gazing directly into the fires of Hell.

"You are the One."

And just like that—his journey was over. Suddenly his belly didn't hurt anymore; he could feel his strength return. Bryan reached over to the front of the truck and untied the rope from the tow hook below the winch and wrapped it around the demon's lower legs. It screamed repeatedly as he tightened the lashings over the broken bone with every turn.

"PLEASE!!!"

But that was the one sound that Bryan would not allow to be uttered. His baby must have cried that word over and over again, but this monster violated her and took her life anyway. He slammed his fist into the Goethe's jaw and left it shattered in a bag of flesh against its throat. *It* would not make that sound ever again.

Then Bryan got up, almost easily, and grabbed the winch control off the bumper; he pressed the button and watched the demon being dragged away across the cobble stones toward the pile of broken boards and dry deadfall he had collected and soaked with gasoline from the can he kept in the bed of his truck.

He had strung the rope up and over the sturdy limb of an old tree that had taken root long before the church cornerstone had been laid. Then, when he saw that Goethe was lifted free of the ground and twisting in the air, he pressed the button again, and the winch shuddered to a stop with the demon's hands dangling a few feet above the pile.

Bryan reached into the passenger window and pulled his rucksack from the floor. He set it on the hood and opened the flap, then pulled out the wooden box and opened it too. The pane of red glass with the amber swirl was smaller now. He drew his fingers tenderly across it and kissed it again where Emma's prints had long ago worn away. This time he didn't bother to cut off a piece like he had done each time before. What was left of it he would use on the demon Goethe, because after tonight he wouldn't need the glass anymore.

The beast hung helpless and inverted under the branch of the great tree. Bryan stood in front of it, but he wouldn't dare to speak its name—names were for human beings and dogs like Molly. He had not thought about what he would say or if he would say anything at all, but staring at it now as he was, he decided it would be best if he just let the flames speak for him instead. He tore open its shirt and in one fluid motion drew the glass through its flesh beginning at the port where the ruptured shit-bag was still attached and across its stomach, drawing straight down its sternum and ending at the base of its neck, where its jaw hung loosely to the side. All it could do was release a hideous yowl and spill bloody mucus out of its throat. Bryan surveyed the wound and was pleased; he had been careful not to cut too deep. Bleeding to death would not be very painful at all.

Being burned alive was an entirely different matter.

There was one last detail he needed to take care of. He grabbed a broken board and used it to pry a cobble stone from out of the drive; it was long and heavy and would work well for its purpose. He fashioned a cradle from a piece of rope and fitted it around the stone like a net; he left a loop projecting from each end that he cinched tight around the demon's wrists. When he let go of the stone Goethe's arms were pulled straight down toward the pile of wood glistening from the wetness of the gasoline. The creature was too weak to resist the weight. Before Bryan lit the match, he thought of the one thing he did want to say.

"You burned my baby's fingers."

Then he tossed the lighted match into the bonfire waiting to be and walked away.

*****

"Which one?" Tom stopped the Suburban at the fork in the dirt road.

"Grainger's map doesn't show this spot." Kate pulled up Google Earth on her tablet and entered Ellis Grove, Illinois. She zoomed in and slid the screen to the right until she found where they had left the pavement. With her finger she followed the dirt trail through the leafless satellite image until she found where it split off in two directions. She could see the blurry roof of the church on her screen just a few hundred feet to their right.

"Find it yet?" Tom sounded anxious.

"Shhh!" Kate held up her hand for him to be quiet. She thought she heard something and rolled down her window; it was faint and hidden in the sound of the frogs. "Tom, over there." She pointed out her window. "I hear screaming!"

Tom hit the gas and barely made the corner at the dry creek bed. When they flew over the rise and back into the woods, they saw the fire and the body burning above it.

"Shit! Hold on, Kate!"

Tom didn't slow down when they plowed into the undergrowth; the scraping noises enveloping the vehicle were deafening. He braked hard when they made the crescent clearing in front of the church; the tires shook angrily over the cobble stones until he rammed into the side of the pickup and they came to a stop.

Kate threw open the door and jumped down from her seat. She ran around the truck and toward the fire; the body hanging over it was swinging from the rope jolted by the collision. She stopped when the heat became too intense to go any closer; the smell in the air was sickening. She shouted to Tom over her shoulder, "We're too late!"

Tom caught up to her and put his arm around her waist as she vomited all over the ground. Just then the rope failed, and the body dropped on the flames; a shower of sparks leapt into the air.

Tom spoke coldly, "That's not Rhodes."

*****

Bryan stepped over the hole in the floor where a two-dollar bolt had kept his captive daughter from getting away and staying alive. He set the bloody pane of glass on the sill where the window had been and slumped down against the wall below it. He pulled off his shirt and pressed it to the wound in his gut, but he couldn't feel the pain anymore, and he couldn't feel his hands. He thought he saw someone appear in the doorway, backlit by the fire, but he couldn't focus his vision. He heard sirens coming, like in his dream. Colored lights were flashing across what was left of the plaster ceiling as if they were shining through the stained glass that was no longer there.

"Emma," he released his whisper to his daughter's ghost in the church, "the picture in the window, I saved it for you. It's called *The Triumph of the Innocents*, in case you wanted to know."

Bryan slowly surrendered to the floor, onto the bed of dead leaves, in the place where her young, broken body had been found, and closed his eyes. He waited for what seemed like a long while, fighting the sleep that wanted to come, but there was something he wanted more.

Then one by one, he felt her little fingers thread between his own...

*****

"Daddy?"

"Yes, Sweetheart?"

"Will you carry me?"

"Always I will, Emma." He bends down so gently to receive her; she climbs onto his back and giggles. Life rings off their old house and into the waking day, but no one else is there to hear.

He stands and tosses her lightness with ease, higher to his shoulders. Her legs drop into his coarse hands and they close securely around her youth; as if he loosened his grasp she might float away—far away from him. They leave the yard through the broken gate that waits to be fixed and turn down the empty gravel road, together.

White picket-boards follow them for a while and then disappear in the blue-green thicket of tall spruce and hemlock. Then for a while more they are accompanied by the familiar line of crooked oak and poplar that grace the lane with long cool shadows in the late summer afternoons. Strands of rusted barbed-wire are strung taut between the nail-scarred trunks. Beyond, cows with bowed heads pray over the rich grass, their tails sweeping at the winged pests that would lay eggs in their hide, oblivious to the passing man with his beautiful daughter.

For a while the barbed fence is close with them, up a gentle rise and down again through a low crossing, before it turns away to separate the pasture from newly manicured yards. The gravel road broadens and hardens with asphalt pavement; the poplar and oak give way to young flowering trees of crabapple and pear. Where alfalfa once thrived, new homes have sprouted up one after another, so closely that their eaves can almost touch.

They pass a dozen homes and then a dozen more, each not much different than the one before. She wraps her arms tenderly around his neck and kisses him just above his brow. They are two hearts connected, much like the stem to the rose.

In a while they arrive at the end of their walk, at the end of the simple world that turns within their understanding. They stand beside the rusted mailbox that was here long before the new homes and wait for the school bus to arrive. It will come soon, and it will take her away. And their morning begins like this, like so many mornings before.

"Daddy?" Her voice, like a song, fills his ear.

"Yes, Emma?"

"Have you ever wished you could fly?" She stretches her arms wide, beyond his shoulders like the wings of a bird and holds flat hands to a gentle facing wind. She raises her face toward the warmth of a hesitant sun. Behind them the rolling, green-gray billows of an approaching storm loom just beyond the homes, beyond the trees and fields, and threaten the light.

"Sometimes, young lady, I wish I could carry you to the top of the sky where the blue darkens to night and glide just below the stars. We would race the world to tomorrow, and when we grew tired, we would sleep on the clouds."

"Would you tuck me in and kiss me goodnight—like you always do?"

"*Yes, sweetheart. I would sit beside you and hold your hand while you fell asleep, like all the nights when you were just a little baby. Then I would sing your song to you and watch your eyelids close. Do you know they dance when you dream?*"

"*Will you sing my song to me now, daddy?*"

"*I can't, Emma; it's almost time...,*" *He paused for a sad moment.* "*It is almost time for you to go.*"

"*Daddy, sometimes I have nightmares.*"

"*So do I, sweetheart; but they're only dreams, and we always wake up in our own house, in our own bed.*"

"*Not everybody wakes up, Daddy.*"

"*I know, baby.*" *He closes his eyes and lets the scent of her linger with him. He is afraid that she will leave him soon.*

"*Do you hear the sirens, daddy?*"

He waits to hear—but there is nothing.

"*It's probably only the wind, Emma. Do you have your jacket with you? Mommy said it's supposed to rain today.*" *In his dream Mary is still sleeping in their house at the other end of the lane.*

"*But it's so sunny, daddy.*" *Her speech is cloaked in a whisper, as if the sunshine is her secret that she chooses to share with him only.*

"*I know, baby, but it won't be soon. Look behind us at the sky.*" *He turns around so that she can see the approaching darkness from his shoulders; it's beyond the new homes and the open pasture and beyond the row of oak and poplar and the spruce and the broken gate.*

"*It won't be long before it's over our house, and soon after it will be here. Do you feel the change in the air, Emma? It's starting to get cold.*"

She sits quietly on his shoulders, but he is all too aware of her presence. Her weight is nothing to him, and at the same time it is everything.

"You know, Emma, I keep one picture of you with me; we have lots of pictures, but I keep just the one. You're waist-deep in leaves behind our house. It was autumn and a morning not much different than this; you were too young to be in school then. I think you were four, maybe five—you were stuffed in that sweatshirt we bought for you at the fair. The sleeves almost touched the ground. I remember that day like I will remember this day. You brought me the biggest leaf you could find; it was from the tree where we hung your swing. It was a beautiful leaf, brilliant yellow and orange like the setting sun. I still have it. I keep it in a very special place. In all this time, the colors have refused to fade."

He can feel her tighten her arms around him. He knows her embrace won't last for very much longer. She is five, she is six, then she is seven... but her age feels wrong to him.

"Will you tell mommy goodbye for me?" She lays her head on his. It is hardly there, just a touch. Her breath washes across his face, and he draws it in—like oxygen. It is a day like every day before and different than every one that will follow.

"She will see you soon. We both will, Emma; I promise."

"I know, daddy, but tell mommy I will miss her. Tell her I didn't want to go to school today; tell her it wasn't her fault."

He looks away to hide the sadness welling up in his eyes. Something feels lost and forever, and he doesn't understand. His heart tells him to cradle his baby in his arms and run home fast, away from the danger he can feel and not see, but he can't. He is powerless to do what he wants; he's following the script of his tragic dream, and he can do only what the dream will allow.

It is a while before the moment passes and he can look at her. Bravely, he turns his face to meet with hers and then manages only a thin smile. "Mommy knows you didn't want to go, Emma. She knows what's in your heart, just like I do. Give me an extra hug, and I'll make sure she gets it."

She hugs him twice and presses each cheek with a protracted kiss. "You're the best daddy in the world."

"Climb down, girl; your bus will be here soon." He helps her from his shoulders and sets her on the ground, close at his side; her head is only as high as his waist. With a gentle palm he strokes her hair and then takes her hand in his. He is every part of her, and at the same time she is every part of him.

"Can't you hear the sirens, daddy? They're getting closer."

"They must be warning of the storm, Emma, I think perhaps this will be a bad one. It can't be very far away now."

The wind combs the grass and pushes between them. Trees twist about their roots and groan in the rising air; the lonely mailbox rattles on its wooden post. His hand tightens gently around hers, and then he releases it to look at each of her little fingers; they are beautiful again.

He kneels to adjust the straps of her backpack and kisses her face. The swirling wind gathers autumn leaves in a tempest of brown, yellow and red that spins around them. Clouds roil overhead and hang black and hook-like from the sky, a precursor to the impending storm. And gray painted the morning.

"Daddy?"

"Yes, Emma."

"We love each other, don't we, daddy?"

"Yes, we do."

The school bus turns the corner and fills the street; its bulk glides silently toward them as if the wheels were turning just above the world. A shadow follows across the yards and flickers below the weakening daylight. In front of them the doors arrive, as if alone, and open wide; inviting her to pass between them. She takes a step forward but hesitates—for just a moment.

Then it all stopped.

The leaves settled, and the wind stilled; the trees came to rest. The clouds opened, and the sun warmed the air; the sirens hushed. Color pushed away the gray, and light flowed all around them like water. They were alone in a place not of the dream or the earth.

He fell to his knees, and she came to him one last time. His hands cradled her face softly. They were so close; closer than they had ever been before. In her eyes was staring back a miracle, and it filled his heart.

"Remember, daddy, how you told me to look for the rainbow?" Her gaze entered the vacuum that was his soul.

"I'm looking at it now, Emma."

She kissed him again and climbed the steps into the waiting bus, turning for a last look before she would be gone.

"Emma, please wait!"

"But I have to go now, daddy."

"I know, baby. I know you have to go, but I love you."

"Pinky-swear?"

She raised her tiny, beautiful finger toward him, and he felt it gently disappear in his.

"Forever I will, Emma."

The doors closed, and the bus pulled away. Amid the reflections of the houses, the trees, the clouds, that danced across the panes of glass, he could see his little girl waving goodbye.

A PANE OF GLASS

*****

R. BYRON STOCKDALE

ACKNOWLEDGEMENTS

Thank you to the following individuals who touched *A Pane of Glass* in many big and little, but important, ways.

Mickey S.—for offering the structural guidance the story needed, but I was reluctant to accept. You were right every time.

Sadie J.—for the character of Kate Morrow, the 'Triumph of the Innocents' and other juicy tidbits. Your presence is threaded throughout the story—*pinky-swear.*

Brad S.—for the added detail and realism you provided to better illustrate the darker side of a Surgical ICU.

Margaret H.—for proof reading every chapter many times over and in no particular order. I hope you enjoy the finished book.

And thank you to my family and good friends, both old and new, for taking the time to read the draft manuscript. Every one of your comments made the book so much better. Your support and enthusiasm for the story helped me get it across the line.